COSMIC HOTEL

a novel

COSMIC HOTEL

RUSS FRANKLIN

SOFT SKULL PRESS
AN IMPRINT OF COUNTERPOINT

Library of Congress Cataloging-in-Publication Data
Names: Franklin, Russ, author.
Title: Cosmic hotel : a novel / Russ Franklin.
Description: Berkeley : Soft Skull Press, 2016.
Identifiers: LCCN 2015045974 | ISBN 9781593766412 (paperback)
Subjects: LCSH: Racially mixed families—Fiction. | Mothers and
  sons—Fiction. | Fathers and sons—Fiction. | Alien abduction—Fiction. |
  Domestic fiction. | BISAC: FICTION / Literary. | GSAFD: Science fiction.
Classification: LCC PS3606.R42255 C67 2016 | DDC 813/.6—dc23
LC record available at http://lccn.loc.gov/2015045974

ISBN 978-1-59376-641-2

Cover design by Jen Heuer
Interior design by Domini Dragoone

SOFT SKULL PRESS
An Imprint of Counterpoint
2560 Ninth Street, Suite 318
Berkeley, CA 94710
www.softskull.com

Printed in the United States of America
Distributed by Publishers Group West

10 9 8 7 6 5 4 3 2 1

For Amy

PART I

CHAPTER 1

In the beginning, maybe I should state some things I did believe in, things that had served me well. Dividends. Face-to-face meetings. I believed in the American business system and everything my mother taught me, and we were successful. I believed in the report she was giving that day, a slide-show presentation—"Final Report: Windmere Resort Properties." I believed in the ten weeks of hard work we'd done at this hotel.

My mother, Elizabeth Sanghavi, stood in front of the room, holding the remote in the crook of her elbow. She stood with such perfect posture that her head touched the edge of the projector's light, her hair aflame with negative cash-flow numbers. She was the best hotelier in the world and nobody was listening. I sat in the dark conference room watching the slides that justified this hotel's closing, this very building's eventual demolition. While she did this, the four men from the hotel's parent corporation sat around the table staring into their personal devices, faces glowing with hockey scores or email jokes or whatever entertained them more than this, her work.

What should I have cared? They were paying us a bundle either way, and we were almost done with this hotel. I had inventoried everything from towels to screwdrivers, had measured the thickness of crawl spaces in an effort to estimate the cost of remodeling versus tearing the structure down and rebuilding a new one. Seven severance envelopes stuck out of my blazer's side pocket, waiting for the next meeting, a meeting these VPs wouldn't have to attend but we would.

Elizabeth pushed the remote to show the white letters on a blue background: "Structured Closure Step 1," and the hidden inlay of her business suit sparkled as if, despite its wearer, it wanted attention.

I sat in a crisp suit, held a nearly empty water bottle, and fantasized about throwing it through the dark and connecting to the rear of a VP's skull. The VP would then turn around, stunned to see Elizabeth Sanghavi's son as the thrower. I would tell him to pay attention, maybe add an "asshole." But then I would see the horror on Elizabeth's face. Then over the next few quarters, we'd slowly lose clients. She couldn't exactly fire me. I was twenty-eight years old and her only employee and the only surviving member of her once successful hoteling family. I could imagine the demise of our consulting business would lead to Elizabeth having a heart attack and with her dying breath she would blame me and the water bottle.

Her shadow extended nearly to the ceiling, and she droned on.

How many meetings have I attended in my life? I wondered. *Can you get cancer from too many meetings?* A heaty panic rose in my body, and I tried to take a sip of the water, and that was when the plastic bottle—that had once been considered for a VP's head—popped. Two of the men glanced up from their devices at me, and I tried to smile with the water still in my mouth and discovered I couldn't swallow.

I was familiar with panic attacks and tried to think positive, but at any second, I knew I could spew water over the room, causing embarrassment to me, the firm, Elizabeth. I covered my mouth and got to my feet.

Elizabeth paused her presentation, trying to see what I was doing, me heading out the door without buttoning my jacket.

I went at a respectable pace down the hallway to the open air of the lobby and finally swallowed. People swarmed through the hotel with the deliberate speed of travelers. I stood at its very center and bent my head back and closed my eyes and concentrated on the feeling of a healthy travel day in America, listening to that sound people's voices make together. I had lived in hotels my entire life, wanted no other lifestyle. I reminded myself we were a normal family trying to run a normal family business. Tomorrow I would be living in a new hotel, which would hopefully be better. If the economy had been good during this period of my life, I'm sure I would have been in a different state of mind that day.

While I'd been fantasizing about the water bottle and the VP's head, my father was in Bangalore trying to find a payphone to call me. I imagine him patting his pockets and asking his handler for the correct change, pretending like he wasn't broke, and making it all sound charming and enduring.

I reopened my eyes to the lobby. Nothing here really mattered, but the severance envelopes still stuck out of my blazer's pocket, and I saw that I had positioned myself uncomfortably close to a guest sitting in a chair. She concentrated on her phone conversation, not noticing me. I saw that she had one shoe planted against the side of her other shoe. Elizabeth had a theory that you could determine a person's economic circumstances by how far apart they held their feet. This woman—one foot on the other—obviously had no respect for footwear, so must have been raised, according to Elizabeth's theory, in a plush childhood.

I watched the woman stand and wave, then walk down into the sunken sitting area to greet someone. Her yellow blouse emphasized her nice figure. She met and hugged another woman. They let go, and I watched the woman in yellow open her mouth like a yawn and swipe a tear with her knuckle.

I buttoned my blazer and went and said to them, "Welcome to the Windmere." They smiled at me, and I motioned for a bellhop to get the new arrival's luggage.

People's first impression of someone with my shade of skin was favorable. I have some of my father's Caucasian features but Elizabeth's Indian color, which subconsciously registers as tan and healthy.

The bellhop took her bag, and I said, "Tony here will have it for you after you check in. Enjoy your stay."

Tony, I saw as he took the handle, wore a blinking blue earpiece, strictly forbidden, but Windmere employees had certainly heard rumors of demise by now. Because of us, the hotel would be closed, demolished, and then another rebuilt on this exact spot.

Across the lobby, I saw the VPs and Elizabeth emerge from the hallway. She spotted me excusing myself from the women.

The corporation's men passed without acknowledging me, went by in a hiss of business soles on carpet, bag straps over their shoulders, checking their return flights' status on their phones. I had this feeling that they never looked up from their phones the entire time they were here in Dallas.

Elizabeth had a soft growth of hair in front of her ears almost like sideburns, her black hair held in a gold clip in the back. Several guests in the lobby were checking her out, including the two women I had been talking to. In this world, Elizabeth—tall, beautiful, sophisticated—was an asset for me, and I knew it, and I was to her.

She glanced at the two women and said to me, "Are you going to get involved tonight?"

"Well, nothing is a given in this business, but . . ."

She sighed at hearing her own maxim and said, "Ten minutes until the meeting with managers, eleven before we go in. Wait until I make the restructuring joke about the Rangers. Then pass the envelopes out."

"It's the Cowboys who restructured," I said, "football, not baseball, and we know how to do this. They weren't even listening to you in there."

She tugged her jacket. "What happened to you?"

"I just needed air," I said.

"The word 'just' is for simpletons. Did you try a positive visualization?"

"Yes, I pictured leaving this hotel," I said.

"Do you have the envelopes?"

"Of course I have the envelopes. Stop worrying."

She began, "Proper planning and practice prevents—"

"*Piss-poor performance.* I know, I know." These were Elizabeth's seven Ps.

"I have to contact Walter Simpson and Chicago." She took a breath and at the same time casually handed me a business card. "This is the address," she said. "Send our things along."

She turned and went away, and as she did, she looked up into the reflection of the lobby in the black marble ceiling.

Then I glanced at the address she'd written on the back of her card. In her nice, neat script was "Grand Aerodrome" and an address in Atlanta. *Atlanta?* I hated Atlanta. It was almost as useless as Orlando.

A bellhop said, "Hello, Sanghavi?"

"Hello, Henry," I said.

The other bellhops stood around the podium at the front doors suspiciously watching Henry talking to me. I smelled some kind of humiliation coming, but Henry only held out a magazine in a plastic mailing wrapper. The familiar label had three hotel addresses marked out until it had finally caught up to me here.

I took it and thanked Henry with a twenty. I also believed that tipping was the cheapest, best investment in life.

Henry said, "And there's a phone call for you."

I touched my phone beneath my jacket.

He shocked me by lifting his hand and pointing.

"Please don't point, Henry. Escort, always escort the guest," I said, but here was Henry holding his hand higher than his shoulder, cuffs riding on his wrist.

"In there. Long distance," he said.

I understood he meant the business suite. Only one person in my life called me on regular phones. I walked swiftly without breaking into a run, knowing if I didn't hurry my father would grow impatient and hang up.

The business suite's hallway was lined with frosted-glass conference rooms on both sides, most vacant, like zoo exhibits whose inhabitants had been set free. The only light came from conference 004B where I peeked around the corner and saw the department heads anticipating our final meeting and the severance envelopes in my pocket.

Directly across from the managers' meeting was a glass room labeled BUSINESS CENTER where the old phone rooms were. I went inside the business center to the receiver off the hook in CUBE 1.

I said, "Hello, Charles."

"*Sandeep!*" he said. "*It's Charles!*"

"Who else would it be?" I tried not to sound excited. "You should call my phone, you know." I put the magazine on the table and glanced through the glass at the department heads across the hallway.

"Lost that number, I'm afraid," he said. "I had to track you down." The long-distance connection clicked and my father's voice surfed along with the static.

"You're the genius," I said, "so *remember* my number." I kept the phone in the crook of my shoulder, and I tore into the magazine's plastic wrapper.

The last time I'd heard from Charles was months ago, a letter. He always began his letters, "Dear Sandeep, my son," as if he needed to point out to some other reader who I was, and I was suspicious that he had read too many books that were *The Collected Letters of So-and-So* and fantasized about his letters being collected.

The reception on the phone faded and came back as he offered empty apologizes.

"Let me call you back," I said, "this is a bad time for me."

"*No,*" he said, "I'm traveling."

I saw Elizabeth stop in front of the other room and look in at the department heads. The shock of not seeing me there registered in her body language as a slight weight change to her heels.

"Charles," I whispered, "I have to call you back."

Elizabeth glanced down the hallway, then at her cell phone to see if she'd missed a message from me. When she went inside the conference room, she tried to smile, and Sylvia Iseman, head of maintenance, circled back to her chair and everyone sat leaning forward. Elizabeth would be opening with a neutral statement.

"Charles, I need to go," I said, "Where can I reach you?"

"I'm at a conference in southern India!"

"*India?*" I said slouching in the chair and throwing my head back. My father was a pain in the ass. He lived in this big house in Palo Alto, had hosted a popular PBS science show years ago, and was once famous, as famous as an astronomer could be. Now I wanted to know what India was like, but I said, "But I *have* to go now!"

Elizabeth continued talking, her gold hair clip sparkling. Carlos Sinclair leaned back in his chair and shook his head.

"I'm still a pretty big deal here," Charles said over the phone, "they treat me very well. Listen, I'm between funding at the moment, but I've got a new book coming out and other things going on."

I noticed a notepad beside the phone with the Windmere logo. Someone had written "Geneva 1000x." I took my pen out to write the amount of money Charles would want so I could hang up and join Elizabeth in the meeting.

"Charles!" I interrupted him, standing up and stretching the cord. "You'll have to call me back. Let me have a contact number, I'll call *you* back."

"Sandeep! If you don't want to talk, I'm hanging up now, but I think you'll want to hear what I have to say."

"No, *don't* hang up." I sat the envelopes on top of the magazine, each envelope with the first name, middle initial, last name printed on it. My chair tilted and its cushion produced a polite flatulence that smelled like mold. I waved the envelopes over my head trying to get Elizabeth's attention and listen to Charles Van Raye tell me he needed a "splash of cash."

"Yes, I know," I said to him. "How much do you need?"

Sylvia Iseman in the other meeting room saw me waving and pointed. Elizabeth turned in her chair. It took her a second to focus through the layers of glass to see me, her eyes narrowing.

Yes, I am talking on a landline.

"And I'd like to tell you something," Van Raye said over the phone.

"Okay."

"It's very exciting."

"Okay."

Van Raye went on about his confidence in me while Elizabeth came through the doors and stood in front of CUBE 1 and looked down at me. She spoke through the glass, "What does he want? Money?"

You would think twenty-five years of being divorced would have distilled the ire.

In the conference room, the managers craned their necks and rose from their chairs to gawk at what was going on.

"Hang up," she demanded from the outside, "this meeting is of the utmost importance."

I put the phone to my chest. "I didn't call him, he called me." I pushed the glass door and stuck the envelopes out for her to take. "Here."

"No," she said. "Hang up. We have a plan."

I tried to whisper, shaking the envelopes for her to take, "I know we do. It doesn't matter. Just get it over with. They'll hate us and we'll leave tomorrow and start over."

"*Are you out of your mind?*" she said.

I stood up, held the envelopes for her to take.

"Sandeep, are you listening?" Charles said. "Is there someone with you? Is it Elizabeth?"

"No," I said to him and then louder, "*She's great, thanks for asking!*"

"He didn't ask about me," she said and snatched the envelopes and turned to walk back toward the conference room where all the managers quickly sat back down.

I took a deep breath and the chair banged against the wall. "Charles, I'm going to have to go!" I said.

"Don't!" he said. "I have found something!"

Found something?

"What do you mean?" I asked.

In the time it took my chair's cushion to re-suck air into its interior, the words "found something" registered as the impossible.

"Yes, I have found something very, very big." He let that soak in. "Do you understand?"

"Okay," I said. I realized I hated the word "okay," but "I have found something" in the context of his life wouldn't be attached to something as mundane as "keys," "myself," or "good sushi." If the economy hadn't been bad, if we weren't delivering bad news all the time, I'm not sure I would have been in the state of mind to listen to him. If we were always extremely comfortable, would we ever really be ready for a change?

CHAPTER 2

If our world of hotels was mundane and normally happy, my father's life could be referred to as exciting and, well, a bit tumultuous. He had written popular science books, was the physicist who people would recognize as the tall, strange-looking man from the PBS series, the one who believed he could find an extraterrestrial sound by listening only to planets that he said, "Remind me of home." I had lived with The Search all my life. The Search was like an imaginary person my father was madly in love with but who posed no real threat because the person didn't exist. One of the personal items that roamed from hotel to hotel with me was the fifteen-year-old edition of the *Sunday Magazine* with Van Raye on the cover. He was young enough in that picture to have only thinning hair, and he had his arms folded as he stared down at the camera, his bell-bottom jeans surrounded by a sea of yellow flowers. In the background was the large dish antenna pointed at the sky—the wispy, impossibly blue California sky. The caption read "Searching Alone."

If I ever thought he would really find something, I certainly stopped believing long ago, but here he was saying words over the long-distance connection, words I'd heard all my life but meaning had abandoned them—"inhabited," "exoplanet"—while I watched the scene inside the conference room where Sinclair stood with his knuckles on the table, his envelope crumpled. Elizabeth nodded and listened to their complaints without me.

"Are you absolutely sure?" I said to Charles. "You've found a signal?"

"Not a signal, but it's the noise of a planet, jumbled noises of a technically advanced planet."

"Sure," I said and whispered, *"Alien . . ."* in such a way I didn't think the phone would pick it up, but he said, "Okay, I don't like that term."

"I know," I said.

I tried to wrap my mind around "inhabited," could only imagine a sparkling city with elevated roadways and flying cars.

Across the hall, Elizabeth calmly listened to the department heads. This scene was too familiar to me. About now, each person would be listing to Elizabeth his or her job description, naming things they thought no one else could do while the hotel was being staged down, but Elizabeth was reiterating "immediate," and that the hotel would be operating for a short length of time on a reduced staff before the complete closure.

I texted Elizabeth on my phone:

> He says he found something

I saw her take a deep breath and push her phone away so her far-sightedness could read it, and she spoke reassuringly to Harrison as she read my message. Then she swiveled in her conference chair and stared at me through the glass walls. I nodded, started a smile, still holding the landline between cheek and shoulder, but then she held up her hands as if to say, *"So?"* and she turned around to face the managers.

Van Raye had written the popular science books *Perfect Randomness,* *Renaming the Sky, My Year of Quantum Weirdness,* and *The Report from Earth.* They were popular enough that I occasionally saw a person reading one in the airport, found a tattered copy of *The Report from Earth* in a beach condo one year. He used to occasionally pop up on a congressional hearing, wearing all black, his white hair styled into disarray to look the part of the mad scientist. His most recent article had been a twenty-five-thousand-word treatise in *World* magazine about strip clubs. He was an interesting character and people wanted to know what he thought of everything, but he was a gangly man who loved women, had dated a few famous women, been married five times, and he had a difficult reputation among his academic peers, made worse when he dressed shabbily and showed up at parties with attractive, younger women. He lived in a big house on the campus of an important university, had made a fortune three times and gone broke four, lost half of Elizabeth's net worth before I was the age of five. He was a great storyteller, a brilliant mathematician, but he still drove a late-model sports car to the liquor store to buy Powerball lotto tickets hoping to defy the odds, and he'd been married five times declaring himself in an essay "a habitual monogamist."

He said over the phone, "Sandeep, I just need a splash of cash."

"Why? Can't you get money now?" I said.

"Good God. You're too sheltered. *How do you think the world works?* I can't tell anyone at this point. Do you understand that? I'm trusting you. Did I tell you I was between funding?"

"Charles, wait, why haven't you told anyone?" I switched the phone to my other ear. "This is what you've been waiting on . . . working on, all these years." I squeezed the magazine so I could get it out of the wrapper.

"I'm in immediate need for some short-term funds. Just to get me through."

"Sure," I said. "Charles, I am going to tell the truth. This sounds suspicious. No one at the university knows? There is a protocol. Even I know that."

"*Suspicious?* Jesus, I'm giving you my word here. If you can't help me I can find someone who can."

"No, no. I just said I would send you funds. I'm simply asking if you're sure it's not a false positive?"

"I'm 100 percent sure of its extraterrestrial origin. I've already tested the chance of randomness."

I tried to see in the conference room if anyone had opened envelopes. I felt horrible for Elizabeth having to do this by herself.

I pinched the phone on my shoulder and pulled the magazine out, glancing around as if Charles might be watching me, then I straightened it out and saw the cover of this month's *UFO Mysteries* magazine showing a formation of World War II bombers and a computer-generated circle around a speck in the old photograph, some bullshit the publishers wanted you to believe was a flying saucer. The caption read "The Real History of the Foo Fighters."

I tried to rub the magazine flat on the table. These UFO publications were for crazy people, but I was alone in CUBE 1, trying to listen to my father complaining about how the world has no cash value for knowledge anymore. Van Raye had dispensed with the UFO phenomenon in his essay "The Modern Religion." I had only started getting the monthly *UFO Mysteries* magazine because I'd attended a conference at a hotel we were working in just to laugh at the people.

"Okay," I said, stopping Van Raye. He'd begged enough. "How much do you need, Charles?"

"Fifteen hundred should do."

"That's all?" I said. "That's not a problem." This would have been a good time to point out to him that Elizabeth and I weren't made of money, but especially today I wanted him to need us.

I said to Van Raye, "Why don't we make it a round two thousand?"

In the conference room across the hall, Elizabeth scribbled on her pad, something she never did.

"That would be great," he said. "This is greatly appreciated. I've got the new book coming out."

"Why don't I make it a little more," I said like it was nothing, and I know it was degrading for him to be strung along like this. What amount would the man say no to? "Why not make it a dollar for every light-year away? How far away is this thing?"

There was a pause. "Three thousand," he said.

"Are you rounding up?"

"Sandeep, three thousand is wonderful! This book is going to be big." He said this like he would pay me back.

"I'll make it four. Is the new book about *this*, I mean what you've found?" I said.

"No, no. But I'm going to give you the bank's routing number, a Bangalore bank's account number, and my account number . . . "

"Charles," I said, "this—what you are telling me—it's true to the best of your knowledge? You aren't trying to just get money from me? All you have to do is ask."

"I'm deeply insulted. Have I ever lied to you before?"

I thought about it and the answer was actually no. Stretched the truth, exaggerated facts, maybe, but never out and out lied.

"Can't you just email me the bank information?" I said. "I'll send you your cash."

"Absolutely. Give me your email address."

I had to spell my email out for him though it had been the same since I was eight, and I glanced at Elizabeth, who'd taught me everything I knew about hotels, and I felt a sense of dread, and realized that for the last few minutes, talking to my father, I had forgotten about the business.

"Geneva 1000x," someone had written on the pad beside the old phone like we were a thousand times happier in Geneva than we are now.

"Charles, use the code word Geneva in the email so I will know that's you and everything is okay."

"What a great idea. 'Geneva.'"

"Yes, Geneva," I said.

There was silence. From thousands of miles away, I could feel his attention waning.

I turned *UFO Mysteries* facedown as if from thousands of miles he could see what I was looking at.

Over the phone, Charles said, "Sandeep, I've got to go, someone is waiting on me. I'll be going on a book tour in the states. Remember, no worries! And I'll send you an advance copy. How does that sound?"

"When are you going to release your findings?" I shouted, but it was too late, the line clicked off.

Still in the conference room listening to the complaining managers, Elizabeth pivoted slowly in her chair to lock eyes on me.

I replaced the landline on its receiver. She had to understand the magnitude of this, if it were true, far outweighed any business meeting we could ever have, especially the final meeting with managers who we would likely never see again. We should leave this hotel and put the business on hold for a little while, connect with Charles, but how does one connect with Charles?

I thumbed backward through *UFO Mysteries*, and then I was trying to comprehend what it would mean if he had found something, and how famous he would be, and I began thinking about his early successful books, and who he was during these periods when he was a guest on talk shows. He was an ass. I remembered the red Alfa Romeo he had the year San Francisco Public Television had produced the six-episode TV series hosted by . . . *Van Raye!*

I had just turned fourteen, and, after not seeing or hearing from him in over a year, I forced him to let me come visit California. He met me at the airport, him wearing green sunglasses like a movie star. I came down the long airport hallway into the real world and saw the green lenses were attached to the front of his prescription glasses, and that unruly white hair was a garland around the dome of his head. For someone raised in Florida, he had pale skin that blushed easily, always seemed a shade of splotchy red, especially the bumpy supraorbital ridge down the center of his bald head that looked like the relief map of the Himalayas.

He put his hand on my shoulder. He squinched his nose and said, "Jesus, look at you," pulling me along, forcing a smile as he studied me, as if I were not the person he'd expected to get off the plane.

I thought something was wrong with me, and the first chance I got I excused myself to the airport bathroom to ostensibly wash my face but really to check myself in the mirror to make sure nothing had happened to me on the flight. Why had he given me that look? In the mirror, I appeared normal, dare I say not a bad-looking guy. Look at the pictures of Van Raye—bushy eyebrows, the ugly head, thin lips, stooped posture that so many tall people get—I could not think of his physical appearance without thinking of the word "bones."

After checking my face in the bathroom mirror that day, I dried it and went out and continued with his escort, him telling me of his plans, stealing glances at me. It had been over a year since he'd seen me. Elizabeth had been against this trip. "Why do you want to spend time with him?" she had asked. I think Elizabeth believed she'd conceived me by herself, like some plant.

In the parking garage that day, Charles and I stood over a bright red convertible, top down, a sports car, a man's car, a cliché that had been illegally parked on the yellow stripes, and he threw a set of keys to me. "You drive!" he said.

I told him that I was only fourteen and he seemed surprised, but that didn't stop his plan.

Van Raye and I spent an hour sputtering and stalling the Alfa Romeo on the top parking deck, him showing me how to give it some gas and let the clutch out, and after a lapse, he asked me if I was ready and pointed to the exit ramp.

I never told him, but I wasn't exactly ready. I stalled in front of the woman taking our money for parking. The woman in the booth looked at him as I re-cranked, and she said, "Aren't you an actor?"

"No," he said, "an astronomer."

She said, "Oh," and asked if we needed a receipt. The price was ten dollars to let us out into the world together.

The gate went up and I made the Alfa go forward, him nudging the steering wheel when we needed to take a certain exit. He pulled a driving hat out from between the seats and wore it backward.

I was two years away from any legal driver's license and very uneven with the accelerator. Van Raye glanced behind us as we merged into the interstate, and he judged things just right. "You're doing fine! Aren't you having fun? Isn't this fun?"

Fourteen and gripping the wheel for the first time in my life, it was all I could do to concentrate and drive through the desert. Back then he worked at a university that had an eleven-mile loop of an underground particle accelerator with the highway built over it that Van Raye used as his personal racetrack. When I hazarded a look, he was rather obnoxiously posed with those green glasses, that hat, his cheeks sucked in so he could hold them between his molars to make dimples. Lining the highway were sterile office buildings crowned with thorny antenna arrays, and the brighter stars and planets came out in the purple sky. Under the ground below us, protons were smashing into protons, like fireworks, and the ends of his hair danced about his hat as if electrified.

Elizabeth's knocking on the glass of CUBE 1 brought me out of the daydream, and I realized I was slouched in the chair, head titled back. Behind her, the meeting room was empty, the chairs sitting exactly where disgruntled former employees had abandoned them.

"I'm sorry," I said through the glass.

"If it's true, he'll be going through one of those periods," she said, her voice dulled by the glass. "He's very hard to manage in popular periods, and he is very unlikeable. Don't let him affect you."

She was right, of course; during high points of his life he never needed Elizabeth or me. *If* what he said he'd done was true.

CHAPTER 3

I got the bellhops to take our twelve boxes to the shuttle and tipped the driver fifty dollars. These were our possessions that traveled the country ahead of us, including my plastic aquarium, five first editions of Van Raye's books, my childhood copy of *Eloise*, my clothes, and the photo album that contained my certificates from seminars. I had completed an online degree in finance, but my real education had been in hotel seminars held by foresters, lathers, magicians, amateur radio operators, celestial navigators, and UFO believers. I was even a certified pruner according to the National Ornamental Fruit Growers Association, a seminar I attended out of boredom in Miami's Grand South Resort when I was a teenager. Elizabeth said only in America can people dream up so many certificates and qualifications.

Back up in our suite, I sat on the couch and barely got my breath before I heard Elizabeth's keycard in the door and the electronic lock spinning. She came in, removed her shoes and slid the multitudes of bracelets off her wrists as she walked toward her room, saying nothing to me.

I thumbed through the *UFO Mysteries* before tossing it on the table when my phone vibrated. It was a text from my cousin on Van Raye's side, Dubourg.

> Where r u? CVG 230-430 tomorow?

I texted back:

> Dallas. Cant do. I have a meeting in PHX, direct flight.

> Ursula is flyin. Tell her that I miss her when you see her in PHX

> Will not see her. There quick and to Atlanta

> You'll see her

Before I could ask him what he meant by seeing cousin Ursula, Elizabeth came out of her room, sari snapping at her ankles, and went to the kitchenette and unscrewed the wine and poured herself a glass, got a container of pasta and came and sat down at the dining room table, opened her laptop, put on her cheap reading glasses, and began tapping out what I knew would be the "Final Report to Shareholders." Her black violin case sat out of reach at the other end of the table.

"You don't care what's happening? He's done it," I said.

Her fingers continued tapping the report and she said, "Did he say if it has been confirmed?"

"He said not yet." I went to the headlines page on my phone and saw only a budget battle in Congress and a color picture of a mass wedding in South Korea, not that I expected there to be headlines that life had been found on another planet. The only sign of Van Raye was an email in my box from an account penjin863@cip.in, which had his bank information.

While Elizabeth told me that nothing was true until it was confirmed, I thumbed through the email looking for and finding no thank you, no name, but the simple secret code word—"Geneva." The man hated email and cell phones until he needed money. I logged in to my First America account.

"But," she said, "if pressed for an opinion at this point, I believe he *thinks* he's done it. Charles is a lot of things, but he wouldn't lie about his work. Which doesn't mean he hasn't made a mistake." She closed the laptop and there was a thin light sandwich for three seconds before the processor went dark.

She came to the sofa chair beside me with her book, *Little Girl Blue: The Life of Karen Carpenter*, and her wine, and I put my phone down.

She eyed it. "Did he ask you for money?"

"Elizabeth, he has made the greatest discovery in human history. Guess where he was calling from."

She hated when I started a statement with "Guess . . ." Her finger continued dropping below each line as she read about Karen Carpenter, this finger moving a remnant of a depressing speed-reading seminar we attended together years ago in a hotel I couldn't remember, though she could surely remember even the weave of the carpet.

"India," I said.

Her finger stopped on the page to think and she said, "Even India doesn't deserve him."

She could talk about India as if it was no part of her, changing her citizenship as the moment and mood demanded, and could certainly make comments as if I weren't half him. She was a self-reliant only child whose hoteling father and her mother brought her to the US when she was five. She had no surviving family members in the states, and she had started telling me early in my life, "The traditional nuclear family is not a necessary unit for success." When I was a kid, I thought "nuclear" meant something to do with Van Raye's work, and because of him we were a special "nuclear family."

"He said it was the noise of an advanced planet."

"They call it an *exoplanet*," she said.

"You pretend like you don't read his books."

"I've never said I don't read his books. I like the science if only he would stick to science." She turned a page to see where the end of the current chapter in Karen Carpenter's life was.

"I don't know if we should go to Atlanta," I said.

"What in the world are you talking about?"

"Shouldn't we wait to see what is going to happen? Everything is about to change."

After she sipped her Chardonnay, the gold meniscus ring shimmered inside like a trapped halo. "What does life on another planet have to do with the price of American Telephone and Telegraph?"

"I hate it when you say that." I was sure this was something her father said to her.

"Will it help us go through middle management in Atlanta? Does it help us determine margins, the *real* margins? Will it suddenly make the next property *and* the existing structure a wonderful investment for shareholders?"

"I don't know. If he's right . . ."

She said, "You are looking for any reason not to do your job."

"God," I said and put my hands over my eyes. "Why don't we buy our own property, huh? We could have had the Desert Palm Inn last year. We've got the capital. We could have financed only 80 percent, conservatively. We are a banker's dream."

"And when the Desert Palm failed, then what?"

"Everything can fail."

"Ha, you've never been there when your own property fails. It's so . . . it's so *public*. Everyone knows. It killed my father and my mother."

She rose and went to the kitchenette. Over the bar I could see her refill her wineglass and pour me a glass.

She said, "You don't know how good it is to have a job to go to. We have no property, but we have this extensive knowledge nothing can happen to. Everyone in the business knows us and respects us."

"I'm not sure it's exactly like you think."

"We do a job that no one in the world can do better and we are paid well. That's how it looks to me."

"We have all this capital, what are we supposed to do with it."

"It'll be yours when I'm gone."

"And what am I supposed to do with it?"

She looked at me as if I were unbelievable. "Give it to *your* children," she said.

I turned my phone and looked at the SUBMIT TRANSACTION for $3,000 to Van Raye, which looked miserly now. Wouldn't $4,000 make more of an impression on him?

She came with my glass, sat down again, saw my phone and began, "He comes into our lives only when he needs something. You mistake this for a relationship. We're going to Phoenix for some business development and then to Atlanta, and we will do our jobs. Control life, don't let life control you." She looked at me over the top of her glasses and said, "Have you tapered your medications?"

"Yes," I said, trying to avoid the subject. "You and Van Raye and me, we had a decent time in Sacramento together."

"*He* had a decent time. I paid all the bills, and he had a vacation.

He'd just published *Report from Earth*, which was an economic failure. Are you following the doctor's tapering guidelines?"

I hit the SUBMIT button for $5,000, and I stood up and tugged the waistband of my pants so that my cuffs sagged an inch and bunched at my socked feet. I got in her direct line of sight and turned so that my back was to her but she couldn't see my right foot. I held my hands out beside me like a high diver.

"What are you doing?"

I spoke over my shoulder. "I'm feeling a strange force in this room."

"You know I don't like magic," she said. Then she mumbled as though speaking to Karen Carpenter in the book, "He knows I don't like magic," and then to me, "Do you realize you've been on that medication for over half your life?"

I faced the balcony doors. In the glass's reflection a mosaic of lights shimmered from our living room and mixed with the stronger airport lights out there in the world, and I tried to ignore her question, which was a statement. I wondered if my cousin Ursula was flying one of those planes right now. I could see my mother's reflection, formless on the couch behind me. I wiggled my toes to get ready to float right in front of her eyes.

"I'm not looking," she said very calmly, but I could tell from her voice that she was, and I did it, I levitated off the ground. Or that was the way it appeared to her sitting behind me—my heels floating off the ground a couple of inches. It's a simple trick done by rotating onto the ball of one foot but keeping your heels together.

"*My God!*" she said.

I landed with a showy wobble and turned to see her face. She had her hand out as if she could block the trick.

I'd gone to my first magic convention in Las Vegas when I was nine, and I got more duping delight out of tricking Elizabeth than anyone else in the world because I could tell that one side of her wanted to believe I had floated off the ground. Tonight, for the first time in my life, she actually said, "How did you do that?"

"It's magic."

She picked up Karen Carpenter. "My God, if you could apply the same passion to the business . . ." She snapped the book shut and picked up the TV remote. She turned to the financial channel. I plopped down on the couch perpendicular to her and took the remote from her and turned on the menu. "You don't need to watch the news."

"Yes, I do," she said.

"No, you don't. It's too real. Did you watch the news when we shut down the Crowne Suites in Denver? No, we watched *Follow That Dream*. When we shut down Sun Resort in Phoenix? We watched *Clambake* and *Jailhouse Rock* back to back."

"Yes, I remember," she said, "but I'm only interested in Elvis's life, his biography, not the movies."

"Bullshit."

"Cursing is a sign of low intelligence," she said, but then, "his movies *are* completely unrealistic, but they are interesting if you know what was going on in his real life when he was filming them."

Under the category "Romantic/Feel Good," I selected *Viva Las Vegas*. "Admit it," I said, "you like to watch Elvis movies when you are feeling bad."

"This isn't a bad night," she said as her eyes actually read the FBI warning on the screen and she said, "Did you know when they were filming this, the tabloids obtained the stills from the wedding scene and published them and started the rumor that he and Ann-Margret really got married."

I knew when Elizabeth was quiet for fifteen minutes (Elvis driving into Vegas with his race car on a trailer), movie flashing on her face, she wanted to enjoy this, and I thought it would make me happy too. All I could think about was Charles.

In this movie, Elvis, a singer/race car driver, is after swim instructor Ann-Margret. Every scene is an excuse to sing, the band always ready, but during the first interior shot of the Flamingo Hotel, Elizabeth said, "Look at that mezzanine. They don't make them like that anymore. He was in love with Ann-Margret, but she was a Hollywood career woman. He wanted a mother figure."

Elizabeth was a sucker for the American celebrity biography, the more sordid the downfall the better. Every biography proved to her how corrupting her adopted country and success could be. She took pleasure in the spoiling and the spoils and the downfalls of the Kennedys, Marilyn Monroe, Karen Carpenter, and Elvis Presley, and I'm not sure that these stories didn't comfort her, showing the high times, just like her younger life with her father and mother, but then everyone had to suffer the downfall just like hers, a once great business of hotels.

In the movie, Elvis looks out his hotel window and sees Ann-Margret teaching a swimming class to kids. Her red hair reminded me of Ursula's, though Ursula's was deeper, nearly brown. Elvis grabs his guitar and heads down to woo her. She wears a red one-piece with buttons up the front and shuns him, though there is no reason for her to do so—he is handsome, charismatic, seems nice—but I think this was what girls were supposed to do back in 1964. Ann-Margret is beautiful, and she goes into a dressing room to change, and Elvis begins singing as he waits for her. She sings back from inside. Pretty soon they dance around the hotel pool, and everyone is watching them. Everything in a musical is perfect, and for a second I believed in Rusty and Lucky, and that perhaps things back in 1964 were really like this, but then Elizabeth's tragic voiceover began, "He started taking amphetamines in 1958 in the army." She put her feet on the table.

"You are using *Viva Las Vegas* as a teaching moment?"

"Look at the people there." She pointed to the background. "Look at those people around the pool and the number of staff serving them. There are too many people in the world today, and everyone has money. Service like that can't be provided to everyone. Everyone expected this treatment back then and we certainly gave it to them." She clicked her tongue.

"Elizabeth," I said, my voice lower, not lifting my head off the back of the couch, "how wealthy was your father?"

"He was trained as a banker in New Delhi before he came here. He worked extremely hard for everything he had."

"I know that," I said, "but he owned motels and hotels here. A lot even by today's standards."

"It was something back then," she said, "but now, how many hotels are there in the world? Profits breed infusion of capital. The security is in the conglomerates."

She had been born Ekaja Sanghavi, and her father made her work at every level in the industry—housekeeping, engineering, and as a bellhop. She liked to claim to others how I'd been brought up the same way, but the truth was that my training as a bellhop had lasted one week and all the bellhops hated me, and I spent the days reading in the employees' locker room. I had lasted about a month in housekeeping, had never valeted someone's car, and she knew exactly how long I worked in all these positions, but she liked to tell people I had been from the ground up like her. She had one picture of the nineteen-year-old Elizabeth in her bellhop uniform, hands down by her side, not smiling but holding her chin up. This was six years before her father died of a heart attack.

"What happened to his hotels?" I asked her. "I mean, I know they were sold, but the buildings?"

"They no longer exist—Nashville, Charlottesville, and Tampa were the last ones to go, and there were some minor motor courts, back when motor courts could be nice. We are incredibly fortunate, but compared to where my father was when he was my age . . . we are far from that. But times have changed. The world caught up to us. The old wealthy are the new middle class. Why are we talking about this? I want to enjoy the movie." She pointed at the television.

Her Indian name, I'd never heard spoken, nor the names of her father's hotels. I was sure the facts and figures of her father's hotels remained in the archives of her mind just like all the others.

She said, "This economy will not survive forever, and we will be fine. My father was a survivor."

"I think he did more than just survive," I said.

She shifted in the chair, lifted her chin to the television, and said, "Shh," as though I was the one doing the talking.

Elvis came through the saloon doors onto a stage and began singing "*Bright light city gonna set my soul, gonna set my soul on fire, got a whole lot of money that's ready to burn . . .*" and it really did make me feel better, and I could tell she was enjoying this too, Elizabeth a classical trained violinist enjoying *this* music. Can anyone explain why something makes you happy?

When she wasn't looking, I turned my phone on and purchased the song "Viva Las Vegas" and started a new playlist, titled it "Songs to Beat Depression." I had in mind that "Viva Las Vegas" would be the first song of many songs to play no matter what depression surrounded me, like a special drug when I needed it, and I could feel like I did right then with Elizabeth.

Even before the movie was over, before Lucky and Rusty were married, Elizabeth went to the dining room table and snapped the latches on the case and took out her violin and bow. I couldn't imagine another night of having to lie in bed and listen to the violin through the wall, or try to sleep with my ears plugged with tornados of toilet tissue.

"The movie isn't over," I said.

"You're paying attention to your phone. We have to leave early tomorrow. I have to wind down. We've seen it a million times."

She tuned and began Beethoven's "Kreutzer Sonata."

"In Atlanta . . ." I said, "I want my own room. I don't want to share a suite. We're getting on each other's nerves. I'm just saying we need a little space."

"Quit saying 'I'm just saying . . .' That's dead talk." Her chin rested on the violin as she played softly. "The Grand Aerodrome is 672 rooms. You'll have your choice. As long as it helps you do your job, and we stay on budget."

I watched Elvis and Ann-Margret eating dinner on a houseboat, but the slow second movement of Elizabeth's violin sonata made the movie tragic, and I experimented plugging my ears with my fingers, not caring if she noticed, and my mind began imagining the sounds in the rooms around us, wandering to events I knew had to be going on in this very hotel, events of the traveling lives of ordinary people: the simple click of a door as a guest looked into her room for the first time, and there were the high-low tones of conversations somewhere; water gurgled through pipes in the walls; people walking in hallways, people plopping in chairs, silverware clicking in the restaurant, someone's empty shoes hitting the floor, and a plopping of a turd in the bowl, a faucet running, one type of snoring became someone else's, a swizzle stick tapped on the bar top, a man standing beside his bed swung an invisible golf club, the simple rhythm of his weight shifting from leg to leg seeking his perfect balance, and there was the distinctive cadence of fucking and the desperate clopping of masturbators, the metal snip of toenail clippers, all the human activity thrumming the building, the girders, waving through concrete and rebar. These were the noises emitting from our planet tonight like the sounds of Van Raye's planet reaching us, and when that went through my mind I knew nothing would stop the sounds tonight.

"I'm going to have a nightcap," I said loudly.

She looked at me over her music.

I went to my room and put on my shirt and quickly knotted a tie. Walking back through the apartment, I said, "I am going to survey the guests in the bar."

She played softer. "I bet you are. You can't stay out all night." She closed her eyes to play. "We have an early day."

I slid my feet into my shoes that were parked beside the door.

"Oh, go have your dalliances," she said, "I know you have to . . . and if it makes you work better, then fine. If you are going to charge another room, however . . ."

I shut the door, stood out in the lonely hallway of the top floor of this Windmere Hotel, the door blocking out a surprising amount of noise, but she was back to playing loudly, and I thought about it disturbing guests in the other rooms but tried to make myself quit worrying.

CHAPTER 4

The woman in yellow turned out to be Fran from Charleston, South Carolina, and she'd changed into a different pair of slacks and a sleeveless batiste shirt to come and sit at the bar with her friend, and that was where I found them, and they kept beginning the stories the same way: "In Charleston . . ." but as the stories became increasingly personal, the preamble began to be "In Mount Pleasant . . ." and then Lisa pronounced that I should call Fran "Franni," and they both, sitting to my right at the bar, shouted at the same time, "*With an 'i'!*" laughing about how Fran tried to convert her name when they were AΔΠs at Clemson University.

Now alone in the elevator with "Franni," I kept feeling her phone vibrate against my thigh as we kissed, and I heard the wind chimes in my mind that always precede an erection.

She had her arms around my neck, and in one hand she had the Amstel Light bar coaster that had "Roberta" written on it, a magic trick involving me ripping the coaster in quarters and throwing them into the bar's trash receptacle and then reading her mind coming up with the name she'd written, and then I made the original coaster reappear completely whole beneath her own cranberry martini glass.

Franni and her friend told me their stories, such as the fact they were going to Saint Clara Island in Florida to "have our tits done." They couldn't believe that I'd never heard of Saint Clara Island. "Go there," Franni had said, "have your surgery and recuperate at the resort. Everyone on Saint Clara is getting something done." I had pictured people dining with bandages wrapped around their heads like Claude Rains in *The Invisible Man*. I drank cranberry martinis and listened to Franni and her friend play the game "Real or Fake?" as other women came in the bar, and when her friend left, Franni had asked me the question as old as hotels—"Would you like to come to my room for a drink?"

Now she let go of me in the elevator and leaned back against the wall with her hips thrust and looked at the coaster. I saw her light on her phone glowing through the material of her pants and that just made me crazier about her, and I tried to put everything else out of my mind and think: *Sex, we are going to open the door in our lives and let each other into the secret room. My father thinks he's found out we are not alone in the universe, but I am stepping into a hotel room seven stories above Dallas, Texas, with a woman from South Carolina, her phone lighting up through the material of her pants.*

I stood on the threshold of her room as though I didn't know my way around a queen single and watched her switch the desk lamp on low.

I let the door go. Like any good hotel, at the Windmere there was a nice consistency to the way a clean room smelled.

Franni balanced with one hand on my shoulder to push off her shoes, and she kissed me, and I tasted a grain of sugar from her cranberry martini. I sat down on the bed and pulled her between my legs and wrapped my arms around her body and kissed her neck. She climbed and straddled me, the wind chimes of erection playing in the pleasure centers of my brain.

She said, "I'll be right back," and went into the bathroom.

I got up and took off my coat. There is something contrarily pleasant about having an erection in pleated pants. I hung my jacket on the back of the chair and glanced at the bathroom door, then held my tie so I could bow my nose into the concentrated scent of her suitcase. There was a feminine flowery smell, and a new Band-Aidy smell inside her suitcase, which was a Charleston or Mount Pleasant bedroom. I'd never been in a woman's real bedroom before, but I'd smelled hundreds of women's bedrooms inside suitcases. Franni's life was in there: the beach where she'd invented the game "Fake or Real?" years ago before she and her friend thought they'd be on this trip to have their own breasts enhanced, and surely there was the bad husband's smell inside there too. The ordinary suitcase and its smell of a home gave me the same feeling I got when our plane was on final approach to yet another airport, and out the window I saw the ordinary neighborhoods with their swirling branches of streets, and the drooping blossoms of cul-de-sacs, the houses collected in curves like seeds in a pomegranate. I had lived my whole life in hotel rooms, wanted to live no other way, a life which made me immune to being homesick except for my aunts' and uncles' houses down in Sopchoppy I used to visit every summer when I was a kid.

When the bathroom door clicked open, I snapped out of my trance and found myself sitting on the bed with my fingers still on the knot of my tie. Franni stood before me in panties and a light-colored camisole, her nipples denting the silk fabric, and her perfect shape— breasts, legs, the slight, beautifully feminine paunch of her stomach and hips as she walked and turned out the desk lamp, leaving us in the light filtered through the shears of the orange parking lot below. She searched my face for a second in the dark, and we were kissing again and she was working my tie loose. I took over and she unbuckled my belt and popped me out of my boxers and rubbed me with her fingers.

We got on the bed, me on top, and I tried to lift off her camisole, but she stopped me, instead rolling out from under me and taking off just her panties, and in a flick of a leg she sent them flying, and she rolled on top of me, still wearing the silver silk camisole.

I felt beneath the camisole for her spine and the fine muscles there, and she made a little sound as she pressed herself on me. I tried once again to remove the camisole but she squeezed her arms and worked her hips harder, losing herself for a moment, and the strap of the camisole slipped off her shoulder and one breast flopped out with the dark nipple and she put her head beside mine and I could feel her eyelashes on my ear, and what I saw in my mind was the betta fish that had lived in the little aquarium on my bedside table whatever hotel I was in, rising and falling with his nose in the corner of the glass, those fine fins fluttering like eyelashes, and that made me think about my cousin Ursula letting me give her "butterfly kisses" when we were kids, and there with Franni on top of me, and in about thirty seconds I came. I tried to keep going for her sake, but the juices and my semi-flaccidness was making it impossible.

She pushed up and put the strap back on her shoulder and rolled off me. We lay beside each other, staring at the ceiling, and I realized I was in one of those moods where the idea of doing something was always better than actually doing it. I was thinking we'd just had the worst sex these walls had probably ever seen, then wondering what had happened in this room in the last forty years of its existence. What was the best sex these walls had ever seen? What loves had been made? What fights and heartbreaks had soaked into the walls? What bad deals had been hatched? Who was the richest person who'd slept here? Who was the poorest person? The most famous? What salesmen missed his family and sat against this headboard and watched TV? For a brief second I could hear the sound of his dry feet rubbing together at the end of the bed. People had laid over here, slept here, fucked who they were supposed to fuck and people they weren't suppose to fuck, masturbated in front of the mirror, and someone missed their flight, people shot heroine, some danced to their own hummed music, washed the travel day off their bodies, a man got on his knees beside this bed and prayed to Jesus, someone tossed pills into their mouth, picked at a hernia scar, puked in the toilet, and another person kept dialing the same number over and over, waiting for the voicemail not to pick up. There had been people inside here who had wished for their regular lives back and people who wished never to have to leave this hotel room, and there was a woman who stopped here and had sex on her way to get her tits done, trying for a new start on her life, and all these people were on their way somewhere.

"Do you hear that?" I whispered.

She wasn't breathing hard but she held her breath anyway.

"A hotel feels different with a lot of people in it," I said. "When the occupancy was low a few weeks ago, it sounded different. Now there's this hum to the walls."

I didn't expect her to understand or care, but what I really didn't expect was to hear her sniff, not like a regular sniff, but one that made me understand she was crying, and a little choke came from inside her.

"Are you okay?"

She swiped tears with her fingertips and pretended to gain composure.

"I'm sorry," I said, which I meant about me and the sex, but also about the cheating man and her old life.

"It's not *your* fault," she said. "I just don't think I'll ever be happy again." Her voice seemed too loud because these were our first normal sounds after we'd made love.

"You will," I said trying to whisper. "This wasn't very good." I wanted to touch her, but I didn't know how she liked to be held.

"Is it terrible," she said, "that I believe that I was always happier in the past than I am now?"

This made me think about the pad beside the telephone when I was talking to Van Raye—"Geneva 1000x"—*we were a thousand times happier in Geneva than now.*

"Sometimes I think everyone feels like that," I said. "If there's anyone who understands, it's me. Listen, you can't let yourself get like this. Emotional pain affects you on a cellular level. You think you won't be happy again, but you will. You and Lisa, you're going to a resort."

She twisted her body and arched on her shoulders and took the camisole off and threw it. It flew across the room and she kept her arms spread, one over my chest. She looked down at herself in the dim light. Her nipples were in the middle of the little triangles of untanned skin. She took her hands and pushed her breasts together. She let them drop. "Real," she said with them flattened by gravity, then she pushed them together, "Fake." She let them go, held them together, saying over and over, "Real . . . fake . . . real." She quickly pinched her nipples as if to punish herself. "You can always remember some time in the past when you were happier than you are now."

"Do you want some water?" I asked her. "Or something from the minibar, or do you have anything in particular you take when you feel like this?"

"You are so weird," she said.

She only took a deep breath, and I waited for it to be released, but it came in a whispered, "Tell me how you did it."

There was the tick of the heater coming on and air blowing through the vent, and I knew what she meant—the coaster trick.

"It's magic," I said.

"Right. Right. It could be. You could be one of those Eastern mystics," she said. "There was a boy who sat under that banyan tree for like a year in India and didn't move, meditating, and never ate. It's true. I read about it."

Someone in the room above us dropped something on the tile floor of their bathroom, a sound that came into the temporary life of Franni and Sandeep and then went.

"But that's bullshit," Franni said. She pulled her knee up beneath the covers and slammed it back down. "You want me to believe it's real *magic*?" she asked.

"Just believe what you want."

"Just tell me how you did it," she said.

I remembered one part of her story, that she had been the last person in Charleston or Mount Pleasant to know her husband was having an affair. Everyone knew but her. I remembered a chapter in Van Raye's *My Year of Quantum Weirdness* about the steps he'd gone through when he'd been let inside the secret Borealis Project for the Department of Energy. Step 1 was disbelief—this isn't real. One of the other steps was that you felt like a fool for not knowing what had been going on all along, and what everyone else knew.

I began explaining the trick. "It's really a variation of a famous card trick, 'The Ambitious Card,'" I said. "Seemingly supercilious motions are usually the most important," and I explained, and in doing so, even to me, it seemed simple and only depended on knowing how to double-card coasters.

After the explanation, there was silence in the room except for the humming of human occupancy around us, and as she was thinking about the trick, I said, "How would you feel if you woke up tomorrow and found out there was life on another planet?"

She began crying again. "*It would be horrible!*" she said. She picked up the sheet and wiped her face. "I remember being twenty-one . . ." she said.

"I'm not twenty-one," I said because I know I looked young.

She paid no attention to my comment and said, "And I remember thinking anything was possible. I always thought I would work in New York. When I was your age, I wondered, 'What is Paris like?' but then I had this feeling that one day I would go to Paris or even to the moon—shit, that wasn't beyond the possibility—and I was happy. You know when you were little, someone mentions the moon, and you can say to yourself, 'I'll probably go to the moon one day' . . ." She started to cry and her voice got higher, and she said, "I'm in Dallas! I'm certainly never going to the *moon*. Why is that so depressing?"

"You can still go to Paris," I said.

"*I've been to Paris!*" she said. "That's not the point. You just keep moving to a state of unhappiness. I mean it's a scientific fact, I mean they've done studies, the older you get, when you take LSD, the more bad trips you have." I tried to follow her. "Because your general outlook becomes bleaker," she said. "When you're young, you have more good trips because you still have time, and more time makes you more optimistic about *everything*."

This was the worst conversation I had ever had, the walls absorbing our bad experience with forty-plus years of experiences, which dawned on me as a stupid theory, as if you could play the room back like a phonograph, the needle playing in the grooves left by the impressions of all the lives.

I looked at the dark lumps of my clothes on the floor. Tomorrow morning I would be in Phoenix in *that* jacket. Then I would be in Atlanta in *that* jacket, those shoes. I heard my phone vibrate as if my clothes knew I needed a reason to leave this room. I was getting a very panicky depression.

I got up and went through the orange light of the room and got my phone to see the text. It had originated as a *865, which meant someone from the front desk.

> call on business center phone. Long
> distance. Can't transfer. Do you want?

Van Raye was calling on the landline again. I began grabbing my pants. "Can you call Lisa?"

"Why? What are you doing?"

"I hate this, but I've got to go. I have an important phone call."

"I think it's better if you just go," she said, angry with me for putting a bow on this bad experience.

"Well, can you call Lisa? I can't leave you here like this."

"I'm okay."

I buttoned my shirt. The room smelled like our earthy alfalfa-sprout sex, and I also caught a whiff of her suitcase/home smell.

"Are you okay?" I said. I put my feet in my shoes, stuffed socks and tie into my pocket. "Look," I said quickly, "you and Lisa are going to start a new life. Leave all the bad stuff here. Write it all down and stuff the note in the razor blade disposal in the back of the medicine cabinet. It'll go into the wall. That's what I do when I want to forget something. This hotel will be gone within a year, and all this will be gone. Call Lisa. You need Lisa."

And I left the room.

CHAPTER 5

I took the elevator down, trotted through the quarter-staffed lobby so I wouldn't keep Van Raye waiting on the line. Why didn't he, a genius, carry a fucking phone and call *my* cell phone? I went down the hallway of empty conference rooms. The phone was off the hook in CUBE 1, and I yanked it up and said, *"Hello!"* I cleared my throat. There was nothing. *"Charles?"* There was only the wash of long distance and then music began—an electric guitar and Elvis's singing, *"Bright lights city . . ."*

I had time to think, *Why is he playing this?* But then I knew it wasn't Charles. Who knew that Elizabeth and I had been watching that movie? My body went weak with confusion, and the dark business center and conference room suddenly felt threatening. Did anyone see me come in here? The conference room across the glass hallway was dark and empty. I took my phone out and scrolled to see the song "Viva Las Vegas" sitting dormant on my playlist, "Songs to Beat Depression."

"Hello?" I said, switching ears.

" . . . and I'm just the devil with love to spare . . . "

"Who is this?" I thumbed my phone to airplane mode to disconnect it from the world. Who had gotten my information? A disgruntled, newly released ex-employee of Windmere? A hacker?

I disconnected the landline by pressing the button, let it go and listened to the ancient sound of a dial tone, and put my finger on the button to disconnect, but something made me wait.

In two seconds the old phone rang beneath my finger, sending a shock through my arm, and I let it go and the line opened and the bongos and maracas and the electric guitar intro began again—*" . . . how I wish there was more than twenty-four hours in the day . . . "*

I swear I thought I could feel someone listening on the other end. "Hello, who is this?"

I waited an excruciating time until the song ended, but then there were clicks and the line went dead and then an annoying *BEEP-BEEP-BEEP*. The piece of paper on the pad still told me "Geneva 1000x," and I ripped it up, threw it in the wastebasket as if it were the cause of my problems.

I waited for the phone to ring again, but it didn't as if the person on the other end knew I wasn't going to answer it this time, and I went out into the lobby, eyed the single bellhop reading his newspaper on the podium, his hands braced on each side like a lecturer.

He straightened when he saw me coming, a night-shifter working alone whom I didn't recognize.

I said, "Did you answer that phone?"

"Yes," he said. "For Sanghavi."

"Who was on the other end?"

"Operator for Sanghavi."

I turned away from the bellhop, fingering my tie and socks balled in my jacket pockets.

I considered that Van Raye was playing some kind of joke on me, which meant he was thinking about me. That made no sense. He wouldn't waste time on me.

As I waited for the elevator, the only guests in the lobby were a group of Japanese citizens holding red passports, talking to each other as they waited to check in.

I took the elevator up and carded myself into the suite. When I finally put my back against the door, I let my breath go. Elizabeth's bedroom was closed, the whole suite dead in the middle of the night, waiting for our departure. I got into my pajamas and slid into bed, staring at the empty place on the bedside table where the betta fish tank normally sat, had been for the six weeks we'd lived here, now gone. Elizabeth took care of shipping the betta fish. There had been nine or ten bettas in my life, the fish being one constant in our moving. I'd told Elizabeth I'd outgrown this tradition, but was happy to be told that she wanted to keep on doing it. Where was the betta fish tonight? In his bag of water in a Styrofoam box in the cargo bay of an airliner at fifty thousand feet? I watched the tiny green light on the fire alarm blinking on the ceiling above me, not really knowing if I ever went to sleep or not.

CHAPTER 6

Before dawn, Elizabeth and I unceremoniously walked out the front doors of the Windmere with one carry-on apiece and Elizabeth handling her violin in its black case, no one in the hotel acknowledging our departure, nor caring, and we climbed aboard a shuttle bus and rode to DFW departures where I immediately checked the news headlines on my phone again as if there would be some news of Van Raye. There wasn't.

Elizabeth had lately begun to think it was useful for business development to backtrack in our journey. If the condemned property was large enough to warrant a demolition party, she wanted to be there. So we were going to fly to Phoenix, see the final moments of the Sun Resort, meet people, and make a quick turnaround to Atlanta by tomorrow morning. That was my life.

We were x-rayed and scanned at the airport, Elizabeth making sure the blue-gloved TSA agents handled her violin properly. Each time I went through security I had to think about my cousin Durbourg who called the world beyond security "the Airport Zone," a place he claimed was the safest place in the world.

Elizabeth and I took the tram to our concourse and rose on the escalator into the chaos of the intersection, walked together past the retail stores and the food court. When you've been up all night, the new day seems like a blurry extension of the last one.

At our gate, I plopped down in a seat and tried not to sigh and tried to look energetic. Elizabeth sat two seats down from me, piled her bag and violin in the seat between us. She knew I had stayed out all night and waited for any sign of weariness so she could pounce.

She put on reading glasses and pulled out her book. Karen Carpenter's face on the cover, that bewildered look.

"Are you enjoying Karen Carpenter's life?" I asked.

"It's a good book. Her brother was a music prodigy. She was a very hard worker."

"She died from anorexia?"

"Yes. She started dieting at sixteen and that was the beginning of her decline. She started a diet called 'The Doctor's Quick Weight Loss Diet.' This was under *doctor's* supervision. Isn't that amazing? One of the main parts of the diet was drinking eight glasses of water a day. Can you imagine that? This is what doctors believed back then. What are we doing these days, *under doctor's orders*, that people in the future will think insane?"

I knew this was a mini lecture, but I relaxed just being in an airport with my mother. Honestly, I loved waiting in airports. We could do nothing but waste time. There was no business, no duties to perform, no people to meet. Whatever she was reading, when we were in the Airport Zone, it seemed interesting. I opened my eyes to listen to her.

As she talked I watched her. She was dressed in a nice pants suit, only her glasses were disturbingly cheap with gaudy, fake stones on the front, dried glue beneath the plastic gems. She didn't believe in the return value of expensive eyeglasses.

Leaning an elbow on my bag, I began re-inspecting the back of my eyelids as she told me snippets of Karen Carpenter's life, me trying not to think about Franni, the phone call, someone playing Elvis to harass me, Van Raye telling me we aren't alone in the universe—everything like a dream. I had gone through all my secure websites and changed the password I'd had forever ("bettafish14") to a new password, "geneva1000x." After you change your old password, you feel like you've left an old life behind.

I interrupted Elizabeth, "Where's Randolph been?"

She searched her mind, and I saw her memory catch but she cracked no emotion and played dumb. Did her face really blush? "I have no idea what you are talking about."

When I was a kid, she would turn into "Randolph" when we got bored waiting in airports or waiting for meetings when no one else was around. When this possession took over her body, she changed her voice to this kind of fay Transylvanian accent and claimed he, this person

Randolph, had possessed her, checking our world out. It was so unlike her to do Randolph; I couldn't even imagine her doing it back then, certainly couldn't imagine her doing it now, but I wanted some acknowledgment that this had been part of our lives. It was Elizabeth's magic.

Randolph always acted surprised to find himself in Elizabeth's body, announcing, "Randolph is here! Randolph, never Randy!" coming to her when we were on the concourse level of terminal 4 at JFK. He would say, "This is one of those ports for aircraft! Which one is this?" It was a good performance. I could barely see hints of Elizabeth's personality coming through, the dry analysis of things around her, filtered through the mind of someone supposedly not from this world. After quizzing me about Earth, about America and this world, never a word about hotels, Randolph would announce his departure, "Until next time, Number 1." (He called me, for no known reason, "Number 1.") When he left, Elizabeth's face would change back to normal, staring at the familiar airport, and I would say, "Elizabeth?" and she would always respond in her own voice restored, "What? What's the matter with you?"

There had been a period of time when I'd begged Elizabeth to fess up that she was Randolph, but she never broke or gave the act up, Randolph coming into her body when I least expected. When she was bored with driving the rental car through the desert, she would suddenly announce in the accent, "*What is this I'm doing?*" staring at the steering wheel. "*What is this machine called?*" I remember her being startled once when I asked, "If you die, would Randolph die too?" She simply said, "I'm not going to die."

I don't remember when she stopped doing Randolph, but it was a part of my childhood that had been helpful, used, and then put down.

"Come on," I said to her now in DFW, "Randolph one more time. You know, I want to hear the voice."

"You're almost thirty years old," she said. I could tell she was mulling it over. Randolph never made requested appearances. Had Elizabeth become even more serious over the years, lost the ability to be Randolph?

"Aren't you over that?" she said.

"No."

"Anyway, I certainly don't know what you are talking about," she said.

I could see a hint of a smile, but she kept reading without that index finger scanning each line in Karen Carpenter's life.

Finally the counter agent called over the speaker, "Passengers Sandeep and Elizabeth Sanghavi please see an airline representative," probably thinking we were some married couple. People either thought it was weird or noble that I'd traveled my whole life with my mother. To me, it was just us.

"Marvelous," Elizabeth said, standing at the announcement. She marched up to the counter, still wearing her cheap glasses, and got our upgrades.

She came back and gave both boarding passes to me. "This isn't an overindulgence," she said. I had heard the upgrade lecture before because she was on constant watch for overindulgence, which, according to her, this country was full of.

"It's not free, we earned it," she said. "The service in business class is the same as coach was twenty years ago. Now, let's walk to some retail stores."

I sighed. "Can't we just wait here?"

"No," she said, "walking around will keep you awake."

"Why do I have to stay awake?"

"It's daytime," she said.

I knew she was going to go into Hammell Brothers Clothiers to take pictures of the inventory like she always did, exclaiming how many choices there were and how full the inventories were. "What kind of country is this?" she would declare.

I told her no, I was staying right here. I couldn't take another speech on the economy and trends, and us looking like we were just off the plane and had never seen Hammell Brothers before.

She took her digital camera out and left her bag and violin with me, and she walked toward the intersection of our concourse.

I leaned my elbow on my bag, closed my eyes, and began con-
centrating on listening to the sounds of an airport, making my body,
mostly my hands and mind, be still. A man's voice raised to cell-
phone level said, "I got no friendly face, I got no yuck-yuck-yuck,"
and then the Doppler shift of his voice as he went away, and his conversation merged into other spoken words and sentences until all
conversations blended into babble that sounds the same no matter
where you are in the world—a hotel in Chicago, the lobby of a busy
theatre in Paris. This reminded me of what Van Raye had said—"It's
like a bunch of patterns of communications unintentionally radiat-
ing into space." He'd called it "the Big Murmur."

I opened my eyes. A pilot stood in front of me with one of those
black bags pilots roll along like obedient dogs, the kind with the
stickers of all the aircraft they'd flown.

Maybe I had fallen asleep, but now I let my eyes make the
roam of the vigilant traveler, a subconscious inventory of things:
our two bags, boarding passes, and a mental alarm went off. Where
was Elizabeth's violin case? I looked behind my seat and saw only
an ugly magazine subscription card on the floor. The nearest person was a woman feeding her baby. I walked toward her, looking
under seats as I went. I carried our shoulder bags, glanced behind a
trash can.

The mother tore bread apart and fed the little girl who sat with her
hands wide on the seat handles.

"Pardon me," I said, "but I had a violin, in a case," I pointed to
where I had been sitting. "It's missing."

"Sorry," she said, shaking her head, "I can't help you."

Obviously she thought I was a crazy person or running some kind
of scam, although people are usually slightly less suspicious of each
other in the Airport Zone.

"It is a violin, my mother's," I said to the woman feeding her girl,
choosing the right word—*mother*—to suggest I was okay. "You didn't
see anyone walking away with it?"

"Oh boy, no," she said. "Sorry. I wasn't really paying attention." The little girl held her mouth open. Her mom turned her head to see the people walking by.

"Shit," I whispered and then saw Elizabeth coming down the concourse. Had she taken the violin to teach me a lesson? It was amazing to watch people steer out of her way as if she were a ship. I looked at her hands. There was nothing but her camera looped to her wrist.

I took steps to meet her, held up my arms.

"What's the matter?" she said, glancing at the bags hanging from my shoulder. "Where is my violin?"

"I can't find it."

"What?"

"It was right here. I was sitting right there." I pointed to the seats beneath a you-are-here map.

"Please don't tell me this."

"It's got to be here somewhere," I said.

We walked around. She leaned over and looked between the rows of seats.

"You fell asleep?" she asked me.

"No! I closed my eyes for a second."

I followed her as she searched the gate area.

"You were supposed to look after my things," she said. "That was all you had to do. Now what has happened?"

People in the gate area began to eye us suspiciously and slowly their legs and hands began guarding their own bags as if to say, *see, this is how you do it*, and the small U handles on their suitcases seemed to be mocking smiles.

I stopped. "We are going to have to report this," I said. We searched the next gate area until they announced the boarding of our flight.

We reported it to the counter person, Elizabeth demanding to speak with the head of security as if this were a hotel. A regular airport police officer came and took the report, telling us that they rarely had problems with theft inside the airport.

Elizabeth said, "That doesn't help us."

She and I were the last to board, Elizabeth holding the yellow police report in her hand.

When we found our seats in the middle of the business cabin, there was already a briefcase in the overhead and a jacket folded on top. To a man reading his *Wall Street Journal*, Elizabeth said, pointing to his bag and jacket, "Is this yours?"

When he saw her, he got up and took his bag and coat down and tried to smile at her, placed his things under the seat in front of him.

Elizabeth snapped the "Missing or Stolen Property Report" for me to take.

On regular days, she always sat in the aisle seat. Today she slid in and faced the window and didn't speak the whole way to Phoenix, the bright new sunlight slowly moving around the cabin in the exact shape of the portholes as the plane banked. I kept going over the contact numbers in fine print on the bottom of the report and her scrawled signature, the description of the missing item, "violin and case, Master Stefen." The estimated value of the violin was an astounding $45,000 and next to ITEM INSURED there was a big check by NO. Under the column PURCHASE DATE, she had written a date that I calculated was when she was ten years old, four years after she'd come to the US, back when her family owned hotels, fifteen years before her father died of a heart attack, followed only six months later by her mother's death.

CHAPTER 7

In Phoenix, the elevator let us out on the rooftop party of the New Sun Hotel. The day was at midmorning, a morning filled with Arizona sunlight, mimosas and the babble of voices, and the crinkling police report in my jacket pocket. I was going to have to pretend that this was business as usual, but I couldn't even smile, kept checking my phone as if that would be the source of good news from Dallas about the violin.

Everyone at the party wore sunglasses, a few women in hats, sipping drinks and rolling foamy yellow earplugs between fingers as they chatted and waited for the main event. The hotel world wasn't that large, and so there were some of the usual people, and it was only strange to see them one week in Miami and then the next week in Phoenix. I noticed an attractive shape blanched by sunshine and inappropriately dressed in blue polyester-blend pants and a white short-sleeved shirt. It looked like my cousin, and only when she picked her phone up and aimed it at me did I realize it *was* Ursula. *Ursula?* Her empty epaulets hunched like inchworms on her shoulder as she aimed the phone at me, her smile crooked. I hadn't seen her in a month, was trying to comprehend why she was here, and also why she suddenly struck me as an Ann-Margret look-alike even down to the nose. I had Ann-Margret on the brain. My legs wouldn't move toward her as she smiled and snapped pictures of my expression.

"You can't inform me that she would be here?" Elizabeth said from behind me.

"I didn't know she was here," I said.

"She has developed a bad habit . . . " Elizabeth was saying, but I found I could move.

"That was a classic face," Ursula said, showing me the picture on her phone. I hugged her, feeling the crush of the aviator sunglasses hanging on her shirt's pocket. She swallowed awkwardly against my ear but didn't lift her arms to hug me back. "Jesus, don't crush me."

When I let go, she caught the sunglasses before they fell. "The look on your face when you saw me . . . " she said, shaking her head, and she wobbled.

I said, "You okay?"

Her dark red hair was pulled back. Her necktie was in the airline's required ugly double-Windsor knot. A pin held the black tie down, the tie's tip flapping, and I tugged the end. "Stop," she said, batting my hand away, repositioning the black zeppelin tiepin.

She blinked at me, then inspected the liquid in the bottom of her plastic cup. "I came to see you, dumbass. It's about time y'all got here."

"Good to see you, darling," Elizabeth said behind me.

"Yes, you seemed overwhelmed with joy," Ursula said. She leaned to return Elizabeth's kiss on the cheek.

"I am. You know that I always am. But surprises are awkward." Elizabeth touched her own elbows, but said, "You look tired. You must have been flying."

Ursula stuck her glasses on her nose. I saw by the way her head bobbed that she was tipsy.

Elizabeth made a big obvious sigh, but Hal Beauvais from Resort Life in Charlotte came over to speak to her.

"How do you know we were going to be here?" I asked Ursula.

"Educated guess. And Dubourg told me." She indicated the party, the sky toward the old Sun Resort building in the distance that was gutted and hollow, no windows, the whole place ready to be destroyed.

The copper-colored hairs on her arms changed blond when sunlight found them. Her rubber watch dangled loosely on her wrist.

"I'm on standby," she shrugged, "and I kind of wandered over here." She let her head roll to port, and I could tell even behind her glasses that her eyes were shut as if she'd fallen asleep, and suddenly I had this image of her and the other cousins hopping around on one foot, heads tilted to get water out of their ears after swimming in the springs back home in Wakulla County. She opened her eyes behind the glasses. "I've always wanted to see one of these things." She pointed her cup to the tops of buildings around us.

Some young guy stepped to her, his hair too long to be anything but an intern, collar too big for his neck, and he apologized and held a pen out to her with a New Sun Hotel napkin and said something to her. She handed me her cup and indicated for me to spin around. She put the napkin on my back, and I felt her swishing her signature as I watched half the party watching Ursula Dunbar using my back as a desk, Elizabeth eyeing me with disappointment. I'd heard Elizabeth's diatribe about the unreality of reality shows, but she'd always ended it with a whistle of appreciation at the amount of money she thought Ursula must have made from *Flight 000*. I happened to know it wasn't much money.

I saw at the bottom of Ursula's cup dregs of brown liquor.

Ursula finished letting the guy's friend take a picture of them together.

I took Ursula by the arm to a corner of the roof. "Tell me you aren't on standby. What are you drinking?"

"Did I say I was on standby? I'm not. Eight hours from bottle to throttle. Always. Sacred. I keep up with it down to the second."

"You're drinking in uniform."

"I'm not in uniform, asshole. These are my personal clothes. Do you see any insignia?"

She looked over the roof's edge and studied the gutted hotel building at the end of the long, deserted street beyond the barricades where official vehicles were parked with yellow flashing lights. The old hotel building faced us like an empty beehive, and by a trick of the eye, appeared to be already listing.

"It's a plain red cup," she said.

"People recognize you, Ur. They know you're a pilot, that pilot, any pilot."

She tried to look at herself. "This is all the clothes I have, thank you. Some people don't have a wardrobe. This is comfortable."

I started to tell her that if you ever defend what you are wearing with "it's comfortable," then you are wearing the wrong thing, but I stopped myself. "How did you even get up here?"

"I told security I was with y'all," she said. "The uniform helps," she fiddled with her tie clip, the black zeppelin on it. "And my charm," she said.

"Dubourg knew you were going to be here, didn't he?"

"I guess. He thinks I've flipped out or something. I'm trying to keep away from the network. They want the follow-up interviews, you know. I don't want to do them."

She'd gained some weight, but she still had the Dunbar good looks. It was hard to believe the two of us shared a common great-grandfather and great-grandmother. Over by the banquet table I saw her suitcase standing straight up, her coat and captain's cap resting on the extended handle like an empty scarecrow, her pilot self. "Your mother hates me."

"She doesn't *hate* you," I said. "It's actually quite the opposite. But she thinks I'll end up in some pub with you or sprawled on the hood of your rental car at the end of the runway watching the belly of jets."

"HA! And you had fun."

"Yeah, and I'm glad you're here, but I really have to work, and I can't upset her anymore. You have to give me a heads-up when you are going to show up."

"And miss that priceless face you made?" She raised her eyebrows. "And if I'd called you, you would have told me some bullshit about working and blown me off." She put a hand on the red railing that went all the way around the roof of this new hotel. "Don't resist, you know you're going to ditch this . . ." Ursula's glasses reflected the sky.

"I can't," I said. "I'm on probation and walking a thin line already, trust me."

This hotel we were on, the New Sun Hotel, was perfect, even the painted concrete of this deck was spotless, and the rails glistened with red glossy paint that still looked wet.

"There's a lot going on," I said. "I lost her violin."

"Her violin?" She turned up the last sip from her cup, tapping the bottom with a finger.

"Yes, her violin. I lost it in Dallas. Do you have any connections at DFW?"

She shrugged her shoulders. "Doesn't she have another one?"

"*No*," I said, "this was her violin since she was a kid."

"*Elizabeth* was once a child?" Ursula said. "I thought she came into the world exactly like that." She pointed to Elizabeth talking in a group.

"I should go mingle," I said but didn't move, and she said nothing because she knew I wasn't going to move. I felt the wonderful shape of a triangle diazepam pill in the secret corner of my pocket. I slipped it in my mouth and when Ursula saw me, she said, "I just noticed . . . *you're a wreck.*" She pushed her glasses up on her forehead where they stuck. "What's the matter with you?" I could see in her brown eyes the specks of black decorating her irises.

"*I lost her violin!*"

"Oh," she said. "Buy another one. What's the problem?" She wiggled her watch to see the time. "Du is in Seattle by now."

"He told me you were in Salt Lake City."

"He told me to come see you. I can get anywhere on a moment's notice, remember. Call and I'll be there. God, why can't the three of us have more junctions?"

"Junctions?"

"Conjunctions or something, what word am I looking for?"

Dubourg and Ursula lived across from each other their whole lives on the misnamed Harms Road in Wakulla County, Florida, along with all my tanned, brown-kneed cousins: Holly, Marissa, Jenna, Good John, and Bad John, their houses scattered not more than a short ATV ride away. If someone had asked them, Ursula and Dubourg would say they were first cousins, which was true if Dubourg's adoption to the Dunbar side of the family trumped the fact that he was Charles's biological son by another woman who gave him up for adoption to Van Raye's first cousin, Louis and his wife Lucy. It's complicated, but if you do the math—divide by pi, carry the remainder, multiply by an estranged father—Dubourg and I know we are half brothers and sons of Van Raye but call each other cousin, and the skin on my knees was pale and the skin on his knees was brown, a peculiar trait of my Sopchoppy cousins I silently studied but could not explain as simple wrinkles or old scars or just the shadow of predominate patella bones. No one seemed wise to their brown knees but me.

Ursula glanced across the party to Elizabeth talking to Susanne Lund who was the banker who worked at least half the properties we dealt with. They saw me, and Susanne waved.

"Are you glad to see me or not?" Ursula said.

"Has anyone ever told you that you look like Ann-Margret?"

She wrinkled her nose like something stank and her sunglasses returned to her nose, and she became more interested in the wind and the gutted hotel in the distance. "I used to get it in college some. Stop looking at me. You've seen me all your life."

I said, "We just watched *Viva Las Vegas* last night. Ann-Margret is on my mind."

She pushed the glasses up on her nose with a knuckle. "Lay off it, okay? I don't like it."

Around our rooftop party, white tulips drooped over their vases, and I forced myself out of the cousin bubble, and it felt horrible outside it. I felt invulnerable when I was around my cousins.

"I'm really very glad to see you, but I'm on the job."

"*Job*, please." She crushed the cup with one hand, but it was one of those brittle plastic cups whose sides split but popped back into a destroyed shape of itself, and she considered its defiance. "I need to tell you something," she said, "but not here, okay?"

Please God, I thought, *don't tell me you are getting married.* I wanted badly to tell her what Van Raye had claimed. "I got something I want to tell you too," I said. "What do you want to tell me?"

"Did I just fucking say *not here*?" she said.

"Okay, okay. Give me a second, okay?" I stepped away and found the number to DFW's lost and found and called, and they passed me off through several numerical choices.

I watched a middle-aged woman in a beautiful blue dress approach Ursula with a pen and a pad ready. Please, I didn't want to go to a wedding. She had been dating a guy from Charlotte but that hadn't been that long, had it? Why wouldn't I want her to get married? Probably the same reason I didn't want Dubourg go be a priest. I would lose them.

Ursula didn't have the normal light complexion of a redhead. I guess it was all those years in the Wakulla sun, but she looked like an airline pilot, straight, true, and smart. She had wanted to be a pilot since she was a little girl, nothing else. I think those looks and earnestness were why the network and the airline had chosen her for the reality show about the crazy cross-country flight, *Flight 000*.

Regular people auditioned to be passengers aboard Flight 000 from Los Angeles to New York, and the airline cooperating with the network was the unknown Shenandoah Airlines. It was promoted as a "test flight" with four crewmembers (pilot, copilot, two flight attendants) and twenty passengers. When the network and the airline chose the "volunteers," they signed a waiver and a confidential agreement that the company could do basically anything to the aircraft and the occupants during the flight. This was the catch: The passengers and crew could never tell anyone what had happened on Flight 000.

The only known flight plan was that the plane would be out of contact with the ground except for normal flight communications, but there were to be no cell phones, no cameras, no recording devices. When the flight was completed, by agreement, the passengers and crew would be given physical exams, would be debriefed and released, and no one could reveal what had happened during the trip. In return, the passengers and the four flight crewmembers, including Ursula (pilot in command), were given guaranteed lifetime gate passes to fly. Any of the Flight 000-ers could walk up to Shenandoah or one of its affiliated airlines, show her ID, and the airline would immediately issue a first-class ticket, bump a passenger if necessary. It was a deal that even airline employees didn't enjoy, guaranteed flight, no reservation, no pre-notification. The only catch was that if one person broke the confidentiality agreement, then everyone—passengers and the four crewmembers—lost their lifetime passes.

When Ursula called and told me that she was one of the chosen cast members, the pilot in command, Elizabeth and I had to watch. Twenty ordinary Americans had been chosen, the passengers interviewed on morning talk shows before the flight. "What possibility most frightens you?" "What is more important, the fame or the lifetime pass?" "What is your worst fear?" "Do you get motion sickness easily?"

One news personality pointed out that Flight 000 might do aerobatics, and then an aviation expert was brought on-air and the aerobatic possibilities of the 737 were plotted along with possible airframe stresses (barrel roll was the most realistic). What about depressurization, a nosedive and pulling up at the last second?

A passenger, an elementary school teacher from Duluth, Georgia, said that she had nightmares that they were going to pipe "strong odors" through the ventilation just to see how passengers would react to five hours of torture. Others speculated on a simulated hijacking. Torture was a big part of the forecasts. What was the airline testing?

Shenandoah said that the captain and copilot would have the same information as the passengers. Ursula was selected because of her experience in the 737 and because you looked at Ursula in her uniform and immediately wanted to know everything about her, including if she was married. At first she told me she was doing it for the small bundle of money the network was paying the flight crew as well as the lifetime pass, but then on a late-night phone call before Flight 000, she told me that the real reason she was doing it was that she would die if she didn't know what had happened on the flight. "I have to know, Sandy. I couldn't stand around and see these people who knew and I didn't. I have to know what happened. I have dreams at night that the flight takes off without me and I'll never know."

"But you'll tell me, right?"

"Fuck off."

Elizabeth watched a few episodes of *Flight 000*, and she told me that this program proved that the world was so big they could find crazy people to do anything. Her opinion of the publicity for the airlines was right on: "The strange thing is that you wouldn't think people want mystery and quirkiness with an airline, but there's something about it that will work. Trust me. The world goes through periods of reverse in logic. The world is crazy."

Ursula didn't sleep for days before the flight, going over every emergency procedure, stealing time on the ground school's 737 simulator (she called it "the stimulator").

On a national network, the world watched as Flight 000 taxied into position for takeoff at LAX, the spotlights shining on the fuselage and the giant black letters painted on the aluminum body: FLIGHT 000. It gained speed and lifted off, wheels up, and disappeared into the night just like any other jet. Viewers could go to the network's website and track the aircraft across the country, but that was all we got: the icon of a 737 as big as the state of Delaware flying a curving path across the country.

The kicker was that Ursula made a smooth Kennedy Airport landing at dawn, and the media immediately approached passengers trying to find any clues to what had happened. Passengers looked sleepy but normal, deboarding and waving to the cameras and the crowd, most smiling and shaking their heads, some ducking and avoiding, some giving interviews that said nothing, but there was no comment from anyone about what had occurred during the flight.

Elizabeth predicted the network never expected them to remain silent. The big story was what happened to the people after the flight.

The network had regular updates with Flight 000 participants, showed them walking up to the airline counter and getting issued their ticket, smiling and waving as they disappeared, five minutes later, into the security line, and if the question was sneaked into the conversation, the standard response: "I have a lifetime pass to the world. Everyone depends on me, and I depend on everyone else. I will not comment."

Amazingly, it took six days for the first person to break from that pat answer. This man was clearly frazzled and was being interviewed in a booth at a bar, a sales representative from Pittsburgh, and he deviated by saying this simple statement: "Maybe nothing at all happened. Maybe everything was normal." Then more passengers began coming forward, and they all said the same thing—*nothing happened.* The flight had gone completely *normal*, they claimed, cocktails were served by the two flight attendants, they said, the chimes dinged when they could safely move about the cabin, some even dozed, most stayed awake the entire flight, wondering what was going to happen. The airline remained mute and revoked no passes.

Of course no one believed the passengers and began thinking that this was the new standard statement controlled by the airline. The louder the passengers seemed to want to say, "Nothing happened!" the less people believed them. Ursula had told me, "What do you want from me? I'm not telling you a goddamn thing, neither confirming nor denying. I made an agreement, and I'm sticking to it."

"Jesus, Sandeep," she said one night over the phone, "I can tell you without breaking confidentiality that it was the longest, most horrifying five hours of my life. I was terrified from wheels-up until I had a visual on JFK."

Pushing buttons on my phone to make my way through the maze of the DFW phone system, I finally got a pleasant woman who took my name and number and said she was adding me to a "list," and before I disconnected, she said, "Have a blessed day."

A woman at the rooftop party in Phoenix tapped her glass and announced, "Three minutes, please."

The spectators stepped out of the shade and into the sunshine, the breeze blowing into our faces.

I said to Elizabeth, "I called lost and found." She stood at the railing. Ursula joined us, still with her shredded red cup in her hand as if it could still hold liquid.

Over the railing, it was a twenty-story drop to the streets below. Yellow lights on security vehicles flashed. "They have my number," I said to Elizabeth. "I'll keep calling to check."

Ursula leaned forward to see past me to Elizabeth and took this chance to glance at Elizabeth's cheap white sunglasses. Beneath the plastic lenses, Elizabeth's eyes focused into the distance at the Sun

Resort. Almost everyone else was leaning back, holding their phones out to record the event.

I adjusted my ears into the wind, and then the Klaxons blared through the deserted street below our party like an animal howling in the empty valley, and then as suddenly, silent white flashes burst in the gutted building ten blocks away and then the sound of popping explosions came to us on the roof. Some first-timers yelped and the thundering rose and deeper concussions thrummed my chest. In the distance, the Sun Resort began to sink into a brown blossom.

The building seemed to claw at that vapor, like the old lives lived temporarily there, and I couldn't help but think of Franni from Mount Unpleasant, and a feeling of old lives lived inside one hotel room, and I had a shocking but unrealistic fear that Elizabeth's violin was in the middle of that building, collapsing, never to be found again.

Along the street, the windows in the surrounding healthy buildings wobbled but held the orbs of the Arizona sun, and the Sun Resort disappeared and the cloud rose. Oohs and ahs came through the crowd and then everyone began applauding and there were a few hoots. Elizabeth, her hands straight beside her, said, "They're building a new hotel on that exact same spot." I waited for it, and she finally said, "What kind of country is this?" and turned and walked away.

Maybe Franni had been right. Surely a person hits a peak of happiness in his life, the happiest point he or she will ever be. I remembered sleeping on the bunk beds in the attic room in Sopchoppy among dozens of cousins and how safe I felt in a room where the freaky air conditioner blew snowflakes, real snowflakes that fell on the dark blanket before disappearing. Elizabeth would tell me that it was only Americans who expect an ever-increasing graph of happiness until the very end.

"Let's split," I said to Ursula.

CHAPTER 8

I touched the keycard to 720's knob and got the green light, opened the door for Ursula. This hotel room smelled new and wonderful. "If only we could capture this exact scent," I said to Ursula, who went past me, rolling her pilot's bag.

She looked around. "Queen interior, no view. Y'all are always frugal."

"Are you calling me cheap?" I said. I loosened my tie, unbuttoned the top two buttons, and pulled the shirt and tie both over my head together.

"Your mama is worth a fortune and she shops at the Dollar Store for sunglasses."

"She doesn't believe expensive eyewear has a good return value, and what makes you think she's worth a fortune?"

Ursula flipped on the bathroom light and looked inside before she let her pilot bag stand, put her shoulder bag on the dresser and unzipped it and pulled out a wad of clothes.

I checked my phone for messages from DFW while she was in the bathroom changing. In a minute the toilet flushed, and she came out wearing a ragged number 20 jersey and boxer shorts. She put her not-uniform pants and not-uniform shirt neatly on a hanger, sat beside me with her tablet, and noticed the alarm clock on the bedside flashing "12:00." The hotel was that new.

"Fuck," she said and grabbed the clock and began setting the correct time.

"What's the matter?"

"Nothing."

Down to my undershirt and slacks, sock feet, I lifted the hem of her boxers and smiled at the design, a penguin on an iceberg with a palm tree print. "Cute," I said and then put my palms against my eyes. "I don't want to think about all the problems I have when I walk out that door," I said.

"Don't be so overdramatic. You're going to have to find her a new violin."

"A new violin? Just like that? All of you think my life is so easy."

"What's not easy?"

"I've got to go to Atlanta and close a hotel down. The violin. And I got this other problem, something that happened. I bought this one song last night, 'Viva Las Vegas,' because we were watching the movie, in Dallas, you know, and I got called to the hotel's public phones, and when I picked up the phone, guess what was playing."

"'Viva Las Vegas.'"

"Right."

"You changed all your security settings?" she asked.

"Yeah. Nothing else was wrong, they just made me go to the public phone and listen to the song. It's just weird." I took a breath and closed my eyes. "I didn't sleep much last night." Then I told her about drinking cranberry martinis in the bar with Franni from Mount Unpleasant, how they were on their way to get their breasts enhanced. "Have you ever heard of an island you go to for plastic surgery?" I asked.

"No, but I don't for a second think there's *not* an island where people go to have plastic surgery. Are you a tit man?"

"No," I said, taking a glance at her free chest beneath the stenciled 2 and 0 on her shirt.

"Surprising," she said, "I could have added that to about a dozen other mother issues you have."

I wiggled into my pillow to get comfortable. "I don't even think I slept an hour."

"Congratulations," she said, "you got laid."

"I didn't say that." I closed my eyes.

"At least one of us is getting laid," she sighed.

"I thought you were dating that other pilot."

"That little experiment didn't work."

"God, I thought you were going to tell me you were getting married."

"Jesus, no. I should be a nun. You know I've always had the fantasy of seeing a nun undress, hearing that heavy cross hit the floor," she said.

"You all blasphemy yet you are psychotic about Mass and the church. I don't get it."

"It was a joke. If I get to heaven and find out God doesn't have a sense of humor, I'll kill myself." She immediately closed her eyes and began whispering, "Hail Mary, full of grace . . . "

Ursula reached a finger into the leg of her boxers, and I heard the nail scratch through a stubble there and then the pop of an elastic band of her panties beneath the penguins.

"Don't snap your panties at me," I said. My face was fifteen inches from her shoulder.

She rested her tablet on her chest to see me. "I'm your cousin, and didn't you just get laid?"

I smiled, heartbeat suddenly throbbing.

"Do you remember the time we kissed?" I asked.

"I think I would remember that *if* it had happened."

"We were in the river, under the dock."

"That? We were like twelve. Have you been pining away for me ever since?"

"I actually kissed Portia and Holly too."

"God, you're an oversexed menace."

"Portia didn't count because we were dared by someone at a church barbecue."

"Trust me, mine didn't count either," she said. "I probably felt sorry for you. That's why I kissed you."

With my finger I reached and touched her forearm, the golden hair there. "We're only *second* cousins," I said. She'd already gone back to reading her tablet. "Do you know how distant that is?"

She made that this-can't-be-crossing-your-mind huff and said, "You think this would be one of your uncomplicated trysts, and you'd move on to the next hotel and forget about me? No, you would fall so madly in love with me." She looked at her watch hanging loosely upside down on her wrist. She wore it like that so that she could see it easier when she was flying.

"More like you wouldn't be able to get over me," I said.

"I'd be over you before I got to the lobby," she said. "But you, you'd be driven insane by not being able to have me, your second cousin. You would be institutionalized. I'd come visit you, though, don't worry. I'd observe you through a one-way mirror, you having not showered for days, greasy, rocking back and forth in a chair, chain smoking and mumbling, '*Ursula, Ursula, Ursula.*' A staff member would ask me why I was there, and I would say you were my cousin driven insane by your unrequited love for me. Gothic fucking city," she said.

I said, "Nobody ever believes it when we say we are cousins. They think it is a joke."

"You're a little browner than me," she said.

"You don't have brown knees anymore." I pointed. "Did you know that?"

"What are you talking about? What's wrong with my knees?"

"Nothing. It was just that when we were kids, the skin on all y'all's knees was brown."

"What *are* you talking about?"

"I don't know, but the skin on your knees was always browner than mine, all of y'all. Y'all's knees were like Rorschach tests. Sometimes I saw Che Guevara's face, sometimes Jesus."

She picked her leg up to see her knees. "It's all the kneeling. That's how we all got Jesus knees. I can't explain Che."

She took the skin over her patella and wiggled it back and forth. Her nails were unpainted and clear, practical and short. In my memory, I could see them plucking a tick from her ankle, pinching it surgically between her fingernails until it popped, her own blood purged from the tiny creature and leaking into her cuticle like a pipette, then Ursula flicking the carcass away.

"You had something to tell me," I said.

She looked at her watch, yet again, as if to see if it were the right time to talk. "Let me ask you something," she said. "What's the weirdest thing that's ever happened to you?"

"Hearing 'Viva Las Vegas' on that phone."

"Yeah, I get it, but I mean something you can't explain. That was a hacker, one of your former lovers. But have you ever been thinking about a friend you haven't seen in ten years, and suddenly you see them in a restaurant halfway around the world?"

"No."

"All the hotels you've lived in and you've never thought you heard a voice, anything? Come on, what's the most unexplainable phenomenon that has ever happened to you?"

"Charles called and told me something that blew my mind."

"*Charles?*" she said. "No, not Charles. I'm talking the opposite of Charles. His whole job is explaining shit. I'm talking about something that astonished you and you have no explanation for."

"I saw a guy levitate once."

"Levitate? You mean you thought you saw a guy floating?"

"I saw it in Key West, a guy on Mallory Pier—"

"No, not *magic* bullshit," she said. "Jesus, Sanghavi, can you follow the bouncing ball here? I'm talking about a fricking *phenomenon*." She squeezed the bridge of her nose. The thermostat on the wall made a tiny click and then the air conditioning came on. I smelled the air-conditioned air, an odor that hadn't been in my life in a few months.

"I don't like the way this is going," I said. "Did something happen to you?"

"I want to tell you something about the flight."

"I know the flight was normal," I said, "nothing happened. You can take it from there."

"You're so condescending when you've got everything figured out. I don't give a shit about that. That's not the important part of what happened to me." She took a breath and let it go. "What if I told you that a couple of hours after we landed, I realized my watch was wrong?" She absently touched her black rubber timepiece hanging upside down on her wrist. "My watch was behind," she said. "Two hours behind."

"I would tell you you screwed your watch up."

"You know I didn't. Don't think I've gone crazy, okay? I went to that fucking convention that time, and I sat there and made fun of people with you. So I'm saying I should be the most skeptical person in the world." She patted the number 20 on her chest and said, "I'm you, Sandy, I mean I'm the same as you, I'm not crazy, but I've seen things that make me, I don't know, ask questions."

"I think you are jerking my chain." I closed my eyes, felt the sleepiness coming on.

"What if I told you I was driving from a friend's house in Sausalito Tuesday night? I did drive back. I got to the hotel just fine. When I looked at my watch, I had only four hours before my flight. I'd left my friend's house with plenty of time."

"How much to drink did you have at the friend's house?"

"Shut up. Just listen. I wanted at least eight hours of rack time before flying, but when I looked at my watch, I had to go straight to the airport. It was horrifying. I flew this flight from San Francisco to Seattle, and I was in the left seat with everything routine, but I keep having these flashes of memory. I realize some things, you know. Are you listening?"

"I'm listening."

"I know that I floated over downtown Sausalito at night. I know I floated over the bay."

"Flying dreams are very common, Ur."

I felt her take hold of the sleeve of my T-shirt. "I'm trying to describe something real here. Don't write it off as a dream."

She continued slowly wadding the sleeve, balling the material in her fist, the collar stretched against my neck.

"Hey, stop, okay?" I said.

When she let go, she pretended to help smooth it back in place.

"What if I told you it's not my only experience?"

"Ur, now you're just freaking me out. This is right off the script of every abductee."

"*Abductee*. It sounds like I'm a leper. What if they are right?"

"There's so much going on that you don't know about," I said to her.

"That's exactly what I'm trying to tell *you*," she said, "if you would have an open mind."

"This is different, but I can't tell you now. But it's important." Sleep nibbled at my brain. "I've got to doze off. I'm about to pass out." I shifted down and put my head on the pillow. "I think your mind just can't handle that nothing actually happened on Triple Zero and it needs something to happen. Listen, whatever you do, don't go blabbing about this. You'll come to your senses eventually. A pilot can't go blabbing about being abducted by aliens."

"I work for Shenandoah," she said, "I could announce over the intercom before every flight that I have been abducted by aliens and no one would walk off."

I tried to let sleep come to me. "Is that really what you're saying? You've been abducted by aliens?"

Her touch on my bare arm made my scalp tingle, and when I opened my eyes her head was on the other pillow, eyes open and looking at me here trying to sleep. "Why do I want you to understand so badly?" she asked.

"Because you love me," I said.

"True. I didn't ask for it to happen to me."

"Ur, I got to fall asleep. You're trying to keep me awake to brainwash me, I think." I hated to lose sight of her with her head so perfect on the pillow, but I lost the battle with my eyes and the curtain began to come down. "Ur?" I said.

"What?"

I cracked my lids so her face was fuzzy. "When it happens to you, what you *think* happens to you, I mean, how does it feel?"

She touched her index finger between my eyes and stroked the skin there to make me blink, my eyes even heavier. "Terrifyingly fantastic," she said.

"You believe with all your heart it's real?"

"I think I do."

"How does believing feel?"

"The world has opened up."

I fell asleep thinking "terrifyingly fantastic." My cousin beside me was more comfortable than I'd felt in a long time. *Cousin, cousin, cousin* mixed in my dreaming brain to become the word *cushion, cushion, cushion.*

Knowing all my cousins almost didn't happen. When I was a nine, Lucy Dunbar, Dubourg's adopted mother, Van Raye's first cousin, tracked Elizabeth down and tried to convince her that I would be much healthier if I knew their side of the family, especially my brother Dubourg. They invited Elizabeth and me to come stay with them in Florida, but Elizabeth said she was too busy, and I heard her explaining that the arrangement with Charles was her total custody of me, and he wasn't in the picture, nor did he have any legal right to be. Lucy Dunbar told Elizabeth that no one in the family had seen Charles in over twenty years, and my visit wasn't about that.

Over the course of several phone calls, I began to hear Elizabeth soften, ask again about the number of kids and the number of adults, and when she finally said, "If he comes, you can't let him get too much sun," I knew I was going to Florida, which in my experience had been Tampa, Miami, Orlando. When she hung up, she told me they were hung up on a traditional nuclear family structure because they were Catholics. Being "Catholic" summed up a lot of things for Elizabeth.

I remember flying alone to Florida, being picked up by a clan of people just outside security. I remember riding in a Ford Expedition, this giant vehicle driving through a forest, sitting in the position of honor (second row, middle seat) where I could see that even the pavement in this part of Florida was different, a lighter gray, almost white, and the headlights were purplish against it, and leaping across the highway were desperate toads trying to get out of the high beams, and everyone talked as if the death of a few hundred toads beneath the wheels were nothing, and there was the constant *thucking* of insects hitting the windshield. That was when I realized my idea of Florida— and certainly Elizabeth's image of Florida—was not this. I fought back tears and the desire to tell someone I wanted to go back, *immediately*.

For the first years I visited, I feared those Wakulla County summers, but every subsequent spring I got excited when Aunt Lucy called Elizabeth about "plans." The more Elizabeth learned about the family's homestead, what we did, the more I wanted to go, shocking Elizabeth with emailed pictures of kids hanging upside down from branches or swimming in an inferior river called the Sopchoppy, which made up for its small size by being crystal clear and populated by alligators. From still pools of water, the cousins scooped up tadpoles, put them in jars so we could watch them turn into frogs, and there were long days when nothing was planned. We simply woke up and fed ourselves cereal and went outside.

They were the kind of families with one ATV for every two grown children, always driven full bore and kicking up dust past single-story houses, each house with at least three satellite dish antennas pointing at the same part of the sky, and you could stop at any house at any time and drink from a garden hose.

We played after supper in a family graveyard, our bellies full of grilled cow liver and fried doves, lying on graves listening for pursuers with flashlights.

Elizabeth thought I was exaggerating these things, and every summer sent me off with the last admonishment, "Don't get too much sun."

In Sopchoppy, a dog whelped puppies and, to my horror, ate two of them, which Dubourg explained meant there was something wrong with the puppies anyway. Equally terrifying to me was the sight of half tadpoles/half frogs growing in the tanks of brown water, rising to take air into new lungs, growing legs that weren't useful yet.

After supper, we played epic games of flashlight tag in the cemetery, and here I was fascinated by the small graves of children, kids dead from childhood diseases or "stillborn," which was a word I was taught and told not to say in front of adults—*stillborn, stillborn, stillborn*, running through my mind.

We watched the movie, *the* movie, at least once every summer, *The Creature from Outer Space*. My heart started pounding when the narrator began, "Since time began, man has looked toward the heavens with wonder . . . wonder and fear." This was the B movie filmed in *Color-vision!* and in which my grandmother was perpetually trapped, perpetually eighteen, and always the first victim.

When the movie was made at the springs, two years before Van Raye was born, Katherine Raye worked as a lifeguard. Young, beautiful, athletic, she was hired to do stunt diving but earned a speaking part in the opening teenage party scene and eventually became Victim 1. She had one line of dialogue. My cousins had Catholic prayers they recited, but we also recited "Meet you on the other side," with my eighteen-year-old grandmother every summer before she dove into the river on the television, where she would be drug down by the Creature yet again.

She had Van Raye when she was only twenty and died of bone cancer when Van Raye was twelve, but every summer I saw the Creature's claw wrapping around her ankle and her struggle to swim, trailing a line of death bubbles, the young Katherine Raye, preserved for twenty seconds on film and dying over and over. She was credited as "Teenage Victim 1."

Of course when we were all kids, we believed the spaceship had really landed in our swamp, and the Creature still came out at night looking for humans. We believed he put his ear to the side of the house every night to listen to how many people were breathing inside.

We believed if there were enough of us in the house—our collective number being our strength—he wouldn't dare come in and try to take someone.

When I had been there enough summers to overcome most of my fears, I could lie comfortably on a grave during flashlight tag and feel the coolness of the stone and listen to my cousins' voices in the dark. They got angry if I pointed the flashlight at the sky because stray lights in the swamp, they said, attracted UFOs and creatures, but I couldn't help but tempt fate when it was my turn with the flashlight, watching how the beam disappeared just beneath the stars.

Ursula woke me in the hotel room in Phoenix. She had already put her not-uniform back on and we walked out into the hallway where a group of middle-aged women saw us, and I knew we looked like lovers emerging from a hotel room in the middle of the day, maybe husband and wife, a feeling I liked, and I smiled and nodded at them as we passed.

Walking out of the new hotel with Ursula I felt halfway decent until I saw a disappointed Elizabeth coming out of the conference room. "I'm sorry," I said to her, "I haven't been myself."

She only said, "Always try to prevent sorries."

When your mother is angry with you, you feel like your clothes are drenched and you can't even walk.

Ursula drove us to the airport in her tiny Shenandoah Airlines car, Elizabeth not speaking. I was clean and rested, but even with Ursula right there in the front seat (I was in the back) I was already missing her, and she hugged me at departures, told me that she was going to see how long she could stay in the air. "Between work and my lifetime pass, I hardly have to touch the ground."

I thought she was joking.

CHAPTER 9

When our red-eye flight got to altitude, the flight attendants turned
out the cabin lights and Elizabeth's silence beside me grew bigger in
the darkness. I was back in my normal window seat, head against
the wall in the dark of the aircraft cabin, trying to ignore her silence.
Ursula would be on another flight to somewhere else in the world at
this very moment.

"I'll find your violin," I whispered, not even sure that she heard me.

"I don't want to become one of *those* families." Her voice was near
my ear, her face in the darkness.

"I don't know what you're talking about."

"You have to work hard," she said. "We don't want to be one of
those families that only bad stuff happens to."

"You've read too much about the Kennedys," I said.

Her fingers found my arm and squeezed. "No. This has happened
to people I know. One or two bad things happen, and then suddenly it
starts piling up."

"That won't happen," I said. "I'll get your violin back."

"It's not just that. Lately things have been getting out of our control.
Maintain control starting with the details, even very small things. I've
given you everything I could," she said in a hushed voice. "Something
could happen to me—natural causes—and you could carry on."

"Please," I said. "Don't talk like that. We don't have to work so hard.
We're fine."

"Work is the answer."

"I know. I'll be better," I said.

I asked her there in the dark, "Elizabeth, are you okay? Tell me."

"Of course I'm fine. There's no need to worry about me. Promise
me something, right now." I said okay and she said, "Keep tapering. Do
you really want to be on it for the rest of your life?"

"No." I tried not to think of where the violin might be, a stranger's hands.

"Let's see what this next place is like," I said.

"Don't let *that* control you, you should control it. Sandeep?"

"I'm here, Elizabeth."

She sighed, which caused her not to say whatever had just crossed her mind. All of this had happened in the dark. She said, "You need to get some sleep. Tomorrow's a big day."

"It is tomorrow," I said.

I closed my eyes and put my head against my hand, knuckles against the cold side of the plane.

I fell asleep on that flight and dreamed that I stood before the lavatory door on this plane. The little window said UNOCCUPIED. When I opened it, the tempest of pressure loss sucked a maelstrom past me, but I stood there, immune to the wind, and below me I saw the darkness of Middle America—fly-over towns twinkling in a flat boring landscape. People in the plane yelled for me to *shut the door*! During the maelstrom of depressurization, the mother from the concourse today calmly fed pieces of bread to her little girl who still had her hands out on the armrests. The dream me shut the door and walked back to my seat and there was no Elizabeth. A female flight attendant touched my shoulder. "I'm very sorry about your mother, Mr. Sanghavi," she said. "You shouldn't have opened the door." In my dream, tears began welling, but I realized I must maintain my composure for the duration of the flight in front of everyone, all these clients, but I couldn't stop thinking about how humiliated Elizabeth must have been when she'd been sucked down the aisles on the floor, the way she must have slid by the other passengers, her nails dragging down the carpet, suffering the indignity of being pulled toward the void and finally into the dark airspace over America. In my dream, the dream me remained composed, sat down in our row of seats, and he flipped the armrest up when it was completely dark. He stretched his legs across where his mother should have been sitting, more comfortable without her, something the real me would never be.

CHAPTER 10

In the morning, rain in Atlanta beat my already dead mood. The hotel van's tires hissed on the interstate, and heat from the transmission rose through the floor, filled the shuttle's interior. The other three passengers avoided eye contact as travelers on buses always do, the cadence of the wipers counted down our fate. Elizabeth sat beside me and appeared impossibly fresh and rested, her suit immaculate.

In the rearview mirror, I watched the driver's eyes scan traffic, his Afro asymmetric. He pushed the blinker and leaned to check the traffic beside him. The flyovers and freeways crisscrossing at this intersection reminded me of my image of Van Raye's inhabited other planet, but here on Earth, in Georgia, this south end of the airport was dirty and abandoned, tarps draped over exit signs that signaled to nowhere, orange barrels blocking roadways, lifeless aluminum warehouses and traffic lights blinking only yellow or clothed in body bags.

We looped until the driver slowed to make a left, nothing but dead businesses on both sides, and when I leaned down to try to see the end of this blight, I saw the glowing red letters on top of a hotel: GRAND AERODROME. The structure had the dimensions of a cinder block and the material was just as gray, the kind of property that every room had a balcony. The whole effect was Soviet-era bunker. On top of the block was a dome, and I said to Elizabeth, "Tell me this place isn't old enough to have a revolving restaurant."

"Did you even read the preliminaries?" she asked me.

Only a high metal fence sequestered the hotel from the surrounding entropy. I counted twelve stories, something I should have known. A large American flag on the roof blew straight and bright against the overcast sky.

When the shuttle stopped, I stepped off under the porte cochere where guests milled about smoking and yelling into cell phones. Two maroon-suited bellhops dispersed to the rear of the van for bags, both older white men with long beards. Another came to the door and held his hand to take Elizabeth's bag, handles of his bushy mustache twitching in the wind.

We went through the electronic doors into the building, and the air seemed to open above our heads. The design was an open atrium, each floor ringed with ornate railing. A businesswoman went past me with the deliberate speed of a traveler, luggage wheels humming on the orange carpet. There was a fake forest in the middle of the lobby, and I went to the railing in the center and leaned over. Below us was a large rectangle of concrete gurgling water from its top, the sides with a healthy growth of real green algae, and below that an array of tables with patrons having lunch.

The walls of the lobby had that dull lumpy look of over a hundred paint-overs. The light had bleached the mulch in the planters pale, and people sat on worn pleather couches working and talking. Across the lobby on the wall above the phone booths, the silver hands of a clock, unbelievably, displayed the correct time.

"Elizabeth," I started, and how was I going to put this, "I can't go through this again."

"Yes, you can."

"What are we supposed to do here?"

"These are our clients," she said.

"This is a no-brainer. Are they going to reinvest some capital or are they leveraging? . . . It doesn't even matter, does it?"

"Keep your voice down," Elizabeth said.

I felt in my pocket for my money clip and tipped the bellhop, and he thanked me and told me he was Richard, and I told him we would need a minute to check in, and when he was gone, Elizabeth said, "It *does* matter. We don't know but there might be some renaissance planned for this section near the airport. How do we know a high-end remodeling won't make this work? How do we know this isn't at some perfect intersection between the airport and the city, the perfect distance of noise reduction and convenience? We study, we observe, we make our report."

I rubbed my shoe on the carpet and several pieces of sand flickered like popcorn. Whatever is on the floor in the lobby will end up on the floors in every room. I'd heard that a hundred times.

"We can concentrate on the accounting," she said, "but don't leave out service and reputation, all the intangibles."

I went to the edge of the fake rainforest. The night's menu stood inside a lighted menu box. The revolving restaurant was called View of the World. I leaned over the railing to see the floor below and that fountain again. On this belowground level there was an open-air bar, and I saw the tops of people eating and drinking, an airport hotel bar being a convergent of time zones, a border town between where you are from and where you are going, the last place in the world where a three-martini lunch was acceptable.

The rain came down harder on the hotel, spraying against the giant windows on the back of the lobby that looked over the Atlanta airport. People looked at the rain and nearly everyone sprouted their phones to confirm with local radar that yes, indeed, it was precipitating, and in the column of air above the fake rainforest, I caught a glimpse of something falling. High above on one of the floors, a young girl leaned over the railing, arm out. The object was a doll, not a cloth doll, but one accelerating with the assurance of molded plastic.

I heard Elizabeth behind me—"My God"—and the thing disappeared on the other side of the forest. High above, the girl who'd dropped it stepped away from the railing, and I saw the white light of an open hotel door behind her and the girl being swallowed inside. Whether she ran in, was pulled in by a parent or sibling, or God knows what, I didn't know. The hotel simply ate her, and I would never see the girl again.

Elizabeth went to the fall zone as fast as her gold shoes would carry her, and when I got there, there was nothing on the ground, and Elizabeth said to a passing bellhop with an armful of courtesy umbrellas, "*Stop.*"

At first I thought he was the same bearded white man whom I just tipped, but he was young and plump, still big bearded and with wind-burned cheeks, his boney wrists coming out of the sleeves of his jacket as he cradled the umbrellas. Elizabeth opened and closed her fingers to indicate to him: *give me an umbrella.*

Elizabeth stood on her tiptoes and poked the tip of an umbrella into the branches of the fake rainforest tree. Rain from the umbrella beaded silver on the shoulders of her dry-cleaned jacket, and she flipped the doll out.

The bellhop and I stepped back to see it plop faceup on the carpet. She wore a blue flight attendant's uniform with nonregulation high heels. It was a Barbie or one of those Barbie rip-offs you get in airport gift shops.

"My God," I said, thinking about my dream of Elizabeth falling out of the sky.

"I know," Elizabeth said, "it is a liability nightmare," looking up through the center of the hotel. Several times I'd heard her say these words: "An air of liability," expressing an atmosphere of dread about a property, but here I was literally looking into an air of liability.

"Nobody in her right mind would design a hotel like this today," she said.

"Let's just walk out," I said. "Catch a flight to wherever."

"Stop," she said.

I picked the doll up and tilted my head back to look up through the hotel.

Elizabeth went toward the front desk and got the attention of a standing agent and introduced herself. Elizabeth believed in announcing herself immediately, the secret-guest approach, according to her, was a cheap tactic employed by nonserious consultants. I wanted to walk up and say, *hello, we're the angels of death.*

After getting the keycards and our accommodations settled, Elizabeth met a Mr. Blaney, a man with a sloped belly and receding hair, glasses on the end of his nose, and she immediately turned on her charming face, introducing me to him, "This is Sandeep Sanghavi. He will be doing the bulk of the analysis, and as such, deserves full access."

When I was supposed to be listening, I couldn't help look at the spectacular view out of the back of the lobby and over a pool deck being drizzled on, and then to the great panoramic plains of the busy airport beyond, the grass in every direction bowed by the weather and another gray phalanx of harder rain marching from the west. Jets blinked in line for takeoff no more than a quarter mile from us, and I had the stupid thought that Ursula could be on one, or maybe Dubourg, and in the distance terminals looked like an isolated city, the spires and cathedrals of control towers. Out the window to the right, to our west, our neighbor was the Gypsy Sky Cargo shipping center with its tarmac full of perfectly aligned green jets with the logo of the Gypsy eye on the tail, actually the pattern found on the wings of the gypsy moth, but it looked like the purple and green eye of a seductive drag queen.

When Elizabeth turned to go with Mr. Blaney to the hotel's "house"—the parts no guest ever sees—I said, "I'll catch up with you. I'm going to get our things moved to our room."

I went and waited for a guest to vacate the concierge, a pretty dark-skinned woman. Concierges are the loners of the lobby, and by trade, snobs. "I am Sandeep Sanghavi, I believe there are packages waiting for us."

"I beg your pardon."

"Boxes shipped to the hotel. They arrived this morning. Last name: Sang-havi."

"There's been no deliveries, sir," she said. "Have you checked with the front desk?"

Before I panicked, I took a fifty from my clip and handed it to her. She gave the tip a glance before putting it away.

"I will be staying here for an extended amount of time, Darlene. Please let me know when packages arrive for me." I handed her a business card and went to the front desk, feeling time clicking down. The betta fish was in that shipment.

I asked the agent if they had received packages for "Sanghavi." I had shipped them for a guaranteed 9:00 AM delivery and told her there was a live fish at stake, and she looked at me like I was unstable, and I remembered I was holding Barbie, right there in my hand propped on the agent's desk. The agent excused herself to check with the shift manager, and I remembered the dream I'd had on the plane, Elizabeth sliding down the aisle and out the door, and now this doll flight attendant had fallen out of the sky. The agent came back and said, "Sorry, no."

Then I panicked.

I put Barbie in my blazer's pocket and went into a cavernous men's room and splashed water on my face. There was a man using a urinal staring at the ceiling as if it were the stars. I dug out the bottle of Rozaline from the side pocket of my bag and tapped out four tablet halves. I often wondered where I would be if we couldn't afford good insurance. I bent and put my head beneath the automatic faucet to drink. The water ran in the corner of my mouth as the faucet's tiny red sensor light stared into my lowered eye as if it were my conscience staring back at me.

I went back out and to the sofa, dug the shipping receipt out of my shoulder bag, and searched the Gypsy Sky Cargo website—that damned Gypsy eye greeting me—and I entered my account number and found that the packages had been logged in two days ago in Dallas. On the page ABOUT LOST OR DAMAGED PACKAGES, I hit REQUEST LIVE CHAT FROM PERSONAL SERVICE REPRESENTATIVE, and I waited.

Had the drivers in Dallas tampered with the paperwork? I don't think it was possible without getting on our account. Should I walk next door to the Gypsy Sky Cargo compound and see if I could find someone to help me?

I had very little to take care of in life. I had never had the responsibilities of cleaning my room or cooking or homework. I had attended formal schools only until ninth grade, which was when Elizabeth discovered that half the freshmen had been "held back" during their kindergarten year, a decision of their parents to make them more competitive, and Elizabeth was furious that ninth grade was populated by should-be tenth graders.

My phone vibrated. The message was from a BLOCKED number and contained some generic text introduction.

I quickly typed my request.

> Missing packages. tracking # IN76102009

There was a ding and I saw the message from who I thought was Gypsy Sky Cargo:

> Hello :)

You never knew when you were getting a human being or a computer programmed to respond. *I hate this,* I thought, *this pathetic excuse for not talking to a human being who I could explain things to.* Then the next message came in:

> How is Atlanta?

> Need Raye. Can you help me find Raye?

Raye? It took me a second to figure out what the name meant. No one called him "Raye." I typed in:

> Who is this?

> I am that I am!!!!! LOL!

I am that I am?

> Can you contact Raye again?

> No. Suggest u call the university

I see you are Elvis fan!!!!

Elvis? Looking up from my phone, there was a man in the lobby rereading the back of his paperback as if he weren't sure what book he had started. There was a woman on the couch wearing running shoes, bouncing one foot as she read from a blue file. Everyone appeared to be normal, then again, what was I looking for? There was a ding and the text said:

Elvis makes you happy right?

I took a breath, typed.

what do you want?

I'm not allowed to have fun with you? :(

To earn a favor, I will help you ;) Agree?

This is how it's done, no?

The world was going on around me like normal—the elevator dinging, people squeezing through the doors before they were even fully opened. I glanced behind me at the faceless clock on the wall. I looked at the texts. Who used so many emoticons? A kid or an old person?

I don't know who you are or
what you are talking about

I need an introduction to Raye :)

I see that you have lost items?

I can help. Do you believe me? :-|

> I don't know who you are.

> I should have a name

I heard the sound of a phone ringing in one of the phone booths behind me. The old-fashioned sound of a ringing bell was so strange that I saw people looking at the source and smiling, but no one stopped to answer it. I turned back in my seat.

This person texting me was the same person who'd called me in Dallas and played Elvis. Now he knew I was here, and that ringing continued in the booth behind me and I tried to ignore it. *It has nothing to do with me*, I told myself, but I eventually took a breath, got Barbie and our bags, and went around to the booth, put my shoulder against the wooden bifold door. Hand on the receiver, I hated myself doing this. I picked it up, heard the hollowness of an open line. *What is the name of this hotel?* "Grand Aerodrome," I said.

There was a click, then an angry squeal—high pitched, then low—then a saddened long dull whining, a sound I'd heard before, the sound of an old modem trying to make a connection, a horrible sound. The metal phone cord yanked my arm when I tried to look around the lobby. I sat in the booth and that rolling drumbeat started and then a guitar and then Elvis's unmistakable singing. It wasn't "Viva Las Vegas," but " . . . *come on baby I'm tired of talking, grab your coat and let's start walking. . . .*" It was "A Little Less Conversation."

Jesus, hell. I put my finger down on the silver tongue to disconnect and make it stop. I needed to remain calm. I texted on my phone:

> This is harassment.

> No, it's funny!!!! :) That song is perfect for this moment! LOL!

> You have our shipment. A live fish is in that shipment!!!!

Its misplacement was random event caused by a 0.05-second power surge combined with a phrase of dead code in a routing program. I could trace it further but you would only find it more absurd

Are u here in hotel?

No. But I *see* you.

I will call you Sandeep.
Give me a name

Are you watching me? Do you have our shipment?

I have located your things (which are literally up in the air at the moment) and I will help you. Yes. I am watching you but I can't see you. LOL! >;)

I'm blocking your texts

You can try. ;(

Be prepared for fantastic things. Are you?

And find Raye. :}

There was no number to block on my phone, just the prefix code. After sitting in the booth—no more ringing—and watching people go by in the lobby, I grabbed my bags and made a dash for the elevators. What scared me most wasn't this hacker. What scared me most was I was going to have to tell Elizabeth Sanghavi that our personal items were not here.

CHAPTER 11

On the way up to the room, I felt the forty-eight-hour recommended limit for my fish running down. I tried to call the only number I had for Van Raye in California to get some answer from him for what might be going on, but I got a recording: "The alumni house will begin taking reservations in March . . ."

I called the physics department and explained to three different people I was trying to get in touch with Charles Van Raye and each person transferred me to someone else.

Holding the phone to my ear, I got out of the elevator and found 1201, our suite for at least the next six weeks, the orange doorbell glowing beside the door welcoming me. When I got inside, I leaned back against the door, and listened to a kind-sounding person named Mary, the "program coordinator" for the physics department, who said Van Raye was "indisposed for an indefinite period of time."

I told Mary, "This is Sandeep Sanghavi. I'm Van Raye's son."

There was a pause and she finally said, "Would you like to leave a voicemail?"

His outgoing message wasn't even his voice but a mailbox number. *Why is he so fucking low-tech?* I tried to gather myself so my voice wouldn't shake, left a message telling him to call me. "This is Sandeep," I added and then said, "Something strange is going on. Call me," and on second thought, I said, "Does anyone call you just 'Raye'?" and terminated the call, intuiting that he would never get this message.

For the first time, I allowed myself to look around the suite, and I would have given it two stars at most. It was large and smelled like an antique shop—slightly homey but "cancer causing" crossed my mind. There were high ceilings. One wall was missing a strip of chair railing. I unlocked the balcony door and pushed against wind pressure to step outside, the vast airport spread before me, wind smelling of diesel and jet fuel, and the patio was a dirty concrete, solid wall on each side for privacy, but twelve stories below me was the hotel's rain-slick pool deck. Beyond the pool deck was a high perimeter security fence separating this property from Atlanta Hartsfield and the Airport Zone.

I went back inside and sat in a sofa chair and waited in the dimness for Elizabeth. One of my great skills was waiting. I'd done it all my life. A trance overtook me, and it was sunset by the time Elizabeth let herself in.

She flipped on a light and glanced at me without making eye contact, slipped her shoes off by the door.

"Where have you been?" she said.

"There have been some complications, I'm afraid." I began with the facts. "Our shipment can't be located . . . "

"Our shipment?"

She always hated when *other* people repeated what you said in order to give them a chance to think.

I told her that the website still listed them as "in flight," though I was waiting on word from Gypsy about their exact whereabouts.

The inner tips of her eyebrows sought each other as I explained, and her movements slowed, her hand stopping at her earlobe when the earring snapped off.

"Sky Cargo could have them here at any moment," I said.

She snapped the other earring off. Then she started to say something and let the gold earrings clatter to the table against her laptop like dice. She suddenly went to her new bedroom and shut the door with authority.

Her earrings lying on the table were supposed to be a gold-braided figure-eight knot, a knot I learned at the Ocean Navigator seminar I took at Bay Front Plaza Hotel in Tampa long ago.

She came out wearing a hotel robe, went into the kitchen, and found the chardonnay she'd ordered in the refrigerator. I hated the silent treatment.

She sat at the dining room table and opened her laptop, and I broke: "You don't think this is my fault, do you?"

Her reading glasses reflected the computer screen.

"I want to know right now," she said, "are you planning on contributing to this analysis, or are you going to make me do it all by myself? You should be taking over. I should actually be doing less."

"Yes, I am, of course, I'm going to do my part, but I'm going to locate, you know, our stuff. That's my first priority. The fish is in our stuff." I put my hands behind my head.

I got up and checked our door to make sure it was secure, glanced out the peephole to the warped image of the Air of Liability beyond the railing, and then I checked that the door to the adjoining suite, which wasn't ours, was locked.

"You have to will yourself to be in control," she said. "When you do that, then good things—not bad things—will happen to you. Bad luck is beginning to follow you around."

I pressed my head against the window and saw Gypsy Sky Cargo to our west, the facility bathed in so much light that it was practically daylight for the workers. Giant coils snaked along the ground and connected into aircraft. Tiny people in yellow rain slickers worked around the ankles of these giants. Nobody stood still. Gypsy Sky Cargo had always been Elizabeth's ideal of efficiency.

"I'll get our stuff," I said.

I went and sat at the table beside her. I put my head in my hands.

"It's a bad sign that *all* our boxes are missing," she said. "Not one box showed up?"

She knew the answer.

I picked up her earrings.

She grabbed my hand to stop me from fiddling. "Listen to me, and listen to me good. The violin, the shipment . . . Now stop and listen to me. I'm not saying this was directly your fault, but you have to stop this trend. You let bad things happen and pretty soon, we're just one of those families that bad things happen to all the time. Trust me, I know families like this. I can't stand them." She seemed to consider what she had just said. "I don't mean to be so harsh, but there is something despicable about how they let bad things happen to them, their inattention to details of life. The Epps, remember them?" I nodded. Susan Epps was Elizabeth's college roommate and she had died of pancreatic cancer a few years ago. "They owned a farm in Virginia. Old money, from canning, of all things. The farm had an airfield for the family plane. The family drove the father in a jeep to the plane, then watched the plane crash on takeoff. A terrible tragedy. The family watched it happen—their father, husband, exploding into the trees with two children aboard. Was it his fault? Ronald was third-generation money, wasn't much of a businessperson. Things were in decline because they were lazy and then he crashed.

"After that, her brother died in a bicycle accident in Spain. There were strange stories about how every time they traveled something tragic happened—family members lost for a month, someone caught a skin disease in Greece, another hit by a taxi in London. She, Susan, well you know that story. Her other brother works at a grocery store in North Carolina now. This is a phenomenon, it's real. I will not be one of these families. It's just you and me, we are a family who has to be vigilant, so you will have opportunities and have the big family."

I picked the earrings back up and felt their weight.

"One of my regrets is that I could not have a large family," she said.

"You never wanted a large family," I said.

"Who doesn't want a large family? But it wasn't right for my generation. For economics, it needed to be only you and me."

"I'm twenty-eight," I said, "I'm not sure I am large-family material."

"Find a younger woman. Find someone you are physically attracted to, a beautiful woman whom you can be attracted to for the *rest* of your life, and this woman should be a woman who wants to take care of you for the rest of *your* life and who will love you because you are successful."

"Seriously? This is Elizabeth Sanghavi's formula for marriage?"

Elizabeth had her suitors, and she'd married two of them—Van Raye first, then an attorney, William (Will) Henry Elrod IV from Savannah, Georgia. Constantly being on the road wasn't suited for marriage.

I said, "Do you want to find someone and arrange this business deal?"

"Stop it! I hate arranged marriages, but Americans want to pretend like marriage isn't business. An individual's success depends on the family; the spouse comes first and foremost."

"Jesus," I said, "will you listen to yourself?"

"A large family is a sign of success."

I thought about all the cousins running around in Florida on hot days, all of us dirty, pulling things out of the refrigerator to eat, tried to picture Elizabeth overseeing such chaos.

I pushed my hair back. "Goddamn it," I said and then very calmly, "This hotel is going to be a pile of concrete in a couple of months. Why should we even care?"

She slammed her fist on the table. "That's what I'm talking about! Stop it! *You* are in control . . . make yourself feel better! Misfortune breeds misfortune, families become cursed! That is not *us!*" She got up and went to her bedroom.

Her door shut harder, and I went out onto the private balcony off of my room and looked at the airport, felt the cold wind sting. I thought I heard something on Elizabeth's balcony but the wall blocked me from seeing if she was there. A mile away there were the pearly floodlights crowning the terminals where people were traveling, constantly traveling.

CHAPTER 12

I dreamed a doorbell was ringing. I woke but didn't move because I didn't want to loosen the bed covers. I looked around searching for a sign to indicate what hotel I was in, what city. The ice in the courtesy bucket collapsed, and then there was clearly a knock on the outer door.

I got out of bed and met Elizabeth going to the door, tying her robe's sash. "Nothing good could be happening at this hour," she said.

I looked through the peephole and saw two figures, the image of their bodies concave like parentheses around a golden luggage cart full of boxes.

When I opened, a Gypsy Sky Cargo delivery person said, "I apologize for the hour, but this was a hot priority per your request. You are Sandeep Sanghavi?"

One of those bearded bellhops shifted his balance to try to see into the suite. He had two luggage carts stacked with our boxes.

"They found them. Good," Elizabeth said.

I quickly signed the DIAD pad and found the important box on top of all the others, a box with an orange sticker: "FRAGILE: Live Fish."

"Again, Gypsy Sky apologizes for the inconvenience of the hour," the delivery woman said, "but I mean with this priority . . . "

"They came from Dallas?" I asked her, carefully taking the box to the kitchen and using the tip of a steak knife to slice through the tape.

She said, "Came to us in Fort Worth, and I'm afraid due to a processing glitch they were never offloaded in Fort Collins. Someone threw a hot-location search on them. Look at this priority." She pointed to the electronic pad.

"I don't understand what that is," I said, glancing as I removed the Styrofoam cooler's top and saw the clear plastic bag. I immediately lifted it and before my eyes was my purple betta fish swimming, his image slightly distorted by the plastic, but alive and well.

"Just what it looks like," she said. "That's a priority five, and I've never seen anything above a three, and I've been doing this for seventeen years."

I lifted the bag in front of my face and watched the fish.

"Priority three is something like you would see for essential industrial or even medical, you know," the woman said. "Didn't know there was a five." While the bellhop unloaded boxes, she looked me up and down as if to determine who I was, and then into the apartment to see Elizabeth.

"Gypsy Sky Cargo apologizes for any inconvenience this might have caused," she said.

"Who did the search?" I asked her.

Elizabeth came and looked at the fish and took it from my hand and carried it to my room.

"Who did the hot locate?" The woman made a sigh but consulted her pad. "There's no ID."

"Thank you," I said.

I showed her the door, which had been propped open by the bell-hop's rubber stopper.

My phone dinged with a message.

> Is everything in order? Don't get carried away with thanking me. ;)

I typed quickly as I went to get a tip for the bellhop.

> You stole our things.

> No I didn't. :(I never get to help people. I can help you.

When I handed a tip to the bellhop to get him out of the apart-ment, I noticed his eyes above the wild growth of brown beard focused past me to the door. I turned. There was a woman in her pajamas stand-ing inside our suite. She held an ice bucket.

I whispered, "Who are you?"

The bellhop had to skim the wall to get around her, but she stood her ground. He grabbed his rubber stopper but held the door open. "Anything else, Mr. Sanghavi?"

I put up my finger to stop him. "Who are you?" I asked the woman again.

"Sandra. I was looking for the ice and vending room."

"Why are you in here?" *Was this person somehow responsible for all this?*

She stepped into the light of the living room, her white fuzzed bedroom slippers snapping. She hugged a bucket of ice. "Look at the size of your suite."

Hearing the voice, Elizabeth came out of my room drying her hands on a towel. "Excuse me. May I help you?"

The woman glanced at her and then down at a can of soda stuck in her bucket of ice. "I was thirsty. I've always loved pop. Is the gift shop open?"

"It's the middle of the night," Elizabeth said.

"I'm looking for the . . . " she contemplated, " . . . the thing. You know."

Elizabeth flipped the towel over her shoulder and put her hands on her hips. "And what kind of sleeping pills did you take tonight?"

The woman thought about this and said, "I'm not drunk."

"Aren't you?" Elizabeth asked.

The woman said lowly, "I'm completely okay."

Elizabeth said, "Then may we help you back to your room?"

We found most sleepwalkers because someone called the front desk to complain that a stranger was knocking on their door. Sleepwalkers in hotels often locked themselves out of their own rooms, and several times had shown up in their underwear at front desks asking for admittance to their room. Quite common.

The bellhop kept the door open with his foot.

"I just came here to find . . . " But she didn't finish.

"I know, *the thing*," Elizabeth said. "Do you understand? You are sleepwalking?"

"No I'm not."

"Let's get you back, okay?" Elizabeth said.

"Yes. I forgot why I'm here?" She turned toward the door. "I'm disturbing a private property."

Elizabeth showed her the way out.

The woman mumbled, "This is really strange. Nothing like this has ever happened to me. I'm Sandra Whitehouse, you know."

We followed the bellhop to the elevators.

Elizabeth said, "Do you remember where your room is?"

"Certainly. It was nice to meet both of you. I'll see you in the morning. Are you going to Frank's lecture?"

"We most certainly will not be," Elizabeth said.

The woman looked confused but walked away without glancing back, hugging her ice bucket until she got to a door. Elizabeth and I both held our breaths until she found her keycard, swiped successfully, and disappeared inside her room.

When the clicking of the door latch finished echoing off floors on the other side of the atrium, I said, "I really hate this hotel."

"The sleepwalkers in the Grand Aerodrome aren't hidden down lonely hallways, are they? This is open and quite dangerous." She pointed out into the Air of Liability and all the rooms we could see. "She won't remember any of it in the morning," Elizabeth said. Her eyebrows of consternation never slept.

The atmosphere of the open-atrium hotel was dreamlike. Tiny room number lights sat beside each door where guests were sleeping or fucking or everything people do inside a layover, airport hotel.

"The problem is that everyone in this country is filthy rich and they don't even know it," Elizabeth said. "We are all filthy rich and everyone takes prescription medications. We have quite literally turned into a country of Elvis Presleys."

My phone dinged.

"Who could be messaging you in the middle of the night?"

"Dubourg," I lied and looked at the message.

> I need you to introduce me to Raye.
> You have to help me.

"We got our stuff," I said to her, and left her looking into the Air of Liability and contemplating a country full of Elvis Presleys. I typed and sent:

> I am not in contact with him. If you can do all this why can't you contact him?

> His introduction to me must be handled gently.

> Who are you?

> I should have a name . . .

> I really like talking to you.

> Do NOT contact me again.

> What you are doing frightens me.

> Don't be frightened. Do you want to listen to Elvis?

CHAPTER 13

I couldn't sleep, not even with the betta fish swimming in his tank beside my bed. His color was coming back, and he was more greenish than I remembered, but they did this sometimes, this slight change of color brought on by the transition.

I gave up on sleep and dressed in my swimsuit and robe and went down to the outside pool. It had quit raining and the water was freezing but for some reason it felt good. I floated on my back and tried to focus on a bright star in the sky. My ears were submerged in the dull thrum of water, making the sound of someone on the pool deck calling my name seem angelic, "*Mr. Sanghavi . . .*"

The security guard stood by the pool looking down at me, walkie-talkie in hand. "Mr. Sanghavi?"

"*What?*"

"The phone in the lobby is for you," he said.

"What phone?"

"The payphone in the lobby."

I hurried to the pool's stairs. "Who is it?"

"The operator said a person-to-person for you, Sanghavi. Would you not like me to take these calls?"

"No, no. Please, always." I grabbed my robe. I noticed his nametag said ALBERT.

I left him on the pool deck, took the fire stairs two at a time, loafers slapping concrete. Out in the lobby, I cinched the robe tighter and noticed all the payphone booths were dark except for the one where a receiver sat on the triangle corner table, door open.

I pushed the door wider and picked it up. "Hello? Hello?" And then the song began, "*A little less conversation, a little more action, all this aggravation ain't satisfaction . . .*"

A message vibrated on my phone.

> It's always funny.

> And it makes you happy, right?

Outside, the floodlights above the main desk shined on a front desk agent bowed to her terminal. One of my loafers had come off and now sat abandoned on the carpet, and an older man worked a vacuum, getting closer and closer to it without thinking an abandoned loafer in the middle of the lobby was strange, the vacuum's tiny headlight touching the shoe and retreating. I listened to the music, trying to think. The old man looked up through the hotel as if to determine where the shoe had dropped from. I responded:

> No.

> Maybe

> Oh

> My mother lost her violin in Dallas on November 9.

These were simple little words. I knew that the violin wasn't the same thing as tracking down lost packages, but I was desperate.

> I don't want to frighten you again.

> You wont

The phone in my booth rang. I picked it up slowly, expecting Elvis, but there was no drum roll or bass beat, only silence and then a man's deep voice cut in, " . . . until five, Monday through Saturday."

"Hello?" I said, but it was a recording: "The Warehouse of Mishandled Luggage is officially warehouse 122-Alpha located on the south perimeter." It stopped and then began again, "Welcome to the Warehouse of Mishandled Luggage! The warehouse hours are nine until five, Monday through Saturday . . ."

> Is this a joke?

> What do you believe?

> What do you want from me?

> Only to be introduced to Raye

I got out of the booth and went and retrieved my shoe.

There was one early-morning guest checking in at the front desk, and I stepped beside him and said to the agent, "If any of those phones ever ring, please see that someone answers them."

"I'm sorry, sir?" the agent, a woman, tried to remain pleasant. "Those are public phones, not hotel phones."

"I know that . . . but . . . " Her nametag said CARLA. "Carla," I said, "it is of the utmost importance . . . "

A voice behind me said, "This is Mr. Sanghavi." It was Albert the security man, looking like some creepy undertaker in his mustache and his thin neck, hands interlocked in front of him and the ugly nylon jacket with his name sewn on.

I said to Albert, "I was just saying, any phone calls on the payphones are very important to me. Even in the middle of the night, text me. I'll give you my number." I got my wallet from the robe's pocket.

"I will make sure you get any phone calls. I hope there was no problem," he said.

As he watched me shakily find a business card, he said, "Is it true that you had everyone from the Springhill Plaza blackballed?"

"Blackballed?"

"Blackballed from the hospitality business."

"That's absurd. Do you honestly really believe that?"

He seemed to be interested in the wire sculpture on the white marble wall behind the desk. "I've worked nights here for twelve years. I heard one person at the Plaza made Ms. Sanghavi angry."

"No," I said, "that's not true. Why would you believe that? Do you really think we have the kind of power to tell every hotel never to hire someone?"

"A few hours ago I didn't believe there was such a thing as the Sanghavis," he said. "I also heard that you travel with your own staff."

"Jesus," I said. "I can assure you we are real, and we have no *staff*, and we are here to help the Grand Aerodrome and all of its employees and associates." I finally found a bent card and handed it to him.

"I have pried. I'm out of line," he said.

"Albert, we don't close everyone down. There are plenty of properties we help become better hotels, and we always educate the staff, which makes the employees more valuable. Please, just let me know if those phones ring. If you answer it and call, I'll be here immediately. Twenty-four hours."

The front desk agent reemerged from the office and held out a package for me and said, "This arrived before I came on duty tonight. I mean, I was told about it but it was late . . . "

The return address was "C. Van Raye" with his California address and a sticker signifying it had been forwarded overnight from Dallas.

I remained poised until I got into the rising glass elevator. I tore open the package and pulled out a book. The title was *The Universe Is a Pair of Pants*, subtitle, *A Survival Guide for the Multiverse*. At the bottom it said simply, "Van Raye," the name the world knew him by. The cover was a beautiful image of the unmistakable Hubble Ultra-Deep Field photograph, showing hundreds of galaxies in the darkness of space— elliptical, globular clusters, spiral arms, like a cosmic Pollack splatter in rich colors. But then I realized this famous photograph of the galaxies had been transposed on a pair of black jeans, a woman's shape filling out the pants. *How does he get away with this?* The truth was that he had a large female readership. I thumbed through the table of contents to look at the chapter titles to see if anything looked familiar, to see if anything had to do with my life, as if one chapter might be titled "Sandeep, My Son," but there was nothing like that, only the Durastock letter folded inside.

Dear Sandeep, my son,

I've just arrived back home. Here is my new book, the best one yet if I'm allowed to say so.

I have to mention to you the subject we briefly talked about on the phone. I will remind you that this information was given to you in the strictest confidence. (Save this letter for posterity sake.)

What many others have searched for, I alone have found. It was a matter of knowing how to narrow the search. I will say this again because it has proven fruitful: It was only a matter of looking for places that reminded me of home.

For people who will wonder about such things, I used an old Craig-48 calculator and performed the loop transformations (like everything else) by hand. This took about three months, between March of last year until June of the same. All my work was done in my house at 211 Gildeer Street, which I should point out has been my personal residence for almost fifteen years, but I, however, first heard the sound when I was alone at the Big Dish antenna above campus.

Enjoy the book.

Your loving father,
Van Raye

This copy of his book—unsigned—and the letter, had cost me $5,000. There was no mention of the money, and I had no idea what a Craig-48 was. I turned the book over and looked at the author photo. The camera had caught Van Raye, eyes right, and he was in the process of smiling, a smile that you could tell was the beginning of laughter. Of course he displayed no hand in the author photo. Van Raye had written in a previous book that a hand in an author photo was a sign of a bad book. An author with his hand to his chin, or an arm draped on an arm, or, God forbid, holding a pair of glasses, was a sign the writer was dull as shit.

He was full of shit. I ripped his letter in half before I realized an old man and woman had gotten into the elevator, now staring at me, both with hands on rolling suitcases, ready to start their travel day. I stuffed the pieces of letter in my robe's pocket and forced a smile.

They got out at the lobby, and I rose in the glass elevator again, seeing Albert in the lobby below, standing with his hands in front of him, staring at me going up, and I felt my eye twitching.

That Wednesday, I went to see a doctor in a strip mall.

CHAPTER 14

By luck of the draw, I got an Indian doctor. He thumped my chest and instructed me to take deep breaths, which took me to the point of dizziness.

Dr. Ahuja was in his fifties, hair parted in the middle, stringy bangs and eyes so small they appeared closed and suspicious of everything. He probably had an Indian mother somewhere out there who was either very proud of him for being a doctor, or who thought being only an internist in a strip mall was a big failure.

When I told him my eye had been twitching, he squinted even harder but said, "No, they aren't twitching."

Redressed and sitting in his office, I stared at the changing pictures in the digital photo frame on his desk. The frame had the swirling logo of the drug company's name on its bottom. A picture brightened in the screen: a pair of bare feet propped on a table framing the Eiffel Tower. Then the picture changed to bare feet framing Big Ben. I was pretty sure these were Dr. Ahuja's feet.

"I think I might be getting depressed again," I said. There was a superficial scuff on the side of my loafer. "I can't seem to relax. I don't think the Rozaline is working. Could I be building up a tolerance?"

"No," he said, looking at my records on his computer from dozens of other doctors in my past. I almost expected him to tell me that America was full of overmedicated crybabies, but I'd listened and heard no accent. I'm guessing, like me, he had been born here.

The digital frame on his desk changed to a picture of his bare feet framing the pyramids, and I tried to control myself from rubbing the mark off my shoe. *Scuffed shoes? No appreciation for the value of things.*

"Can you describe in greater detail how you are feeling?" he asked.

I crossed my leg to bring the shoe closer. "I have this twitching in my eye, like I said—"

"Stop. It says here you are refusing an influenza shot? I want you to tell me why."

"I never get the flu," I said.

He made a distrustful sound in his throat and a small laugh, and I used the moment to lick my thumb and wipe the scratch off my shoe.

The picture frame on his desk changed to his legs propped on a backpack, his bare feet framing sharp snowcapped mountains.

He asked, "You were how old during this period here . . . when you were last paralyzed?"

"Last time? Fourteen," I said, "but I had milder cases at six and eight."

"Ventilator?"

He'd just examined me and seen no scar on my throat, and this mistake made me picture a disappointed Indian mother frowning at him. "No," I said.

That episode of paralysis happened after I had visited Van Raye with the Alfa Romeo in the desert. I'd flown back to Elizabeth who was living at a hotel in Baltimore. Tingling began in my extremities. In a matter of hours I had even been unable to talk.

Dr. Ahuja asked me, "Did anyone ever give a firm diagnosis?"

"No. It just went away."

I remembered how doctors had examined the fourteen-year-old me, trying diagnoses on me like shoes—"He has Guillain-Barré syndrome," ruling each one out—West Nile virus, MS, mercury poisoning. There seemed some comfort in Elizabeth telling them that it had happened before when I was six, once when I was eight, and it simply had gone away both times.

Dr. Ahuja's brow wrinkled, and for the first time I could see his brown eyes, but then he squinted again as the picture changed to his bare feet framing an alpine chateau.

"I was stressed then too, like I am now. That's what I'm worried

about," I said. "I haven't been sick at all since. I mean not even the snif-
fles. I don't need a flu shot. I just don't want to get emotionally unbal-
anced or I'm worried about the paralysis happening again. The flu shot
is unnecessary. My mother says I have an Indian immune system."

He said, "That's absurd."

"My biological father is from rural Florida. I've got a weird combi-
nation of third-world immune systems."

He said, "May I see your medical degree?" Idiotically, I touched
the pocket of my jacket, but he said, "No, you don't have one. I do.
What you are saying has no scientific facts." He looked down at his
computer and began rapidly typing. "What happened to you has a
medical reason, it just hasn't been found yet. Stay away from supersti-
tions. I would suggest that you let good medical professionals collect
the facts and let them give you answers. Calcutta and Miami immune
systems have nothing to do with each other."

"I didn't say Miami, I said *Florida*. There's a difference."

"I know the difference," he said. "And I would also strongly suggest
you take a flu shot." He asked me, "And you think you are depressed?
Describe how you feel." He squinted into the fluorescent lighting, prepared to analyze my answer.

How could I explain? I thought about my playlist, "Songs to Beat
Depression."

"You know how when you are listening to music?" I said. "Okay, on
the shuffle function, it gives you random songs supposedly designed
for you by your previous choices, right?"

"Of course. I know this."

"And some days every song the computer sends me makes me
feel great, like the best song I've ever felt. On other days, it shuffles
songs . . ." I shrugged my shoulders. "You know, every song makes
you feel terrible, they're all bummers. Then I realize it's not the music,
it's me. I only listen to one song, basically. Only one song makes me
feel good."

"You listen to the same song over and over?"

"Kind of," I said. "I just have this feeling everyone is happier than I am. I just want to feel like everyone else."

"That's exactly what *everyone* else says," Dr. Ahuja said. He tapped the keyboard to go back over something. He nodded his head. "Okay, okay . . . " He tilted his chin at me. "Do you have any thoughts of suicide?"

Suicide? I thought.

Before I could answer, he held up his hand to stop me. "What was that in your mind?" He admonished me with his hand, "Stop! Free association only. The thing that popped in your mind. Close your eyes."

I did. I backed my mind up and saw a cart full of cleaning supplies and I saw housekeeping women pushing the cart. I realized that it had always been the morning staff that found suicides.

I said to Dr. Ahuja, "Morning maids, hotel morning maids."

His chair squeaked. "Interesting," he said. "What are they mourning?"

"No, *morning* maids," I said, "like housekeeping, like in hotels in the morning, cleaning. I don't think that will make sense to you—"

"It makes sense to me," he said.

"But morning maids is what I thought about. My mother and I live in an environment where everyone resents us."

"Everyone *resents* you? Interesting. Okay, the question again, and I'll let you answer it. Any thoughts of suicide?"

"No," I said.

"Let me ask you this." He touched his fingertips together beneath his nose. "Are you getting ready to go on a trip?"

"What?"

"A trip, *travel*?" he repeated.

"Always," I said.

"See, I knew it. I can tell." He smiled, pleased at himself. "Travel is very stressful."

He swiveled in his chair and picked up a brown box from the floor, set it on his desk, took sample boxes out, and slid them across the desk to me. "This is going to help you," he said. He explained this was a "new common help" people took, and explained the dosages, and told me to taper off the Rozaline. "This is newer, more effective, fewer side effects. This is my preference," he said.

He waited. It was called Elapam. When I didn't say anything right away, he pushed three more sample boxes to me. I finally said, "Sometimes I have trouble sleeping too."

"My choice for my patients is somatropin."

I turned the box of Elapam over. On the back were words and complicated chemical contents and warnings. Shaking the box, it rattled with tinfoil pill sleeves, and on the front of the box was a formless figure dancing, sexless and twirling with arms overhead, and I realized that the swirling at the feet was the drug company logo on the frame of his digital photo frame.

Dr. Ahuja was working at the computer, the mouse clicking faster. It took him about ten seconds to send the prescriptions to every pharmacy in the world.

"That's it! Godspeed!" he said. "Enjoy your travels!"

I checked out with the woman who had been the nurse who'd weighed me and took my initial blood pressure, now sliding the translucent glass open and taking my credit card. All the magazines in the waiting room were business magazines, and she handed me the receipt for my visit, rather expensive for what he'd just done. It reminded me of the warning Van Raye had written in an essay in *My Year of Quantum Weirdness*: "Every doctor thinks he can be a businessman, and every businessman thinks he can be a lawyer, and every lawyer thinks he can be a writer, and every writer thinks he's right about everything."

CHAPTER 15

On Thursday, Elizabeth and I woke early for a trip to Chicago for her to attend the Host Resorts board meeting. Elizabeth's standard procedure was to be through security two hours before our departure time. I wore a gray suit and a red tie, and when we sat down at our gate and I had just begun enjoying the Airport Zone, I glanced at our itinerary on my phone and was shocked to see that our flight had been rebooked through Birmingham. When had I done that?

I had some vague recollection of changing our flights, as if I had dreamed it, but yes, it was me, not the hacker. I'd changed our reservations after taking my sleeping pills, under the influence, and believed the violin could be in Birmingham, at this place called the Warehouse of Mishandled Luggage. Now I wasn't so sure. We'd be wasting our time going.

On my phone, I found where the post-sleeping-pill me had searched for the Warehouse of Mishandled Luggage. There was strangely no website, only an address in Birmingham. Sitting in the gate area, I found a street view of the address and saw a standard-looking warehouse warped in the fish-eye perspective.

Elizabeth took out the CEO report and began rereading it using her speed-reading finger.

On my phone, I also discovered a text conversation with Dubourg, my cousin. I actually had typed these words:

> There's weird shit going on.

I was embarrassed and annoyed.

> Something big has happened with Van Raye. Tell you tomorrow.

Tomorrow? I scrolled toward the end of the conversation. The conversation went on with Dubourg trying to figure out what I was trying to get at, trying to follow my explanation of ringing payphones, Elvis, and Elizabeth's lost violin, and he'd said:

> I can fly through ATL in AM.
>
> Meet concourse C tomorrow.

The last balloon was time stamped this morning:

> Im here.

I looked at my watch seeing that our rendezvous time was fifteen minutes ago, and quickly texted:

> I'm here! On way!

"I've got to go walk some," I said to Elizabeth, standing suddenly, lifting my attaché and putting the strap over my head. "Stretch my legs."

Her eyes studied me over her cheap rhinestone glasses, and she knew I was up to something. But as she was forming a question, I turned away.

On the train to concourse C, I noticed people wearing identify-me lapel pins—Christian crosses, Rotary Club pins, and different-colored ribbons signifying some cause—and the tram let me out on C, and I took the escalator up and stopped in a bookstore, searched the "New Arrivals" display until I found *The Universe Is a Pair of Pants* on the lower shelf and bought a copy and a pack of Marlboros and stuck them in my bag.

Midway down the concourse to the smoking lounge, I started encountering the smoke smell and the red-eyed people with the general gray complexion of addicts. I'm sorry to have to report that smokers in general show poorer personal hygiene than other people.

Outside the smoking lounge, I leaned to see into the glass room, the fishbowl of cancer, where my cousin—really my half brother—sat on a bench with a cigarette. He wore his black jacket and priest's collar, and that valise between his feet, and he uncomfortably listened to a middle-aged man in a goatee smiling and talking animatedly.

I hadn't seen Dubourg in over a month, but he looked older to me, and more like Van Raye than he ever had, though these features were handsome on Dubourg, perhaps the right amount of DNA from his biological French mother. We looked nothing alike. On one of my first visits to Florida, two of the aunts had put Dubourg and me back to back, made us slowly turn as though we were in a police lineup, looking for a resemblance, but there was very little. Elizabeth always claimed the Indian genes stomped all others.

I'd gone to his ordination in New Orleans on the last official day of spring for that year, and in the heat of the cathedral he vowed poverty, celibacy, and obedience, and he had pissed off someone because ultimately he was not given the assignment of a parish priest, but he was made a courier for the church, having to tote around that black valise now protected between his knees, the contents of which he was not even privileged to.

I watched through the glass, saw his hand absently touch the valise as the stranger talked. This man spoke excitedly, cigarette between his fingers. Dubourg's brow wrinkled with concern.

The man finally looked at his watch and stabbed his butt out. They stood and shook hands. The man grabbed the long handle of his suitcase and left.

Dubourg began writing in a notebook and I went and sat in the seat directly in front of him and waited for him to notice me.

He finished what he was writing and stubbed out the cigarette, turned his head sideways to see the words. He lifted his head and blinked at me sitting across from him. His heavy glasses had slid down his nose.

A smile eased onto his face, and he shook his head, smiling, closed his book. "How long have you been here?" He stood and held his arms open to me. His long brown hair and beard made him look like the velvet portraits of Jesus in truck stops. He took me in a hug, and I felt the familiar strength of his arms. He gave me hardy thunks on my back.

When he looked at me again, I saw he had a crusty white remnant on his mustache from a recent swig from an antacid bottle. I pointed to my lip to let him know, and he wiped it away.

"Got a smoke?" I asked.

He bent to perform a reassuring touch to the valise, then turned to a woman and asked politely while making the international sign to bum a smoke. The woman said, "Certainly, Father," and he got two, Dubourg lighting mine, and we went around and sat in the row of black vinyl chairs that faced out of the fishbowl of cancer and watched the rest of the world walk by.

I felt the rush of nicotine. I only wanted a cigarette when I was around him, and I had toured all smoking lounges in major American airports because of Dubourg and his assignment, that black valise that he had to keep moving for the church.

"Jesus, when's the last time you slept?" I said.

Instead of answering, he straightened his posture, and he filled me in on the cousins he'd talked to lately—Holly, Good John, Curt, Benita, Bad John, and Cecil, and updated me on the recent births and babies and children I'd forgotten about. He snuck an antacid tablet into his mouth, then he pulled a thin package of wet wipes out of his duffle. He offered me one, and he rubbed his on the back of his neck and under his ears.

He had been a great athlete in Wakulla County, had gone to a private college in West Virginia on a baseball scholarship.

I blew smoke from the side of my mouth.

"What's so big that's going on with Charles?" he asked, flicking his ash casually as if this wasn't what he was aching to know.

I wasn't ready to talk about Charles. Van Raye's limited contact with Dubourg—all meetings happened through me—heightened Dubourg's fascination with the man. I said, "You know all that stuff I said about the hacker sending me messages, you know, like cloaked messages to find Elizabeth's violin?"

He nodded.

"Somebody's fucking with me."

"Yeah, I get that."

I handed him the phone so he could see the texts from the hacker.

He said, "You don't really think there's one place that all the lost luggage in the world ends up, do you?"

"No," I said. "I was a little tipsy last night. I took a sleeping pill. I kind of don't remember having that conversation with you."

He looked at my phone.

I tried to keep my hands from shaking, kept bringing the cigarette to my mouth sooner than I normally would. I said, "I will admit that how much he knows about me is a little scary."

He tilted his head to read the phone through the bottom of his glasses. He scrolled with his index finger. "What am I supposed to be looking at?"

He handed the phone back to me. It was on the menu of all my texts, mostly from him and Ursula, but there was no text conversation from the blocked number. I kept thumbing back and forth from the text page as if it would magically reappear.

"You're shitting me," I said. "It was right here!"

I sat back and looked around the smoking lounge. "I'm going insane." I rebooted the phone, the technical move of the truly desperate.

Dubourg asked another man for a cigarette.

"My God, you think I'm crazy . . . " I shook my head. "It doesn't make sense. Could a hacker erase the conversation on my phone?"

"I don't think so. Change all your passwords right away."

"Oh, great advice, thank you. Do you think I haven't done that?"

"I'm trying to help."

"I know, but I'm telling you something is going on."

I turned the screen back on as if it would magically reappear.

I asked him, "Ever heard the phrase 'I am what I am'? It sounds like it's from the Bible. I know I've heard it."

"No. That's Popeye. But 'I am *that* I am,' that's Exodus, when the burning bush starts talking. Moses asked the voice to identify itself, God said, 'Yahweh,' or, 'I am that I am.' It varies among texts, but there you go, basically speaking. You don't think it's God texting you, do you?" I waited for him to crack a smile but he didn't.

"*Seriously?*" I said. "You're asking me if God is talking to me?"

He didn't change his studious, serious expression. He said, "There are plenty of ways God talks to you."

"Du, through my *cell phone*?"

"The manifestation of His words might be a hallucination that your phone is doing this."

"You're not helping. You can't understand how unbelievable this is. Forget God. It's not God."

He slouched and said, "You don't really think God would direct you to your mama's violin, do you? Doesn't quite work like that."

I was frustrated. "I'm not an idiot," I said.

Around the smoking lounge the other addicts seemed to be talking to each other. Very few had their phones out. It was suddenly annoying that a smoking lounge is the friendliest place in the airport.

He put his hand on the valise and watched the non-addicts strolling in the regular world on the other side of the glass.

He said, "I know you want to find her violin. Sometimes desperation makes us believe anything."

"Goddamn it, I don't believe anything."

He shushed me. "Keep it down, okay. Maybe," he said, "you are having a vision."

"I'm not having a vision."

"Maybe a religious experience."

"Du, please."

"Do you have any proof that this is happening to you, something you can show me?"

"I can only *tell* you what has happened to me."

He nodded his head and smiled. "If something happens to you, are you ready?"

I put my head in my hands. "What if I told you that Charles found something," I said. "Would you believe that?"

He leaned away to see me better. "What are you talking about?"

I glanced behind us before saying, "He found a noise."

He looked from my right eye to my left. Smoke drifted between us. "You're joking, right?"

"No. He told me the other day. Over the phone. It's a big secret. I'm not supposed to tell you, anybody."

"Well shit. He's actually done it?"

"It hasn't been confirmed. But he says yes."

"Holy mother of God," he said, closing his eyes, and when he opened them again they followed the people on the other side of the glass, his eyes jerking as they picked up the sight of each person. "But if it hasn't been confirmed, it means nothing," he said.

"I know."

He stretched out his leg and reached into his pocket, took out a chalky antacid and put it between his teeth and crunched.

"Come stay with us in Atlanta," I said. "We got to go to Chicago for the day, but we'll be back tonight."

"Can't," he said, searching each stranger's face as they passed the smoking lounge.

"Are you looking for someone?"

"No one particular," he said, "just the annoying interfaith chaplains." He shrugged. He touched the valise. "Do you have any clothes I can borrow?" He eyed my carry-on.

"Not with me. Go to the hotel and I do."

He shook his head. "I'm going to have to go kick the bishop soon."

"What does that mean?"

"Just a euphemism. I wish I were having visions. You're lucky, you know that, right?"

He held his cigarette between thumb and forefinger to smoke and think. "I'm slowly losing touch with the church, and I don't think that's exactly healthy, but I don't want to stop what I'm doing with this." He touched the valise. "You know, when I travel, it's a good time to talk to God. You should try it."

"I hope you aren't talking to God out loud when you're walking around airports."

"Traveling alone, it's a giant meditation with God. I can feel Him sometimes, like He's right there with me. It can happen to you, you know."

"Yeah, your life seems so sexy," I said.

"You think life is a grand hotel?" he said. "Well, it's not. It's serving a higher purpose. I didn't ask to do this service," he tapped the valise, "but this was what He chose for me. I released myself to God. The other night in the Denver airport, I clearly heard a voice tell me, 'Wash your hands.' I did it literally, you know."

He shook his head like I was a child who would never understand, and he crossed his arms on his chest.

I said, "Sometimes I just want my cousin back."

"You got your cousin. You got your brother too. Where do you think I've gone?"

"You can't talk like we used to." I wanted the regular him back— back from before his big moment on the hiking trip in college when he felt God on the mountain and cried for a whole day.

He said, "I know you're not a believer, but He's here. Sometimes I go days without talking to anyone. I mean I'm right here among all the people, but I'm silent for days. To be silent among everyone is wonderful."

His ordination ceremony in the cathedral that hot spring was three hours long. When I showed up, a Knights of Columbus in his commodore hat and sword seated me in the back until Aunt Lucy, Dubourg's mother, saw me and moved me forward, a big, deep-voiced, strong woman whom I loved for finding me and bringing me to them when I was nine years old.

Aunt Lucy cried during the ceremony; lots of people cried like it was a wedding. I leaned forward and saw Ursula dry eyed with her brother Cecil and Aunt Myra and Uncle Ben.

In the airport smoking lounge with Dubourg, I pulled the copy of *The Universe Is a Pair of Pants* out of the satchel, and the pack of Marlboros, and gave it to him.

"His latest book," I said.

He leaned away from the book as if to see it better before touching it. "Maybe that's not what I need at this exact moment."

"What do you mean? He can't have fucked up your life that much. You've barely known him."

"But all the science. Maybe I don't need his rich thicket of reality at the moment."

"Maybe you do," I said.

He saw my puzzled face. He took the cigarettes but left me the book. "But thanks for the smokes."

In the ordination ceremony, Dubourg had to lay facedown on the altar while a woman in the balcony sang out for the blessing of every saint upon him. I remember seeing the soles of his shoes up there on the altar, which were unscuffed and a symbol so blatant it was laughable. The ceiling's mural depicted Christ showing his scarred hands to his disciples, and I noticed that the woman singing in the balcony was standing near the railing, and through the gap in the marble railing, I, the only one in the cathedral whose head wasn't bowed, looked up into the shadow of her short skirt. I sat in the ceremony realizing that if all this were true, then I was going to hell, but I began to hear the wind chimes in my brain that proceed an erection, the exact sound, I realized, as the church's Sanctus bells rang, *those* bells that signify a supernatural occurrence, and I thought about how happy Dubourg seemed when I went to see him in college, before he ever mentioned wanting to be a priest. He had boyfriends in college, and I have this image of him when he was joking around with a guy, grabbing him by the wrist to pull him out of a car. I can still see Dubourg's hand around the other guy's wrist, playfully pulling. I can still see him asleep on the train when we went to New York, boyfriend's head on Dubourg's shoulder, Dubourg watching out the window.

I was surely going to hell, but I wondered how Dubourg gave up the happiness of tugging his boyfriend by the wrist, the way they were laughing together, or giving up ever having someone to sleep with you, to protect you at night from the Creature listening through the wall. On the altar he repeated, "I vow poverty, chastity, and obedience to my superior in the Society of Jesus . . ."

"Father Dunbar?" someone said in the lounge. "Is that you?"

"Yes? Oh, hello," he said to the man.

The man had a suit on, a red tie he rearranged with a flick. "We would love to have you come worship with us today. Would you?" His nametag said:

Deacon Donald K. Cook

Airport Interfaith Services

(Baptist)

The man squinted his eyes, not used to being in the smoking lounge. He tried to smile at me and resisted the urge to fan the air in front of his face. "You too, my friend," he said to me.

"Oh, right," Dubourg said, rising. "May I have a minute?"

The man nodded, and we watched him walk out the door. Through the glass we could see him smiling at passersby.

"Are you in trouble?"

"No," he said. "Interfaith people," he rolled his eyes. "The hazard of spending too much time in airports is they start to recognize you." He faked a smile to the man.

"Can I pray before we leave?" Dubourg asked me, and he didn't give me a chance to answer, only put one hand on my shoulder and bowed his head. "God, this is Dubourg Dunbar in the Atlanta airport. I say a prayer of safety and tranquility for my cousin, if it's Your will. Look after him on his journey. You are all powerful and loving God, and it is in Your son's name, Jesus Christ, we pray, amen." He patted my shoulder.

"Well, thanks," I said, picking up my bag.

He frowned. "Sandy, do you need a sign as literal as the dog's eyes to believe something?"

Dubourg and I stood inside the fishbowl of cancer, being watched by the interfaith man through the glass, and I searched my memory for the meaning of "the dog's eyes."

"I remember the dog's eyes," I said. "Was that when you had the experience? I thought it was that camping trip."

"These feelings of understanding God's love happen a lot," he said. "It's ongoing and magical. One aspect that William James observed with conversions is that the experience can't be explained. The feeling I got when I saw the dog's eyes couldn't be explained."

This was before we were teenagers. We were playing in the grave-yard at night. Someone dropped the flashlight and ran. This was my memory: A dog barked and cousins ran in different directions, and there was stifled yelling and laughter. Dubourg picked the flashlight up. One of the dogs stood in the beam of light. The dog's eyes were floating gold orbs, disks, reflectors, and Dubourg saw me behind a grave marker, but he didn't turn the light on me. He shook the light at the dog's eyes and said, "That's proof God exists 'cause they protect him from getting run over by cars at night." He turned the flashlight up at the sky as if to search for God. "He made dogs with reflecting eyes!" Dubourg had yelled and claimed he was overcome with comfort, a feeling of ease in the universe. It scared the shit out of me. What is an anxiety attack and what is a religious experience?

I said to him on concourse C, "Come stay with us. Please, Du."

"I will when I can." He opened his arms and we hugged again, me taking a good whiff of his body odor to remember him. Elizabeth and I were going to Chicago, and at some point I was going to have to tell her we were going to Alabama too because I had this feeling I would find something there, maybe not the violin, but it was important to go.

I said, "Have you ever lost your luggage?"

He let go and held me at arm's length, his legs straddling the valise. "Are you shitting me? I can't lose contact with this."

"You don't have any idea what's in the case?"

"Nope."

"And yet you carry it around because *the church* told you to?"

"Faith," he said, "sacrifice."

"You must have pissed off the wrong person to get this assignment," I said.

"I can't imagine it being any other way now."

"Hey, have you ever heard of this place in Birmingham with the lost luggage?"

For an answer, he pushed his glasses up with a knuckle, exactly the same way Van Raye did and shrugged his shoulders. He waved. "Thanks for the cigarettes," he said. "I've got to go."

He turned and began walking fast with the big case beneath his arm, duffle hanging on the other side of him, and I saw that his white shirttail was untucked and hanging below his jacket. His shirttails never stayed tucked.

CHAPTER 16

In Chicago, while Elizabeth attended the board meetings, I sat in an empty waiting room and read the *Universe Is a Pair of Pants*, a chapter titled "Musings in a Quake Zone." He wrote, "Twenty-five years ago I had a wonderful little theory. This was before planetary science distracted me. I arrived at it while in San Francisco where I met a wonderful violinist." He described the violinist as "sophisticated and worldly." He wrote, "We went back and forth in my tiny apartment above Beulah Street, each playing separately—my French horn, her violin—then together, working ourselves into a frenzy, and not a single neighbor complained. It was a perfect night." Van Raye wrote that they had a "continuous concert" together, and the chapter was really about cosmology and his "wonderful theory." "When we were done and almost asleep," he wrote, "a mist fell through the open window on my face, and I heard a junkie puking on the street below, some guy who'd wandered off of Haight, retching right beneath the window, and I thought—*Exactly!* And that was when I began to formulate the shape of the universe in my mind, which could be both infinite and *bounded . . .*"

I read through eight pages of cosmology but then I kept rereading the beginning.

When Elizabeth came out of the meeting, I told her that we were going to fly through Birmingham. "I have to show you something in Charles's new book."

"Birmingham?" she said. "Why?"

"There's a store I want to go to," I said.

"What store? Another magic store?"

"Did you hear me? There's something in Charles's book I want you to read."

In the gate area, waiting for our plane, I watched her eyes beneath the cheap rhinestone readers go over the words about the violinist in San Francisco.

"You can stop when you get to the cosmology part," I said.

She finished and shut the book.

"That's about you, isn't it?" I asked.

"Yes," she said, "who else?"

"It's the only time he's ever mentioned you in a book!"

She handed the book back to me. "He mentions everyone in his books."

"Not you and me."

"Is that what you want, Sandeep? To be a couple of paragraphs of an excuse for him to talk about what he wants to talk about?"

"I just don't think I've done anything interesting enough for him to write about."

"Self-pity isn't productive," she said.

I leaned back. "Well, we're going through Birmingham."

"I don't mind spontaneity," she said, "but don't spring it on me."

It was late afternoon by the time our Airbus glided out of the overcast and touched down in Birmingham.

We got a green minivan cab, and I gave the driver the address. I asked him if he'd heard of the Warehouse of Mishandled Luggage. He'd simply replied, "No," and put the address into his GPS and sighed because he saw the fare would barely earn him over his minimum.

"What is it?" Elizabeth asked.

"Just somewhere I wanted to go."

He drove us through the same indistinct buildings and warehouses you'll find at the southern end of any airport. The driver turned off the main boulevard and went down a narrow street, then across a small bridge, and I had this sinking feeling that there wouldn't be any kind of store here, not even a pawn shop.

Big drops of rain spotted the windshield, and the wipers smeared the pollen. A simple green utility sign beside the road announced WAREHOUSE 122-A and had an arrow pointing to the next street.

A single piece of hard-cased Samsonite luggage was wrapped to an oak tree with yellow crime-scene tape. A single word, LUGGAGE, had been spray-painted on a board against the fence.

Up the drive, through woods, we left the rain shower. The cab pulled up to the indistinct warehouse I had seen on Google Street View—blue aluminum, no windows, no sign of people other than a few cars in the lot. A big Dumpster in the parking lot was filled with construction scrap, but on second look I saw it was full of dead suitcases, ones that had been unzipped or cut open and discarded.

I told the driver to wait.

"Why are we *here*?" Elizabeth asked, getting out and looking over the top of the car at me. I could hear the rain advancing through the trees and waved her to take my arm and run. We got under the shelter and I said, "I just heard about this place. It's supposedly where all lost and unclaimed luggage ends up. I thought it would be interesting."

She wiped the water off her shoulder. "Used to, when the airlines lost your luggage, they found it and delivered to your front door. Now they give you a voucher for the value. Everything is expendable."

When we stepped through the door and saw the expanse of the place, saw the rows and rows of merchandise, I felt around inside my bag, dug her camera out, the one she used to take pictures of the merchandise in the retail stores in the airports, and gave it to her without a word.

The warehouse was a giant thrift store filled with smells of used clothing, old plastic, warm electronics. I saw no other shoppers. Only a mannequin guarding the entrance dressed completely in scuba gear and holding a spear gun, guarding the wall-to-wall forgotten merchandise, a graveyard of lost things.

"Welcome to Mishandled Luggage!" a man shouted over the full rain on the metal roof. He was behind a sales counter working on the interior of something electronic. His cash register read a green "00000."

I caught up to Elizabeth at the glass jewelry case. Inside, mannequin hands reached out of the lake of a mirror, plastic fingers garishly adorned with rings—lost wedding bands, cheap green stones, ugly turquoise jewelry, white price tags dangling.

"Look at this, Sandeep!" She took the camera and aimed into the display case, trying to get a picture through the glass. We went to the next case where watches hung from horizontally placed golf clubs, hundreds of watches.

Somehow I knew which direction to walk. Maybe it was the increase of electronic noise from the back, but I saw guitars on the back wall, old ones and shiny new ones, a few without strings. Guitars? Who lost guitars? And each one represented someone's broken heart, like Elizabeth with her violin or the girl who'd dropped Barbie into the Air of Liability.

There was so much stuff here I didn't even notice the young woman until she moved, lifted her head to see us. She sat on a stool behind a counter, and her chin dropped to continue reading an old paperback held open on her knees.

On the wall were beat-up trumpets, shiny flutes, and empty instrument cases with plush red-velvet interiors. Beneath the pounding of the rain was my heartbeat because I saw high on the wall a violin in its open case sitting on pegboard hooks. I could see the Master Stefen label liner, the gold script on black cloth, one that I had seen all my life. It is a popular maker of violins, but I felt the remnants of raindrops reach my scalp and tingle. "Elizabeth" was all I could say, but she had seen it.

"That," she said to the girl reading on the stool. "Get that down."

That's it, I thought, *that can't be it.* The coolness of the raindrops made me dizzy. *This can't be happening.*

The girl pulled an aluminum ladder over, legs clattering. Elizabeth put her hands on her ears to block the racket, and the girl stopped and climbed.

Elizabeth pivoted to me and said, "That *is* my violin. Sandeep, *how did you know?*"

For the first time that trip, I noticed her earrings (clip-ons)—were gold frogs sleeping on her ears.

"I don't know how to tell you," I said.

The girl took the Master Stefen by the neck, no strings.

"Be careful," Elizabeth said, "and the case too. It is all delicate."

The girl put the violin under her arm and grabbed the case.

When a pegboard hook fell, clanging through the ladder, Elizabeth put her hand to her mouth, but the girl made it to the ground and came forth and put the violin on the counter. An orange tag had $800 written on it.

"This is my violin," Elizabeth said to me. It lay before her, but she seemed unable to reach out to touch it. Her right hand came out slowly and for some reason the violin reminded me—this thing without strings—of something dead in a tiny coffin, the children's graves I had seen when we played flashlight tag in the cemetery in Florida, and she lifted it.

"Is it okay?" I asked her.

"This is my violin," she said to the girl.

The girl said, "It's eight hundred dollars."

Elizabeth twisted around, eyes wide in disbelief. "I should not have to pay for my own violin!" She looked at me, tears streaking. I couldn't bear to look at her. "*Should I have to pay for my own violin?*" she said.

I took my money clip out, hands shaking.

The girl said, "You don't pay me."

We had to go to the man up front. He scanned a barcode on a sticker and the register went from 00000 to 00800. Maybe I should have explained that the price was badly wrong, but I was shaking and stunned, only wanted to get out of there.

I gave him the money to get us back out in the world with her violin, which rode in its case on her lap in the cab. Classic music played on the cab's satellite radio as the driver retraced the path back to the airport, Mozart's Symphony No. 15. Elizabeth wiped tears away as soon as they came, trying not to sniff, both of us wondering what had just happened.

Her tears cleared up and she asked me, "How did you know it was there?"

"Are you absolutely sure this is yours?"

"Without a doubt. How did you know?"

My hands squeezed my knees, and I said, "Magic."

"Dammit," the driver said and touched a finger to the radio to change stations until the screen said "Sports Talk 250" and the music was gone.

My phone vibrated. I pulled it out and saw a new conversation had begun:

> Some people call them "miracles."

I texted:

> Thank you for the lost luggage
> tip. How did you know?

Now Raye?

Somebody out there could obviously sort through data and track a violin down. The explanation would be complicated but it would be a rational one. I kept reminding myself of this. It wasn't really magic. Nothing was but I had this wonderful feeling of being confused by what I saw.

I quickly turned my phone for Elizabeth to see. "Do you see this conversation?" I said to her.

She cleared her eyes and tilted her head back even though she didn't have her reading glasses on. "What?"

I looked at the phone and there was nothing but the phone's menu, the conversation gone.

Everything could be explained, maybe explained with a long-shot scenario, like the fact that all information exists on the web and a hacker could get information and track down a violin. I think we all have this sense that a shadow exists in this other space—each name, place, thought, theorem, video—entire lives could be constructed from the information. I had once noticed how my fingers were more blunt than Elizabeth's, and the thought crossed my mind to search "Sanghavi Aardarsh's fingers" to see what my grandfather's fingers looked like before I realized the absurdity.

The satellite radio on the dash changed from sports talk back to Symphony No. 15 without the driver touching it. Everything was becoming a message to me, or I was going insane.

For a second I thought my phone was vibrating in my hand, but realized my fingers were tingling. *Not the tingling. What is happening?* I shook the hand to increase circulation.

I wanted Charles to help me figure everything out, but on that flight back to Atlanta that small tingle became numbness and progressed inward. If this thing, this paralyzing thing was happening again, I wouldn't be able to talk to anyone. *This isn't happening, this isn't happening again.* I had allowed myself to get stressed out, that was all. I was too scared to mention it to Elizabeth sitting right beside me.

CHAPTER 17

By the time we got back to the Grand Aerodrome, it was almost a comfort to see the ugly orange carpet. I only wanted to get in the bed, give my body rest. The numbness would go away.

When I walked by the payphones, the one on the end began ringing. I motioned for Elizabeth to go ahead, and when I picked it up, I didn't even say hello, just waited for the music, that drum roll and beat and the bass pick up—"*A little less conversation, a little more action, all this aggravation ain't satisfaction in me . . .*"

My phone dinged and the text appeared:

> LOL! I still love doing that to you!
> Life can be so wonderful, Sandeep!

I glanced around the lobby before taking a breath and typing with numb fingers:

> Where are you?

> I am everywhere and nowhere at the same time, a clump of data like you. I need Raye in order to travel on.

> I think I'm getting sick.

It took a few seconds as though he were thinking or searching.

> The paralysis?

How could he know about the paralysis? My medical records? I opened and closed my left hand, shook it.

You know what is happening to me?

Yes.

I rode the glass elevator up, went to our suite. My throat tingled. *Would I stop breathing?*

The paralysis hadn't happened in fourteen years. I remembered weeks of lying in a bed and being so incredibly thirsty, waiting for someone to hold a cup of water to my lips. *Was the thirst only in my mind? Is the paralysis somehow up to me?*

Alone in my room now, I took off my clothes and slid into the tight covers of my bed. The aquarium water had cleared and the betta swam inside, gills flared, him fighting his own reflection.

Through the wall came the first tuning of Elizabeth's strings.

The rising tide of tingling had reached my knees. I didn't want to have to go and tell her.

The music she played seemed brand new, like nothing I'd ever heard before, though I'd heard Sarasate's "Carmen Fantasy" a thousand times. Maybe it was the new strings, but I also realized that Elizabeth, like every musician in the world, was a bundle of organic compounds and neurochemical reactions with feelings and experiences that converted the chaos of the universe into the best order she could make.

I was going to have to tell her it was happening again, but first I got up and got *The Universe Is a Pair of Pants* and went to the bathroom, poured a glass of water, shut the toilet lid and sat backward on the toilet with the book on the back of the tank, and I began where I'd left off, and I drank glass after glass of water as if I could fill up my body for this long journey. Elizabeth finished "Carmen Fantasy," started and finished all of "Moonlight Sonata."

I pissed and drank one last full glass of water.

In my room, Barbie sat stiff limbed on the dresser, back against the wall. I had to find Van Raye. I texted the hacker, thumbs feeling like nubs.

I am getting sick again. This sometimes takes awhile

I am very sorry this is happening.

I have gotten used to talking to someone.

I will miss talking to you but I'll be here when you are well

I opened the door to the suite where Elizabeth played in the low-wattage light of the fake living room. Her arm stopped when she saw me against the doorframe.

"Sandeep, what is it?"

"Elizabeth . . . " It seemed like the hardest thing in the world to tell her what was happening. I felt like I was failing her. I waited for a jet to finish landing, the thrust reversers shutting off. She stepped toward the lamp and the few strands of frayed string floated away from her bow like spider webs. I said, "I want to go to India."

She puzzled over my statement but said, "Look," holding the violin up. "This is wonderful. How did you do this?"

"You've never taken me to India," I said.

She held her breath then carefully put the violin in the case. She walked to me and put her hand on my forehead. Elizabeth had always told doctors, "My son never has a fever." This gesture tonight of putting her hand on my forehead was just what mothers had done for a thousand years when they were worried.

"I've never been to India," I repeated.

"Stop it," she said. "You're delirious. You've had a long day. Look," she pointed to the violin, "it's here."

"In India," I said, "I can let my body have its way with all the diseases its supposed to have. Right?"

"Why are you thinking about this now?" she said and stepped back to see me. "You don't want to go to India," she said. "In India, I've seen Americans get sunburned through their hats and die."

I held onto the doorframe. "Can I have a glass of water?"

She went into the bathroom, leaving me leaning against the doorframe. When my phone dinged, I fumbled it out of my pajama pocket. It said:

> I can't believe you are going away.

> Can you stop it? I'll do anything. I can't get Raye if I'm paralyzed

> No. I can't stop a disease.

I started to put the phone away, but another text came in.

> But I can give you a method.

> It will help time go by quickly. Take it.

> Ask me a question about the near future.

> I don't understand.

> Do you want to know the date you will get out of the hospital?

> ?

> Providing the answer will make you jump there in time. You will still have the experiences.

> But for the moment it will feel like you've leapt forward in time.

> Do you want to know how?

> Who are you?

> I'm not from this planet, so call me Randolph. :)

I read the word again, "Randolph." This was impossible. I was losing my mind. A hacker couldn't know about a childhood game that Elizabeth had played on me, one in which an alien took over her body.

> When Raye contacts you, he'll have a dog. Take care of the dog.

Dog? This was bullshit.

> Do you want to know when you will be out of the hospital?

> Telling you the future will make you leap there in time.

Elizabeth came out of the bathroom with a glass of water.

"Tell me now," I said. "You did Randolph, didn't you? Randolph is you."

"This again? Sandeep, please."

I could see my hand gripping the glass of water but not feel it. The coolness of the glass felt a long way from my head. Elizabeth watched me gulp. "Why are you drinking water?"

"I won't be able to drink when it's done."

"*Stop that talk.*"

"You know that's the worse part," I said. "I get so thirsty."

"It's not happening again. Tell yourself no. Please, Sandeep. It's not true."

"It's not my fault," I said, and tried to adjust my hands and the glass fell, almost hit Elizabeth's feet.

"Sandeep!"

The water splashed on the floor, the floor an impossible distance from my head.

"It's the tingling," I said to her, the horrible, magic word we never spoke.

"Oh no," she said, her eyes big, "you're wrong!"

"Tell me! You are Randolph. You did Randolph."

"Of course I did," she said. "Why is that even important? Stop, you are frightening me."

I leaned against the door, her eyeing me suspiciously, and I texted.

> ok. Tell me

And he, Randolph or whatever he was, gave me the answer to the question—What day would I be out of the hospital?—though I still have the experience of the EMT shining a light in my eyes that night I was driven to the hospital, the ambulance leaning into a turn and all that was to follow, but as it was happening I did not think about the date, worry about the date, the date never crossed my mind but now seems to have been there all along, waiting for me to remember it. Every experience from that episode is in my memory, but here I am typing this, knowing that I knew the date of my release all those weeks, the date Randolph had given me of my body's reprieve.

Riding in the ambulance, I thought about my phone sitting on my dresser in the hotel room—"Viva Las Vegas" stuck on my "Songs to Beat Depression" playlist—and also that I hadn't sent Dubourg and

Ursula a message about what was going on. My body was shutting me inside. I hoped like all the other times it would only be temporary. I was becoming just a brain.

I remember the EMT, a woman, putting the plastic oxygen mask over my face and remember how clean the air was and Elizabeth sitting on a jump seat, arms wrapped around her body, rocking as if praying, which scared me the most.

PART II

CHAPTER 18

A couple of thousand miles away from me, a woman sat on a campus bench that afforded her a view of both entrances of the physics building. She sucked an unlit cigarette for a cheap tobacco buzz, her first "cigarette" in over a year. She wore a dirty insulated jacket, though the air temperature in Stanford, California, (I've checked archives for that day) was 65°F. Students probably thought Ruth Christmas sitting and listening to an old radio in her lap was a homeless woman who'd wondered over from town. It didn't help that her hair had been chopped off so she looked crazy.

(When she was telling me this story, filling in the few gaps left by Van Raye's journals, she told me she didn't consider what she was doing as "stalking," but then she laughed and told me, "That's what every stalker says.")

If anything showed her state of mind that day, it was that she sat nearly six hours listening to big band music on that radio, no eating, drinking, or relieving her bladder or lighting the cigarette. (She told me, "I have the perfect bladder for an astronaut.")

When Van Raye finally emerged at 17:25 from the north entrance, he was wearing the same button-up sweater he'd been wearing when she'd followed him to work that morning.

A minor heart palpitation took Ruth's breath. *Jesus*, she thought, *why do I want him now?*

Remembering that people walk 1.3 meters per second, she counted to thirty-three before she pushed the radio's antenna down, shut the front cover, and began trailing him. She noted the way his body swayed back and forth as if it contained more lazy muscles than enterprising muscles, leaning to his left to counterbalance carrying the single book in the other hand, and Ruth suddenly realized she was out of breath, needed to lean against something. She'd forgotten gravity was a bitch.

From Van Raye's perspective, he had no idea Ruth Christmas was back on Earth.

Two weeks ago, she'd left the space station via emergency pod, the pod coming to Earth dangling from four parachutes and landing not so gently in Mongolia. There, she traveled via horseback, then bus, then a Roscosmos flight to Star City where she was given a physical, which included peeing on a stick, her condition confirmed, and then she'd hopped a MAC flight to California without telling anyone where she was going.

From Moffett Field, California, she'd taken a cab to the storage lot in Redwood City and liberated Van Raye's Jaguar, technically *her* Jaguar because she'd gotten it in the divorce settlement two years ago, though she hated the car, hated driving. She had stopped at the first 7-Eleven and bought a pack of Marlboros and a three-pack of lighters, and then went to Empire Vintage Electronic in Palo Alto. She settled for the solid heaviness of a Trans-Oceanic model 600, bought a new IL6 capacitor, and replaced the old one just to cover her bases. She drove to campus, left the Jaguar in the overflow parking lot, took the Trans-Oceanic, and now she was hiding behind bronze statues of weeping people and watching Van Raye climb the stairs of the auditorium.

She sat on a marble wall to catch her breath, opened the panel on the back of the radio, and checked the tubes, the battery leads. Then she stared at the sculpture garden around her: Rodin's giant "Gates of Hell," a twenty-foot bronze, spectacular with the inlaid suffering people, screaming and melting into the surface of the door.

Hell, hell, hell, Ruth thought.

She noted in particular the bronze babies cast along the left column.

The babies made her quit the "Gates of Hell" and take the radio and work up the courage to go inside the auditorium. Why did she want him? He would be a comfort, but she also knew he was the least qualified man in the world to discuss family.

Van Raye looked out at the scant audience in the auditorium, not yet recognizing Ruth sitting in the back. This was depressing, he thought. He used to pack this auditorium, used to pack the lecture room even for a simple Physics 211 lecture.

In the middle seats, he saw the three old string theorists—ruined men who now spent their time attending any lectures. One of them, Gabriel Zepler, was doing something on his phone. Besides them, the audience was older book-club types, no candidates to take home to sleep with tonight. He'd been having an on-again-off-again relationship with a married system administrator from Sunnyvale who had become less and less available, and there was the woman across the aisle on the flight from Seattle to San Francisco yesterday who had recognized him. As soon as she said, "I saw the *Report from Earth* when I was a teenager . . . " he knew that he would sleep with her that night, and he did.

The auditorium's giant coffee maker gurgled while a woman from the university bookstore gave an introduction and he went to the podium, thanked her, and read the chapter in *The Universe Is a Pair of Pants* about the time he drove the Pacific Coast Highway with an "actress." He referred to her in the essay as "Jessica," and they stopped at an alfresco Mexican restaurant, were eating at a picnic table above the beach when she said that a friend had told her that you could unlock your car from anywhere in the world by simply broadcasting the signal of your electronic keyless device through your cell phone.

(I kept up with all of Van Raye's writings. This essay that he read was "There Are Neutrinos in My Hair," and it first appeared in *Playboy*, which I had bought several years before, and I will always associate the "actress" with that Playmate of the Month who appeared to enjoy being alone and naked in the desert and eating plums.)

He read about how he told Jessica that even if he weren't the world's foremost expert on electromagnetism, if he knew nothing about electronics, he would know that broadcasting her door lock over her cell phone was impossible simply because he could feel how badly she *wanted* to believe it.

Jessica said, "My friend told me she's done it. It works."

"Don't you feel it?" he said to her.

"Feel what?" she said sitting at the table in her bikini top and a gold hunting horn dangling from a necklace. (He, a French horn player, wrote these details.)

"Don't you feel this thing inside you," he said. "This is emotion-driven logic, this feeling of how you *want* something to be true? How wonderful would the universe be if we could discover this one little thing that tied everything together—phones and door locks? We could unlock our car doors from *anywhere*! Wouldn't that be wonderful? When it feels that kind of wonderful, it's never true."

To prove it, he used his charm to borrow a server's cell phone, and left Jessica at the table and went alone to the gravel parking lot and held the phone to Jessica's Porsche. Behind the restaurant Jessica held the remote keyless fob to her phone (open line to Van Raye) and tried to broadcast its signal over the airwaves. Nothing happened.

"Nope," Van Raye said on his end of the phone.

Her voice came from the hollowness of cell phone reception: "Are you holding it to the car?"

"Yes, darling." He blandly turned the phone to the Porsche and smiled at the waitress who looked out the open window of the taco shack to see what he was doing with her phone. Lifting it back to his ear, he said, "Nothing, dear. Sorry."

He writes that Jessica was angry: "As if it were my fault that she'd believed this thing."

He hated the term "skeptic," but he wrote in "There Are Neutrinos in My Hair" that the more we want to believe in something, the unlikelier it is to be true.

Back eating tacos behind the restaurant, Van Raye took Jessica's keys off the table and said, "But watch this." He held it up in the air, pushed the button. He showed her that it was still out of range, her car silent.

"Now," he said, "put it under your chin like this." He put the fob beneath his chin in the V of his jawbone and pushed the button. When the wind rested, when the waves were in lull, Van Raye and Jessica could hear a beep coming from her car in the parking lot each time he pushed the button. She wanted to try, pushed it into the tender spot beneath her jaw. Her Porsche beeped and then beeped again.

"Your body is an antennae," he said to her.

She was underwhelmed, he wrote.

"What's the difference," she asked, "in believing this will work, and my idea . . . besides the fact one of them was *my* idea and one was yours?"

"My idea isn't very grand. It's not something I felt I wanted to *believe* in, the way a part of us wants to believe in the supernatural or horoscopes. I could feel how much you *wanted* to believe that the universe is built like that. Always be suspicious of what you feel yourself wanting to believe. Couldn't you feel your imagination being played with? I actually felt myself wanting to believe in the idea too.

"Professor Marcello Truzzi said it best: 'Extraordinary claims require extraordinary proof.' My idea just uses your whole body as an antenna," he said. "Of course, some bodies are better than others."

If you watch the archived video of him reading this essay that night in the auditorium, you'll be able to distinguish the exact moment when he saw Ruth Christmas.

He noted this person in the audience, a woman in an oversized puffy coat, and he did think she was a homeless person who'd wandered in to eat the free food.

He was wrapping up the reading, "The universe itself is a wonder but often completely unfascinating to ordinary people, and therefore they want to believe in little green men, monsters, or God . . ."

Here, in the video, he does a double take, adjusts his glasses with his knuckle.

He said she mouthed words at him, holding an unlit cigarette beside her head and he recognized Ruth Christmas. Her gorgeous dark hair was gone.

Van Raye stopped the reading midsentence and tried to hear what she was saying. Here was his most recent ex-wife.

"I'm sorry, darling?" he asked.

Annoyed, she spoke louder from the thin audience, "I have something for you." There was percolating from the coffee boiler in back, and the shifting of the few people in the audience to see who was interrupting.

Van Raye cleared his throat. "Wonderful," he mumbled.

He found the place in the book and wrapped up, "Why do human beings find such outrageous beliefs comforting? Can they not find satisfaction in reality? Has reality not served them well? Why isn't the neutrino, which can pass through matter, not as exciting as a ghost?"

CHAPTER 19

To write this book, I have researched websites and personal blogs of people who attended some of the public events of his book tour, and I have noticed that quite a few of the women posing with him have their hands on his stomach.

The reception at his university that night Ruth showed up was in a room adorned with portraits of dead university presidents. He signed all twelve books presented to him in the same way:

> On the night
> of the noisy coffee maker.
> Van Raye

Ruth, who sat at a table by herself, watched people posing with him, and she said she felt at ease for the first time since she'd returned to Earth, watching him with his arm curled around the book, trying to pay attention to the people he was signing for, but his eyes kept finding her, her fake smoking an unlit cigarette.

When the caterers were clearing away the one table of food, he went to her and stood without speaking.

She said, "Not a big crowd, huh? It's a sad thing when people no longer find you interesting. If only they knew what you've found."

"Let's keep quiet, shall we? When did you get back?" He straightened his posture and asked the bartender for a beer, got it and guided her away. He swigged from his Heineken and smiled at a couple with their coats over their arms, wanting to talk to the author before they left, but he turned his back to them.

"This is my home," Ruth said. She touched her head as though she could fix the stubble of hair. "What? You don't want to see me?"

"I didn't say that." A server came and put a new Heineken on the table and took the empty bottle from Van Raye.

"Should you be doing that?" she asked, pointing to the beer.

"You knew all along I didn't have a problem."

Three years ago he'd shown up to a department meeting with ice cubes in a glass of Guinness beer. When asked by the chairman what he was drinking, Van Raye had told him it was iced coffee. The department had formed an intervention (not including Ruth who was training in Houston) and gave him the ultimatum that it was AA or face serious reprimands. AA seemed like such a commitment that Van Raye had quit drinking, and in the last several years he'd gotten into the habit of *not* drinking, and he'd kept on not drinking until now.

Now he tried to look at Ruth, put the Heineken bottle to his lips. He'd forgotten the perfect click a Heineken bottle makes when it touches your incisors. *No other beer bottle is made so perfect*, he thought. Also the hissing foam in the mouth. That sounded like a large audience applauding. He took swigs just to hear applause.

He felt electricity when he touched the sleeve of Ruth's insulated parka as he swallowed and thought about her body beneath it. He remembered her strong legs and her daringness in bed, the way she would hop around. Now she stank a little.

"Would you like to go back to my place?" he asked.

"I was surprised to find that it was still *your* place."

"It's still my house," he said. "Barely. Is that yours?" He pointed at the radio in the chair beside her.

"Yes," she said without taking her eyes off him. "I have to tell you something: I'm pregnant."

There was the sound of bottles being placed on the serving cart, the last caterer walking across the room.

"Oh," he said, thinking. "How long have you been back?"

She pulled the sleeve of the parka to see her watch. "Ten days. I think. I lost track."

"That was fast," he said.

She narrowed her eyes and waited for him to think.

"Oh," he said. "Up there?"

She nodded.

"Is that why you came back down?"

"It played a part in my decision, yes."

They left the auditorium, walking through the sculpture garden, "The Gates of Hell" illuminated by spotlights.

They walked through the dry lakebed toward home, Van Raye with two beers in his sweater's pockets stretching the fabric, bottles tapping against his thighs. Above the trees was a dome of light pollution cast from the university golf course's arc lights.

"Let's see," Ruth said counting the brighter stars with her finger. "Now where is it?"

"Don't point," he said.

"There are the twins. There's Capella," she said, her hand held straight out, "so I'd follow it east. It would be about . . . there, third star down. There's a planet there full of life. Chava Norma!"

"Don't say it out loud, please," he said.

They were on a small pedestrian bridge. Van Raye glanced to see only a student walking through the grass using her open laptop like a flashlight, illuminating the ground before her.

"Please don't be flippant about this," he said. "I'm not ready for anyone to know."

"Why not?" she said.

"Soon," he said. "But I have things to do first."

Moonlight highlighted the lakebed's grass. He took a breath. "Sometimes I don't believe it's real," he said. "What if I made it all up in my mind?"

"You're forgetting I heard it too," she said. "I'm not crazy."

She stopped and put the radio on the railing of the bridge. She unhooked the gold latch on the front of the radio and lifted the front cover to reveal the old radio dial. She extended the antenna and turned it on, illuminating the eight bands on the dial.

"You don't think you can . . ." he started. "That's not possible."

Big band music played until she pushed the button for the dial labeled NIGHTS & EVENINGS and then there was the whining of white noise. She dialed through voices, Spanish and more Spanish, an Australian calling out numbers, then more music, and she fine-tuned to a silence among the chaos and then a humming interlaced with a pattern of clicks like a needle stuck at the end of a record.

"My God," he said sitting back on the railing. "How?"

"The space station's high gain is still trained on it. When I fell to Earth, I made sure it would keep tracking. It's broadcasting down to old Cold War repeaters, which in turn broadcasts it over Earth."

"We shouldn't do that," he said.

"Why? It's hidden in plain sight. Do you think anyone knows what this is? The telemetry of your signal isn't there, only the sound. Does it sound a little like a didgeridoo to you?"

"No," he said.

She took out a plastic lighter, lit the cigarette.

"Should you be doing *that*?" he asked, pointing to the cigarette. "If you are pregnant."

She fanned the smoke away from her face to see him better and said, "Every expectant mother has her cravings." She rolled her neck to loosen it, then quickly switched the radio off, shut the radio, pushed the antenna down.

He thought: *Her problem is not my problem*, and he grabbed her and kissed her on the bridge over the dry lakebed. She enjoyed the kiss, but opened her eyes to look at the sky while she did it.

CHAPTER 20

While the Van Raye/Ruth reunion went on in California, I was paralyzed in a hospital bed, living through nights while my roommate incessantly snored and the old woman in the next room shouted her name: "This . . . is . . . Rose . . . Epstein. I want to go home!"

Wouldn't I have focused on that date the hacker, "Randolph," gave me for my release: December 12? I don't remember remembering. It's a classic paradox.

Nurses came into my room all night long, green phosphorescent ID glowing as they took our vital signs in the near darkness. I'd gotten to a point where I barely woke when they slid the pressure cuff on my arm, pressed the thermometer to my ear, or stuck a small gauge needle into my abdomen, though I felt the cold shot of heparin spreading beneath the layers of my dead nerves, medicine that kept my blood thin so I wouldn't get clots.

The 11:00 PM shift was good at reading my face, and one of them would get out the tablet Elizabeth had loaded with *The Universe Is a Pair of Pants*. The nurse put the headphones over my ears and moved in my line of sight to see if the volume was okay. I blinked once to signal yes, my father's voice announcing, "Chapter 19, 'Elements from the

Tiger's Tail,'" and began the essay about the most dangerous elements on the periodic table. I had no choice but to drift off while he spoke, my ears sweaty in the headphones.

When I woke, still the middle of the night, there was a reprise of light but the hydraulic door was closing, and I had enough time to see Ursula standing in the darkness. There is always an awkward moment when people step into your darkness because you see them better than they see you: her uniform was sloppy, her captain's hat crooked on her head.

She let her eyes adjust to see me and then let her bag plop on the floor. My roommate's snoring continued.

Ursula took off her cap and stepped to my bed, patted the cap twice against her leg as she looked down at me. She'd never seen me like this, only heard stories about the episodes when I was younger.

She tossed her hat in a chair and then removed my headphones and listened to them for a second and said, "Seriously? You'll get brain-washed." Then she leaned over the rail and kissed my forehead, not at all scared I was contagious.

She smelled like a cockpit—sweat and electronics and a shower-less winter day. At the spot her lips touched my skin, the chaos of tin-gling nerves stilled as if they tried to decipher the touch. When she took them away, the tingling swarmed back in like a hive of bees.

"Do you think your mama calls me and tells me what's going on?" She stood in silhouette against the window and tried to smooth strands of her hair that had escaped from the barrette and floated away from her head. "Hell no. I couldn't get you, and so I finally called her." She walked around inspecting things in the dark, the network of the hexagons in the safety-glass window cast a shadowy net over her body. She went to my sleeping roommate, his mouth wide open. I had no idea what was wrong with him, though his name on his computer monitor was JAMES LEGGETT and had a green cartoon heart beating just like mine. The room was filled with his breath and the bitter metabolized morphine stench of it.

"I can't find Dubourg," she said. "He's probably going through one of those times he keeps his phone off." She wiggled out of her uniform jacket, carefully folded it on the chair, and then rummaged through her duffle and came out with tiny bottles of Jack Daniel's. She lined them up on the tray table, got two cups from the wall dispenser.

"Want some?"

I heard the seal break, and I blinked deliberately when she looked at me. She turned her head sideways, eyes scanning my face. She swigged from the tiny bottle and said, "That's it, then? Blinking?"

I blinked once—yes.

She squinted and said, "Have you stopped masturbating yet, Sanghavi?" She waited until I blinked twice—no. "Got it," she said and put the cup to my lips, and I tried to get only a taste, enough to spread on my tongue.

I wanted her badly to touch me again, to still the tingling anywhere.

She poured the remainder of my cup in her cup and poked at the Foley bag hanging on the end of my bed. "Let me see. I pour whiskey in this end of you and it comes out this end? Interesting." She took another swig and looked over her shoulder at Leggett as if she didn't trust his being asleep, and then put her hands on my railing and said, "And you don't know why this keeps happening to you?"

I blinked twice, no. Through the wall, the old woman's voice called out to be recognized—"I'm Rose Epstein!"—shouted like she was on a phone with a bad connection.

"They come and get you at night. Do you have recollection of this?"

I blinked emphatically no. *I was not getting abducted.*

"Jesus," she said, and for the first time I saw a little fear. She looked out the window and felt around the seal to see that it couldn't be opened.

She went to her bag and took out a thin book and two more tiny whiskey bottles. She pulled a goosenecked lamp over to a chair and clicked its rheostat switch and judged just the right amount of light. She poured both bottles into her cup and made herself comfortable in the chair under the light, propped her legs on my bed. The lamp's light shined on her face. She held the book up to show me the cover: C. G. Jung's *Flying Saucers: A Myth of Things Seen in the Skies*.

"Carl fucking Jung." She wiggled to get comfortable and began. "Chapter 1, 'UFOs as Rumors.'" She waited to see if the snoring would be interrupted, and I could hear the tiny sound of my father's voice coming from the headphones still on the bed, like he was reduced by a mad scientist's shrinking machine.

Ursula continued, "'Since the things reported of UFOs not only sound incredible but seem to fly in the face of all our basic assumptions about the physical world, it is very natural that one's first reaction would be the negative one of outright rejection. . . .'"

I wanted to laugh. I could barely make the face of laughter, my right side particularly droopy. No sound came from me. Clicking my tongue hurt. I didn't have enough breath to whistle. There was a paper calendar on the wall directly in front of my bed, a clock beside it that I had no choice but to watch.

While she read, I moved my eyes to watch her face and then back to the clock's hands moving time forward. You would have thought with those big calendar numbers in front of me I would be thinking about December 12, but I wasn't. It didn't seem to be in my mind.

Ursula fell asleep curled in the chair. More than three hours passed on the clock until she stretched, put the book away, and stood over me.

Please touch me.

"I could stay here with you," she whispered. "Do you feel vulnerable? Do you want me to stay through the night?" She looked at the sleeping roommate in the other bed.

Yes, climb in bed next to me, I thought, but I blinked no. I'd been there for fifteen days and, no, I wouldn't let her think that for a second I believed aliens were coming to get me in a hospital.

She leaned over and finally did it—put her hand on my head, lips to my skin, stopping the tingling. She whispered good night and got her bags, jacket over her arm. As the tingling flooded back, she was out the door.

I noticed my roommate was awake, and when he and I were alone, he said from the darkness, "This guy rides into a Southern town and sees an old man on the porch . . . He says to the old man, 'This is a godforsaken place. What do y'all do around here?'" The old man says, 'Fuck and hunt.' 'What do you hunt?' the guy asks. The old man says, 'Something to fuck.'"

He always waited for me to laugh at his jokes, and I mercifully heard the solenoid click in the machine by his bed, and the red ✖ on his monitor turned to a green ✔ when the morphine dose was released and he fell back to sleep.

You know it is really late in the hospital when you hear the bundle of keys go swishing down the linoleum hallway outside your door. These were the keys to the narcotics cabinet. Late at night, this is how nurses passed them around.

A hospital is an ugly hotel where you share your room with a complete stranger, a world that is never fully asleep or awake, and when you are paralyzed, head facing the unavoidable clock, nothing much changes except eyes open or eyes shut—dreams, reality, half dreams, thinking, thinking, thinking, thinking.

December 12 should have meant something to me but it didn't.

CHAPTER 21

In California, morning light and hammering woke Van Raye. He had once again spent another surprisingly comfortable night wedged against Ruth's hot pregnant body. He lifted his head off the pillow and noticed the cold air coming through his bedroom window, flowing with a velocity that made him understand that the downstairs doors and windows were open, and the work crew had let themselves in for another day.

Ruth shifted in bed next to him, and from downstairs came the screeching of an impact hammer.

He stepped over Ruth's clothes and toed her underwear on the floor, these unsexy men's boxer briefs. What had started out as a one-night stand with an ex-wife had ended up as days of bedroom debauchery, days sequestered in the bedroom with the concert of construction noises playing downstairs, and then the nights in the silence when he and Ruth turned on the Trans-Oceanic radio and listened to the signal bouncing off the space station and down to terrestrial repeaters and broadcasted over Earth for them to catch. Or anyone else, he worried.

Her duffle bag on the dresser had slowly deflated and spewed its content of clothing and books over the room. She had, he worried, quickly made herself back at home here.

He went out on the balcony and looked over his front yard and pulled a metal pipe from his robe's pocket, inspected it, and flicked the lighter and smoked. (In *The Universe Is a Pair of Pants*, in the chapter "Cursing in Sunday School," he discussed the creative powers unleashed by cannabis.) In the distance, a flock of pigeons flew over the terracotta roofs of the university, first forming a boomerang and then an awkward O.

Down in his front yard he could see the bleached roof of his old Jaguar. When she had gone up to the space station, she'd obviously not stored it inside because now the black roof and hood had been baked for nearly two years in the sun and bore the symmetrical gray ovals of oxidation.

Trucks and vans were parked in his driveway and on his grass. Construction junk littered his property, technically the university's property, and he looked down into the contents of the Dumpster and saw parts of his old house, what he still considered *his* house, though it had been "given" to him by the university when he was hired and was now being taken away. The guest bath's old lime-green toilet was now in the Dumpster, so were the cabinets from over the bar. Van Raye was thinking that once he announced his discovery, the university would not only halt the conversion of his house to an alumni inn, but they would probably give it to him on a permanent basis. But he wasn't ready to tell the world. Not quite yet.

When the computer had kicked out the anomaly, Van Raye had been alone in the control room of the Big Dish antenna, and he'd done something he always promised he wouldn't do at that moment: He piped the actual sound through a headset and listened. The edges of the signal were empty, like an open line on a phone, like a calmer outside layer of a whirlpool, but then fine-tuning onto the planet produced the electronic sparks and pulses, washing of waves, and burps.

Eight hours later, he'd contacted Ruth aboard *Infinity*. She was shocked to hear his voice and see his face on the monitor. He was charming as always, calling her "honey" and "sweetheart" and explaining why he'd called.

Per his request, she'd turned the station's little-used low-gain antenna to the coordinates he'd given her. Her exact words over the secure link to Earth—after the computer confirmed the chance of this "noise" being a random pattern was of the magnitude of 10^{-23}—her words were: "You got something extraterrestrial."

Van Raye, leaning against the doorframe of his balcony now, smoked his pipe and watched the vehicles in his driveway and yard, observed yet another truck turning slowly into his driveway. Not just another construction truck but one with kennels on the back. *Animals. Animal control?* A gold seal reflected from the door when it opened, and a woman got out, a nice-looking young woman in a tank and a billowing skirt and black tights on her legs and practical tennis shoes, and he heard the dogs in the kennels yelping, lots of dogs.

She opened a kennel box, stuck her head inside, and Van Raye noticed her shapely calves beneath the black material, and the hounds inside the kennels bayed louder as his thoughts went to *shapely calves* and she lifted a gray-haired dog and gently put him on the ground. When she came toward his house, Van Raye instinctively hid behind the wall. Did one of those workers have a dog being delivered? It made no sense.

From the bed, Ruth blinked at him, wondering what he was doing flat against the wall.

The doorbell rang.

He put his finger to his lips.

It rang again.

"*Don't answer it*," he whispered, though she was only stretching beneath the sheets, giving the headboard an isometric push. "What's happening?" she said.

"*Nothing.*"

When the hammering and sawing on the first floor stopped, a worker's voice yelled up the staircase, "Professor? Professor? Someone's at the door."

"Shit," he said.

He went down and through the big living room where workers stared at him in his robe and bare feet, a few mumbling, "Morning, professor."

He went to the front door, which was propped open with a five-gallon bucket of scrap, and there, on his stoop in the morning light, was the smiling, young attractive woman holding a leash in one hand and an electronic pad in the other. The old gray dog sat calmly on the stones of the stoop, hair shading its eyes.

The woman saw Van Raye and she simply exclaimed, "Wow," and began shaking her head, "I can't believe it's you . . . I can't believe . . . "

Being recognized was a fine feeling, like Heineken bubbles popping in your mouth. The dog, he noticed, avoided looking at anyone, eyebrows twitching.

"Hi, darling, what can I do for you?"

The young woman said, "Okay, I look on my list, right, to see who's my next client, right, and I see your name, right, and I'm thinking I won't really see you, but it is you, right?"

Van Raye leaned against the doorframe.

"I can't believe I'm standing on Van Raye's steps. When I was a freshman, I went to your lecture on redshift galaxy formations."

Normally he could have invited her in. "Fantastic, darling, what can I do for you today?" *Why are attractive people so fascinating?* he thought.

She bent to give the dog a hearty pat on the shoulder, and he admired her bare back between the straps of her double tanks.

"Look who we found here!" she said.

"Who?" he said.

"I bet you missed this boy, didn't you?" She held out the leash for Van Raye.

He took it but then immediately tried to give it back and said, "Oh no, there's some mistake," he said. The dog sat obediently, tongue out. "This isn't my dog." He shook the leash for her to take back.

She looked at her electronic pad. "You've got to be kidding me. This isn't Chava?"

"*What did you say?*" he said.

"This isn't Chava? Isn't that a girl's name? Sometimes the scanner picks up another dog in the truck."

"Let's not say that word."

"Ah, I'm not saying anything, professor," she said. "But if this isn't your dog . . . I am so sorry. What kind of dog do you have?"

He glanced behind her for possible eavesdroppers, looked up and down the street at the houses.

"Why do you say that's its name?" he asked. "Who are you?"

"I'm Kathy, an associate at the shelter." She looked at her pad.

"That's not my dog. I don't know what it is, but it's not mine." After thinking for a second, he added, "It's impossible for that to be its name."

She squinted her eyes at him and then looked at the pad. "His name is Chava Norma Raye," she said. "His registered name."

"Okay," he said, "this is not my dog and there is a huge misunderstanding."

"Hmm . . . a mix up," she said.

She pressed buttons on the pad, knelt and touched the pad to the dog's neck. The dog held its breath and there was a pleasant chime. "It might have scanned a nearby chip . . . " she said, "that happens sometimes."

"That can't be the dog's name," he said.

"Ah, yes." She stood up. "You are Charles Van Raye. And this is definitely . . . Chava Norma, registered to you at this address." She turned the pad so he could see. "This is you, and this is Chava. Do you call him Chava or Norma? I think he's underweight. How long has he been gone? Maybe you don't recognize him."

"He hasn't been *gone*," Van Raye said. "Can you change that?"

"Change what?"

"The name," he said.

"Sure," she said. "I mean, you'll have to fill out the necessary forms, but you can change your dog's name, though at this age we don't really suggest it. He'll always respond to Chava," and she rubbed the dog's ears. "Good boy, good boy, Chava."

"Please stop saying that!"

She considered his face and then his robe. Was he crazy? The dog didn't seem to mind that anything was going on around him. He panted. Slobber was about to drop.

"I'm very confused," Van Raye said, "where did he come *from*?"

"Probably a Good Samaritan picked him up and brought him to the animal welfare center. Happens all the time. Can you just sign here?"

"I can't sign, this isn't my dog! I've never seen this dog in my life." He looked behind her at the houses across the street as if neighbors would see him.

"He's been your dog—the records show . . . " the woman glanced at the registry, "for seven years."

"Seven years? Wait. I have a theory," he said, "could someone be doing this to me? There are parties interested in harassing me. I have several ex-wives."

"Ah, professor . . . " she said, "this isn't a joke. These records are meticulous. No one can register you as an animal parent except you. You are accepting responsibility for your family member, aren't you?"

"Absolutely not," he said.

He thought about the dog's name. How had that happened? It was the name of the exoplanet, given by some other astronomer years ago, existing in the registry of known exoplanets among several thousands, and he'd discovered the Sound coming from this Chava Norma and now a dog shows up on his steps with the same name. It made no sense. Someone was behind this. He would take the dog and have the name changed with as little ordeal as possible and give the dog back to the shelter and someone's little harassing joke would be over. Someone less dense than this woman would understand.

"Professor?" she said. She handed him a pamphlet and turned to take experimental steps away from him and the dog.

He realized he was still holding the leash. Van Raye mumbled, "This isn't my dog, but it *will* be straightened out."

When she was going toward the truck, she glanced over her shoulder and stopped. "Ah, Dr. Van Raye, it is my responsibility to tell you that the Veterinary and Animal Society, and I'm sure the university, takes dog abandonment very seriously. You do know it's punishable by municipal laws?"

"I didn't abandon this dog!"

"Good," she said and kept going.

He started back into the house, kicking a box of construction scrap over with his bare foot. The dog stretched the leash to get away from the sound, and he dropped it but the dog stood still. He heard the animal welfare truck beep backward down his driveway.

He turned the pamphlet over. It was titled, "How to Welcome Your Dog Back Home":

#1: Although you might be angry at your dog for running
away, welcome him or her back with open arms,
enthusiasm, and love!

He bent down and unhooked the leash. The dog didn't move, still panting, cocking his brows. Dogs, he thought, were the best creatures at pretending nothing was going on.

He left it downstairs, the dog free to go on about its business in the world. Maybe a worker in the other room would take it. He hated them all, them turning his house into something he didn't want.

Upstairs, without the dog, he found Ruth standing topless by the open window, wearing only those ugly briefs pulled below her slightly swollen belly. She'd told him that she was eighteen weeks "along," and to him the belly looked like she'd drunk a milkshake—maybe two milkshakes and a few beers—and the skin was stretched tight enough to be mottled red, and her breasts hung full. She leaned against the wall and smoked as she studied the world outside the open patio doors, the canopy of trees.

"You shouldn't be smoking," he said still standing in the doorway.

"What was that all about?" she asked.

Ruth Christmas was the only other person in the world who knew that Chava Norma was the planet in question. The dog had to be Ruth's doing, he thought, but she wasn't a person to play a joke.

He explained to Ruth what had taken place downstairs. His theory, he said, was that someone was harassing him, and he waited for her to show some sign of guilt.

"Who else have you told about this?" she asked.

"No one," he said. "I did tell my son."

"Which one?"

"Sandeep."

"The one with money. Not the priest?"

"He wouldn't have told anyone," he said.

"How do you know?" Ruth held the cigarette beside her head to think. "Someone else obviously knows what you've found," she said. "The dish has logs. Someone can go through them."

"That won't tell anyone anything. It was a scan. It scanned large sections of the sky. This makes me anxious. Time is running out."

"For what?" Ruth asked him.

"I don't know." Van Raye got on the bed, flat on his stomach, took his glasses off.

"Tell me how this would make you feel," she asked, "if the dog thing, this problem, just disappeared?"

"Problem? Don't change this to *your* problem." He sighed, not in the mood to be analyzed by the space station's chief of biomedical problems. She was, ironically he thought, her own biomedical problem.

She went to her duffle bag and pulled something out. "I guess I should give this to you." It was a box about the shape of a coffee grinder, orange. She tested the weight and then underhanded it to him. The orange box flashed through a streak of sunshine and came toward the bed. He rolled, and it bounced heavy, and he put a hand to stop it from falling off the bed.

"Jesus!" he said. "What are you trying to do? What is this?"

There were two white stripes around the box, a handle on one end, Cyrillic letters and multipronged, female outlets on the side.

"Is this what I think it is?" he said. He had to retrieve his eyeglasses from the floor. "You've had this all along?"

"Courtesy of Roscosmos. It was a backup unit."

"Jesus, there was a *backup*?" He held it in both hands. "Do you know how much this little orange box is worth?" he said.

"That's not the point. It's a loaner until we . . . I don't know what . . . until we finish. You do want to send something yourself, don't you? That's what this delay is about, right?"

"Yes. Don't throw it around!" he said.

"It's for you. From me. I'm guessing we can use a dish as small, as what, two meters?" She stared out the window, letting the smoke rise from the cigarette. "Sending something? A message from you? It's not going to reach Chava until long after you're dead. That's so unlike you." She turned her head sideways.

"Why not? Isn't it normal to want to send something real before the others do?"

"When do you care about something that will be around long after you're dead? You'll get no reward from sending a message. That signal will take three thousand years to reach the planet. You'll be dust. I know you and there has to be something you want now, from sending a signal now."

He took the gain booster and put it gently on the desk and stared at it.

"I want to send my own message before the others get theirs off. That's simple."

She blew smoke toward the outside world. "My God," she said. The smoke balled in the air. "Yes, the size of your ego never fails to impress me. I don't have the software, by the way. If we don't have the software that thing's nothing more than an anchor for a boat."

"We can get the software, can't we?"

"Yes, I have someone on board who would be willing to trust me with it. He'll send it to me if I ask."

"The father?" he said.

"What difference does that make?" She stretched her neck.

He sat on the edge of the bed. "Ruth, you have to tell me something. Are you responsible for the dog thing?"

She took a second then smirked, stepped back to the window, the sun on her face. The curtains flapped on both sides of the doorway and she gazed into the canopy of trees.

"Darling," he said gently, "someone will see you standing there like that, come here."

She picked up one of her breasts and inspected it and let it drop, sucked on the cigarette. "Why do you think I would harass you? What would my motive be for doing something as contrived as this? I've got other things on my mind." Her face was beautiful in the light. Her hair, he thought, would grow out and be beautiful again soon.

She leaned against the doorframe and crossed one foot over the other. There was a bruise on the back of her leg that had been there since she'd disrobed that first night, something suffered on reentry or during the caravan journey out of Mongolia.

"I have nothing to do with the dog," she said. "You've never had anything bad happen to you, have you?"

"My mother died when I was twelve. I never knew my father." Van Raye was looking at the dirty underside of her foot and had been thinking of something his mother always said. His mother called black-soled feet "7-Eleven feet."

"Boo-hoo," Ruth said, "there's that, but you've gotten everything you've ever wanted. You're an expert in your field. You've written books that people actually read. Women throw themselves at you. You hold court at every party you attend, but you don't have any family. Are you okay with that?"

"Don't torture me with your analysis. Ruth, why are you here?" he asked. "In this state, why did you come to *me*?"

"I am still employed by this university," she said. "And my car was here."

"You hate that car. You're eighteen weeks pregnant."

"Nineteen. I came to you, I think, because you're the only other one. You're like me, having a family is not your first priority, and you're all I have to help me figure this out."

"Nineteen weeks?" he said.

She nodded.

Van Raye got that helpless feeling of an approaching deadline. "Are you at a point when you can't make a decision?" he said.

She flicked the cigarette out the door into the backyard.

"No. Not quite."

"But you need to be making arrangements?"

"*Stop*," she said, "okay, I get it. I'm not mother material. I know that."

She came and crawled over him and pinned him down by the shoulders. She had one knee up against his crotch and looked down at him. "I'm not the most nurturing person on the planet," she said.

Something like a bundle of wood clattered on the floor downstairs.

"I'm not the most nurturing person either," he said.

"Exactly. What's the matter with us?"

"Ruth, some people are here for other reasons. Some people have bigger reasons. We've been burdened with this task, not anything else."

Her eyes were ringed with black construction dust; the dirt and grime surrounding her eyes had been smeared.

"Have you been crying?" he said.

"No."

The dust covered everything in the house and it was probably on his skin too, and she was breathing it in.

"Why don't you make arrangements, go somewhere?" he said.

She rolled off of him and on her back. She whispered while touching her stomach, "Because I hear something."

"You what?"

She took a deep breath. "I know it's not real, okay? I know what audio hallucinations are. But anyway, to me, I hear music."

"You're hearing the music from downstairs."

"No," she said. "It's different music. It's comes from inside me. I feel it too, like vibrations. Like music-box music."

"Sweetheart," he said, matching her quiet tone, "you have been through a lot."

There was only the light coming through the curtains flapping in the breeze.

"You are hallucinating because your mind, well," he said, "you're overloaded. You're struggling, and you have conflicting instincts. Your mind is looking for some way for there to be something that will make you feel better about having feelings for this . . ." He waved his hand over her belly.

"Fetus?" she said.

The room was silent. The curtains still.

"Are you hearing it now?" he said.

"Maybe. I shouldn't have told you."

He said, "I can assure you that in reality, there is no music." His ear was against her chest. "There's no music."

"How do you know? You're on the outside."

When Ruth had been aboard the spacecraft *Infinity*, and she'd found out she was pregnant—this was after she'd listened to the broadcast for Van Raye—she'd started packing to come back to Earth, stuffing personal items in her bag, and then grabbed the gain amplifier just in time because Cosmonaut X stuck his head in her quarters and asked what she was doing.

No one knew her condition, especially not him.

"Leaving," she said, fanning away a group of monarchs fluttering about her cabin. Her sleeping bag was hung on the wall like a giant chrysalis itself, butterflies decorating its outside, hundreds of pulsing wings. It was nearly impossible not to occasionally smash a butterfly, and the crew was constantly vacuuming up carcasses, an experiment on growth and flight that had gotten out of control.

Ruth floated her duffle down the trans-tube, then followed it, and then Cosmonaut X followed her to the bay where orange monarchs were disturbed into confetti fluttering up, down, and sideways. She braced her feet on each side of the escape pod's hatch and strained to open it.

Cosmonaut X went to the intercom and said, "We have a crew member loading her things into the emergency capsule."

In seconds the other five crewmembers were watching her entering information on the computer.

"It's been rough on everyone," Jane said.

"I can't do it again right now," Ruth said, "I just can't."

The station began emerging from Earth's shadow and the sunlight hit the station's skin and began creaking.

Cosmonaut X floated in the high corner, arms folded. Ruth stuck her head in the escape capsule and scanned to make sure there were no butterflies there. What would butterflies born in zero gravity think of gravity?

"You volunteered for that walk," Jane said. "You don't have to go out anymore, okay? Don't do this."

Ruth's hair floated like the Bride of Frankenstein. "It's not that," she said. "I've got other reasons."

There was a loud pop as the sunlight intensity peaked on the space station's exterior.

Ruth quickly gripped the handle and went into the capsule feet-first, stuck her head back out like an angry gopher. "There's shit going on that none of you can imagine. I'm getting the hell out of here. There are two more seats on this thing, anyone else want out?"

No one spoke.

"Then start the sequence." She reached to pull the hatch closed but the leverage was awkward.

"That is a big mass," Cosmonaut X said, not uncrossing his arms, as if the hatch would stop her.

"You don't know where you'll come down," Jane said. "Give us twenty to come up with trajectories."

"And then I'll have to wait for a window and have time to think about this? No." She struggled with the heavy hatch but no one helped until finally Cosmonaut X pushed himself off the wall in a flutter of butterflies and grabbed the hatch. He touched her hand first. "Because of me?" he said.

"Jesus, don't flatter yourself." His flight suit was smeared with more black protoplasm than the others. "A port in a storm," she whispered, looking around to see if anyone else heard or understood this slight of intimacy.

When the hatch was shut, through the round window she saw everyone exiting the airlock. In six minutes, after she was buckled in and the pressure had fallen inside the airlock, she watched through the porthole as the butterflies froze into unrecognizable specks, and when the pod separated from the station and the tiny boosters hissed, stabilizing her into a decaying orbit Earthward. The computers came up with an emergency-landing target, and she heard Uree over the com say, "How's your Mongolian?" and the signal faded as *Infinity* contin-ued over Earth's horizon and Ruth's pod fell behind like a dropped

buoy and her porthole began to glow in the fire that separated space
and Earth, and she felt the first g grab her in her center of mass where
it always started, in her gut near where this thing lived inside her,
and the pod began shaking, and Ruth began grunting, contracting
the muscles in her stomach and legs. She had always grunted "monster" when reentering. Everyone had his or her own g-load word to
grunt. She grunted "*monster*" to dam the blood flow in her head—
"*Mmmmmmm-onster . . .*" taking a quick breath and repeating,
straining, "*Mmm-onstersss.*" She flinched when something fell out of
the instrument panel, and she watched the cosmopolitan butterfly
beat dying in the crook of her arm as she began to pass out.

CHAPTER 22

When his house was quiet for the night, Van Raye and Ruth made
love, and she fell asleep, but his eyes were wide, trying to listen for
signs the dog was downstairs, but there was only the hiss of distant
interstate traffic coming through the open balcony doors. He tried to
shut his eyes. No more dog. Problem solved, but then he was thinking about the freeway and the possibility of the dog wandering into
traffic. He bolted upright.

He got dressed, left Ruth sleeping, and as he slid on his bedroom shoes he noticed a pack of cigarettes on the dresser. He thought
he'd secretly taken them all. *What is she doing?* He grabbed the pack
and wadded it into his pocket and went quietly down the back steps
to the first floor and through the grand dining room. He held his
breath for a few minutes, listening and watching the tiny lights of
power tools recharging, and he looked around for the animal. *Dog,
be safe,* he begged, and then: *Why do I care?* A black shape on the
kitchen floor raised its head. Van Raye fumbled around to find the
leash on the counter.

In the middle of the night, he took the bus to the animal shelter, the dog riding obediently in the aisle. At the front of the shelter—a strikingly modern building—he peeked through the glass doors into the dim waiting area inside and saw one luckless night watchman at the desk. Van Raye took a circuitous route to the rear, the dog walking slowly on his leash. A single tube flickered over a loading dock and cast purplish light on the wall of empty cages and the words NO QUESTIONS DROP-OFF.

Van Raye pulled his lighter out to see the list of instructions by the cage. They were too long to bother reading. He wasn't stupid. It was simple. He opened the mesh-steel doors and kneed the dog to get inside the cage. He pushed its neck to keep him inside, the dog swallowing against his hand. He tried to think about all the work he had to do, his upcoming book tour, finding an easy way to get rid of Ruth before the pregnancy or another decision became an issue, deciding what message he would send to Chava Norma, and reminding himself that this wasn't his dog. You couldn't abandon what didn't belong to you.

He got the door shut and secured the latch, smelling the dog's sour panting.

He went down the dock stairs and through a gate at the back of the complex and into an open-space park, a long expanse of grass sparkling dewy in the moonlight. He headed toward the electric whine of a bus in the distance and the warm glow of campus beyond. He saw a clump of something he'd thought were bushes but were actually resting cows. A beast disturbed, stood. A glint of stray urban light shown off the cow's side and Van Raye stooped forward to see. He'd been waiting for the dog to bark in the cage behind him but nothing happened, and he found his lighter and flicked it on so he could see what was on this cow's side. The cow—a good research cow from one of the dark pharmaceutical companies surrounding the field—was patient and still, let Van Raye get closer with the lighter. There was only the sound of grass being ripped from the ground and the crunching of cud in molars. The thing on the side of the cow was a porthole, a medical porthole into the gut of the animal. Van Raye saw gummy pink intestines smashed against the glass. Van Raye let the lighter's flame go at the exact moment the cow startled and began to trot, Van Raye high-stepping in the other direction, stopping only when he was out of breath and realized his right shoe seemed heavier than his left.

CHAPTER 23

The sun slid down into the frame of our hospital window and the parallelogram of yellow moved across the tile floor as my roommate watched a news show about a man who'd killed his wife on their Jamaican honeymoon. Luckily our door had been propped open, and I could cut my eyes to study people walking past, the parallelogram of window light stalking me, finally climbing onto the side of my bed like it did every afternoon. I watched every old woman going by our door—walkers, wheelchairs, shuffling in bedroom slippers—to see if I could determine who Rose Epstein was, the woman's voice that called through the wall. I was a little obsessed with finding out who she was.

Elizabeth came in the door carrying a new paper sack with a change of clothes, and Leggett watched her go over and take my cup from the table and fill it with water. She put it to my lips, and a pewter charm dangling from her neck caught the sunlight—the elephant head of Ganesha. I didn't even know she had this charm, this remover of obstacles.

She saw me looking at it and leaned in and kissed me on the cheek, stilling the nerves for a second.

She opened the paper bag to get my new pair of pajamas and the nurse came in and rolled me on my side to change my diaper. When they did this, they had no idea the dead weight of my high arm crushed my chest, and for these fifteen seconds I couldn't breathe. They folded the dirty diaper beneath me. The nurse inspected the Foley catheter going into the tip of my penis, ran the tube and the bag through the leg of my pajamas, hung the bag on the end of the bed, and pulled the pants up. She gave me the cold shot of heparin in the gut and went away.

"Are you okay?" Elizabeth asked me, watching me swallow one more cup of water.

I blinked once, yes.

Leggett's news program was interviewing the husband in his orange prison jumpsuit.

Elizabeth stepped on a pedal beneath the bed, and the motor hummed and the whole bed rose until she could put her hands on the railing, bracelets pushing up, and she bent to whisper, "Sandeep, think about how happy we are going to be when all this is over."

She straightened herself. She went and got the paper bag, stuffed the old pajamas inside, and put her purse on her shoulder. She straightened her posture. "I'm going to run away and work for Sky Cargo." When she stopped to look at herself in the mirror above the sink, putting her hair back in place, she looked like a stranger. She turned and smiled at me. "I'm joking, of course, but I look at Gypsy every day, the people working, loading and unloading. Everyone seems happier than we do." Inside the bracelets was her watch, and she noted the time. "She's coming to see you tonight, right?"

I didn't blink because I didn't know. Some nights Ursula did, some nights she had to fly.

"I know she comes here. I smell whiskey on your breath every morning." She kissed my cheek. She sighed. "I'm glad you have each other. You know that, right?"

I blinked yes.

On her way out, she ignored Leggett in the other bed as usual. She left my bed a good four feet in the air.

When she was gone, Leggett stared at the shut door and said, "What did the Buddhist say to the hot dog vender?" I hated him. "'Make me one with everything,'" he said.

At night, after the last chimes had played over the PA to signal visiting hours were over, Ursula came in trailing the light from the hallway, put her things down, poured one cup of whiskey, which she gave me a sip from, and pulled up a chair, propped her feet on the railing of my bed, and began reading Strieber's classic, *Communion*, "'This is the story of one man's attempt to deal with a shattering assault from the unknown.'"

During her late-night visits I had to lay and listen to how abductees supposedly recovered lost memories through hypnosis, though I knew that hypnosis had been scientifically proven to create false memories. Leggett, when he was awake, seemed to listen to her, making no comment, mostly looking at her as she read the words of some third-rate journalists and hokey scientists with titles like "Harvard *educated . . .*"

When she finished for the night, her steps were often too deliberately careful, and she always came and touched me one last time for the night, kissing my cheek and then left.

When the darkness took back over the room, and Leggett fidgeted in pain, grunting, the night belonged to Rose Epstein who came alive shouting her name through the wall.

Leggett grimaced and said in the darkness, "Did you hear about the deaf gynecologist?" He gripped the railing with one hand, his gold Masonic ring glinting. His other hand raised the morphine clicker like he was a contestant on a game show of pain, and he finally said, "*He reads lips!*" and pressed the button, and there was the snap of the solenoid, and on his monitor above his rising heart beat, the green ✔ appeared.

I began dreading his passing into sleep each night, the dose of morphine taking him away because then I heard the narcotics cabinet keys go swishing past our door, and I waited what seemed forever for Rose Epstein. "*I'm Rose Epstein . . .*"

It was hard to tell the difference between sleep and just living through the night, stranded inside my head, but this made me vulnerable to an experience that I have to write about if I'm going to tell the truth about everything.

A teaching hospital such as this is a surreal place where people often came into the darkened room—doctors and interns administering tests just outside the dome of light surrounding my bed, asking each questions about my condition, trying on diagnoses. I was often taken to different exam rooms in the middle of the night, once waking to a woman outside the light surrounding my bed, asking, "Babinski reflex?" I wanted to answer no I wasn't Babinski Reflex, but someone uncovered my feet, which seemed a million miles from my head, like looking backward through binoculars. The man rubbed a tongue depressor along my sole, something I didn't feel, and when my toes curled, everyone seemed to be impressed and said, "Babinski reflex," and took notes on their phones.

I once woke in a strange room where doctors spoke Spanish and inserted needles below my skin delivering shocks that convulsed dormant muscles and produced peaks and waves on a computer next to my bed. The only English was "This will be a little uncomfortable," though I wasn't sure who spoke it. The needle pricked into my leg, and the electric stimulus was delivered to my thigh, then my calves, and when the needle and the wires were taken away, doctors in the dark began asking me questions.

"Do you have any thoughts of suicide?"

Thoughts of suicide?

"Are you generally happy about the world?"

No.

"Have you had unexplainable missing or lost time?"

No.

"Do you have any unusual scars or marks on your body you can't explain?"

Just outside the dome of light, I saw the reflections on the surfaces of blank eyes, saw their slender bodies and the large heads of the classic Greys. *It is happening to me*, I thought, even though I write this with the confidence that it was a dream. In the dim light I saw the four-jointed fingers I'd read about, and a great wave of relief washed over my body, not because the pain had stopped but because there were aliens around my bed. I tried to catch my breath and at the time I only felt terrified and wonderful, thinking that at last something fantastic was real.

"Do you have memories of floating through the air?" one asked.

Yes. I was communicating my answer telepathically.

"Have you ever been paralyzed for unexplained reasons?" said another. These were all classic abduction questions.

Yes.

"Had any unusual nose bleeds?"

Yes.

"Have you had long-time problems with insomnia, the cause of which is puzzling to you?"

Yes.

"Are you more comfortable being in crowds, more comfortable with sleeping among people?"

In hotels.

"We will be releasing you from this paralysis."

You are doing this to me, I said without speaking, and I remember floating out in the hallway, just my body, floating down the hallway toward the elevator and back to my room.

The next morning I simply woke in my room, and the nursing staff and Elizabeth rolled my body and I began the fifteen seconds of suffocation that started every day as my diaper was changed. Everything was normal, but I felt wonderful. When Elizabeth asked me if I was okay, as she did every morning, I blinked *yes, yes, yes, yes.* This was the euphoria of understanding.

During those strange few days of believing, I gave up my obsessive search for Rose Epstein. I didn't intentionally stop, I just knew that every woman I saw was Rose Epstein who wanted to go home, and every man was Rose Epstein, and I was Rose Epstein and Rose Epstein was me, and I was also James Leggett and his jokes, and I liked his jokes, even the simple stupid ones. The jokes were funny. *Why hadn't I known this before?*

I'm glad I couldn't speak during this stage of my life because I would have shouted to everyone who would listen, *It's real!* The lunacy of a new convert. It might be lunacy, but I think anyone would want it. If you make fun of people who believe in UFOs or Jesus, then you just can't remember how great it feels, how fucking great it feels, to believe in something fantastic.

When Ursula read at night, I wanted to talk to her—*yes, I know!* My God, what would have happened if I could have talked? I would have become the most obnoxious convert. I was saved or destroyed by paralysis, whichever way you want to look at it. I was forced into a cooling-off period, and I went through a cold reawakening to reality, the tiny voice of my father through the headphones when she wasn't there.

Let me dispense with my experience in the strange room. It was a dream, my brain filled with Ursula's reading and convoluted by boredom and depression. What the doctors administered me that night was a real test to measure the conductivity of your nerves—an EMG, an electromyogram.

If conversion is a lightning strike, coming to your senses takes a few days, and that was what happened to me, slowly coming back to reality.

One night I just simply watched Ursula's face as she read out loud and felt the same skepticism I always had, but I would have done anything to get that feeling back of believing something fantastic was real. I would have gone through the electroshock again, been paralyzed longer, anything.

In those days when the euphoria faded, the movement came back into my body. Ursula read from Jung: "'These people are lacking not only in criticism but in the most elemental knowledge of psychology; at bottom, they don't want to be taught any better but merely to go on believing . . . '"

One of my promises was to kiss those lips. I would declare my love for her as soon as I could speak.

A few days later, very normal human nurses loaded me in my wheelchair and took me down several floors to an MRI machine, a small tunnel fed by a gurney.

The motors pulled me along rails into the machine's throat, and over a tiny speaker inches away from my nose, the tech gave me the absurd command to "stay completely still." There was music to relax me: flute and Tibetan bowl. Air blew down the tiny tunnel, and then the music went off and then the drum roll began and the bass beat—"Viva Las Vegas" cued. It seemed like music from another world, a signal from a friend, and a bit of the euphoria of believing came on me and a drop of my body's own saline leaked from my eye and found its way down my cheek, trickling in my ear. There was one last fantastic thing left, I thought, or was this a dream too?

CHAPTER 24

Van Raye's California book tour was disappointing. After a reading at a legitimate bookstore in San Francisco, he went home with the bookstore's manager who was painting her apartment. He slept with her that night and picked up a hangover and latex paint that dried on his body and itched on the flight to Palm Springs.

In Palm Springs he had been booked to read in a new-age bookstore, and he'd gone home with a woman who'd told him afterward, "This is the best book you've written."

Later that evening in the tub with the new woman, she sat with her legs draped around his waist and picked the latex paint off his leg with her nail. She wasn't the least curious how he'd gotten paint on strange parts of his body, a non-curiosity that Van Raye took as a sign of low intelligence.

"I have found something," he whispered to her while leaning back in the tub, rubbing his pubic hair beneath the water, letting the tiny bubbles tickle up his hand like champagne. He would try his news on a stranger, and he was drinking wine in a bathtub with her. The nice thing about returning to drinking after a sabbatical was that everything—when drinking was added—seemed much more fun. *Drinking in a bathtub, telling someone* you have found something.

She sat against the other side of the tub, and she used the sides of the tub to haul herself close enough to stare into his eyes, oblivious to his statement.

"Do you understand?" he said. "There is life on another planet."

"I've already seen them," she whispered but continued pealing latex paint from his leg. The hair ripping out was excruciatingly pleasurable.

She told him that she was a sculptor specializing in statues of aliens. "Anyone who buys one has a visitation," she said. The chips of latex paint floated in the water and collected around the shoreline of her body.

Van Raye was glad to return to Northern California and the rational world of Ruth Christmas, but he carried in his suitcase a green alien figurine.

He returned to comfortable exile on the second story of his Palo Alto house, staying awake nights with Ruth, tuning the Trans-Oceanic radio to listen to the sound of Chava Norma. Ruth found the ceramic alien statue in his suitcase and pulled it out and held it with both hands, the size of a green cantaloupe with a belly and large black eyes, sitting in lotus, an alien Buddha. "Someone you fucked?" she asked.

He didn't answer, and she put it on the dresser under the lamp.

He woke in the morning and didn't feel her heat next to him and half-consciously searched with his foot, then reached a hand and found nothing but empty bed. By the sloping of the sun, he determined it was past midday and the drapes flapped dots and dashes to wake him. "Where are you?" he said.

He saw her figure rummaging through her bags. She turned to him and said, "You're taking my cigarettes."

"Why would I take your cigarettes?" He remembered the exact way a pack of cigarettes wadded awkwardly, always forming a non-aerodynamic ball. He'd felt like a kleptomaniac, stealing and throwing them off the balcony into the Dumpster below. Why did he do that?

"I left a pack right here on purpose." She pointed to the bedside table. "*You* are doing this."

He sat up on his elbows. He could no longer deny he'd been destroying those cigarettes, so he said, "Why would I care if you smoke?"

A worker shouted from downstairs, "*Professor?*"

"Damn those people," he said.

"Professor!" the person shouted again. "Someone is here! Professor? *It's someone with your dog!*"

"Shit."

When he got his robe on and went downstairs, a woman—not the attractive young woman from before, but another—waited on his stoop, holding the dog on a leash. The same K-9 truck was idling in the driveway. "Dr. Van Raye, look who we have. Lucky we found him."

"I know what you are going to say," he said, "but that's not my dog."

Van Raye didn't put up much of a fight. He even took another copy of "How to Welcome Your Dog Back Home."

The dog followed him to the kitchen and Van Raye took out a Tupperware bowl and filled it with water and put it on the floor.

He had run out of money. They were taking his house away. He had a dog that wasn't his responsibility. But the dog was also registered with the planet's name for his name. Why and why and why?

The dog panted and didn't drink. His eyes shifted around the kitchen but didn't look at Van Raye.

"Suit yourself," Van Raye said, turning his back and walking out of the kitchen.

He would have to find a way to leave Ruth. Would she be suspicious if he told her he was going on another book tour? Could he somehow retain the gain amplifier and the car?

As soon as he was at the top of the stairs, he heard the dog's paws following him. Van Raye stopped, closed his eyes. *Please just go away.* The phone in the nook in the hallway made a chirp. The red light flickered. This was a new phone system for the B&B. He sat on the recessed bench, and the dog came up the last step and cautiously smelled the floor.

Van Raye picked the phone up, put the receiver to his ear, and muttered hello, but there was a voice, loud and clear, "Welcome to the Grand Aerodrome reservations. To make a reservation dial one . . . "

A hotel? A hotel calling me? Was Sandeep doing any of this to him?

The dog came and smelled Van Raye's feet.

Van Raye pressed zero, and when the operator answered, he said very slowly, "Is there a Sandeep Sanghavi registered?"

"One moment," the woman said, "I'll connect you."

He held the phone out and looked at the receiver and put it back to his ear. When Van Raye wiggled his foot, the dog backed away.

His hand reached to touch the dog as the transfer began ringing. The dog glanced toward the stairs as if it might leave. The line clicked open.

"This is Elizabeth Sanghavi," she said on the other end.

"Elizabeth?"

There was a pause, and she said, "Charles?"

"My God," he whispered. He looked at the new gray phone, the buttons marked for different lines to call different rooms and a sticker that said 9 FOR OUTSIDE LINE.

"Did you call me?" he asked.

He heard a sigh on her end. "Are you drunk?" she said. He heard the wind blowing over her receiver.

"No," he said. "Elizabeth, it's me . . . Elizabeth, is everything okay?"

"I know it is you. Why are you calling?"

"I didn't. Is Sandeep there?"

"Yes. No." He heard her switch ears, then the momentary stilling of the wind. "He's in the hospital," she said in a lower tone.

"*Hospital?*" he whispered.

"The paralysis, but it's over. He's getting out soon. He's recovering. They don't know why these episodes keep happening. Do you know why they keep happening to him?"

"How would I know?" he said.

"*Well, I know you don't know.* I'm thinking out loud."

"People expect me to know everything."

"You are, as usual, no help."

The dog sat down and put its head on its paws.

Elizabeth explained: paralysis again, six weeks in the hospital but getting better.

Van Raye began to formulate a plan in his mind. He would suggest Ruth carry on with her decision, and he would slip away and stay with Elizabeth, hopefully somewhere on the West Coast because he couldn't afford to fly. But Ruth had the radio, and the gain amplifier, *and the car.*

"Where are you?" he asked.

"The roof," she said. "Sorry about the noise. Is that better? I have to find somewhere to play when it's this late."

"You're playing your violin, aren't you?" Van Raye scooted his foot over until it barely touched the dog's leg. "I love your music," he said in a whisper. "I always have. What city are you in?"

"You never said you liked my music."

"Sure I have. We used to play for hours together. I can see you playing in my mind. You were playing Bach, weren't you? You are in a long coat. You are wearing a scarf and you are beautiful."

"I have on a coat because it's forty degrees in Atlanta. I can imagine you too, and let me guess, you're in a bathrobe and there's a woman within fifty feet and an empty bottle."

"Elizabeth, you and I have a connection. We have a progeny together."

"This isn't a sharing arrangement."

"Jesus, I know that."

There was the silence of the open line until she said, "Do you still play your horn?"

"My horn?" He crossed his ankles and pulled the robe over his knee. "It's been a long time. I do need to start again. It'll be a lot like starting over."

"No, it wouldn't," she said. "It won't be like learning the first time."

"I wouldn't mind a beginning," he said. "Beginnings are good. I remember it being quite fun to be getting to know the instrument, and you too. I can see you now, on the roof of some hotel, playing under the stars. I would very much like to be there with you."

"You were right about the Bach," she said, "the Presto from Sonata No. 1."

"That was what I was hearing in my mind!" he said. *Hadn't I been humming that? What if things worked like that, an old lover on my mind, her passionately playing Sonata No. 1?* He sat up on the bench, startling the dog. "I will come see you." He tried to think of a way to ask for money.

"Charles, why did you call?"

"Me?" he said, thinking about the phone ringing here in his house. "The strangest thing happened," he began.

"What?" she said.

He shook his head and rubbed his eyes beneath his glasses. "Did you call me?" he said to her.

"What are you talking about?"

"Never mind," he said. "Somehow we *are* having this conversation."

"Charles, may I tell you something?"

"Anything."

"A lot has gone on. My life is changing. I need to start planning on slowing down. Whatever I've been planning . . . I have to say that you . . ."

"Are you saying you and I?" Charles asked.

"Is that outrageous?" Now the wind blew over the phone and covered one word she was saying. He imagined her looking up at the sky.

"Elizabeth, I have found what I was looking for."

"I know."

"You do?"

"Yes, of course."

"I've still got important work to do. I need somewhere to do it. Elizabeth . . ." he whispered. "Are you crying?"

"No."

The dog stretched on his front legs. Van Raye could smell its panting breath and he had a flash memory of being a boy with a dog. He pushed its muzzle away.

"I've been through a lot!" she said. "I'm fine. I'm babbling. I'm going to retire. Sandeep will have a head start, and he'll be much happier and healthy without me. He's completely capable of doing this on his own. His health is related to his happiness. Do you want to come visit?"

"I haven't felt like this in years," he said, rubbing the bridge of his nose. He glanced down the wide hallway to his shut bedroom door. He tapped his knuckle on the wall as if trying to locate a stud, trying to figure out a way to ask her for money. Instead he said, "Did you hear that I have a new book out too?"

"Yes," she said. "Why don't you call him?"

Someone with money? he thought. "Who?" he said.

"Sandeep."

"I absolutely will," he said. "Did you say that you read my new book?"

"Yes, Charles, we've all read it."

"Sandeep has?"

"Of course."

"Elizabeth, are you okay? I won't hang up this phone until I know you are okay."

"I am fine. I don't even know why you ask if I'm okay. We are staying at the Grand Aerodrome . . ."

He shut the bedroom door before the dog could come inside.

Ruth smoked a new cigarette staring out the window, flicking ashes directly on his floor and letting them blow inside on the breeze.

"Something has come up," he started.

"Yes, it has." She threw her phone to the foot of the bed. "Read that."

He picked it up. It was in the middle of a *Times* article, and he went backward to read the headline, CREW DEAD.

"*What?*" he said. "This isn't real."

"There was a fire in the forward bay," she said. "What's not real about six dead, no survivors?"

He scrolled down the article where it mentioned that Ruth Christmas had been the seventh crewmember but had made an emergency return to Earth in January because of "acute appendicitis."

Cold night air flowed through the open French doors.

"Oh my God," he said. "This is impossible."

"It's not impossible. They're all dead. That's a fact." The muscles in her cheeks flexed as if to form a smile, but her mouth pulled straight. "So how would you feel if your dog problem just went away?"

"I don't have a dog problem," he mumbled, but then he understood what she was getting at. "The father?" he asked her.

"What about him?"

Van Raye didn't speak.

She said, "Yes, he's dead. He didn't know about . . . you know, this." She pointed to her belly.

"I'm sorry," he said.

"Trust me, there are worse things than death."

"They were all your friends."

She tilted her head back and blew smoke. "Asphyxiation isn't a bad way to go. Burning alive would be bad. That place was an accident waiting to happen. Now it's an orbiting mausoleum, a big charred mausoleum. I'm sure people are going to make a big fucking deal out of that, a perpetually orbiting crypt. Isn't that a kick?"

"Ruth, do you have someone you should call?"

"Why?" she said.

"I don't know. They'll be coming after you. You'll want to attend services. They'll want you . . . You'll want to go, right?"

"Are you trying to get rid of me?"

"Certainly not, but I just thought . . . I don't know what I can do. I'm not good at these things."

"What do you have to be good at?" Ruth said, and she put her hand on her belly. "The weird part about this is that when I saw the news, I realized I'd had a premonition about this."

"There are no premonitions," he said.

"Shut up. I know that."

"Let me ask you this, and I don't mean to be insensitive, but how are we going to get the software for the booster?"

"I don't know," she said.

"Do you know anyone who can, you know, get it?" he asked.

"Sure. And guess what? *They're all dead.*"

"We'll get it, somehow, though, right?" he said. "Is the station's antenna still tracking on the planet?"

She went and turned the Trans-Oceanic radio on.

Please, please, he thought.

He worked the knob and the hum and clicks of Chava Norma tuned in strong. These sounds began three thousand light-years away, traveled to space spreading out and losing energy, but a tiny bit arrived at the space station, was gain-boosted there and rebroadcast over the earth.

He watched Ruth crawl back in bed on all fours, roll over, and put her hand on her belly. She held her breath.

He clicked the radio off.

"You're hearing it now?" he whispered, using his eyes to indicate her belly.

She put the other hand on her stomach. "You can't hear *that*? It's as clear as day to me. Music."

"Is it a song?"

"It's just . . . like music-box music," she said.

He waited for her to tell him to come over and listen to her stomach. She waited for him to say he wanted to listen. Neither happened.

CHAPTER 25

I don't remember the first words I spoke. Recovery happened too slowly. What was a loud breath, or what was a syllable? One week I was flexing fingers; the next week there was movement at my wrist, the tingling, like an occupying army, decided to pick up and retreat, and the elation of the vivid dream that night had long faded though the memory was there, and I did not anticipate the coming of December 12 because it wasn't in my mind.

After six weeks and two days Elizabeth pulled the December 11 off the wall calendar in my hospital room, and suddenly there was December 12 staring me in the face, and I remember Randolph telling, and the memory flooded in. I had the sensation of falling, heart palpitating and my breath short. There was nothing to grab but the bed's railing. Time imploded, and I had the sensation that one second ago Randolph had told me this date when I was standing in the doorway waiting for Elizabeth to get me a glass of water, and in a blink of the eye here I was seeing Elizabeth crumbling up the eleventh and dropping it into a wastebasket, but I had all memories of what had happened here at the hospital. It was like waking from anesthesia, thinking not enough time had gone by for everything to have occurred, but yet all the memories were there, including Ursula reading, the experience of the vivid dream, the elation of having believed.

Elizabeth kept talking as she walked around the room, but I wasn't listening. I was dizzy with fear, hand to my chest. The sensation was terrifying. I knew then that I didn't ever want this to happen again, my life leaping forward. I opened and closed my hand; I moved my fingers, watching the tendons in my wrist flex.

I heard about the disaster on the space station when we were on the old plum-colored shuttle going back to the hotel. Of course I didn't know this had anything to do with my life.

When I finally went back to the Grand Aerodrome, when I finally pushed the door open to my room, I hobbled to my dresser and found everything exactly as I'd left it six weeks ago: my watch, my wallet, my money clip, the hardcopy of *The Universe Is a Pair of Pants*, and Barbie, and my phone. It was like I'd left it yesterday.

I plugged in my phone and waited for it to get enough charge to power on.

Elizabeth stood in the door watching me. I angled the phone so I could see her reflection in its black screen.

"Sandeep, there are things that I don't understand, and you can explain them to me."

I turned to her. "Did something happen?"

"I have my violin," she said. "How did that happen? And then you got sick."

I waited for the phone, adjusted Barbie's arms so that they were down beside her and not reaching out as if she wanted me. I sat her on her bottom and loved that smile of hers that was like a smile that was beginning to blossom, as if she were about to face some life-altering happiness.

"I know," I said. "I don't understand it all either. Charles will know. He'll tell us when he gets here."

"What does he have to do with this?" she said. "We don't know for sure he's coming."

I watched my phone finally come alive. "Can you play now?" I said to Elizabeth. "Please." She looked to see if I were serious and turned to her room. There, I heard the latches on the case open.

My screen turned a light gray, and the home screen came up. I scrolled to my text conversations and found nothing there from Randolph. It was as if it had never happened. I had no proof that he existed other than that the violin was in our possession. Then a text dinged in:

Hello Sandeep. Welcome back.

Elizabeth began Sarasate again just as she'd played the night I'd gotten sick, the night she first got the violin back. I texted:

Was that you in the MRI?

:)

Did you do all this to me?

Please don't be one of those people who blame me for everything. The universe is chaotic.

Are we ready for Raye?

Will I have to go through this all my life?

If we realize the future, we will only jump to that point. It's better not to skip the journey.

But I didn't skip it. I have all the memories.

But doesn't it feel like I just gave you the answer?

Don't do that again.

> Do you want me to believe you're God?

> LOL!

Elizabeth was at the point that the bow was drawn slowly. I knew if I went to show her this conversation, it would disappear.

> Why can't I show this conversation to anyone?

> We must handle this in a delicate way.

> Do you want me to believe you're an alien?

> :)

> Are you?

> :)

> Why can't you find him yourself?

> It is best that you introduce me to him

> He has called your mother. If he calls again tell him it is important that he look after the dog

Dog again? What dog?

> You think you're God?

> ;}

> You are not God

I am not God.

When Elizabeth's music changed to the next movement—sad and slow—I typed and sent:

You are God

The answer came quickly:

I am God

You did this to me

I did not do this to you

Can you stop it from happening again?

No.

I thought of ways to trick him, try to run to Elizabeth and show her the text, try to copy the text.

I used my cane to go to the bathroom and I ran water in the glass, drank it, refilled, indulged myself by spitting it in the basin and drinking more and more, no longer thirsty now that I could drink all the water I wanted. I splashed it on my face. There was me in the mirror, wearing a tracksuit a size too big for my body, my hair over my ears. I got the old tinfoil sheet of pills out of my shaving kit and punched out two of Dr. Ahuja's antidepressants and looked at the medicine's box where a dancing figure spun as if in a fit of euphoria, and I thought about Elvis movies, musicals, and happiness. I was ready for the musical based on my life to begin.

CHAPTER 26

In the middle of the night, Van Raye and Ruth left Palo Alto. He felt good behind the wheel of his old Jaguar, headed out on the nearly deserted causeway to the interstate.

"He smells awful," Ruth said.

Van Raye glanced at the light crossing over her closed eyes. The dog was in the backseat making snotty noseprints on the window, the smears twinkling brighter.

On the dashboard, the alien statue stared back at him. "Do we really need this?" he said.

"Yes," Ruth said. She'd drug it out of his suitcase the other day. "Because," she said, "I can tell you hate it. Whoever gave you this, you fucked her." He saw her rubbing her own belly. "Let's call it therapy," she said.

Forty-five minutes into the trip, she asked, "When are we going to stop?"

She wore her standard green unflattering flight suit. When she'd thrown her one duffle into the trunk on top of Van Raye's three garbage bags of stuff, he'd noticed the bulge of her belly in the jumpsuit.

Now there was starlight overhead and dark forests on both sides of the road, woods thick enough to do what was best, and he had a pregnant ex-wife in the car, a whole country to drive across, had another ex-wife to find, and he told himself that he had to start organizing his writing so he could perfectly tell the story of his discovery and how he sent his own message to the planet before anyone else did.

Van Raye found the right spot to pull off the road. Ruth pretended to stay asleep against the passenger door when he shut the engine off. They'd discussed this, agreed it was best, but he stepped out alone, scared by the silence of the woods. Lightning bugs tricked his eyes. The concrete of the highway sparkled moonlight, and the heat of the Jaguar's engine smelled good as it ticked and cooled. Van Raye opened the back door. "Come on," he said to the dog.

Ruth was a dark, unmoving, silent mound in the passenger seat. The dog hopped out and never lost momentum, zigzagging back and forth, nose going over the ground.

Ruth's door creaked open. She shoved it wider and grabbed the doorframe. "What a son of a bitch you are," she said calmly. She hauled herself out.

"Don't . . . " he said.

How, he thought, *did I end up with a pregnant ex-wife who was hearing music in her belly, a hundred miles from nowhere, letting a dog go in the woods?*

Her flip-flops scraped the pavement as she went to the driver's side, slid behind the wheel, and started the car.

The dog stopped, turned and looked at them, tongue out. Van Raye got in the passenger side and pulled his silver pipe out as she got the car going. *I will sleep it off*, he told himself.

It was Ruth who said, "You let him go rather easily."

"What dog wouldn't want to be free in the woods?" he said.

Ruth ran the car up to ninety, the hand on the bottom of the wheel, the car swaying, and put another cigarette in her mouth.

"Be careful," he said.

"What does it matter?" she said. "This is dark. Dark, dark." She pushed the lighter in. "I'm going to remind you in the daylight what you are capable of, what we are all capable of, and see how you feel then. This isn't a 'never talk about it' moment."

"You don't believe in those, do you?" he said.

"I don't think we can just forget letting a dog go."

The lighter popped out.

"Don't mention it if we're in Texas, please," he said. "Texas is depressing enough. Wait till we're through Texas, if you must. Maybe we shouldn't go into Texas."

"I'll save it for Texas. Let's heap the shit on and see what happens." One hand on the wheel, the other with the cigarette rubbed her belly in the jumpsuit, and he knew she was hearing the music.

"Who was the father?" he said.

"A cosmonaut," she said.

"What happened to you up there?" he said. "I'm not talking about *that*."

She didn't answer at first but then said, "I got a glimpse of the big thing that scares everyone."

"What 'big thing'?" he asked.

"Nothing," she said.

"Like nothing 'never mind,' or like nothing *nothing*?"

"Capital-N Nothing," she said. "I saw Nothing. I saw it when I was up there. Nothing is horrifyingly bright. That was the scary part—it was bright and nothing."

"Quit talking like that. I'm not in the mood," he said.

She made a defeated sigh.

He said, "You need some professional help. You've been through a major trauma."

"I am professional help," she said.

"Doctor, heal thyself?" he muttered.

In a few minutes, after staring at the road, watching the trees go by, she said, "What does this Elizabeth look like?"

"Don't be petty. My son is sick, and we are going to visit him for a few days and see what progress we can make on finding an antenna to send my message."

Smoke filled the car.

On one of the trees she drove past, there was a small white sign, and Ruth had time to read it as they flashed by. It said HELL IS REAL, and Ruth said, "Hell is real. Why not send that?"

"Quit," he said.

"That is succinct and it's very helpful."

He didn't say anything and then softly, "Poor baby."

"What did you say?" she said.

"I didn't say anything."

When Van Raye fell asleep against his door, he dreamed he was in the woods trying to re-catch the dog. The dog stood still long enough for Van Raye to see a medical porthole in the side of the dog. He looked inside, expecting intestines like in the cow in the pasture, but instead there was clean blackness of space and one bright shiny point of light. It was, Van Raye knew, the star with Chava Norma orbiting around it, a whole other world inside the dog. In his dream, he tried to get closer, but the dog ran away.

PART III

CHAPTER 27

I got the adjoining room to Elizabeth's suite, room 1212, and didn't have the energy or the initiative to go out in public. My waking hours were spent texting Ursula and then Dubourg, pressing redial for the only number I had for Van Raye and getting a recording for the university's bed and breakfast. My companions in my room were the betta fish and flight-attendant Barbie sitting unladylike on the dresser, legs spread, and out my sliding glass doors was the wide-open dome of sky over the Atlanta airport. I ran a search for "World record" + "living in a hotel room," and got directed to Howard Hughes biographies.

Elizabeth would come and speak through the adjoining door to me, "This is very unhealthy."

I sometimes gathered myself into one of my new tracksuits and went to dinner. In the revolving restaurant, she updated me on the Grand Aerodrome's wrap-up. I sat slouched in the chair. She told me that I looked like a gangster. I told her that my wardrobe was comfortable.

"If you ever have to defend what you are wearing with 'it's comfortable,'" she said, "you've made the wrong choice."

She explained that I had to get back to work, to write this report myself. My phone sat beside my dinner plate, the last conversation with Randolph clearly visible in green and purple text balloons.

"I'm preparing you to run the firm alone," she said.

"And what are you going to do?" I touched the screen to make the light come back on and slid it again in her direction. *Just look at my phone, see this conversation!*

"I will not travel with you," she said, "if that's what you are asking. I think you would be healthier without me. You're completely capable of doing it when you get back to 100 percent."

"No, I don't think I can. Are you looking around?" I used my eyes to point to my phone. All she had to do was glance down at the conversation.

"What? What is wrong with you?" She picked up the phone. She tilted her head back. "What am I supposed to be looking at? I don't have my glasses on."

"Jesus!" I took it, but the screen was blank white, conversation gone. "Dammit!"

The restaurant revolved, slowly turned on its axis. After dessert, we drank coffee. If she retired, if she never said a word about business, would our whole lives be like it was when we were waiting on a flight—no worries, no business, only the moment? Her eyes kept looking to the west, and Gypsy Sky Cargo inched its way into view. The jets were being unloaded and loaded under the lights, cargo doors wide open, and containers going up on accordion lifts. They had floodlights mounted in clusters on high poles making every worker on the ground have multiple shadows emanating from his or her feet like a Swiss Army knife of selves.

CHAPTER 28

Back alone in my room with the doors shut and locked, I took Dr. Ahuja's sleeping pills when I felt like I needed a break—they were like pushing a button—and I would wake into new light, my phone on my chest.

I turned my head on the pillow and watched the betta fish and wondered if he was somehow changing colors. Now he looked a plasmotronic blue as if he'd changed color for a different segment of life, and he went up and down in the corner of his tank, fighting his reflection. A jet's thrust reversers rattled the balcony doors, the sounds of the womb to me, and another gray day trying to leak through the shears, and I thought, *Is the day ending or beginning?* I'd become jetlagged inside a hotel room.

I was thinking "*jetlag*" when something on the other bed moved, a lump of a human beneath the covers, and somehow my mind already knew it was Ursula. She was on her side facing the wall, the shimmering light from the aquarium undulating on the comforter over her body, and I had some vague recollection of the happiness of seeing her last night. *Ursula is here.*

On the bedside table were a martini glass with two dead cranberries and my bottle of sleeping pills.

I whispered, "Ursula?" and wondered why I was whispering if I wanted to wake her. "*Ur!*"

She rolled, squinted at me, and immediately squeezed the button on her watch to stop it. "What?" she said, eyes swollen from sleep.

"What are you doing here?"

"Sleeping, dumbass." She rolled back toward the wall, and I heard the watch beep again.

"Are you really here?"

"Are *you* really here?" She didn't turn over to see me, only took a deep breath, and her voice reflected off the wall. "You don't remember anything, do you?"

Her watch beeped again, and she rolled over to see me, then checked the time.

"A little bit."

"I found you downstairs," she said.

"You're lying."

"You were at the bar. I'm extremely pissed at you, by the way."

"At the bar?" I pulled up memories that were like dreams. "Elizabeth doesn't know about this, does she?" I asked. "Did she see me?"

"No, but you were quite the hit there in your pajamas. It's freezing in here." She pulled the cover tighter over her head. "Why did you invite me here?" she said. "Do you even want me here?"

"Yes, of course I want you here." I had a dull alcohol headache.

She rolled her eyes and pulled the covers over her mouth; she was only eyes and a nose. The empty martini glass sat on the bedside table, sugar around the rim reminding me of the night with Franni from Mount Unpleasant.

"There's a front coming, an ugly storm," she said, words veiled, her lips beneath the fabric. She reached a hand out and picked the brown pill bottle and shook. "Look, don't take this shit."

"I know," I said. "I just—"

"No, you don't know," she said. "I mean, it knocks you out, and, you know, erases your memory. You don't want to be that deep asleep. Ever."

She got out of the covers, slammed the bottle down and it bounced on the floor. She said, "Too many people take these. You don't want to be that out."

"Aliens aren't coming to take me."

She had on that worn-out fake jersey with the peeling "20." She put her feet on the floor so she was facing me, had on gray cutoff sweatpants. "You think I'm crazy, don't you?"

"No," I said. "You believe what you believe. In a weird way, I can completely understand why you do this. It makes you feel good, doesn't it?"

"Feel good? To live in constant fear it's going to happen tonight?" she said. She got back under the comforter.

"If someone could snap their fingers," I said, "and make it never happen to you again, would you do it?"

She thought about it. "No."

"But you're scared all the time."

"Like a cat on a windy day," she said.

"Ur, just don't get hypnotized. Okay?" Almost all the abductees she read about got hypnosis to supposedly regain memories. They only engrained false memories. She had read this too, but I still wanted to make sure.

"Did I say I was fucking getting hypnotized?"

"Stop cussing so much. It just means you don't know how to express yourself."

"Jesus, I'm freezing," she said.

Her fingers were holding the covers beneath her chin as she ceiling-stared, and she said, "I wish you would just open your mind for once. I have several floating experiences I remember, I mean when I was a kid. I remember flying over the woods, seeing the highway. I literally have seen the V wake of snakes swimming in the river at night, moonlight reflecting on the water. They aren't dreams."

"Ur, we literally grew up thinking there was a spaceship crashed in the swamp, or wanting to believe it. We were kids. I think we liked to believe. We liked to watch the movie and believe an alien was in the swamp. I think you're just doing that now."

"The *Creature*," she corrected me.

She waited until everything was completely quiet and still in the room and she said, "They took my eggs."

"Stop it."

"They did."

"No, Ur, you're just trying to find a reason for why you are the way you are, you know . . . "

"*Barren*, you mean?" she said.

"That was because of the cyst, or related to it," I said and watched her shift beneath the covers. "I'm speaking honestly, okay. We all remember when you had that problem." Ursula, since she was fourteen and had the cyst removed and the doctor told her that she'd probably never have children, always openly declared herself *barren*. She had always said it as if she just wanted to get over it.

"But why did I have a cyst?" she asked.

"Look, forget that for a second. I really think Triple Zero affected you. I know nothing happened on that flight, and when *nothing happened*, that triggered something in your mind. You wanted something to happen."

She got up and went over and grabbed a new Adidas jacket from the chair and put it on. The tag stuck out of the collar, and she walked around and sat on the bed across from me. Her eyes moved back and forth from my right eye to my left, inspecting me, and there was a part of me that wanted to put my hands on the side of her face and pull her and kiss her. I had promised myself to do this.

"Are you lucid?" she asked. This close, I could smell her, and I had a flash of the house in Sopchoppy, the taste of fresh river water and then the salt of the gulf.

"You think I'm crazy?" she said. "You're the one who thinks God is sending you text messages."

"*What?*"

She nodded.

"What else did I tell you?"

"You said it was a hacker too and it's all related to Charles's discovery."

"I told you about Charles?"

"Yes," she said. She paced and pulled the elastic band out of her hair and casually said, "And conveniently can't you show me this conversation?"

"Whoever it is makes the texts disappear."

"What a fine predicament," she said. "You think I'm crazy, and I think you're crazy for believing anything Van Raye says. He's got that Southern mouth of a liar, you know." She spread her mouth thin with her fingers. "You know, Southern liars all got a thinness, a shape."

"I don't think he's lying about this."

She held the elastic hair band in her mouth as she collected her ponytail again. I watched, jealous of the dexterity of her hands looping the band in her hair. Then she went and put her feet into a pair of my Nike high-tops and pulled a fifth of Jack Daniel's from her duffle, held it up so I could see it and said, "I'm not keeping this very sophisticated." She got two glasses from the bathroom, shook the protective covers off, and let them fall to the floor as she plodded back. She pushed the martini glass out of the way and put the glasses down too hard.

"What's the matter with you?" I said.

When she poured, the brown liquid washed up one side of the glass, left an oily after-wave that slowly retreated.

"You got your head so far up your daddy's ass. You and Du."

"Why are you angry?"

"Do you understand the magnitude of what is happening to me? People like me have been chosen. I don't know why. Something comes to me and takes me away. I *fly*. It has happened when I'm in my apartment, and once recently when I was staying at this motel in Twentynine Palms, okay. It happened once when I was driving through the Muir Woods in a goddamn rental car. This was last month! Whenever I'm alone. Do you understand? They take me. I fly, I mean, just my body. Van Raye might hear something but he's about five hundred years behind. There are dozens, hundreds, whatever, of civilizations out there. So what? Something is *here*," she said.

We waited in the relative silence of the airport hotel room. She took her feet out of the shoes and sat on the other bed. She said, "I'm here with you because I don't want to be alone."

"Stay with me as long as you want," I whispered.

"Don't get weird on me, okay?" she said.

We took a sip of our drinks.

She lifted her glass. "To life somewhere else in the universe . . . besides here. To aliens."

"Don't ever let Charles hear you use that term. I think he's coming here."

She turned and put her legs up on her bed and crossed her arms. "I've never met the man," she said. "When you're not around, Dubourg tells me what an ass he is, but Dubourg is totally in love with him. Dubourg put his own name on Van Raye's Wiki page. He put himself under 'children.'"

"Why?" I asked. "He's a pathetic excuse for anything resembling a father. Dubourg's got Uncle Louis. I can't think of anyone but Uncle Louis as Dubourg's father."

"Would you trade Van Raye for Louis?"

"Louis is great," I said.

"No, that's not an answer. Think about it. Van Raye's a son of a bitch but he's bigger than life."

We sat still. I listened to the hotel room, felt the humanity around us, the rooms full of lives.

She got up and went to the bottle on the dresser and poured us both more whiskey. I watched her calves flex when she adjusted the thermostat, and the Sanctus bells stirred in the nether lobes of my brain. I hadn't had an erection in weeks, not even the healthy morning kind, and I'd begun to wonder if it was the depression.

I glanced at my phone and saw a whole conversation from last night that I had no recollection of, Randolph asking me:

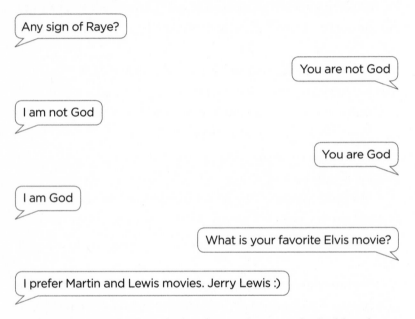

Any sign of Raye?

You are not God

I am not God

You are God

I am God

What is your favorite Elvis movie?

I prefer Martin and Lewis movies. Jerry Lewis :)

Ursula came back with the glass and got on the bed beside me, pushing the comforter tight over my body. I turned the phone quickly to her and she studied it, and then shook her head, said, "Nothing. Yes, you are crazy." She put legs straight out on the covers.

"Sandy, do you remember that you once flew down to Sopchoppy because Dubourg left a pair of pants in Baltimore?"

I twirled my whiskey in the glass before gulping some. "Yes. I was like twelve." But there was the memory emerging from the background. "It was actually a pair of swim trunks," I said. "And it was in Washington. That was after you stayed with us at the Marriott. I remember it because y'all wanted to run up and down the hallways."

"Right!" she said.

"You and Dubourg sprinted up and down the hallways because you said that you could run faster inside than you could outside."

"I still believe that, by the way," she said.

I realized how good it feels to have a shared experience with someone and told her, "Isn't family about having someone around to share experiences with?"

She said, "Then Elizabeth caught us and jumped all over our asses, and Du and I went back home, and the next thing we know you flew down with his pants." She laughed. "You looked pathetic standing on the porch holding the bag."

"All right," I said.

"You stayed for weeks."

"I know," I said, "I've always wanted to be part of y'all."

"Not that you couldn't have just come down and stayed if you wanted, but we all thought it was a little weird."

"I wish you would just forget that," I said. "I was twelve or whatever."

She handed me her glass to take a sip and crossed her arm over her eyes. "Can I tell you something? This is the best I've felt in a long time. Right here. I love you," she said.

She took her arm down to see me.

I said, "You know I love you . . ."

"Like a sister?" she said.

"Of course." The whole room was quiet.

She said, "Do you remember we used to believe that the Creature wouldn't come after us if we were all together in the kids' bunk room?"

"Of course," I said.

"It was a great comfort being together, wasn't it?"

After a few seconds of silence I thought she'd drifted off to sleep. Without opening her eyes or removing her hand, she said, "This is the same thing, isn't it, except it's only us, and it's not the Creature from the movie. It's something else that we are scared of."

"And that we make ourselves want to believe in," I said.

I got the remote and turned on the TV, the light filling the room. I searched the movie menu until I found *The Creature from Outer Space*, and when she saw, she said, "Seriously?"

"When was the last time we've watched it?" I asked.

We took turns sipping out of the same glass as the credits played and the music started, and she got under the covers against me.

"What are you doing?" I said.

"Watching the movie that scared the hell out of me when I was little."

We sat, the length of our bodies touching. I could feel her heat trapped beneath the blanket with mine, and I could smell her, and this feeling reminded me of once being alone with her in a pub in Dublin years before, and we'd started holding hands because we had realized that the patrons who'd befriended us in that pub thought we were traveling college students who were lovers. We simply held hands in the pub, her thumb rubbing my hand, and we drank our beers, and people went in and out of the door like life was normal, and a man at the end of the bar asked if he could sing us a song, and as he sang to us, we let go of each other's hand because holding hands while he sang so beautifully would have been like stealing something that wasn't ours.

"Even this music starts to freak me out," she said as the movie began.

The voice-over narrator said, "*Since time began,*" and Ursula and I recited along with him, "*man has looked toward the heavens with wonder . . . wonder and fear. The interstellar distances have kept us safe . . . until now,*" and her voice and his voice made a tingling, a good tingling, spread from my back into the base of my skull.

"There's something sexual about that fear," Ursula said, "I've gotten that same feeling when I was about to have sex."

"Are we about to have sex?" I said.

"You'll only fall madly in love with me and be driven insane by your cousin-lover—"

"Ursula, quit. I've always been madly in love with you." I stared at the movie. I felt her take my hand beneath the covers and pull it to her lap, the heat like a fever.

"I tremble, okay?" I said. "My muscles are weak, that's all."

"I'm trembling too," she said. "It'll never work, will it, we'll never work?"

I was about to ask her why not when I felt myself getting hard, heard the Sanctus bells chiming in the pleasure center of my brain responding to the one person in the world who I most desired, but there was also an unfamiliar stretching pain as if the growing erection were caught on something.

"Eventually you'll get tired of me," she mumbled, unaware of my discomfort, which only made me harder, made more stinging and stretching. "Then where would we be?"

"I don't think I ever would get tired of you," I said, the pain not stopping. I closed my eyes to make it go away, but when I did, I suddenly knew what the date was, new what the time was.

"Hey," she said, "you're squeezing my hand."

"Sorry."

My heart palpitated, but before letting her hand go I lifted her arm so I could see that rubber watch she always wore, dangling on the bottom of her wrist. Its time and date confirmed what I already knew. Worried about my impotency, I had asked Randolph when I would get an erection, and he'd told me, and now here I was. Now here I was tumbling, falling forward in time again.

"Holy shit," I whispered, putting my hand to my chest, my breath taken away.

"What?" she asked.

"Nothing," but I had felt my life leaping to that moment my penis was burning. I rolled to try to inconspicuously shift the erection.

I went quickly to the bathroom.

By the time I got the door shut, I heard her shout, "Are you okay?"

"Fine!"

I undid the drawstring and pushed the pants down, inspected everything, which, miraculously, didn't have blood on it, and I pulled my pants up and made myself breathe. In the mirror I looked more hollow eyed than ever. It seemed only a second ago that I had been alone in my room and had forced Randolph, once again, to answer a question about the future. Now here I was. Jesus, would more of these moments just pop into my life, throw my life forward?

I went back and slid in bed beside her again.

"What's the matter with you?" she said.

"Nothing," I said. Glancing at the television, I said, "Good, I didn't miss it."

In the movie it was daylight on the river. A group of young people were having a party on a bluff, which was the scene with my grandmother, Harriet Raye, Victim 1. Dance music came from a transistor radio on a rock, and I could only think about how most of these actors were dead now, their lives gone in probably what seemed like a couple of blinks.

Ursula whispered, "I've seen this movie so many times . . . I swear I'm getting that same feeling I used to get when we were kids. This shit freaked me out, okay? Now it's an extremely corny movie to me, but I still get the same feeling . . . " She held her breath, then let it out. "Here it comes," she tensed and relaxed, "and there it goes. It comes in waves. I want to hold onto it for a second but can't completely do it."

We both had our backs against the headboard, and at some point I realized she was watching me.

"What?" I said.

She stretched her knee until it touched me.

On the screen, Harriet Raye, my paternal grandmother, Ursula's great-aunt, unbuttoned her shirt and revealed a black bathing suit.

"See you on the other side!" Harriet Raye says in the movie. The movie cut to a longer shot from across the river and she dove perfectly from the bluff. This was really my grandmother diving.

The Creature's theme came up loud.

Right then, as our ancestor was becoming "Victim 1," I felt the same fear and excitement *The Creature from Outer Space* had given me when I was a kid, but like Ursula said, it was there, then gone, and even though it was a kind of fear, you wanted it back, and when I looked to tell her this, she had turned away. While Harriet Raye was pulled down by the Creature, claw around her ankle, struggling through the crystal-clear water, Ursula's watch beeped and then there was her gentle snoring.

CHAPTER 29

Ursula slept. The Creature was eventually killed by spear guns.

I slowly lifted her hand to see the numbers twirling on her stopwatch as she slept. She was trying to somehow quantify real sleep time versus lost time if the aliens came to take her away.

I turned the television off and put my back against her back and tried to sleep, but the bed covers were loose and frustrating.

I had no choice but to get up, but I didn't get in the other bed. I put on my red tracksuit and went down to the empty nighttime lobby. I shut myself in the phone booth on the end and waited. The sign on the phone said:

> 1) STOP!
> 2) Listen for tone.
> 3) Deposit coins.

When it rang, like I knew it would, I snapped it up without speaking. It was the old favorite "Viva Las Vegas," and it did seem like the best song ever—"...and I'm just the devil with love to spare ... Viva Las Vegas ..."

I glanced outside to the lobby but saw nothing out of the ordinary, just the lobby at low staff, and I closed my eyes to relax. The tight confines of the phone booth was wonderful, slouched with knees braced against the metal wall, but then my leg tingled—tingling, tingling?—but I realized that my phone was vibrating in my tracksuit pocket. The message was from "UNKNOWN," which meant Randolph:

You are very happy tonight.

How do you know? Why can't I show this conversation to anyone?

At the right time everyone will know. They aren't ready.

You are from another planet.

:)

And I need Raye's help.

You know what he has found?

Yes.

Do you have something to do with the noise?

Is the noise your planet?

No.

No, but . . .

But that is where I want to go.

I am going to have to locate the dog again. He didn't look after the dog. There will be a slight delay.

The dog? I looked at the world outside the phone booth as if I would see a dog among the late-night check-ins. On the concierge's desk, a small sign apologized for the inconvenience of her not being there.

> Forgive me if there is a long period of silence.
> I must search and solve problems for the dog.

I fell asleep in the comfort of the booth, one of those deep, paralyzing sleeps from childhood, and dreamed of being back in the hospital bed beside Mr. Leggett. I happily waited for Rose Epstein to call her name and tell everyone she wanted to go home. I wanted Mr. Leggett to tell one of his stupid jokes even though I had always agreed with my father about jokes being the shallowest form of human conversation.

In chapter 9 of *The Universe Is a Pair of Pants*, "Mediocre Men," Van Raye ranked them:

3) Talking about sports.

2) Talking about television shows.

1) Telling jokes—"Did you hear the one about . . . ?"

"It is slightly interesting to wonder where these jokes come from," he wrote. "The 'farmer's daughters' jokes, 'a guy walks into a bar' jokes? Nobody knows who creates dirty jokes, nor why such categories evolve and remain. How do the jokes survive in the world? How do they become popular enough to be repeated? Why do these appeal to people, appeal to them enough that they are memorized and stored? They spread like the most proficient virus. Why?"

In the chapter, he tells of an experiment. He made up a joke, told it to a friend when they were on a hiking trip on Russia's Kamchatka Peninsula (picture a woman in a tent). "I told my English-speaking friend the joke on top of a volcano," he wrote. "It was funny, if I say so

myself. I told no one else the joke, and I will not write it here. This is
about what spreads among human beings by shear desire to have this
superficial contact with other human beings. I hope to one day hear my
joke repeated to me somewhere far away from Kronotsky."

I woke in the phone booth the next morning, sat blinking my eyes to a
new, dull-gray day dawning through the hotel, and I was surprised to
see Elizabeth get out of the elevator at that moment, fully dressed in a
navy business suit. I started to fold the door open but Elizabeth's speed
of walking made me stop to see what the hell was going on. She was
looking at someone. He was in the direction of the bank of courtesy
phones on the opposite wall, and as soon as I saw the rounded Bob
Cratchit posture I knew it was Charles.

CHAPTER 30

Charles wore a big blue arctic parka and a knit cap. He still had on sunglasses like he was a movie star, and the heavy coat couldn't hide that
stooping posture. They went toward each other like a bad movie, Van
Raye with his arms open, Elizabeth moving too fast, not even caring if
anyone saw her. She hit him with an embrace that knocked him slightly
off balance, then took his cheeks between her hands and stretched her
neck forward to kiss him on the lips.

He appeared mildly shocked.

I rose awkwardly out of the booth, stood with the help of my cane
and the doorframe.

I walked to them and said, "Elizabeth?"

She let go of him and kept his elbow in her grip and simply said,
"Charles is here!"

"Look who's here!" he said, eyes behind the glasses. "*Me!*"

"Charles," I said. He came and hugged me, pinning my arms so that I could only touch his elbows. "It's really you," I said. "Thank God. Charles, let me go. You're squeezing me."

He did and said, "We're all here!" He took in the sight of Elizabeth, down to her gold shoes. "I've never had a greeting like that! Darling, look at you, you look fantastic! I look horrible. It really took too long to get here. It wasn't supposed to be this long. And the storm." His parka squeaked as he moved. He had on black pants and boots with zippers.

"It doesn't matter," she said. "You're here."

The waterfall ran in the fake rainforest. The Air of Liability was clear. Guests pulled their luggage by us. Everything was quite normal except the girlish look of delight on Elizabeth's face.

"I've got a lot to tell you," I said. "I don't know where to start."

"Well, we have plenty of time." He clapped his hands. "You look fine," he said to me. "I love the getup," he pointed to my red tracksuit. "Very urban." He took Elizabeth's arm, me with the other, moving us along as if we were guests in his hotel.

"My God. This is just like you to call when you are already *here*," Elizabeth said. "I wasn't even dressed. I could have used some warning."

"We had to beat the storm."

"Have you had breakfast?" she said. "Do you want a room? Of course you want a room. There's an extra room, Sandeep's old room. I could see what else is available. I'll book you something."

"Elizabeth, slow down," he said. "I've got some things." He pointed toward a gold luggage cart where a homeless woman sat on a pile of cheap bags that included two garbage bags and a drawstring laundry bag. The woman's hair had recently been sheared off. She wore sandals, her legs spread so that hairy shins were revealed.

He herded us to the cart and said, "This is Ruth Christmas."

The woman didn't attempt to get off the cart. She had an unlit cigarette in her fingers and she had the expression of careful, objective observing.

"This is Elizabeth Sanghavi, and this is Sandeep."

She only nodded and reached up and hooked her hand around the top bar of the cart and let it hang there as she took an imaginary drag of the unlit cigarette in the other. She was clearly deranged. My thought was, *Where had he picked her up?*

"This is . . . " Elizabeth said, "this is your luggage? I mean, this is it?" Elizabeth was staring at the woman, but then tried to occupy her eyes with scanning the bags. "I thought you were bringing your horn."

"My horn?" he said.

"I don't see your horn." Her voice had changed.

"Elizabeth, I haven't played my horn in years. Ruth did most of the driving. I'm starving."

"You don't have your *horn*?" Elizabeth said again, and I wanted her to stop repeating herself. She'd told me a thousand times that only dullards repeated things in order to give the dullard time to think about what was going on.

"I haven't played a horn in years. You know that." He smiled.

"You mentioned starting back," she said.

The bellhops in their maroon uniforms wore *ushankas* that made them look like ice fishermen in band uniforms.

"Ruth and I were wondering," Van Raye said, "if we might see the hotel's roof."

"The roof?" I said, being the dullard now.

"We're searching for a certain type of dish antenna—"

My phone chimed and Charles looked at it as though it were a turd.

A message from Ursula said:

Dubourg is here

"*What?*" I mumbled.

Van Raye maneuvered Elizabeth and me by the arm again as if to talk to us in private.

Elizabeth glanced over her shoulder. "She's with you?"

"Now, sweetheart, before assumptions are made . . ." He turned slightly back at the other woman—"Ruth is . . . "—who still sat on the bags on the cart and out of earshot. She put the cigarette in her mouth and drug on it as if it were lit; she even squinted through nonexistent smoke.

I saw Elizabeth's focus in the distance, and her eyes became sleepy the way she did when she was playing a particular difficult piece of music. She refocused on Charles talking about driving, and she slowly lifted her hand and tucked her fingers, and I saw the meaty paler part of her palm rise, and I had a flash memory to the executive self-defense course we'd taken in Trenton, New Jersey, years ago, and that meaty part of her hand traveled on a path toward Van Raye. He could only flinch before it struck him on his cheek, half slap and half fist.

He stepped backward, mouth open. "My God!" He still had those horrible sunglasses on.

Travelers stopped walking, stopped talking on their phones to see this spectacle.

The woman sitting on the luggage began to laugh.

Elizabeth covered her mouth. "Dear God, are you okay?"

"Violence?" he said. "Seriously?"

"He's okay," I said. "You're okay, aren't you?"

"NO!" He leaned away from me.

Elizabeth recovered and dropped her hands. "Go find another hotel! Get out!"

"Elizabeth, darling . . . "

"Elizabeth," I said, "wait a minute, okay?"

I saw the front desk staff dispersing, one woman quickly coming out of the door.

Van Raye said to Elizabeth, "Please don't. I have nothing." He finally took his glasses off and folded them and put them in his parka's pocket, withdrawing a pair of tortoiseshell eyeglasses. "I don't have anywhere else to go," he said. "I don't have *nothing* exactly. I do have one thing. Sandeep knows. I've had a bit of success. For what I was searching for."

Someone had summoned potbellied Mr. Blaney, and Albert from security followed.

"What has happened here?" Mr. Blaney said.

"Nothing," I said.

"Was someone struck?" Albert in his brown nylon jacket and tie wanted to know, his aftershave arriving with him.

"I'm handling everything," Elizabeth said. "This is a family matter, and I apologize."

"I'll go get an incident report," Albert said.

"I don't need an *incident* report," Elizabeth said. "Please leave us."

"Yes, ma'am," Blaney said and motioned for Albert to disperse, and Blaney left without a glance back.

Van Raye unzipped the jacket and said, "Seriously, Elizabeth? It takes a lot to admit this to you, but I am broke."

"Broke you should be familiar with," she said. "And we are always here to bail you out, aren't we?"

"It's not like that. That's not true." In a lower voice, he said, "You know what I've found."

"Yes," she said. "That has nothing to do with us."

He let out a breath. "It has everything to do with everyone. Look, I need a place to stay. Ruth is here to help me work. She's the only person who can help. She's a genius."

When we turned to see Ruth Christmas sitting on the luggage, she shrugged.

I reached out to Elizabeth, but she turned and stormed toward the elevator.

I hobbled on my cane to catch up to her. She pushed the button and waited for the elevator. I turned to Van Raye and held up a finger for him to stay away.

Elizabeth tried to control her breathing as she watched the numbers above the elevator. "The man will never change. I don't want him here."

"Yes, you do. Who was that back there that I just saw?"

"You mean the *genius*?"

"No, I mean you."

"Me?" she said.

"Yes. You were someone else, asking about his horn. And then you hit him."

She closed her eyes and made a visible shudder. "Sandeep, look at me, I'm shaking. Yes, I struck someone."

I leaned on my cane. "We can let him stay."

"He's using us."

"What does that hurt? He's going to do this anyway. We can let him work here. Just don't get too close."

Elizabeth considered the chandelier in the ceiling, then casually glanced at the woman across the lobby dressed in a green flight suit and with no hair.

"A *genius*?" Elizabeth said sarcastically.

I quickly typed Ursula a message that I was coming to the room.

Elizabeth said, "'Genius' is a term tossed around too much, don't you think? *You're* a genius, Sandeep."

I stopped typing and looked at her. "What do you mean?"

"See, you can label anyone," she said.

She took in a deep breath.

"Holy shit," I said, "for a second there, you scared me." Elizabeth and I watched the other woman put her feet up on the bags.

"His discovery won't make this elevator any faster, will it?" she said.

"Dubourg and Ursula are here."

She turned to me. "We're supposed to be getting back on task here. I'm ready to put this hotel behind us." She looked back at the two geniuses. "Book only one room for the geniuses. What do I care? Put them away together. We'll pay for everything, of course."

CHAPTER 31

I went to my room to collect my cousins. We hugged and then divvied up my ski gear because I told them Van Raye was going to the roof to check out some antenna. Ursula cursed me for leaving her alone in the room and ended up putting on Dubourg's wool pea coat, and Dubourg put on my hooded ski jacket. We took the service elevator to the attic storage room, and Dubourg and Ursula followed me through aisles of fold-up bed frames from some forgotten era, me following the path of ceiling lights Elizabeth had flipped on only minutes before, purplish and buzzing as they warmed inside wire cages. A set of steel stairs on the far wall went up to a landing and a single metal door. Halfway up, I had to catch my breath and my phone dinged:

Raye is with you.

I turned the phone to them. "Can you see this?" I said.

"No," Dubourg said, patiently waiting behind me for my legs to rest.

Wind shook the door at the top of the landing and drew our attention, and I kept trudging upward. Ursula reached the door first and pushed its handle and the wind threw it open. Dubourg and I covered our eyes, blinking into the snow. This was the top of the hotel, literally in the sky, swirling with cold that immediately bit at my ears.

Elizabeth stood calmly in the wind shadow of a giant metal utility box, only the triangle of her wool overcoat lifting, her cheap sunglasses on. She pulled her scarf down to say something I couldn't hear, and pointed. The flagpole's halyard dinged a rhythm. Ducts leaked clouds of steam that tumbleweeded and thinned and disappeared before it got to an old satellite dish, and there was Van Raye marching toward us with arms raised, a giant smile on his face. "*There is more here!*" he shouted. "*Look at the people!*" The ends of his white hair were damp, snow collected on his cap.

Something heavy dropped and Dubourg stepped past me to intercept Charles. Dubourg's hand went toward Van Raye in slow motion and struck him on the right side of his face. My first reaction to Charles being punched for a second time that day, I'm sorry to say, was to laugh. Maybe it was seeing the physics of Van Raye's twisting body again and the expression on his face change from the bullshit of his greeting to total candor and the shock of a Munch scream, and then there was the miraculous catch he made on his way to the ground of his eyeglasses in midflight.

He rolled to his elbows and shut his mouth and blinked up at us. There was the slow blossom of a laceration above his eye.

I said to Dubourg, "What was that for?"

Dubourg, hopping around opening and shutting his bare hand to stay the pain, yelled at me, *"Why did I do that?"*

Van Raye's gloved hand, the one not holding his glasses, was on the ground beside my foot, and because it was an easy thing to do, I adjusted my weight and lifted my right foot and put it on his hand. The glove was thick, but I pressed through the cushion until I felt his hand inside. I tried to remember if Van Raye had wronged Dubourg lately or if this was just some kind of reaction. Their last meeting was a few years ago, back when Dubourg was in seminary, and the three of us met in Southern California on a day that couldn't have been more different from this. That meal had been completely amicable, though afterward Dubourg had mentioned that the man talked down to him.

"My God," Van Raye said now. "More violence? What was that for?"

Dubourg spun like a dizzy kid and tucked his hand between his leg. "Oh fuck, oh fuck. That was pent-up anger. Oh fuck, I'm sorry. I really have hated you all these years. But I'm sorry!" Dubourg's breathing produced condensation, but the curses were cloudless *Oh fuck*s, and he began mumbling in the blizzard, *"Tadyatha diri tishta taskara . . ."* his eyes closed, hands on his knees.

"For what?" Van Raye snapped. "Jesus, I've never done anything to you."

Then there was laughter behind us and Dubourg's chanting stopped. Through the falling snow, standing and in front of a satellite dish antenna, the "genius" had her jacket hood over her head and was laughing, trying to clap but she had a tool in her hand. A utility box on the pole of the satellite dish flapped.

When the genius saw Ursula and Dubourg staring at her she put a hand on top of her head to keep the hood on. Her face was in the shadow, and we could see only her breath and that unlit cigarette. In her other hand she worked a pair of pliers as if deciding whose teeth to pull first. She stilled the control panel's flapping door without taking eyes off us. She still wore flip-flops. Her toes must have been frostbitten. Obviously she was crazy.

Van Raye shouted up at me from the ground. "*Sandeep!* You're on my hand!" Blood trickled from the bridge of his right eye.

"*Oh, sorry!*" I shouted. "*I don't have normal sensation in my feet!*" A gust rocked me off balance.

He raised himself to his knees. Dubourg and I grabbed him under his arms and hauled him to his feet.

"*Don't touch me!*" Van Raye yelled, shaking us away, touching his cheek and smearing the blood.

I pulled a moist towelette I happened to have in my coat pocket and handed it to him.

"What is the matter with you people?" Van Raye said. "That could give me brain damage! Then where would we be? You ass! I'd punch you back if I weren't a pacifist." He took off his gloves and with hands trembling tore open the towelette.

Dubourg had scooped his case back under his arm. "I couldn't help it. It was like I was possessed."

Holding the towelette to his eye, Van Raye shouted to the woman, "*Can you make one work?*"

She turned toward a field of dish antennas of different sizes across the roof and said, "What we have here is an anthropological display of the decades of technology." She pointed to the group of bigger dishes, "The eighties, and the nineties," she said and pointed to a smaller farm of gray dishes, "and the aughts. But here: C band, steel. Nine meters, but its azimuth is rusted over. I can see when the star will drift through the field of view. Maybe we can make small adjustments." She tilted on her heels and looked at it, holding her hood on her head, then back to him, "Yes, we could do it if we had the software to make the amplifier work."

"We'll get the software!" Van Raye said. "Somehow."

She shrugged her shoulders. She wiped her hands. I saw the woman's tongue come out of her mouth and spit out the worthless cigarette, and it bounced along the roof and into the sky. "If we can get the software . . ." she said. "Ifs and ifs and ifs!" Her hood finally fell. She had that punk, fuck-you haircut but there was something else. I'd been in a hospital for over a month and had seen people in their worst states— sick, underweight, broken bodies, heads shaved and scars across their craniums—but I recognized Ruth Christmas was beautiful. Unlike all the sick hospital patients, I didn't have to reimagine her with hair, didn't have to take away the dark circles from her eyes nor try to magic-erase twenty years or try to put her in healthier times to understand that simple fact: she was beautiful.

Elizabeth stood by herself in the wind, her arms wrapping her shoulders, those sunglasses on in this weather, and trying to look into the gray horizon.

The alcohol in the towelette had decreased the viscosity of Van Raye's blood, and it ran down his chin. A bit had frozen on his collar. It wasn't much of a cut, but it was just one of those places of the body that bleeds greedily, and I had time to notice the wind had let up some.

The genius suddenly spun and squatted with her hands on her knees. It was as though she'd discovered ants crawling around her ankles, but wrenches spilled out of the pockets of her jacket, and she made a horrible sound and projected a tan vomit that splattered between her feet.

Van Raye said, "Don't worry, she's just pregnant." He put the useless towelette to his nose and tilted his head back, the bloody end of it lifting in the breeze, but he seemed to suddenly remember something and said, "Relax, *it's not mine, people.*"

Ruth Christmas, squatting and spitting, stuck her hand up and hung Van Raye a bird without looking at him.

Elizabeth turned and went toward the door but stopped.

He pointed his bent glasses at Ursula, and said, "And your Ben's daughter that Sandeep is always talking about, aren't you?"

Clear snot hung from one of Ursula's nostril and she touched it with the back of her glove.

"Are you going to hit me too?" he said to her.

She pulled a bottle of antacids out of the pocket of Dubourg's coat she was wearing and looked at the label as if the answer was there. "I'll wait until you can feel it!" she said and tossed the bottle through the wind to Ruth Christmas. Van Raye flinched as it passed in front of his face.

The genius caught the bottle and threw them back to Ursula. "I've got nausea, not heartburn."

Van Raye squinted at Ursula, then burst out one laugh—"*Ha!*"

He smiled and turned toward everyone. "We're all family here, so I might as well tell you." He paused for effect. "You know what I was looking for, right? I've found another planet! With life!" He held his hands up in victory, glasses in one hand, bloody towelette in the other.

Elizabeth said from the doorframe behind us, "It hasn't been confirmed yet." She had pulled down her scarf to say it, and she turned and went inside, shutting the door behind her.

Dubourg tried to help the puking genius up, but she shrugged him away.

I touched Charles's elbow and yelled, "*Do you have a dog?*"

He leaned back to see me better. "*A dog?*"

"*Yes! Dog!*"

He held out his hand as if to stop me from advancing, and he shut the bad eye to focus. "*You did the dog to me, didn't you?*" He stabbed a finger at me. "*YOU DID THE DOG TO ME!*"

"*What?*"

The woman snapped the hood back over her head and stepped over to a pipe to try to let steam warm her bare feet.

"*Let's get out of this!*" Ursula said.

As Ruth Christmas walked by him, she pointed a finger at Charles to emphasize when she said, "We don't have the software."

He ignored her, holding the towelette to his eye. "What kind of swimming facility does this place have?"

"I want to talk about the dog," I said.

"You can come swim and talk."

My cousins walked by me.

"Why do I have to follow you?" I said. "This is my hotel."

Van Raye ignored me, seemed to notice the bent glasses in his hand. "Watch this," he said, "it never ends well." He tried to bend the glasses back, but of course they snapped. "Fantastic," he said, "just fantastic."

The snow drifts went by us, obscuring the roof-scape, and when I turned, Van Raye was going toward the door, a piece of his eyeglasses in each hand, the bloody towelette tumbleweeding past me and in two leaps going over the edge of the roof. Just before I pulled the door shut, I glanced at the black dish antenna they wanted to use for something, frozen like a net cast against the sky.

CHAPTER 32

No matter what hotel we were staying in, Charles had to go swimming. Most of my childhood talks with him took place sitting side by side in lounges as he dripped dry, his dark glasses on, fresh drink in hand, me sneaking glimpses of the Möbius strip tattoo on his right shoulder blade.

That day of the snowstorm was no exception. Everyone but Elizabeth went down to the small indoor lap pool because that was where he said he'd be. He immediately turned the gas heater on high.

Even when I was hanging the CLOSED sign on the door, I admired Elizabeth for being able to stay away from him. Here the rest of us were already doing anything Charles wanted, ready to see what he said next.

Ursula and Dubourg sat and ate cheeseburgers, while Charles unbuttoned his shirt, immodestly dropping his pants to reveal plain, vertical gray-striped boxer shorts. I caught a glimpse of the Möbius strip tattoo on his shoulder and remembered the noise of the tattoo gun tattering as he stoically explained the characteristics of this geometric shape, which went right into an essay I read months later about how painkillers block the opioid receptors in the brain to prevent pain. He didn't mention his son attended the tattooing.

That memory must have been fifteen years old, but Charles swimming in the pool was in exactly the same shape—pale, boney, skinny. He hopped into the shallow end of the pool, his eyeglasses repaired with a bundle of white surgical tape. When he got used to the water, he began catching us up on his story, including the drive with Ruth across the country.

Ruth worked on a laptop beside a giant leather radio, an antique thing that played a salsa station. Without taking her eyes off the laptop, she turned her head sideways to take large bites of her burger, and Charles told us about first hearing the sound on the Big Dish antenna.

Ursula went into the utility room and changed into a black sports bra and red tennis shorts and got into the water. Van Raye reached the pool's edge, took a sip of his whiskey, pushed his mended glasses on top of his head, and gingerly placed the baggie of ice to his darkening eye. The Möbius strip tattoo on his shoulder had certainly faded over the years, and when a cold drop of condensation hit my hand, I realized maybe I hadn't actually been with Charles when the tattooing was done. Had I only read his essay, "My Non-Orientable Surface," and internalized it?

"Are you going to write about what is happening now?" I interrupted him.

"This is the most important discovery ever made."

I tried to study the details of the room as he might—the way the ceramic tile in the old gas heater glowed orange. Condensation dimpled on the ceiling like contact lenses about to turn into rain, and as Dubourg walked down the steps into the water, his green cargo shorts filled with air then burped. I was the underweight guy in the red tracksuit.

I said to Charles, "Why did you say I did the dog to you? What does that mean?"

"There's no dog," Van Raye said, and I could tell that he and Ruth glanced at each other. "We had a problem in our neighborhood with a stray. I made a bad association."

"What kind of dog was it?"

"Just a stray and the humane society took care of it."

"Can you call the humane society?" I asked him. "Just to make sure this dog is there?"

"Why would I do that? I have no way of telling them what I'm looking for."

"The person, the hacker, contacted me, said to look after a dog."

Charles stopped in the pool below me, crossed his arms over each other on the side, stared up at me with that bluing eye. "Don't you find it rather convenient that these supposed conversations you are having disappear before you can show them to anyone?"

"How do you know that?"

Dubourg sat on the top step, his hair slicked back, glasses off, making him look younger, and he stared into the cup of coffee on his knee. "We only want to help you," Dubourg mumbled to me.

"Seriously, you've been here four hours, you slug him, and now you get together and talk about me?"

The only thing Dubourg did was straighten out his leg and take a tiny bottle of energy drink from his shorts pocket.

Charles said, "There is a reason you think God is contacting you."

The seal on Dubourg's energy bottle cracked.

"Dammit, I never really said it was God, but it did say it wasn't from, you know, here."

Dubourg poured the energy drink into his cold coffee and swirled it with his finger.

"Somehow you've internalized what I have discovered and processed it," Charles said, "now it is manifesting itself into this thing you believe you see on your phone. We can help. Ruth is a doctor."

"I don't *need* a doctor."

One of Charles's loose white hairs had gotten stuck in the hornet's nest of white tape that mended his glasses, and that single hair swirled from his head like a thought that couldn't break free.

The door shook in its frame and we all turned to see the silhouette of Elizabeth through the translucent glass inserting her keycard. The tumblers spun in the lock and the door opened. She was dressed in a hotel robe and slippers, book under her arm as if she were going to the beach.

"Elizabeth! Welcome to the grotto!" Van Raye said as if he owned the place.

"What, have you got the heater on?" Elizabeth said.

Ruth glanced at Elizabeth—from her slippers up to her hair, Elizabeth dressed exactly like Ruth was, in the hotel robe with GA on it.

Elizabeth made her way toward the table. She picked up the bottle of Jack Daniel's, studied it, and then considered everyone in the room and pointedly asked to Ursula, "May I?"

Ursula nodded.

Elizabeth poured two fingers' worth, and I got up using my cane and got her covered plate from the room-service tray for her.

"I was just discussing some work I need to do," Van Raye said.

Elizabeth sat in the lounge beside mine, straightened the sash, kicked the slippers off, and crossed her ankles as I set her plate on the table beside her. She thanked me with a glance. She rested her book on her chest, a local library copy of *Get Happy*, a Judy Garland biography.

"I know there are procedures to follow after a discovery of this magnitude," Elizabeth said, "so why aren't you following them?"

"Wait a minute before you jump to protocol," he said and then nodded to Ruth.

Ruth narrowed her eyes and turned the old radio around so she could see the dials. The rear panel had been folded down and revealed glass tubes with glowing points of light inside them, and the air was filled with ions of electricity and the oniony smell of the cheeseburgers. Ruth pulled a long wire from the back of the radio and stretched it to a metal fire sprinkler that had the placard warning DO NOT HANG FROM SPRINKLER. She opened the alligator clip on the wire's end and connected it to the fire sprinkler, the wire drooping back to the radio, salsa still playing strong. Ruth sat and punched a button with her finger, and a different static came on. She tuned through intermingling voices and electronic noise.

"Listen to what this radio is picking up now," Van Raye said in a stage whisper, and she slowed her tuning, let it stop on music and then human voices—Japanese, then Spanish, more music and a preacher proclaiming, *"This is a time when you don't want to be messing with Abraham's seed . . ."*

Charles said, "Hear all of what is being broadcasted tonight. Think also of all the electronic sounds playing together at once in all the atmosphere, the cacophony." He waved his hands in the air. "Remember that, okay? That's our planet's Big Murmur."

Ruth kept tuning. She stopped on a humming vibration. Inside the noise was a cadenced electronic *twap-twap-twap* and a sound like an airplane propeller increasing pitch. Ruth sat back and crossed her arms behind her head.

"That's it?" Dubourg said.

"That's the planet?" Elizabeth said.

"Yes," Van Raye said.

Elizabeth turned her head to listen.

"We can hear it over a radio?" Ursula said. "That's impossible."

"Shortwave," Van Raye said. "The space station is receiving the signal and amplifying it and then rebroadcasting it to Earth where receivers at different relay stations rebroadcast it over the planet via shortwave. Atmospheric skip does its magic." He shrugged his shoulders. "It's hidden in the white noise of the shortwave lengths. The rebroadcast is of no scientific value, has only the telemetry of the space station's broadcast. We aren't listening directly to the planet. It's like looking at an art book photograph of Van Gogh's *Irises* instead of the real painting. I wanted everyone to hear it. Everything will change after I make this public, but before then, I need a place to stay so I can compose and send a message and we have an antenna here that can do it."

"*You're* sending a message?" Ursula said.

"The message wouldn't have to be a large amount of data. Ruth has checked and confirmed that the star, the planet, will track through the beamwidth of that dish on the roof. I'll send one little tiny message blurb."

"My God, the ego," Ursula said.

"You're not supposed to be doing this, are you?" Dubourg said.

"It's not morally wrong," Charles said.

"I think it is," Dubourg said.

"I think I deserve to send my own message. It won't matter in the grand scheme of things."

"They," Ruth said, "whoever is on the other end of this noise, they probably won't even pay attention to it."

"But, so, why shouldn't I do it?" he said.

"This will be the longest ego trip in history," Ruth said. "Even after you're long dead, your ego trip will be carrying on in outer space."

Ruth began explaining how she used the space station's computer to prove that this was not a random pattern of noise. She added, "It's just going to make for a better chapter in the book."

"That's not totally why I'm doing it," he said.

I used my cane to stand and think: Charles is going to send his own message because it makes a better story for a book. He, Van Raye, would be the rogue who sent his own brief message to the planet before he would tell the world what he'd done. Would he even tell the world what the message was or would it be a better story to leave it a mystery? I stood beneath the fire sprinkler and stared at the alligator clip biting the metal pipe. I took it off and the airplane sound stopped, leaving only the hum of white background noise. "Sorry," I said to everyone. I replaced the alligator clip and the noise came back on the radio. The radio was connected to the pipe, and the hotel plumbing was an antenna seining the atmosphere of those broadcasts Ruth had dialed through, broadcasts as ethereal as snowflakes. The noise flowed by and if you missed it, you missed it, like time flowing by. I also understood that Charles needed the hotel.

I said to him, "You're going to write about this, aren't you?"

"I don't understand the significance of that question," he said.

"Of course you're going to write about this," I said. "You'll have to name the hotel, right? Will you talk about the antenna on the roof, or that Dubourg punched you?"

"Certainly the important facts will have to be recorded for history."

"It's called the Grand Aerodrome Hotel, by the way," I said. "You can get the antenna to work, right?"

"We'll need some equipment," he said.

"How much will this cost?" Elizabeth said.

Ruth said, "The dish is the right size but it's a fixed-azimuth mount. We'll have to wait for the star to drift into the field of view. If we finish rigging and the programming, and if—a big *if*—we can find the software for the gain amplifier, we would have one chance in March."

"*March?*" Elizabeth said. "We're not going to be here. This hotel will be closed by then."

"Elizabeth, this is of great importance," Charles said.

She looked at him in the water. "Yes, I know. But we always mind costs."

"But we *don't* have the software," Ruth repeated.

Van Raye said, "We'll get the software. Somehow. Help me, darling. No problem is insurmountable. Don't you know someone who could get the software?"

"Yeah, and they're all dead," Ruth said.

"Wait," Dubourg said. "You were on *Infinity*? You were the one who left the station?"

"Who?" Ursula said.

Dubourg said, "There was one astronaut who come back to Earth . . ."

"I told you she was the station's chief of biomedical problems," Van Raye said.

"And I stole a gain amplifier," Ruth said, "but we can't get the software for it."

"You stole something?" Dubourg said.

I noticed Ruth's bare feet crossed beneath the table, the bottoms as black as if she'd walked from California.

Charles said, "I'm not sure 'stole' is an accurate word."

Ruth said, "It's a little magic box that can make low energy into ultra-high energy." She put her hands behind her head and leaned back. "But we need the software a friend of mine wrote or the magic box is just a box. The software is just a spell to cast on the magic box."

Elizabeth slapped her hands on the chair arms and pushed herself to a standing position. "You don't have to over oversimplify. We understand what software is."

Elizabeth twisted her hair on top of her head, tucked it in, and inserted a hotel ballpoint to hold it in place, then she undid the sash and took off her robe, revealing her full figure in a black tank swimsuit with a gold accent braid. My mother's skin, even at the age of fifty-eight, was beautiful. All those times in our lives when she chased shadows—shadows of telephone poles while waiting on the bus, finding shade anywhere we went, the sun her enemy—kept her skin incredible. She took her time stepping into the pool, her rings tinging on the metal railing as she descended by Dubourg in his existential hunch on the steps.

"I'm just saying," I said, a statement Elizabeth abhorred, "we can make something happen. This is important."

"I'm not delaying the process of our business," Elizabeth said to me as though no one else was in the room.

"Do you want him here?" I asked.

"Me? Don't worry about me. I can take care of myself." She sank in the water up to her chin and began fanning her arms to swim, a strand of her hair trailing in the water.

My phone dinged in my hand.

Tell Ruth I will get her the software.

All the sweat inside my tracksuit suddenly chilled. I concentrated hard on the words. What would it look like if I were hallucinating? I typed a message, concentrated on seeing my letters pop up, and I sent them:

Let me show them this message.

No. I am scared to make contact with too many people.

"Something important is happening," I said, "okay?" I tapped my cane on the ground to think of words that would convince, and that's when Ursula burst out crying. She sat forward and put her head in her hands.

"Ur?" Dubourg said.

She took her hands away from her face and shot her index finger at Dubourg. "Stop! I'm fine! Stay away." Her face was mottled. "It just hit me, okay?" She looked to everyone else. "I know it's real. Why aren't y'all crying?" She wiped her nose on the back of her hand. "Why am I the one crying? I've known longer than he has." She was in the chair beside me, so she hooked a finger in her pocket that was gaping open. She patted her chest and said, "I know you think I'm insane, but I know what happened to me."

"What is she talking about?" Van Raye said.

"Ursula," I said, "not now."

"I know what you are going to say, but *I'm* an abductee."

"You're a what?" Ruth said.

I tugged at Ursula's pocket to stop her.

"She's had abduction experiences," I said.

"Oh God," Charles mumbled, shaking his head.

Ursula slapped my finger away. "Don't make it sound like I'm a goddamn leper."

Dubourg stepped around a lounge chair and Ursula pointed her finger at him again. "Don't you dare come over here! Just leave me alone. What sucks is that *he*, he's right."

"This has nothing to do with what you think is happening to you," Van Raye said.

"Shut up," Ursula said. "*I know* what you've written about abductions." She counted off on her fingers that were shaking, "I know what Jung has written, *and* Kelly *and* Mathieson."

"Ruth," Charles said, "Jesus, what's going on?"

Ruth peered over the radio as if we were all a distraction to her. "She's hysterical," she said. "She's suffering from some type of stress-related shock. She's been given a reality her mind can't handle . . ."

"Bite me," Ursula said. "I'm getting lectured to by a knocked-up astronaut?"

"You, I like," Ruth said pointing at Ursula. "I have auditory hallucinations myself."

Van Raye said quickly, "That's not important right now. You're not *delusional*."

"What are hallucinations," Ruth said, "besides personalized visions? It's like listening to your own music through headphones." She pointed to her ears, once again oversimplifying. "You can hear it but no one else can. We only look crazy when we dance to our own music."

"Oh God," Van Raye said. "Everyone is getting distracted from reality."

"But I have a hacker," I said, "or whatever, who is telling me stuff that has to be real." I had my phone against my chest. "I have more information."

When everyone was quiet, Ruth pulled out a lighter and flicked the flint and lit her cigarette. She fanned the smoke to see me better. She kicked one leg up on the chair, her dirty black sole facing us.

"You think you are seeing a message now?" Van Raye asked.

"The person calls himself Randolph." I looked at Elizabeth. "I know it's unbelievable, but it's real. I don't know how he knows things, but he does."

The gas heater diffused the chlorine, the smell of a clean hotel pool, a healthy and good hotel smell I'd sought all my life that was real. Ruth's smoke drifting out of her corner, that was real. My phone was in my hand, and I looked at the message again. I texted:

> How are you going to get the software?

> I'll work on that. But tell her.

"Most people believe what is most comfortable to believe," Ruth said. She leaned up and turned the knob on the radio, leaving the broadcast. Then a voice clearly preaching said, *"God has given us a choice to believe . . ."*

Ruth said, "No, no, really, *that's* the noise from the planet." She tuned to a pattern of dots and dashes, clearly someone's Morse code. "Nope! Never mind! That's it!" Then she tuned until a woman's voice said, *" . . . at the tone, one hour, seven minutes, universal time . . . "* "No, no, no, *this* is it."

"Stop, Ruth," Van Raye said.

Ruth said, "I still think you should just send the message 'Hell is real!' I think everyone on another planet would want to know we all had this in common—'Hell is real.' How much data would that be? Beep, blurp, bang, there goes your message."

"Ruth, darling, stop."

She ran the dial back and found the original sound.

"What's the difference in truly believing something and reality?" she said.

"It's not a good idea for you to be smoking, is it?" Dubourg said.

Ruth sat with one leg propped up and stared at him through her smoke as if he were a new kind of bug she'd found crawling on her arm.

"It's probably not a good idea for the baby, I mean," Dubourg said, sipping his energy-drink-spiked coffee. "Obviously you got pregnant on *Infinity*," he said.

"Well, look who is figuring things out," she said. "Is it outrageous, Father, to think about astronauts fucking?"

"No," he said calmly. "I took a vow of celibacy in order to take a different journey in life, but I'm not outraged by *fucking* or discussing it, or the importance it takes in so many lives," he said. "I'm trying to imagine what you are going through. You lost friends. One of them was the father of this baby."

"What would you say, Father, if I said I wasn't even going to have this baby?"

He got out of the pool and grabbed a towel and roughly dried his hair and wrapped it around his waist, went over and took a cigarette from her pack, and right in front of her turned his head and lit it. Dubourg said very calmly, "Hell is real. Maybe the music you are hearing from the womb is God telling you something."

"You know all about me, so let me make sure I understand your story. You're a priest who carries a bag around?" she said. "You don't know what's in the bag? Yet you're prepared to dedicate your life to keeping it moving?"

Dubourg said, "That's what faith is. God has told me to do this."

"Literally, you heard God talking?" she asked. She looked at Van Raye. "We are at an impasse. Very little of individual realities are overlapping here."

"The baby might as well be smoking too," Elizabeth said. "Mothers everywhere frown on you."

"I'm not a mother," Ruth said. "What would you do to protect him?"

Everyone looked at me.

"Anything," Elizabeth said, "absolutely anything."

"Right," Ruth said, "I don't get it. I know your instinct is real, but I just don't have it. This is one fucked-up quixotic endeavor." She slammed the laptop shut. She dumped the cigarette in her glass, and she got up.

Elizabeth gently swam toward the other end of the room.

Ruth, standing on the edge of the pool, undid her sash and let her robe fall, revealing that she had on nothing beneath her robe. She stood with a wide stance, her belly plump.

Ursula mumbled, "Great."

Dubourg looked at Ruth with bored eyes as if he'd expected her to do this all along.

Elizabeth swam oblivious to the nakedness behind her.

"What are you trying to do, darling?" Charles said to Ruth.

"I didn't bring a bathing suit," Ruth said, not lifting her eyes from the back of Elizabeth's head, waiting for her to turn around.

Elizabeth fanned her arms, slowly turning.

Ruth's pubic hair was a bushy funnel that went from the wide stretch beneath the belly and twisted into a tiny tornado between her legs. Her toes flexed on the edge, a thigh muscle twitched.

Elizabeth saw her and continued to swim. "There's nothing more pathetic than someone trying to shock you. I'm not a prude. How many weeks *are* you? I will not keep you here unless you stop the cigarettes and the drinking. I'll have nothing to do with it."

Ruth dove in, torpedoing past Elizabeth. Her hands cushioned her momentum on the far wall and she did a flip turn underwater.

Elizabeth took the opportunity of her being submerged to say to Van Raye, "She has lots of problems."

Ruth came up and spit out water and drank from Van Raye's remaining whiskey on the side of the pool. Asian techno music played on the old radio.

Ruth took Dubourg's old place on the steps, her elbows on the step behind her so that her body floated outward. There was this archipelago of Ruth Christmas sticking above the water: shoulders, breasts, a palm-tree navel island, the sub islands of her kneecaps, and then her feet.

A text dinged in:

> On the night of the 27th, tell Ruth to listen to Infinity. I will send her the software.

> They won't believe me. Let me show them this text.

I said out loud, "Is the software you are talking about, can you get it from the space station?"

"It's there," Ruth said, "but there's no one to send it to us. We can retrieve it."

"I think I can help."

"How is that?" Van Raye said.

I put my phone against my chest. "I think the software you want will be sent down on the twenty-seventh. He's talking to me now."

Van Raye stood up in the water.

"Can you 'listen' to *Infinity*?" I asked them.

"Why would I do that?" Ruth said. "There's no one there."

Randolph said,

> Tell her you know about the Bright Nothing.

"I want to tell you this," I said, "and I want you to believe me. This thing who is texting me, he's not from here, he's not from Earth. I'm pretty sure that's real."

I sent the message back:

> Is the noise Raye hears, the noise we're listening to, is it from the other planet?

> Yes. And that is where I want to go

"Does the 'Bright Nothing' mean anything to you?" I said to Ruth.

"The what?" Van Raye said.

Ruth turned pale, but her face also relaxed slightly, a mask having fallen away, and again the word "beautiful" came to my mind, but trying to understand what beauty was is like trying to see individual fish in a large school of fish.

CHAPTER 33

Van Raye and Ruth gathered their things to go, Ruth re-robed and, slightly frantic at my mention of the Bright Nothing, though she would not elaborate, only said, "It's impossible for anyone to know that."

Ruth carried both the laptop and the heavy radio with her, Van Raye following.

Elizabeth put on her robe and collected her book and asked Ursula if she could have another bit of whiskey to drink on the way to her room.

I stopped Elizabeth at the door and whispered, "Are you okay?" I felt her tighten beneath my touch. "I know you don't like being asked that, but I'm worried about you."

"Me?" she said. Then she took a breath, held it, and let it go as if that was how long it took her to make a decision. "I will have to get used to you asking me that, won't I?" Her nostrils pinched as she inhaled and smiled. "Now I'm going to play my violin. Make sure housekeeping knows about the dinner tray. I don't know how often they—" she cut herself off. "Never mind. You handle it now, can't you?"

When she was gone, only the three cousins were left, Ursula going into the utility room to change out of her wet clothes, and I pulling Dubourg over. "What is happening?"

"I don't know," he said.

"Listen to me, Du, don't get chummy with him. He'll suck you into believing he's forming some kind of attachment and then he'll suddenly cut you loose."

"Look, I'm sorry about discussing your problems, but we are all family."

I snorted. "Come on, Du. We're family, but he's not, not really."

"Are you and Ur okay?" he asked.

"Of course."

"It's not like everyone doesn't see you are madly in love with her."

"We both love her, don't we?" I said.

He shook his head like I wasn't getting it. "You two have always been in love. You just don't know it." He crunched an antacid that I didn't know was in his mouth. "Ur is not in the best place." He pushed his glasses up on his nose.

I held my phone out to him. "But what is going on?"

"I think I'm qualified to say it's not God," he said. "God doesn't work like this."

"But you believe it's something, right?"

"I don't think you can hallucinate something so specific, so perfect. It doesn't make sense. I guess we'll find out on the twenty-seventh," he said.

When Ursula and I stepped onto the twelfth floor, Dubourg stayed inside the elevator and put out his arm to block the door, told us he was going to the attic to help Ruth and Van Raye.

Ursula and I were walking to our room to change, and I touched Ursula's arm to stop her. Gentle music played through the Air of Liability and the sound of the chorus of voices rose from the lobby, the Big Murmur of snowed-in guests.

On our corridor, I noticed one of those clamshell light fixtures flickering between rooms. The bulb inside the translucent glass blinked a random pattern barely hanging onto life. I pulled Ursula by the sleeve of her robe and we went into the corner under the flickering light.

"What the hell?"

"It's the feeling from the movie," I said. "I feel it now."

I felt her chest deflating against mine. I reached over her head, and as my face came close to hers, I tapped the clamshell lamp with my finger and the light went out.

I felt her arms come up around my back, and she turned her head and let me kiss her on the mouth. What I realized was this: I had tasted her my whole life, tasted her when I drank from the same glass she had, when I put my head on a pillow she'd laid on, when I got in a car she had been in, the smell of her bedroom at home. She suddenly stopped and pulled away and said, "Stop, okay. Dubourg's somewhere."

One kiss and we were breathing heavy like we'd been holding our breaths under the water.

"We need to stop," she said. She pushed my arm up and ducked away.

I leaned in the corner for balance, watching her go away.

She turned down the corridor in the center of the hotel. I watched the empty glass elevator rise to her, watched her step into the gold box and it sank while she squeezed her ponytail to get the wetness out, not glancing at me there under the dead light.

I reached up and tapped the light's dome, and it flickered on, tungsten buzzing, a connection I knew couldn't last long, this whole hotel not far behind, and I wanted to freeze everything, to make sure this hotel was there if I ever wanted to come back and remember what was happening to me right now.

CHAPTER 34

The low-pressure system dumped its snow and twirled over the Atlantic to fizzle and be forgotten. I attended meetings in the hotel and watched committees that lacked enthusiasm because they were shutting this hotel down, and when I left meetings, I put myself into a phone booth in the lobby not caring if I looked crazy sitting there staring at the world going by.

I mumbled, "Call me, dammit," because I needed proof that Randolph had happened to me, but he wasn't responding—no ringing, no Elvis songs, the last conversation having disappeared.

Out the big windows on the back of the hotel lobby was the sky over the airport. The storm had left in its wake harsh sunshine that lasted for days as though the great factory of weather was spent of raw material, and there was little proof that there was ever a storm except for tiny patches of snow around telephone poles or in the northern shadows of buildings. That's the crazy part about the present: there is rarely satisfying proof that anything really happened in the past.

I wanted everyone to believe that Randolph was someone not from this planet who was a great finder of lost things, but no one would come out and say they trusted me, not even Dubourg or Ursula.

What Ruth was doing should have made me feel like she believed in me. She and Elizabeth purchased a small military satellite dish for the twenty-seventh, but instead of feeling good about this my stomach was constantly churning. The setup had cost $5,125. What if this Randolph was some mad professor in some snowbound laboratory who hated Van Raye, some guy with a T3 connection and a ham radio wanting to make Van Raye look like an idiot? The number "27" loomed in my mind.

Sitting in the booth, I caught the eye of the middle-aged bellhop with a beard like Moses. I waved. He didn't wave back. Honestly, these employees were taking the closing better than any group we'd ever cut loose. Maybe this was because—though I was one of the Sanghavis—I was also Van Raye's, "the professor's," son.

Over the days, Charles's eye had turned from black to purple, and if he were working on a secret plan, he was anything but incognito in the Grand Aerodrome. He greeted maids in Spanish, talking and laughing with them. He knew every employee's first name, from engineering to front-desk agents.

While Ruth spent most of her time crawling through access passages, dragging cable or bowed over her computers in the attic, Van

Raye barhopped the three hotel bars, his favorite being the Outer Marker on the convention level where he always sat at the corner stool and shouted, "Ron, my favorite mixologist!" Ron would place a hand-written RESERVED sign at Van Raye's place when he wasn't there, and Ron would quickly mix a gin and tonic every afternoon while Van Raye scribbled in his black-and-white notebook, the kind he always used, the notebooks mottled like dairy cows. He didn't look like a man recording history, but rather a man on vacation as hotel employees, people he knew by name, disappeared into unemployment, and eventually Ron the bartender was gone and all the liquor in the Outer Marker inventoried and taken away. Only one bar on the lobby level remained open.

I came out of the phone booth to intercept a Gypsy Sky Cargo man strolling across the lobby with a package under his arm. Of course it was addressed to me, and I signed and took it, expecting it to be the usual heavy hardware, but it was surprisingly light, though lightness, I had learned, didn't mean inexpensive.

I rode the glass elevator with the light package under my arm, wondering where the concrete of these walls of this hotel would be in a year's time. Where would the pump to the fake rainforest fountain be? Would it ever be used again, or would it sit out decades in storage or be sent to a landfill? Would birds and dragonflies one day fly through the air that had once been this great hotel, sensing for a second the thousands of old lives that had lived in this space? Would Van Raye be not just *science* famous, but *famous* famous?

On the twelfth, I went through the laundry room, which was still perfectly stacked with white towels and linens that might never reach a guest's hands again. Where would they go? On the far wall, I punched the service elevator's button and noticed words scratched on the metal plate. Some employee had etched "heaven" over the elevator's UP button, and on the DOWN button scratched "Atlanta."

The elevator took me to the attic, and the doors opened onto the big, open room, the full size of the hotel's floor plan and interspersed with load-bearing columns. The old furniture from past years was stored there, and there was my whole family in an oasis of light in the center, five players in The Musical Based on My Life: Elizabeth playing her violin; Ursula sitting sideways in a King Henry chair; Dubourg at a table and gluing what looked like ping-pong balls to clothespins. Van Raye was lying on the couch and reading from his milk-cow notebook held awkwardly above his head. Ruth was at a table burdened with five CPUs stripped of their casings. Sitting in the center of the rug was the $5,125 portable receiver and dish, deployed like a metal daisy.

Dubourg saw the box under my arm, put his glue gun down, and took it from me.

"What is it?" I asked.

He judged the box's weight and said, "Charles, I think it's the hats."

"Hats?" I said. It pissed me off to be in the dark about expenditures.

Elizabeth stood with her violin, and she wore the same clothes she'd had on the day before, her eyes closed as she played Bach.

Charles put his notebook on his chest, put his arm across his eyes. I asked him, like I did every day, "Isn't there someone else to call, some way to check on the dog?" He was trying to doze now, his lips slightly parted. The days were marked by the metamorphosis of his eye, and I realized looking at the new avocado color, nearly healed, that it reminded me of the Gypsy Cargo logo of the Luna moth's eye.

"I wouldn't even know what to ask them," he said.

The back of Ursula's King Henry chair was at least five feet high, and she was sideways in the chair reading *Flying* magazine.

Dubourg, straddling his valise, slit the new package open with his pocketknife and pulled out a stack of baseball hats, white *A*s on the front.

"Atlanta Braves hats?" I said. "I'm not paying for those. Who ordered *hats*?"

"They are important, actually," Van Raye said. "It'll help us in the dark."

"What dark?" I asked.

"We're going hiking on the twenty-seventh. At night," Van Raye said.

"What? Jesus, I'm funding this project, and I demand that I approve everything and be told. Why the hell do we need hats and why are we going *hiking*?"

Elizabeth played softer and said, "I decided we should go away from the city lights on the twenty-seventh."

"Why?" I said, "That's not necessary. This thing can receive from anywhere there's a clear view of the sky."

"To see the space station," Elizabeth said. "It's for her." She indicated Ruth. Ruth's back was to us. She was lost in her four computer monitors.

Dubourg put his baseball cap on, the bill straight, and said, "We all think it might be good for her."

"Great," I said, plopping down on the other couch in this living area under the dome of floor lamps and table lamps. "I don't think we need to make it a big production. We don't know what will happen. If anything will."

I held my breath and stared at Ursula's profile until she told me, "Stop."

When Elizabeth finished the song and was putting the magic violin in its case, Dubourg set the old Trans-Oceanic radio on a table, stretched out the wire, and clipped the alligator clip to a pipe in the ceiling and began searching the bands.

Ruth swiveled in her chair as if discovering us behind her. Solder smoke hung in the lamp's light. Her hair had grown longer and was spikey, and her eyes were sleepy. She carefully lowered herself from her chair to the floor, eyes closed before she was totally supine. She grabbed the corner of the old area rug and rolled inside like an enchilada. She only slept two hours at a time. If we didn't bring meals for her, I don't think she would have stopped to eat.

I wondered about Ruth's life, about how we were supposed to take a break and go watch the space station fly over on the twenty-seventh and hope to get the software so Van Raye could send his damn message to the planet.

Only the top of Ruth's head stuck out of the rolled carpet. Did the baby sleep when she slept? On nights when we forced her to eat and go to the pool, she stripped off her robe as usual and dove in. What sensation did a baby conceived in zero gravity have when its mother dove into the pool, a momentary weightlessness during her dive?

Dubourg tuned to a strong music station, a female singer, and turned the volume down.

Sitting in the chair beside Ursula's, I tried to understand why listening to a faraway broadcast was any better than finding music on the Internet, but it was, something about how these signals broadcasted for someone to listen to at that exact moment. There was this idea in my mind that this song making me so happy would simply evaporate.

I watched Ursula's leg bounce to the sultry sound of some woman singing in French and the guitar being passionately plucked and then strummed. I leaned and held my phone to the speaker so the app could identify the title, so I would know this song, put it on my "Songs to Beat Depression" playlist, and remember Ursula's bouncing leg. The French voice was incredible, and I felt myself getting hard without pain. My phone chimed with the song title, but I didn't look.

I never found out the name of the French singer or the name of the song, and I've never heard it again, and I reached out with my hand and put it on Ursula's thigh until she parted her legs enough for it to slide between them. It was halfway between her knees and all the rest of her. Everyone else was paying attention to what they were doing.

"I want you," I whispered.

"They came and got me last night," she whispered back. "You don't remember anything?"

What I remembered was only that Dubourg and I had ended up falling asleep on the same queen bed, Ursula on the other bed.

"They can get me while I'm here," she said. She was on the verge of crying.

"Please don't," I said.

She slid her hand to mine between her thighs, and I felt the familiar heat of her, and this was a gesture of lovers, people who'd slept together, and as stupid as this sounded, I had to think about if we had slept together, had sex together. Of course not. It seemed the only thing left that we hadn't done.

At night when Ursula, Dubourg, and I went to our room for the night, we fell asleep like we were kids again, back in the house in Sopchoppy with all the cousins, sleeping wherever we ended up, but combinations and permutations burned my mind in the Grand Aerodrome: three people and two queen beds. There could be three people in one bed and zero people in the other bed, which would be represented DSU+0, or two people in one bed and one in the other (DS+U or DU+S or US+D). When it was DU+S, Ursula and I watched each other across the gap, the undulating reflections of the aquarium's light on her face, the betta fish fighting his own reflection. When it was US+D, both of us in bed together, Ursula and I touched each other through the night and slept at times with my erection against her. Dubourg in the other bed started the deep breathing that indicated sleep. What did he dream of, his case on the ground beside his bed? He had his hands under his chin, exactly the same way he slept when he was a kid.

In bed without kissing, nothing else, I placed my hand flat on Ursula's chest, felt her heart beneath her shirt. She took my hand away and guided it beneath the shirt, letting me feel the sound her whole body made, hearing it through my hand.

Her watch always beeped within a minute of her falling asleep, her pressing the button, some last-ditch effort before falling in the wormhole of sleep, and on some nights I woke to the limpness of her paralyzed body next to me, completely consumed by sleep. I whispered her name but I didn't want to wake her, only comfort her in whatever dream she was having.

CHAPTER 35

With Mr. Blaney, the general manager, we closed the hotel from top to bottom. It took six days. When even Mr. Blaney was gone, Dubourg went with me to lock the front doors. I started to kneel, using my cane for a brace, to put the thick brass key into the lock at the bottom of the revolving doors, but Dubourg took the key and did it.

It would be weeks before auction people came and cleaned the hotel out. I glanced around the dark lobby. Did it really already smell stale? A 1,439-bed hotel for six people? We could let it fall apart around us for the next few days if we wanted to, if Elizabeth could let a hotel decay around her and still keep her sanity.

This empty hotel changed my life. It was devoid of human beings. I took Ursula to the tenth floor, took my plain white master keycard, and I showed her how I could open a room in the middle of the day and how the rooms were still perfect with perfectly made beds. I always threw the metal safety latch across the door as if we needed extra protection from the outside world, and when I was supposed to be arranging for venders to start collecting the contents of the hotel, Ursula and I began discovering the clandestine light that exists in hotel rooms in the middle of the day when you are in bed together. Our clothes littered the floor, Ursula always keeping her black rubber watch on. We tumbled into exotic positions, but always found ourselves quickly back to positions in which we could wrap our arms around each other, that watch of hers pressing into my back. Words were brief because our own voices reminded us of who we were.

Only once did she say, "This isn't going to last forever."

I felt her hold her breath. "What do you mean?" I asked.

"We aren't going to be here much longer. What are we going to do then?"

"We can meet anywhere," I said, "nothing will change."

"Something important is happening to me," she said. "I'm not going to just get over it."

"Let's see what happens," I said.

For a few seconds we watched the steady green light on the fire alarm above the bed. "Do you believe," I said, "that you reach some point in your life, some peak happiness, a point you'll never be as happy as you are now?"

"You think this is it?" she asked.

"It can't be," I agreed, but just like starting the Movie, listening to the narration and badly hoping that your grandmother doesn't die again, you still know something has to go wrong or it wouldn't be a movie. The hotel business teaches you something is always going wrong. Now this hotel was decaying around me, and I was only delaying emptying it out.

CHAPTER 36

The night of the twenty-seventh, the six of us wore our Braves caps and the elevator took us down through the hotel, me looking out of the elevator's glass and being spooked by the emptiness, the lack of travelers, the darkness broken by only the lowest-wattage security lighting and glowing exit signs as we sunk into the basement.

We looked like a gang in some heist movie all wearing identical hats, Dubourg walking in the parking garage with his black valise in his hand, Ruth with the black laptop case, and Van Raye carrying the nylon bag with the satellite receiver inside. We were on a grand mission to get software to send a message to a distant civilization, but as I walked through the parking deck, I was thinking, *What kind of car is Charles driving?* Then I saw the old Jaguar.

"A Jaguar?" I asked. "*That's your car?*"

He'd always said that a Jaguar was a shitty automobile that people bought only because they were expensive. I think he was actually applying it as a metaphor to a Baltimore private school Elizabeth had enrolled me in at the time.

"We'll not be comfortable in that," Elizabeth said and turned on her boot heels to see the plum-colored shuttle van parked along the far wall, its windows stained by time.

Dubourg mapped the Civil War campground on his phone, as Elizabeth drove, the heater in the shuttle on full blast.

"When was the last time I saw you driving?" I said to her, smiling.

The bill of her cap was straight, her hair falling out the back. She kept her eyes on the dark road ahead, hands at eleven and one. "Are you asking me a question? You don't expect me to remember, do you? It was probably in Nashville." Even in her insulated coat, she looked small in the seat with the seatbelt rising above her and going into the wall.

"Listen," I said so only she could hear me, "if nothing happens, it doesn't necessarily mean I'm hallucinating. I don't have a history of hallucinating." The others in back watched out the windows, the light from the streets crossing their faces. Ursula had curved the bill of her hat so severely that it shadowed her eyes.

When we left the lights of the city behind, went miles on a single lane and turned off the country highway, we parked at the entrance of a Civil War park, the iron gate flanked by two stone columns.

We abandoned the shuttle at the entrance, stepped over the gate. Van Raye and Ruth stopped, and I realized they were clipping their ping-pong balls to the bills of their caps, the ping-pong balls that Dubourg had glued to the clothespins.

Van Raye said, "Place the ball over your eyes like this. We won't need lights. No phones please. Think about your night vision."

"What is this?" I said to Dubourg. He shrugged.

We did as told and began following a trail. It was awkward having the white orb hanging on the bill of my cap. Even with my cane, the terrain twisted at my ankles. It was too dark to see our breaths, but in a minute, the woods and the dirt below the ball became clearer. I saw

individual roots and stones, stepped on the wooden erosion steps perpendicular across the trail. The ping-pong ball seemed to emit some
kind of glow, but that wasn't it. The ball kept your focus; out of the sides
of my eyes everything was bright. Focus on the ball and everything in
your peripheral vision was clear and bright.

"This is amazing, Charles," Dubourg said.

We went up until the woods gave way to the open space of a field,
the stars a brilliant bowl, the Milky Way bisecting it.

"It's a beautiful night," Dubourg said. "I thank God for this."

"Do it in a hurry," Ruth said. "The station will rise from east-
southeast. That direction. We've got to set up."

A meadow was bathed in starlight, scattered with brush. Some
kind of primitive fencing zigzagged toward a mountain that blocked
out a quarter of the sky, and I smelled a campfire and cooking grease.

"Here are tables," Ursula said. Dubourg clicked on his cell phone.
Van Raye said, "You're killing my vision!"

Dubourg's light caught the table and showed a shocking scene of
a mini disaster of a recent meal—plates with chicken bones on them,
and a pot of congealed liquid, and that was when a voice yelled out of
the darkness, "Hark, who goes there!"

"Sentry!" someone from the other direction called, and there was
movement at my feet and voices.

"*Sentry, sir!* A-LARM!"

"Good God," Van Raye said.

Dark shapes rose from the ground around us. The one nearest
hauled his blanket shawl-like over shoulders.

"I am Dubourg Dunbar. Who is there?"

"Christ, shut up, old ass, it's cold," mumbled what I thought was a
log at my feet. "Get down!" the voice said.

The six of us stood among acres of sleeping humans, maybe some
encampment of desperate people, down on their luck, but then I saw
one with a rifle. Someone let out a fart and there was no laughing.

Dubourg aimed his fading phone to reveal a shocking scene of scraggily faces and beards at our feet, men trying to remain under blankets, their eyes squinting at the light. "Who's there with a lantern?" one said.

The yelling voice said, "Eighteenth corps, third division. Dodge's regulars. Identify yourself!"

"Oh hell," a standing man said, "a civilian is here." He cupped his hands around his mouth to yell, "Lieutenant, let the lines know there are Beauregarders."

The lieutenant with a Civil War cavalry hat shouted over the field, "BEAU-RE-GARD! BEAUREGARD!" He turned in another direction. "*For God's sake, BEAUREGARD!*"

Someone down the line picked up the alarm and repeated it, "BEAUREGARD!" Shapes grumbled under blankets. More voices in the dark: "*Oh, for shit's sake. What is happening?*"

The interior of a tent lit and shadows moved on the canvas.

"They're reenactors," Ursula said.

"'Living historians,'" a voice from the ground said and added, "ma'am."

A man came out of the tent holding up a lantern; I saw blue military pants and a nightshirt and a sleeping cap. He stepped over his men and came at us with an entourage following, hands on the swords at their belts, very cold Civil War actors in unbuttoned tunics.

"Jesus Christ, what are you civilians doing here?" the man in charge said.

"We were searching for dark skies," Van Raye said.

The man held the lantern up. I recognized him, had that flash that he was someone I didn't like. He was the muttonchopped security man, Albert, from the hotel, but he said, squinting, "I'm Major General Joseph P. Rosenblach of the Army of the Potomac. Who are you?" He held the lantern closer, and when he saw me, he seemed to snap out of it. "*Sanghavi?* What the hell? Professor Van Raye?"

Elizabeth had her head turned slightly so she could see him around the ping-pong ball, her muffler pulled over her mouth, unrecognizable.

The general looked back at his men, then said to me, "The park closes at sundown. Douse that light! This is a battleground."

The two men in his escort wore blue uniforms with gold buttons, and I recognized them as former employees of the hotel too—bellhops.

"We apologize, General Rosenblach," Dubourg said. "We're out here looking for satellites."

"Satellites?" He turned from Dubourg to Van Raye and said, "You do understand that this is a mindset, don't you? Do you know how rare it is to have an actual new *goddamn* moon on the night before the battle? You do understand—a *mindset*? What we are doing is important."

"I'm sure it is," Van Raye said.

"Yes, it is. If we are as accurate as possible . . . it's real, you understand? I mean I can smell you all. You smell like the twenty-first century. My God. What is on your hat?"

All six of us had the ping-pong balls on our bills.

Albert straightened, became this General Rosenblach again, and a command voice came from the back of his throat, "My men are tired, hungry, and cold. There is a confederate encampment beyond that branch. Douse all the lights. I'll have you escorted to safety immediately."

He turned with his lantern and whispered to two soldiers. I heard my name—"Sanghavi . . . "—and then he looked back at us and fanned his hand as if to make the smell go away, and his men came and indicated which way to march. There was the sound of metal on metal as they put their bayonets on their rifles but Charles led the way, veering off toward a hill to the north and the escorts said nothing.

CHAPTER 37

Charles led us up a trail to the plateau of an empty parking lot with historic markers too dark to read. Our small band encamped above the battlefield in a picnic area. Below was the waiting battlefield with hundreds of tiny red specks of campfires warming reenactors who were too far away to see. Ruth and Ursula opened the box of the satellite dish, me holding the flashlight on my phone. They adjusted the three flat legs until the bubble level was centered, holding their breaths whenever fine adjustments were called for. When it was ready and aimed at the eastern sky, Van Raye, Dubourg, Ursula, and I sat on a crosstie fence watching the valley bellow, hearing Ruth clicking on a laptop as she sat in lotus, stomach beneath her coat. Elizabeth sat on a picnic table, the two reenactors beside her as if we needed guarding.

Van Raye lit a joint, puffed it alive and gave it to Dubourg. He smoked and handed to me, and I smoked, not liking the light on my face, handed it to Ursula who took it, kept it going. She had clipped her ping-pong ball to the collar of her coat. Without hesitation, she handed the joint to Elizabeth who took it and handed it to the former bellhops, no reenactors, sitting beside her. "Thank you, Ms. Sanghavi."

Van Raye got off his seat and went to the reenactors and said, "Give me that; that's certainly not historically accurate."

The guy took quick puffs before giving it to him.

"What time is it now?" Van Raye said. He twirled the joint in the lighter's flame.

"Quit asking that," Ruth said. "We're here. We're set up." She touched the screen to start different applications.

"I can't feel my toes," Van Raye said.

"This isn't all about you," Ursula said.

"I never said I wanted to come here to do this," Ruth said.

"Working so hard can't be good for the baby," Elizabeth said. "We are taking a break."

The fires of the union encampment below were single dots of amber. Over that scene, jets winked against the stars, and occasionally there was the high-to-low-pitch banshee whine of jet engines decelerating out of high-altitude holding patterns and headed down to the airport. I wondered about Albert's mindset. Ursula lay back on the table with her hands behind her head staring at the blinking jets and the stars.

There was a yell from the troops in the distance.

"Who are they shouting at?" Dubourg asked.

"Rebel taunts," a reenactor said.

"They're shouting '*Chickamauga*,'" the other said. "They beat us up pretty bad in Chickamauga, but we'll get them tomorrow."

"You'll *get them?*" Van Raye said. "How absurd. Do you not find it disturbing to recreate the scene of horror where men shot and killed each other in mass? My God, we are on a field of hell, and you are celebrating this? It's disgusting."

"Shut up," Ruth said. Tracking motors whined beneath the dish, a short test, and stopped. "Everything is so fucking academic to you. I'm sick of it. I'm doing all the work of this project. Without the instrumentation, you wouldn't be shit. *Oh, the horror, the horror*," she mocked. "What do you know about horror? There's only one thing that really scares us," she said.

"And what is that, darling?"

"Don't be so quick to want to know," she said.

Van Raye took out a metal pipe and his baggie. I heard him tapping it on the fence and then the relative silence of him stuffing it. "I want to know," he said. "I want to know what happened to you up there."

I smelled the natural rot of decay on the wind from a nearby trash can.

"Maybe we shouldn't talk about this," Elizabeth said. "We are out here to get the software, and the space station . . . we will see it pass over. Have you seen it, I mean, watched it since you've been back?"

"No," Ruth said. "Why would I?" She touched the screen in the lower left and all the light went away, and we could see the stars better and the campfires below. "We had a slight problem up there," Ruth said. "Did anyone know that? EVA-ing? That's spacewalking. We became a little unhinged by it. Kind of an epidemic we couldn't explain. At first, I diagnosed panic attacks, but nothing like this had ever happened to anyone. It started happening to a few of us as soon as the doors opened. Like agoraphobia but on a grander scale—hyperventilating, increased heart rates, adrenaline spikes, and the screaming. Yes, they screamed. I'm talking hysterics. But it wasn't that simple. Nothing is. Even safely back in the station, people continued to scream. I tried to calm them.

"Some of the crew were parents, you know." She sniffed in the cold air. "And they were the ones to compare what was happening to the night terrors their kids experienced. Nothing can calm kids in this state and nothing worked on us either. I mean besides a good cocktail of Ativan and Haldol."

Ruth stared across the valley of the battle, legs crossed beneath her. "Kids having night terrors, they have their eyes open, appear lucid, but they can't communicate and there's no amount of reasoning or reassurance that can bring them out of that state. Children in all cultures experience night terrors. What was happening to the crew, I guess, it was similar in a way, and it would start the second the airlock opened—sudden-onset hysterics.

"I volunteered to be forcefully EVA-ed on the BEAR arm. You know, the BEAR . . ." Ruth extracted her arm, fist balled. She pointed to her fist to show she was on the arm. "Supposed to haul twenty-ton satellites, but it's me on the end. I told them stick me out there and don't stop, no matter what. I've got to see what this is, right, to see what's making us like this? I'm the chief of biomedical problems, right? So I'm strapped to the cherry picker and it moves me out there, and I'm screaming but I force myself to shut up and take it. I can't see Earth. It's behind me, so all I'm seeing is empty space. I'm in the station's shadow, right? There's darkness all around. Darkness only happens when you are in the shadow of something, like we are now, the only way the stars come out at night is we're in the shadow." When she moved, the material of her jacket squeaked. "From a shadow of the space station, you can see stars," she said. "Stars to focus on. So I'm on the end of the BEAR arm, and I'm under some modicum of control with stars as reference, but I'm still panicking and I'm moving out of the shadow into the light, the thing comes back on me, this dread that there's nothing waiting, and the arm extends me into the sunlight, and that was when it hit me the hardest: everything is black, but it's a *bright* black. That's the terrifying part: there's nothing there, and it's painfully bright, but I also feel the presence of nothing. I started screaming so loud that I overloaded the audio."

Everyone but Van Raye had turned around on the fence to see her. Ruth pulled a cigarette out of her jacket pocket and lit it, looking like she was asleep with her eyes down into the lighter for a brief second.

Dubourg hopped down and took the cigarette from her. She didn't argue. He sat on the other table and smoked it.

"The strange thing about this experience," Ruth continued, "was that I realized this thing, this bright nothing, I'd always known about it, but something had made me forget it. When I was a kid, I knew it was there. It had been every dark shape caught in the corner of my eye, every sinister shadow. We don't understand how horrified children are, but at least the adults are there, you know. Can you imagine, these other beings in your world telling you with good authority that everything is *okay*, that things are fine? At some point you start to believe it. You have to believe it or go insane. Adults have blocked out the knowledge of nothing. Adults provide meaning for kids as they live through childhood and tell them what's real and what isn't. In American culture, we get them fucked up on Santa Claus and the tooth fairy, but then they figure out that's bullshit, right? Then we get them fucked up on God, and God is just Santa Claus for grownups. Pretty soon, you subconsciously start believing in this order of the world or else you just go insane. Don't you remember feeling when you were a kid that anything could be just around the corner, anything?

"Here's the irony," she said and leaned back, the nylon of her jacket rubbing together, and she tried to wiggle her belly. "See this? This is what happens when you seek comfort by fucking a cosmonaut, which is what I did first thing after I came out of the terrors. Safety makes you want to procreate. That's cruel because safety never lasts long."

The two Union guards seemed to be frozen, sitting and leaning into their rifles.

Dubourg stubbed the cigarette on the crosstie.

"It doesn't make sense that I had the instinct to procreate after what I'd experienced. I'm only producing something that will suffer and that will probably cause me more suffering, though, I'm sure, some pleasure too, right?"

She clapped her gloved hands so hard everyone jumped, then pointed over the battlefield. "Well, look who's here."

A tiny point of light rose over the mountains. The receiver on the ground beeped, servomotors on the dish began high-speed clicks, and Ruth squatted over the equipment, like the squat she'd done that very first day I saw her, vomiting onto the roof of the Grand Aerodrome.

In the sky a moving star grew brighter as it came away from the horizon.

"Right on time," Van Raye said, hopping down to see the screen.

Ruth, arms over her knees, typed and hit "Enter." Two sets of numbers on the screen rolled as the antenna whirred to track. "I don't see how this is going to work," Ruth said. "There's no one to answer us up there."

The point of light moved swifter than a terrestrial airliner, was clearly made up of a different kind of light from the stars, reflecting sunlight from the coming tomorrow.

Ruth said, "We're tracking a dead space station, people. Nothing's happening."

Dubourg whispered, "Ruth? I'm sorry you had that experience."

"Yeah, that really helps me," she said.

The dish's purring sounded warm, keeping pace with the station that hadn't reached it zenith. I took off my glove to hold my phone, waiting for something to happen.

The station rose higher, luminosity making silver spikes.

"Ever wake up hungover in zero g?" Ruth said. "Realize what's sticking in your hair is semen? Wake looking out the porthole at nothing? Then you'll know what a fucking wasteland the universe is. What are the odds of getting pregnant anywhere? I was so skinny I missed like three periods. What are the fucking odds?"

We were all huddled around her now, staring at the screen. She kept touching the command "check run," "check run," but nothing happened. The star transited the zenith, us craning our necks as if to see little parachutes falling out of the sky or a beam of light, anything. Elizabeth's face was lit by the screen, expression blank, the tops of her ears tucked into her Braves cap. "Wait," Ruth said. "There's incoming."

READY SOURCE A

Ruth said, "Someone is asking us to open the line. There's no way."

She hit return and saw CONNECTED, and even she glanced at the sky. "Hey, everybody back up, away from the dish. Don't jiggle it, okay?" The screen popped full of code and began scrolling. The light around her changed to yellow. "Oh shit, holy shit," Ruth said, "*Capture, capture* . . . please." There was a tiny sound as the light of the monitor flashed with more data.

"That's it?" Van Raye said.

"Yeah, that's it," she said. "Yeah, that's it. Okay, okay, it's downloading. Un-fucking believable, okay?" Ruth put the keyboard down and then got up off the ground, Dubourg helping her up.

"Sandeep was right," Elizabeth said.

I held up my dark phone.

Ruth had her head bent back to follow the track of the station, the moving star that was the space station now falling toward the other horizon. "There's no way," Ruth said. "My God, someone is sending that to us. Is someone really still alive?"

"No," I said. "I'm afraid there's no one up there. It's whoever . . ." I held up my phone, ". . .whoever's on the other end of this."

Van Raye said, "Ruth, darling, there's no one there. You really know that."

"Fuck you," she said.

Dubourg put his valise down on the picnic table and put his arm around Ruth. The station got dimmer as it went back toward the horizon, turned a deeper yellow, but the data was still scrolling on the screen. Ruth pushed Dubourg away. "I know there's no one left, people. It means we have other problems we haven't figure out yet. Is it finished downloading? Let's hope we get all of it." She watched the station changing to deep amber.

A window popped up on the computer screen. "There you go. Done." Ruth touched the screen, checking the files, then shutting things down quickly and mechanically. "Somehow we got the software, and if someone asked me how we got it, honestly, I wouldn't know what to tell them." She looked around with her laptop under her arm. "You goddamn people, you have no idea what just happened, do you?"

The troops in the valley began their normal taunts and wild animal yells across the lines in the predawn light, ready for the reenacted horrors coming in the next day, oblivious to anything that happened in the skies, or dismayed by such witchcraft of it.

But this dark section can't be over yet.

CHAPTER 38

Dubourg helped Ruth into the shuttle and sat beside her. She seemed so groggy, I wasn't sure she hadn't taken something. Elizabeth got the engine going. We glanced at each other as if expecting the other to tell us what was wrong with Ruth.

As Elizabeth drove, I looked in the long mirror above the windshield and saw the shapes of everyone in back. Van Raye sat beside Ruth in the side seat, and Dubourg and Ursula bounced in the very back seat.

Elizabeth's eyes concentrated to navigate the roads back home, shadows crossing her face, Braves hat on, no ball, and the way her eyes shifted from one thing to the other out the window, I could tell she was thinking, and as always was vigilant and keeping us safe.

"I don't know how to explain it," I said. "You do believe this person is contacting me?"

"Yes," she said.

We passed an oasis of lighted gas stations with no one in them and there was a feeling of emptiness like we were the last people on Earth, and we drove county roads through one-stoplight junctions, and finally spiraled up and onto the desolate interstate south again. Ursula's head was on Dubourg's shoulder. Van Raye watched the night out the window, happy to have his software, so he could send some goddamn message to the planet and write a book about it.

Near the airport, we exited down from the interstate and then took Airport Loop South to the Boulevard of Desolation. When lights moved across Ruth, I saw her eyes closed, and she had the blank stare of the overmedicated. Her baseball cap had been taken off and her stubbly hair looked terrible. I had this sinking feeling this baby wasn't going to make it, and that possibility seemed like the most horrible thing in the world.

The shuttle accelerated as if Elizabeth read my mind.

Dubourg glanced at Ruth and said, "We need to make sure that she's healthy, stays healthy from now on. She's working too hard. To hell with anything else. The baby is priority."

"As soon as possible," Van Raye said, though I had no idea what he was talking about.

"Yes," Elizabeth said. The engine hummed louder and the automatic transmission downshifted, but the shuttle refused to go faster. Only the lateral rocking quickened the tempo of one squeaky shock. I had that last-day-in-a-hotel feeling, a feeling there was no water in the fish tank, no fish, and tomorrow could be a different time, a different place, if we just left this behind.

We shot through the dead sprawl of the Boulevard of Desolation beneath out-of-order traffic lights shrouded in black body bags. The road was dirty with things piled against the curves and blinking barricades anchored by sandbags. A gust of wind rocked the shuttle. Up ahead, a plastic bag lifted and moved along the road, the shuttle missing it by inches.

Van Raye said, "Everything is going to be okay. I can't stand this. Tomorrow we'll be back to work."

"Did you hear the one," Ursula said, taking her head off of Dubourg's shoulder, "about the human being who found a magic lamp on the beach and the genie came out?" Ursula's head wobbled with the swaying. "The genie said, 'You can have two wishes.'"

I thought about all the jokes I had to listen to Leggett tell in the hospital. Ursula's only depressed me more.

"Two wishes!" Van Raye yelled from the backseat, trying to be jovial. "I know this joke."

"Are you seriously telling a joke?" I asked.

"Just listen," she said and continued. "And for his first wish, the human being says, 'Give me one pill that will make me happy forever!'"

"Happy forever!" Van Raye shouted. Van Raye, the man who hated joke-telling. "I believe I know this one," he yelled over the engine noise. "This is unbelievable."

Elizabeth's eyes scanned the road, not paying any attention. The tires hissed.

And Ursula said, "So the guy takes the eternal pill of happiness and the genie asks him if he's happy, and he says, 'Yes! So happy! I've never felt like this in my life!' And the genie says, 'Congratulations, and you will feel like this forever,' and the genie says, 'So you get one more wish, what do you want?' And the human being says . . . "

Van Raye shouted, "'*I want another pill just like that one!*'" delivering the punch line.

"*Right!*" Ursula shouted. "'*I want another pill just like that one!*'"

Van Raye from the backseat shouted with his finger in the air, "*That's my joke! I made that joke up!*"

I remember turning back around, trying to think of what this meant. I put my hand on the dashboard. The joke meant something to me, Leggett on my mind. Out the big windshield the hotel loomed at the very end of the boulevard. Another piece of trash blew in front of us toward our lane, a tumbleweed of a trash bag, but I clearly saw the bag stop and sit with two shiny eyes staring into the headlights, glowing like silver dimes. My mind had time to think, *God is in the headlights, God is in the headlights,* making no sense, and then the eyes were gone as if they'd never been there. *I am not God, you are God, I'm not God.* "Elizabeth," I wanted to say, but all I could get out was "God."

"God?" she mumbled but then I could tell she saw the dog, staring again at the oncoming shuttle's headlights. I heard her foot release the accelerator, and the world moved very slowly, and time stretched into a song in my head:

> *You are dog.*
> *I am dog.*
> *You are not a dog.*
> *I am not a dog.*

The only word I could say was the most important word in my life—"*Elizabeth.*"

It would be a long time before I remembered the details of the accident, like the way the seatbelt seemed to click angrily to lock me down. One tire screeched and the van spun. I saw the dog out my window, the shuttle continuing toward him standing stoically or blinded, and my side of the shuttle bowed. I heard Ruth shout as the forces began, "*Monsterrrrrrr—*" and Dubourg, "*Holy mother . . .*" The creature disappeared beneath the van, and I waited for the sickening thump. The shuttle seemed to stabilize but the forces were only in the apogee of changing directions before the flipping would begin.

I had seen the glowing eyes, the very thing that had made Dubourg believe in God when we were little, and there was the clear quietness of new flight. We were floating before the noises began, only the yanking tug-of-war between gravity and the seatbelt. Gravity was a whirlpool and there was a boil of sparks vomiting through the van, which I could taste, and then the noises stopped, replaced by the long silence and the smell of steam and rubber. There was only this silence afterward and finally someone whistling for a dog, someone very far away me.

PART IV

CHAPTER 39

I am under water, and it is dark and I cannot breathe, I thought. My senses rebooted one at a time, including my sense of surrounding, and it was this: Air coming to me, and I swam quickly, sensing the others looking at me as if I'd done a belly flop and they wanted to see if I was okay. There was nighttime humidity and the relative coolness of the water. I stood in the shallow end, not wanting them to know it had happened again. *It?* I thought. *It? It what? Forgetting? An "episode"* . . . And I held onto a constant in my life, my mumbled prayer of the Seven Ps: "*Proper planning and practice prevent piss-poor performance. Proper planning and practice prevent piss-poor performance.*"

Humid night air weighed on the pool deck, and instinctively I knew which way the pool steps were. This was the big outdoor pool. I found the metal rail and hauled myself out, and I understood that I had no clothes on. I turned around, standing as my undressed self in the darkness before Ursula sitting on the steps. Behind me was the calm movement of the tip of Dubourg's cigarette. I knew Charles was that form laid out in the lounge, and Ruth was swimming in the dark pool. Ruth scooped up my floating boxer shorts and threw them at me.

If anyone knew about my mind rebooting, they didn't move or say anything as I stepped into my shorts. I went over what I knew: *I am nude and dripping and looking down through the metal fence at the wide-open space of a great airport beneath the ever-blind windows of the Grand Aerodrome Hotel. We are alone and no one is looking out of those windows because the hotel is vacant.*

The wind changed direction and brought a whiff of dog shit, and the smell brought on a big happiness. In my mind this equation:

Happiness = the dog. A light from an open stairwell cast a shard of orange on the ground and there the old dog stood with his hind legs in his chariot. The cart held his rear legs off the ground, and he hobbled with front legs forward, trailing a loose stool in the grass, the globs of shit glistening in the moonlight. I found the shovel against the wall where I knew I'd left it last night—it felt good to remember such details—and I took it and leaned on it to make a posture of calmness—*nothing is wrong with me*—so the others wouldn't know that I had an "episode." An episode of what, I wasn't sure.

I searched for the happiness again, something about the dog. I began to reconstruct facts from feelings. *I feel good because the dog is taking a shit. I feel good that the dog is taking a shit because? Because the dog is alive!* But even happiness comes with dread because time moves on and nothing stays the same.

The reflection of lights on a jet taking to the sky wobbled unevenly through the dark glass panes of the dark hotel, the image disappearing for a split second in the vertical columns and then popping out through more panes, in fits and starts like my memory.

The gray shaggy dog rolled his chariot forward finishing his business, and glanced at me with those eyebrows. *Now it makes me sad because? He is old and dying.* He was a terrier mix, knee-high and with scraggily beard and wise eyebrows that moved as he thought, his back haunches strapped to the cross-frame of the chariot and his ankles strapped and held up. I kneeled and pushed the hair back to see the blackness of the eyes, and I had a clear memory of these eyes reflecting. *When was the accident?* In my mind that night before the accident was a marker, like a surveyor's stake on the edge of a cliff. Beyond the stake was a giant excavated pit of nothing in the middle of my life.

"What is your name, dog?" I whispered. *Rally? Rally? Something like Rally, or was "rally" a prayer Dubourg had muttered for the dog?*

The vibrations of the pool pump tingled through the concrete and up into my legs, and I stomped it out like fire ants. The bag in Ursula hands crinkled. I remembered, *Ursula eats pretzels.* She squeezed and the bag popped open. In my memory, I could see her bending and plugging in a vending machine in the empty hotel, feeding it coins. *Pretzels are always D7 in every vending machine left in the Grand Aerodrome.*

I could feel the exhaustion of our group, palpable as humidity. A debate had been taking place. I remembered that. I had an elated emotion that Van Raye had been deposed. Were we not going to send his message?

Ruth swam through the dark pool with her head above water. *Ruth*, I thought, *Ruth swims at night, and she has no clothes on and the baby is still floating in her belly and it is okay.* My mind continued to reboot: *The dog is alive, but I hated the alien inside the dog, hated the whole ordeal of what Van Raye had brought on us. Hate?* I begin following the breadcrumb trail of emotion back to memory: *I hate the thing inside the dog because it's an alien. Randolph. Randolph is trapped on the microchip inside the dog. I strongly dislike Randolph because?*

The dog's eyebrows fluttered beneath my touch and sent chills along the dome of my head.

From the pocket of my robe hanging on the back of a pool chair, I got my phone because I knew it was the center of our circumstances, had to do with Randolph, not *the* Randolph of my childhood, but an alien trying to make me feel comfortable and believe in him, so he could travel on to Chava Norma, continuing his journey through the universe. Everyone knew I was right about Randolph.

The clock on my phone said 10:55 PM, almost eleven, which made me happy too, a secret happiness I knew to hold within me. *What happens at 11:00?*

From the darkness came the familiar sound of the safety cap on a prescription bottle clicking and then the sound of Charles's mouth opening. *The mouth belongs to Charles and the pills are painkillers.* I heard him swallow liquid and then a wineglass base tinged against the concrete and then the roar of another jet coming to a halt after hurling itself from the sky.

Why is eleven a happy time? I glanced through the fence to the compound of Gypsy Sky Cargo to our west. That's why. Shift change at eleven. Elizabeth will be going on duty at Gypsy Sky Cargo. I texted Randolph:

> How long have you been trapped in the dog?

I said to the others, sensing where to pick up the argument, "We don't even know how long he's been in the dog," knowing somehow this was Charles's argument: to postpone the sending of Randolph to Chava Norma, basically, to keep him here. Everyone else wanted to send him on his journey. Ursula and Dubourg's agreement was that we had no right to keep him. Ruth wanted to send him for the simple reason that she'd changed this whole hotel into an antenna, molded the software, and she simply refused to not see if the thing worked.

"He's been on the microchip fourteen and a half years," Dubourg said. "You know that. Are you okay?"

"Absolutely." *Proper planning and practice prevent piss-poor performance.*

"We could just wait," Van Raye said. "That's all I'm saying."

Without being able to see him in the dark, his presence was a smacking of lips, slurped saliva, breathing through his mouth, searching for words.

Van Raye continued, "Take the dog . . . somewhere else . . . to a safe facility to download." *What is wrong with him? There's something wrong with him that I can't remember.* "We have so much to learn," he said. "We can't let *that* slip through our fingers." He held his hands up as if testing his fingers in front of his face.

Ursula said, "It is a *he*. It annoys me when you call him 'it.' You haven't humanized him yet."

"Human? We don't even know it has a gender," Van Raye said.

He, he, he, I said to myself.

The text came in from Randolph asking me:

> Are you forgetting again?

I knew to be angry at him, and my fingers typed it out:

> Fuck you.

> If you are having an episode, please tell the others. We are preparing for tomorrow.

I listened to the dog panting. I put my phone in my robe and shoveled the congealed shit patties and hefted the clumps over the fence where it floated and then clopped on the ground on the Gypsy Sky Cargo side. I gripped the fence's wire, gazing down the hill over a flat no-man's land to the Gypsy tarmac sparkling beneath the clusters of spotlights as if it were a world without nighttime. What wouldn't Elizabeth like about this place that prided itself on such efficiency and order? Aircraft were parked in perfect rows. The spotlight clusters reflected on the top of the fuselages like decorative saddles. Trains of cargo carts snaked around the giants. The compound was far away, but I knew I could recognize Elizabeth's height and posture anywhere. *I come out here to watch Elizabeth at Gypsy, and it is part of an old sorrow for her leaving me. I was on my own. I could do anything I wanted.*

I also knew for some reason I didn't want the others to know I was watching Gypsy Sky. It was my secret. *Is everyone angry at her?*

"What are you doing?" Dubourg asked me. I heard an antacid roll ripping open.

"Nothing," I said, letting the fence go, turning away. The tip of his cigarette touched the concrete and went out, and some part of me worried about the black stain on the patio, but then I immediately stopped myself. *This hotel will never see another guest.* Not worrying was freedom.

I lifted my long hair off the back of my neck to feel the coolness.

"Where's Butch?" Ursula said.

BUTCH! The word had come to me at the moment she'd said it. "He's right here," I said, and I remembered what Ursula said when we'd scanned the microchip and gotten his name off the chip and a metric shit ton of data. "There's something wonderful about . . . " she said, tears going down her cheeks, " . . . about finally knowing a stray dog's name. When you say his name—*Butch, Butch*—it's like a secret password that lets him know that we are okay."

Dubourg flicked one of those kitchen matches on the pool deck, and the flame leapt to life and he lit another cigarette, and I could momentarily see Butch's scraggily shape struggling to kneel while his haunches remained in the chariot. He yelped at sharp pain.

"Shit," I said.

But when his head was on the ground he panted.

Yet another pretzel snapped in Ursula's teeth, and I felt the sound move through me, and I gripped my wet hair on both sides of my head and squeezed, *Stop, stop the snapping!* but I knew not to say this out loud. Instead I concentrated on the sound of Ruth moving through the water, and looked to the sky to see the dim star between the two brighter stars that I knew was our star. *We come out here every night to watch the path of the star get closer to the aim of the antenna on the roof.* I remembered waiting for time to pass and wondering what a future point would feel like when it would finally point at the star, but I also stopped myself from thinking about the future because I didn't want another answer about the future to come to me, setting off another time bomb from Randolph.

Watching in the distance for Elizabeth at Gypsy Sky Cargo, I tried to access the memory when Randolph had contacted me after the accident. Where had I been? I remembered the inside of the empty restaurant, Dubourg serving us string beans he'd scavenged from the pantry, putting them on buttered toast he'd made.

On the pool deck, I scrolled through the history of my texts, back to the very beginning, messages Randolph had allowed the others to see. The first one:

I am Randolph.

Ha! I'm not crazy!

I am trapped inside the dog.

He came to Earth on August 15, 1977, and had lived first among military computers, and then personal computers, inside the stock exchange's network, skipping to different data-storage sites—inside Disney World, a register at a Whole Foods in Los Angeles looking at barcodes twinkling in the red laser, in the system of the Bibliothèque nationale de France.

I found another memory: Ruth kneeling over the unbelievably alive dog on the carpet in the middle of all the computers, the shelves of computers that had recently begun to make the strained noise of hard computations, Butch lying flat, his back legs useless. Ruth waved a yellow wand over his body. Ursula was crying. Ruth knelt and waved the wand like a metal detector over the animal, then concentrated it on his shoulders. The computer beeped and then the screen began marching with 0s and 1s. Ruth whistled. "That's a lot of data." And my phone had beeped:

I am this data. Don't remove me.

I would like to be sent to Chava Norma but no transfer. Storage can corrupt

Please.

Ruth had said, looking at the information from the chip, "By the way, he's a neutered male, up to date on shots, owner's name is . . . 'Charles Van Raye,' and his name is Butch." And that was when Ursula had told us about finding out a stray dog's name and she'd cried, saying *Butch, Butch, Butch*, watching him raise his ears and happiness registered in his eyes, him thinking, *They are one of those people, those people who know my name.*

Randolph had explained to us how he went from one electronically alive planet to the next, a kind of cosmic tourist, but never getting involved, never leaving a footprint, but learning and traveling. He was older than 150,000 Earth years. Twelve years ago, he had been passing through the systems of a small veterinarian clinic in Santa Cruz, California, where the animals came and went, all the personalities—the happy, the sad, the scared, nervous, and the owners who loved them. He "watched" the pets, though didn't explain other than, "I see without seeing." When a litter of strays were brought in, he said he forgot about moving himself. The microchip was physically picked off the data pad by a technician and inserted into the neck of six-week-old Butch before Randolph could move. Otherwise he would have gone to Chava Norma when someone discovered the new planet was a new neighbor three thousand light-years away—and nobody on Earth would have been the wiser, and he wouldn't have affected our lives.

This is the hatred I feel, I thought while standing on the pool deck. *I dislike him so because he* affected *our lives.*

I leaned on the shovel, looking at the hollowness of a shadow by the blooming azalea bush, the shadow that was this Butch who'd gone through nearly his whole life with Randolph inside him.

My phone vibrated, and a text from Dubourg was bright in my face:

> You remember the plan?
> Don't wig out *now* please

I thumbed it off. Yes, I remembered the plan. We were sending Randolph to Chava Norma. I looked at the faint star in the sky and remembered the plan hatched to keep Van Raye calm; a plan us four coconspirators had forged in what seemed like a dream.

The dark, flat shape of Van Raye was sunk in the lounge chair and he didn't know how close the star really was to moving into the field of view.

Ursula snapped another pretzel stick and I cringed. I was on the verge of yelling at her, *STOP! I hate the fucking snapping*, and then Dubourg's teeth broke an antacid.

Ursula came to the fence to see my face. "Why are you standing here?" she asked.

"I don't know," I said. "I like the view to the west there. I'm just saying . . . " *I'm just saying* was a statement that Elizabeth loathed. "Empty talk," she would tell me, and I felt sadness coming on.

I said to Ursula, just because I could, "I'm *just* saying! Why don't we get married?"

"Don't start on this again," she whispered.

"He's lapsing," Dubourg said.

"I'm not," I said.

From the pool, Ruth said, "Short-term memory is a strange beast. It has to take its natural course."

Van Raye's snoring stopped. I know how he felt when he woke among the others, felt us watching him.   •

"I'm not a goddamn patient," I said to Ruth. "I'm right here."

"And you're displaying unusual anger," Ruth said. "Very common with head trauma."

"It was a *concussion*," I said, "days ago."

"Weeks ago," Dubourg said.

"That's what I meant."

That was when I heard another clicking, felt it rise through my legs, making me cringe because it was another snapping, but this was the pool light's timer, the underwater light spreading down the length of the pool, Ruth's body dark and surrounded by sparkling, floating microparticles, her belly flashing white like a keel beneath her.

Ursula was on the steps, hair slicked back over her head, freckles on her shoulders, one bra cup gapping so that I could see the crescent of her burgundy nipple. *Happiness, sit. Happiness, stay.* But her eyes were red-rimmed and swollen, and her face lax with worry and unable to break the trance of staring into the palm trees where the light from the pool wiggled. Dubourg was reclined in the deck chair, his legs astraddle and his valise beside him.

Charles's new eyeglasses mirrored the light, dull stipples going across his body. He was pale, his boxer shorts dry, left foot hanging over the side, and his right leg only a stump with a rubber swim cap on the end. *He has a stump!* It was true: his leg was gone. These forgotten facts of my past rebounded into place. His temporary prosthesis stood upright on the ground beside his lounge chair.

"Charles lost his leg," I mumbled, and I couldn't help myself, I smiled. That was all—*Charles lost a leg,* which seemed much less than the lurking sadness that had been in my brain. I said *"AAK, AAK, AAK,"* and everyone looked at me.

"Not this again," Dubourg said.

"Why am I thinking AAK? Laughing?" I asked.

"'*Amputation above the knee,*'" Dubourg said.

That is why I am angry. If it weren't for Randolph, Van Raye would have his leg!

"Are you okay?" Ursula asked me.

"Sure."

Charles put his hand on his bare thigh. His remaining foot was bare, toes flexing, and the stump had a white rubber swim cap on its end, a child's swim cap with black rubber flowers on it. I remembered he'd found it in the pool box. His crutches were on the ground beside him. I also now remembered he wanted to take Randolph out and present him to the world and be really famous. Frankenstein and his creature. I remembered a scene from yesterday, or maybe it was the day before. Butch went missing, and I had found him in the empty underground parking garage standing obediently in his chariot beside Charles's Jaguar. His leash coiled beneath the seam of the car's back door, and there Charles sat in the backseat. Charles didn't move even when I peered through the window, him frozen in a painkiller haze, desiring to steal the dog. I looked in the car and saw the other end of the leash still looped to his hand. I got in on the other side, moved his crutches to sit, and he'd explained to me that he was running away with the dog but couldn't manage to lift him into the Jaguar. On the dashboard of his car was this ugly statue of the alien Buddha. This was the first time I'd ever seen the thing, the long eyes of a classic Gray but plump and fat as Buddha. I remembered the way the statue seemed to be staring and smiling at how ridiculous we were in the backseat of the car as if waiting for a chauffeur who would never show.

In the lounge chair beside the pool, Van Raye grabbed his thigh and shouted, "Why won't it go away?" He held his palms up to heaven and made fists, "I can feel the wind tickling the hairs! The ultimate irony, people: *It hurts like hell and it's not even there! My toes are curling painfully! For fuck sake, these painkillers are worthless.*" He sat up and raised the stump, tore the swim cap off the end, revealing the puckered brown end. He threw the cap in the pool.

The metal shaft of the "shin" of Van Raye's prosthesis stuck out of the boot on the ground, brushed aluminum that matched his new aluminum-framed glasses.

Ruth didn't break her swimming stroke, capturing the swim cap in her hand. She went to the edge of the pool and looked at Charles. She put her arms on the side of the pool and said in a whisper, "One of you, please be his leg. Dubourg?"

Dubourg didn't respond immediately, but reluctantly rose and went over to Van Raye. He stared down at our father who had his eyes closed, Charles's chest rising and falling. Dubourg lay flat on the ground beside the chair and scooted beneath Van Raye's lounge, Dubourg in only boxer shorts. He turned his hips sideways so that he could stick his foot between the plastic straps of the lounge in front of Van Raye's stump, holding his head off the concrete to see what he was doing.

Van Raye stirred but didn't open his eyes. Dubourg's leg was positioned on the lounge as though it were Charles's leg, left leg in the place of Van Raye's missing right leg. Dubourg, half beneath the lounge, fiddled with his phone, holding it above his head to type. His text came into me.

I know you just had an episode. U ok?

Launch is tomorrow night

VR thinks it's two days away

I'm fine. I remember

We knew that if Van Raye knew it was tomorrow, he might sober up and cause trouble. I think Charles fantasized about being in a crowded grand lecture hall. I imagined the alien in a glass beaker, the substance inside glowing magnificent blue. He would be *famous* famous and the audience would clap for him and his "alien." Monster movies rarely ended well for the monster. Randolph wasn't light, he was data; he was sentient, a living being on the microchip inside the dog. "Aren't we all data?" Ruth had said when she'd made this discovery that day in the attic.

The submarine light in the pool casted a V through the particles, and the surface settled around Ruth as she braced on the pool's edge watching Dubourg beneath Van Raye. She put the swim cap on her own head, pushed her hair, now grown several inches, beneath it. Dubourg still lay on his back halfway beneath Charles, fingers interlocked on his stomach holding his phone, staring at the sky, the brighter stars that could shine through to the dome of the airport.

I spoke quietly to Dubourg, "You don't believe it's God, do you?"

"No," he whispered.

When Van Raye's eyes opened, I said to him, "Are you angry with her?"

"Who?" he said.

"Elizabeth," I said.

"My God, you're breaking my heart, Sandeep, simply breaking my heart." Dubourg raised his leg, which simulated hyperextension of Van Raye's "leg." "How could I ever be angry at your mother?" Charles said, finally seeing his "leg."

Why couldn't he understand that the big toe was on the wrong side?

"How's your leg?" Ruth asked him.

"I can feel the nice temperature of the night against it," he said again, keeping his head still, moving only his eyes to the leg. "My toes have uncurled, mercifully."

"And the pain?" Ruth asked.

"Much, much better," he slurred.

"Wiggle your toes," Ruth whispered to him.

Dubourg wiggled his toes, and Van Raye watched the toes wiggle, eyes in the bottom of their sockets like he was seeing a monster awakening and a wicked smile appeared on his face and he closed his eyes again.

"Are they wiggling?" Ruth asked.

"Yes, wonderfully so," he said. Then he whispered, "Thanks, Dubourg."

She pushed gently away from the wall, still wearing the swim cap, which accentuated her beautiful face. Van Raye drifted into la-la land. I wondered: *In the book he will write about all this, will he refer to me as Sandeep or Sandy?*

The dog seemed to be sleeping, bowed down on his front legs, butt in the air. I pushed his fur back on his face. His eyes were closed, but his chest moved. Was this all there was to being alive? I tried to imagine that Being was inside Butch, a being with language and all of the knowledge that he had gained traveling through the galaxy. I asked Ruth, "Are you sure we should send him on? I mean, it's a matter of waiting. He'll still be able to go eventually."

"It's been decided," Dubourg said. "He wants to leave."

"Yes," Ursula said. "He's got a right to go."

I looked at my phone and saw the clock had ticked past eleven.

I didn't hide the swiftness. I went to the fence, climbed up on the concrete skirting with my bare feet. Through the fence, down the hill was Gypsy Sky Cargo Center where the dozens of jets were lined perfectly under the bright fake daylight of the never-sleeping Gypsy Sky Cargo. Some jets had cargo-bay doors closed, were warming up, engines going, red lights blinking. From this distance, I couldn't tell which people had dark skin and which had light skin, but I knew Elizabeth wore the earphones that went around her neck, not over her head. Only supervisors wore that kind.

Ursula stepped up on the concrete skirt with me. I looked at her and smiled, but she didn't smile. She looked at my right eye, then back at my left as if trying to find something. I leaned and sucked on the tip of her bare shoulder, tasted the chlorine and her salt. I wanted to trace the perfect line of her neck with my finger and into the cleavage and that one spot in the center of her that I loved. "I'm hearing Sanctus bells," I said to her but she turned to search Gypsy Sky.

"Did I say something wrong?" I asked.

"No. What are you looking at?"

I straddled the corner, feet hurting, hands clinging to the wire mesh. "Down there," I said and pointed to where people conversed in groups, debriefing and briefing. Over the acres of black tarmac, mirages of heat wobbled upward as if the Gypsy Sky Cargo Corporation were casting spells on the sky. Someone could ship the most insignificant package to the smallest village in the world and do it overnight. I could hear Elizabeth in my mind saying, "What kind of world do we live in?" Now she was part of it, shipping those boxes.

Then I realized I'd been staring right at Elizabeth over there. I recognized her head held straight, her crisp movement, her long hair in a ponytail down the back of her yellow reflective vest. She pointed to a cart of cargo and gave people instructions, took an electronic pad from a man. I waved overhead to get her attention, and she saw me, put the clipboard over her eyes to block out the light. She raised her gloved hand and waved.

"That's her?" Ursula asked.

"Yes." I gave a hearty overhand salute.

Ursula didn't wave. It was too late anyway because Elizabeth had turned to get on a tractor to go give other people instructions on what to do.

Ursula dropped from the fence. I heard her feet hitting the ground hard, reminding me of childhood in Sopchoppy, her dropping from a tree.

"I'll carry him up," Ursula said and the unhappiness of Butch's short life with us came upon me.

Butch's head was down in the grass, one front paw bent as he slept. I texted to Randolph:

> When will the dog die?

> Giving you the answer will only make you jump there in time.

> Is it before or after you are gone?

> You all have already made this decision. Do you remember?

I could feel the others watching me. My heart pounded. We'd decided to let Butch go and the sadness flooded in.

> I know. But if we don't have to do it, when will he die on his own?

> You will only jump to that point in time and it will be too late to make a decision to stop his suffering now.

> Then we'll euthanize, but I just want it to be over, stop the suffering

His suffering will stop tonight as you have decided it would.

After that, he will no longer suffer because he will no longer be capable of storing memory.

When will the dog die? Tell me, answer because I only want it to be over with.

The future-you will not know the difference. You will still have the experience of the death of the dog and it will not shorten the dog's suffering.

Tell me

It's of no value to your future self to do so. It's only valuable to your current self

Tell me and let it be over with

What is the exact time the dog will die!

Ok

And Randolph told me the answer.

CHAPTER 40

As with everything I've told you, I have told you the truth. I have a memory of the time from when Randolph told me that answer to when Ursula asked, "Is he gone?" This is what I remember about Butch dying: I see Ursula lying across the bed in our hotel room, arms over her eyes—"Is he gone?" I remember the way her legs hang off the end of the bed. The time was 12:38 AM, the exact time Randolph had told me, but it only seemed like the snap of a pretzel since he gave me the answer. I have all the experiences: I felt Butch's weight in my arms as we rode the elevator up to that room, the way I had tried to synch my breathing to his breathing to feel who he was. I have the images in my mind: The white paper sack in Ruth's hands. Dubourg placed a hotel sheet on the bed where I put the still-breathing Butch, the place he always slept, making sure his back legs were not folded uncomfortable beneath him. All of us stood around the bed. Only Butch's eyes moved, wondering, without lifting his head, what we were doing. From my vantage point at the foot, I wondered this thought: What must we look like to him, the five us wearing our white bathrobes, smelling of pool chlorine and speaking a language he only understands one word of: Butch, Butch, Butch. Did he know there was something alive inside of him?

He was sunken into the middle of the comforter. Only a bedside light illuminated the room. I had my knees against the bed. Dubourg sat beside the dog, rubbing from his eyebrows down his head. Ursula fell backward into the disarray of covers on the other bed, putting her hand across her eyes, that image burning into my brain. Van Raye slouched in an armchair, shoulders hunched, letting his crutches fall to the floor. Ruth sat near the dog's head, working what she needed out of the white bag beneath the lamp. The betta fish in his tank swam against the glass.

I pushed Dubourg's valise slightly aside so I could lean over Butch and touch his chest. I felt the rising and falling of breath that was this creature who occupied space, his body forming the crater in the comforter. He was created by his parents, came into this world, created space and stored memories for thirteen years, that's all there was to us: created space and memories.

Ruth sat sideways on the bed facing away from us, her belly, her Cal T-shirt visible in the gap of her robe. She worked her instruments beneath the light. I watched her profile, eyes downcast as if closed. She turned with the metal syringe in her hand, loaded with a clear vile of liquid. She felt up and down the dog's front leg. She said the first shot will relax him, and he would feel good. What was feeling good to him? A memory of running in a field? A park? The voice of a person he loved, calling his name—Butch? Butch? Who had loved Butch?

Ruth felt along his leg and put the needle into his fur, her other hand holding his paw. She took it away. Dubourg held Butch's hair so we could see his eyes.

I could only lean my knees against the bed, not knowing or thinking to look at the clock. I had no awareness to stop Ruth from reloading the syringe with the last solution, nor awareness that the time Randolph had told me was approaching. Maybe none of this happened, maybe Randolph didn't tell me 12:38, but the needle was real and Butch is not here because Ruth reloaded the syringe and swung away from the light and back to Butch. There was a blue fluid in the vile. When she was done, out of habit, I'm sure, she rubbed the spot the needle had entered, and she said, "Shh, shh." Butch's eyes closed, not in a way that he was falling asleep. Butch opened his mouth twice as if to gulp air. There was nothing similar in these two things: sleep and dying. I didn't understand why anyone ever calls this putting your animal "to sleep."

The room filled with the smell of urine. Ruth took a handheld scanner out of her gym bag and waved it over the dog.

"Still there?" Van Raye mumbled from the chair.

She looked at the scanner's screen and switched it off without answering Van Raye, but I could tell that Randolph was still on the microchip inside.

"Is he gone?" Ursula said, not taking her hand away from her eyes. I had the startle reflex as if I'd just fallen in a dream, and the bedside clock said 12:38, and the horror of having time blink by struck me completely unaware. *Jesus*, I thought, *how many more of these leaps are there?* But I knew that I had asked for it. Butch was on his side with his legs bent together like he was in mid-gallop.

So what is the difference if Randolph had not given me the answer? Did I somehow cheat? Did I trade the feeling of time passage and gain anything? How many more of these questions had I made Randolph answer? How many of these time bombs are out there in my life? Could I just ask him when I would die? This would be a kind of suicide, but the others around me would not be robbed of my time with them. I shuddered at the thought and helped Dubourg change the sheet beneath Butch, then shroud him with a clean one, something I would think about weeks later when I swaddled a baby.

CHAPTER 41

We left the shrouded body of Butch on the other bed in my room, the place he slept every ordinary night in the Grand Aerodrome. When I asked Ruth if it would be okay to keep him here until the broadcast, she'd only smirked at my not knowing even these small details about life beyond hotels, life beyond life, and she went out with Charles who crutched along stoned on painkillers, his one leg beneath his robe, Dubourg close behind him, patiently watching his foot, ready to catch him if he fell, his other hand carrying the valise, Charles's prosthesis beneath his arm.

Dubourg turned to Ursula and me before shutting the door, "I'll come back about five."

When they were gone, I went to the bathroom and took my afternoon dose of the antidepressant. I glanced at my watch to make sure I had enough time and decided to take a sleeping pill too.

I had on only boxers, climbed in the bed and felt the heat of Ursula without her clothes on. She was on her side facing the wall. She rolled over and reached for me and began kissing my neck below my ear, then on my mouth. Her skin tasted like the saltiness of sorrow.

"Can't we lay off each other one night?" I said, struggling to slide my boxers down. When she didn't answer, I added, "This isn't a happy time. Why are we doing this?" I whispered, still taking her.

She wrapped her legs around me and said, "Whoever said this only goes with happiness?"

I said, "I just had a déjà vu. You're about to tell me how it's natural to have the drive to procreate after a tragedy."

"Now I don't have to say it," she said.

"We've already talked about this?"

But she didn't answer. I pulled out of her, which she hated, and she bit her bottom lip, and I watched her face in the wavy light from the aquarium. The next thing, according to the déjà vu in my mind, was that she was going to tell me that she couldn't procreate anyway. I began to be fearful of another time bomb about to explode, so I kissed her neck.

She stopped me with her hand and said, "Let me ask you a question, an important question." I waited and she said, "Do you think Charles is better off believing he can see his leg?"

"He doesn't really believe it's his leg. He can't."

"But if you were him, would you want to keep on believing the leg was there? Listen to me," she said. "It's important. Answer me: Do you think he's better off believing that *is* his leg even if it's not?"

"I think he's letting himself believe. Deep down he really knows it's not there, the real him does. And the hydrocodone . . . you know . . . He's not himself. He'll eventually come around."

"But then he won't have the relief of believing anymore?" she said.

"Maybe he's going to be so fucking famous he's going to hire someone to be his leg forever. His leg man."

"Don't be sarcastic," she said. "Just let me have this night, okay?"

I didn't like the way she said this, as if there would be no other nights.

We worked slowly, and the feeling of déjà vu came on because it was the sadness of Butch being gone, but the betta fish poked around in the yellow plastic plant, and I quit watching him to extend this time with Ursula. Time flies when you're having fun is the truest maxim in the world and must have been dreamed up by someone during orgasm, the quickest moments in a human being's life never to be captured, like shortwave radio broadcasts. I tried to hold on to this moment with Ursula, being connected to her as the sleeping pill took over and I came, and we passed through the hypnopompic badlands of sleep together, each in our own dreams.

CHAPTER 42

I don't remember my last thought about Butch's body being wrapped in the sheet on the other bed. I don't remember Ursula's pressing the button on her watch as she always did when she drifted off to sleep, measuring her time away from reality. I don't remember turning off the aquarium's light when we were done, nor sleeping or dreaming, only of a gentle annoying sound of knocking on the adjoining room's door that woke me.

I got up, quietly pulling on my tracksuit, and returned three quiet knocks on the adjoining door before opening it. Elizabeth's suite was dark. I quietly closed the door so as not to wake Ursula.

In Elizabeth's room, her lamp's shade cast a perfect circle on the ceiling, and Elizabeth sat on her bed facing away from me, the thick ponytail down the back of her uniform.

I shut the door quietly and heard her laces hiss through the eyes of her boots. The sheers filtered the blue light from the airport, and I wasn't sure I didn't smell Charles's scent in here—old cars and his musk. She glanced over her shoulder. "You need a haircut," she said.

"Do you have to say that every night?" I asked.

She felt the weight of the boot in her hand. She put it on the floor beside the other, adjusted them until they were perfect. She lay down on the bed, still in her green Gypsy uniform with the triangle of a white T-shirt showing at her neck, and her white socks glowing. She looked ten years younger. "Why are you still angry at the thing inside the dog?" she asked.

"I don't know."

"Is everyone mad at me?" she said.

"No one blames you," I said, and then I told her, "You have to be there in the morning for the launch."

"Why?"

"It's just important for you to be there. We're going to send him on, you know."

"'*You know?*'" she said. "And the word 'just' is for simpletons." She unclipped pens from her pocket and put them on the bedside table. "I'm not going to take a night off. This is my job now."

"What's it like?"

"Sandeep," she said, "it's wonderful. I'm extremely tired, but it is *so* worth it."

So? So worth it? She'd never talked like that.

"Better than you could ever, ever imagine. I mean I'm working hard learning the system, but it is like I've always known their system. It's the system I would have designed."

I could smell sweat from her uniform.

"So why isn't it for me?"

She made her it's-impossible *shish* and said, "This is for you. This is what you've been trained to do. You have a knowledge base that no one else in the world has, and you are young with your whole life ahead of you, and you come from good stock. You can have a big family, the family I never got to have. Is Ursula sleeping?"

"She is."

Though I couldn't see them I knew her eyes were closed, her arms crossed on her chest in the posture of being dead. "She still believes she is being abducted?"

"Yes," I said.

"Why are you sighing like it's a horrible thing?" she asked me. I hadn't realized I'd sighed. "You don't know how wonderful it is to believe in something fantastic," she said. She crossed her arm over her eyes.

"You think people like that are fools," I said.

"No. If we remembered how good it felt to believe in the fantastical, like we were kids again," she said, "we'd give up anything else to feel that way."

"I just don't understand why you won't be there for the launch. Don't you care that this thing is happening?"

She took a few minutes to think in the dark. "That was a different part of my old life. I can't dwell on that. I'm very proud of you. But time flies by."

We sat in the blue silence of the room for a while, Elizabeth lying on the bed with her hands crossed on her chest until she spoke. "We might not get to talk like this often so I want to tell you one thing, okay?"

I agreed.

"There are times," she said, "when you have to forgive someone you don't think deserves it."

"You mean Charles?"

"I'm telling you an important lesson. Are you listening?"

"Of course I am."

"In order to carry forward in a productive manner, you have to learn to forgive completely. Give this forgiveness to someone who you might not feel deserves it. Say it out loud to them—'I forgive you.' It sounds simple, but it starts working from that point forward. I think Dubourg's Jesus had this right, and also that thing about being a child to be enlightened. Anyway, you will not be very productive until you learn to forgive. Some things in life just happen, and sometimes there's a person who caused the event, but we go through life causing events, don't we? Forgiveness starts with saying it."

"Do you forgive Charles?"

"I'm very tired now," she said.

"Do you think I should forgive *you*?" I asked her. "Is this what this is about? There's nothing to forgive. I love you more than anything. There is nothing else in the world to me but you."

"You know," she said, another non-Elizabeth prelude to a statement, "you have always wanted me the most when I was walking out of the room," she said. "Did you know that? I could be sitting with you for hours and as soon as I got in the doorway, you'd go, 'Mom . . .'"

"I never called you 'Mom.'"

"I supposed that's my fault."

"No, it's not," I said. "Why are you talking like this? I'm worried about you."

"You are worrying about *me*?" she said. "Don't make me angry right before I fall asleep. It'll only give me bad dreams. Good happy thoughts before you fall asleep . . ."

I looked at her work boots beside her other shoes, and I left her there to sleep, closing the doors quietly behind me—her door, then my door—and I snuck back in bed beside Ursula and just as I was thinking I would never fall asleep, I heard gentle knocks on the main door and then the silent form of Dubourg letting himself in the room, putting his bags down, and getting on the floor with a blanket and falling asleep below us with his fists beneath his chin just like when he was a kid.

CHAPTER 43

I startled awake from a dream, found Ursula asleep beside me, and Dubourg on the floor between the beds. The world through the shears was not yet showing the dawn of the next day, but Ursula's watch alarm was going off, the blue dial light blinking as she raised it to her face. She reached to find me in bed and only then did she let her breath go, and Dubourg from the floor said, "I'm already here."

I hobbled to the door to Elizabeth's room. I put my ear to the solidness and listened, felt her presence on the other side. I raised my hand, thought I should give her one last chance to go with us, but then I didn't knock.

Dubourg sat on the end of the bed putting on his black shoes, his priest shoes, and he had his valise, of course, but he also had his carry-on duffle packed.

"Are you leaving?" I asked him.

"Yes," he said. "We all have to after this."

Ursula's eyes followed me as I walked across the room. "What's the matter with you?" she said.

"Nothing," I said. I got Butch's leash off the counter expecting him to perk up when he heard the sound of the buckle sliding on the counter, and I looked around for his chariot in order to strap it on for his morning walk.

"Oh God," Ursula said.

But I saw the bundle of white sheets sunken into the comforter, the dead Butch, and of course I remembered.

"I can't take it anymore," she said.

"I had a momentary lapse," I whispered, "I remember last night, don't worry," and I threw the leash back on the counter where it hit flight-attendant Barbie sitting drunkenly and staring straight ahead. She always looked like she was focused into a world we couldn't see, one filled with her tiny friends and family.

"Why do you keep doing this?" Ursula said, grabbing both sides of her head. "I can't go through it again."

"No. You won't. I remember."

"Everything?" she said.

Ruth and the needles seemed like a dream.

Dubourg slid his hands under the bundle that was Butch and lifted. "We've got to go," he said.

The service elevator took us up to the attic. It opened into the heavy air of the big room, and Dubourg mumbled, "Welcome to the inferno." We walked between the frames of foldaway beds, and in the center of the darkness were the oasis of the light and furniture. It was like a lit stage at a theatre, this stage a messy set: equipment, computers opened and gutted, CPUs running, soldering irons, notebooks spread open, tools, spools of wire, an empty gallon jug of water, stacks of unused hard drives, and of course the Trans-Oceanic radio among stacks of plates from the restaurant.

Dubourg went over to the table beside Ruth and set the bundle of Butch down on a pad and draped another pad over his body, a heavy pad.

Van Raye was lying in one of the pool's lounge chairs with his prosthesis standing beside him, the leg wearing a black zip-up boot as if it were dressed and ready to go.

"You goddamn people," Van Raye said. "How many times do I have to be *right* before people start listening to me?"

Ruth screwed the wire leads to metal eyes on the pad on Butch and went back to work in front of four screens.

Dubourg looked down on Charles. "He knows?"

"Yes," Ruth said without taking her eyes off the screens, monitors shining on her face. "Cat's out of the bag." A rotating fan agitated strings of the frayed fabric of her cutoff sleeves.

Ursula went over to Van Raye and took away his crutches.

"Stop that. Shit. Those are mine!"

Dubourg sat in front of the Trans-Oceanic radio.

"If you send it, go ahead and kill me," Van Raye said, "Okay? *Okay?* I'll have nothing."

Dubourg turned on the radio. It took a few seconds to warm up to a station playing organ music but he tuned past it and past a voice— "Four cats, three dogs, a bundle of sticks has been delivered . . ." and then the tapping of Morse code—until he found our sound, like a twin-engine plane warming up for takeoff, the sound having traveled three thousand years to get here. Every sound we were hearing was three thousand years old.

"You'll have the planet," Ruth said to Van Raye. "You'll have Chava Norma."

"Fuck that noise," Van Raye said. "There's an extraterrestrial *here*." He pointed to the bundle lying on the banquet table between the two plastic pads, a corner of the shroud hanging off the table. On a metal shelving unit was the orange box, the spell of software supposedly cast upon it making it a magic box capable of sending the burst of data that was Randolph, or whatever his real name was, to Chava Norma.

Ruth had her chin resting on her hand as she watched a graphic version of the Earth rotating. She rolled her chair over to the gain booster and toggled a switch and watched a bar on one screen begin: "10%" then skipping suddenly to "15%" and stopped in a dimming of lamps. "Don't surge on me now," Ruth said, and the lights on all the hard drives remained green and the noise from the radio was strong.

On the other end of the table there was a hole—a hole, like a blind spot in my vision. It was like a bubble in an aquarium, but this sphere was purer than air. I made myself watch the clock go through 00:00:5:00.

"Are you okay?" Ursula said. She sat in her regular spot in that wingback chair.

I nodded.

"What do you see?" she said.

"*What?*"

I could tell Ursula's eyes tracked to the hole on the end of the table.

I knew from past experience this thing on the end of the table was disturbing to look at. I closed my eyes. I heard Ursula get up. I put my feet on the couch and drank from a water bottle. *What was on the end of the table?* I forced my eyes to look at it—a bubble in the air, a crystal ball of cosmic clarity with nothing in it.

Van Raye was in a half stupor on his lounge, and Dubourg smoked and stared at the radio as if this hole in the universe wasn't right there at the end of the table beside him. I squinted to see it better and it changed to the green alien Buddha from Charles's car but alive and opening its mouth, a grotesque black tongue licking as though it had just swallowed something, its blank black eyes watching all of us. I knew even as I was seeing it that it wasn't real. I understood I was hallucinating.

"We can ask him anything. What do we want to know?" Dubourg said, but he meant Randolph, not that Buddha.

"Go ahead. It's now or never," Ruth said. "You wanna know what's in your case?"

I heard Dubourg say, "*No.*"

My phone dinged with a message from Randolph.

Calm down. You are hallucinating.

The small alien Buddha persisted, moving, licking, fingers flexing as if coming alive.

Before I go, I want you to see through the hallucination. You must see what it is.

Ruth called out coordinates as if there were someone listening: "Right ascension, less than ninety seconds."

"You don't understand!" Van Raye tried to push up on the chair. "Don't any of you have the least bit of desire for knowledge? *Where does it come from? How long does it live?*" The fan whirred in Ruth's face. "Damn all of you," he said.

"Do his leg," Ruth said to Dubourg.

Dubourg looked over at the radio as if just discovering Ruth there. He started to get up, but I stopped him. "I'll do it," I said, making myself not look at the living Buddha.

I was able to squeeze beneath Charles's chair, took off my shoe, rolled up my track pants, and carefully put my darker right leg in the place of his right leg, positioning it through the plastic slats. I waited beneath him, the back of my father inches away from my face. I looked out and saw Ursula resting her head sideways on the arm of her chair, her eyes red from crying and staring at me on the ground.

"Sandeep," Van Raye whispered. His hand found my arm and squeezed it. "You understand me. Stop them. Stop them so all this isn't a useless endeavor. You are the only person in the world who understands me, always have been. You and Elizabeth."

I wiggled my foot to get his attention, and turned my head to see the alien Buddha. The Buddha continued smacking his lips as though he were looking for a teat, eyes big and embryotic, pre-birth. The 3-D Earth on Ruth's computer spun slowly, dots of satellites like bees swarming it. Ursula's head sat sideways on the arm of the chair watching me.

My phone dinged, but I thumbed it to voice, the same generic voice of millions of phones, but it was Randolph:

> You have to see the object for what it is.

I can't, I thought, *I can't.* Ruth tested the connection of the heavy pads on top of Butch's body. The clock counted down.

"YOU ASSES, YOU FOOLS!" Van Raye shouted. I felt the prosthesis being snatched up from beside my head, and he threw it across the room. The leg clattered to the floor halfway to Ruth.

I heard Dubourg's whispered prayer, *"Jesus, Mary, I love you, save souls . . . Jesus, Mary, I love you, save souls . . . "* and the radio played the planet's noise, slaloming in and out of high and low humming, as mesmerizing as a didgeridoo.

"Ask it questions," Van Raye said, "someone. We're blowing an opportunity, the biggest in the history of the world."

I closed my eyes and repeated my Elizabeth prayer: *Proper planning and practice prevent piss-poor performance,* and opened them and saw that the Buddha was gone. Instead, on the end of the table, sat a simple white vase, and even the taste in my mouth changed. I knew what was in the vase.

Randolph spoke through my phone:

Are you ready?

Are you leaving?

"I can see my leg," Van Raye mumbled above me.

Do you understand what you are seeing?

"I feel it," Van Raye said, "it's right there. I can wiggle my toes."

I wiggled my toes for him. Ursula watched me, her head sideways on the arm of the chair. She was worn out. "I'm sorry," I said to her. How many times had she had to tell me my mother was dead?

"She's not here, is she?" I whispered.

Ursula closed her eyes and held them closed against the pain of having to tell me once again that Elizabeth was gone.

"But I see her at Gypsy."

She almost imperceptibly shook her head.

"Those are my toes," Charles said above me. I felt the vibrations of his chest as he spoke.

The vase on the table. It was Elizabeth's ashes. I had simply forgotten where I'd stored this information and the sadness came back on me again. I was living in a world without my mother.

Water from Ursula's eyes dripped onto the floor, the nice reliable pull of gravity, Butch's leash wrapped tightly around her hand, her fingers turning blue.

Dubourg was in a trance, bobbing before the radio and mumbling, "May the most bold, most sacred, most adorable, most mysterious and unutterable name of God . . ."

It's almost time. Please send me.
Would you like to listen to Elvis?

Ruth said, "What the fuck? What is this?" The tip of her finger bruised pixels on the screen. "It's asking for a password, *a goddamn password*," and Dubourg prayed, " . . . in heaven, on earth and under the earth . . . " and Van Raye said, "I feel tingling in my leg."

"You feel what?" I said to him.

"Tingling, it's tingling. It's terrible."

"A *password*?" Ruth asked, typing frantically.

He can feel my leg? Could I feel tingling in my leg? Was I going to get sick again?

"If Randolph wasn't here," I said to Ursula, "then Elizabeth would be alive."

Ursula looked frozen to the chair.

> Elvis makes you feel better?

"Go fuck yourself," I said, not caring if he heard it or not.

> Elvis always makes you feel better.

I closed my eyes. "My mother loved Elvis movies."

"Ask it about the other planets . . . other worlds," Van Raye said above me.

I ignored him.

> My journey will be longer because I have your mother to think about and you. You are the only other being I've spoken to.

> I'm sorry to have gotten involved.

> This journey will be long. But send me.

I wiggled my toes.

"Password?" Ruth muttered. "*What password?*" I heard her typing and pounding the "Return" key. "Fuck me. This isn't right. What fucking password?"

"Try 'Geneva,'" I started.

Her chair squeaked as she leaned backward. "*Geneva?*"

"Stop, not yet!" Ursula sat up. Through tears, she said, "Will Ruth's baby be okay? Ask him! Ask him!"

My phone chimed and the message came:

> If I answer, you will only jump there in time.

"Do you want to know the answer?" I said to Ursula. "There are consequences."

"Yes," she said, crying.

The clock said six seconds.

I said to Ruth, "It's Geneva 1000x. Geneva 1000x."

"Geneva 1000x? As in x-ray? Hold on," Ruth said, "here goes."

"We want to know the answer," I said to Randolph, and then I whispered, "I forgive you."

I clearly heard Ruth hitting the "Return" key, like a pretzel snapping, like a bone breaking, like someone's life going away forever. The second Ruth hit the key, the sound over the Trans-Oceanic stopped, and there was nothing but gentle static, and silence in the attic until my phone dinged, and I looked at the answer to Ursula's question—*will the baby be okay?*

CHAPTER 44

The first time I become aware that the baby is okay, that he is truly safe, he is in Dubourg's arms, but he is not a baby anymore, and Dubourg is carrying him with his hand around the boy's chest and through his legs, carrying the boy flat as if he is flying over the yard as Dubourg runs, and I have the sudden falling feeling that comes even through my paralysis, and I realize another time bomb has gone off in my life and I've leapt forward.

I am paralyzed in the reclining chair in the Desert Motor Court's yard. The desert sun has set beyond the faraway cobalt-blue mountains, and this is when the single specks of satellites move through the sky and lend perspective to how far away the stars are.

Feeling safe took a long time, and I remember the stages of the boy being a baby, especially the gelatin stage that was the most worrisome to me. The boy is twenty-two months now and healthy, though not much of a talker. As Dubourg carries him through the little stone yard behind the Desert Motor Court, the boy tries to aim a flashlight at bushes, but Dubourg pretends to almost drop him, purposefully bouncing him so the beam of the flashlight he holds can't focus on the thing they search for: *the mole.*

The mole is really just a black sock stuffed with other socks and tied to the end of thirty-pound test line, which has been pre-strung through the yard by Ursula. I am paralyzed in my reclining chair for the third time in two years, and I have begun to think of it as timeouts, the opposite of time bombs, when life stands still and I can observe it.

Ursula sits alone on the swinging chair diagonal from me. She has one leg folded beneath her. The toes of her other foot barely touch the ground and keep her chair moving, her belly swollen with a child inside her.

The mole (the sock) sticks on the bottom of a fairy-dust bush, but the boy doesn't know it, and Dubourg runs by and kicks it free. "*Where is it?*" Dubourg shouts. Ursula tugs the line and the mole starts moving across the yard again.

"Where does the mole live?" Dubourg asks the boy, allowing the beam to shine in the wrong direction, momentarily at his black valise safely on the ground by the water pipe.

The boy has a real name on his birth certificate, but we have never called him anything other than "Boy" or "the boy," though Ursula and Dubourg sound more natural saying it than I do. What will we call our next baby if it's a boy? I don't know. Of course Ursula doesn't consider it "our" baby.

We are at the Desert Motor Court built in 1969, a space-age design with a marquee out front that has a series of concentric disks that reminds me of a laser shooting toward the sky, and this is where I go when the Disease With No Name takes over my body. Mr. Leggett, the former letter carrier from Atlanta, my old hospital roommate, is in charge of security here, a position I secured him through the owner-ship, friends of Elizabeth's, though managers complain that Leggett thinks he runs the place, and he has an endless stream of jokes, which he still tells me when I come here for my episodes.

The motor court is good, though the neighborhood in the valley below us is known for meth houses. The pool is spring fed and the res-taurant at the end keeps its doors open, and other guests take note of our special gang, but read their paperbacks or sip their cocktails.

The ownership warns everyone that it's not a good idea to leave the grounds after dark because of the crime, but this only adds to the isola-tion and feeling of security when we are here together, though Ursula says that they—the Others—come freely to take her away at night here in the desert with her family around her. She still flies for Shenandoah, but she has written a book about her abduction experiences, and is often the keynote speaker at UFO conventions, but she has refrained from telling her audiences that the baby growing inside her is of alien stock, though she reminds me constantly that it is not my child.

At this stage of pregnancy, she is round and plump, a baby she thought she could never have, practically a miracle. One of those eggs harvested by the aliens when she was young, she says, fertilized and replanted inside her.

During the mole hunt, she stares at the blinking lights of air-liners in the sky, and I know that being up in the air is what she really loves, almost as much as she loves this boy, the boy whose mothers are from the sky.

Ursula transferred her Triple Zero lifetime pass on Shenandoah to Dubourg, so he didn't have to rely on the church, but can still spend the rest of his life keeping the valise safe, safe inside the Airport Zone, and he can talk to God.

The boy calls me "Dad" because I am legally his father, and he calls Ursula "Mama," because Ruth told her that she wanted it that way. He calls Dubourg just "Du," which sounds like "father" in a better language. We tell the boy about Ruth, his mother in the sky, traveling back in space, which is confusing to him, and we know that we will one day tell him about his biological father who died orbiting Earth, Cosmonaut X. They'll be abstract to him, and his mind will build myths around this, surely. Will he want to go to the sky?

Now I watch the boy and imagine putting my fingers through his hair when I'm well, something I promise myself I will do more often than I've done, show him love no matter what, breaking the cycle of bad fathers.

When we are all here together at the Desert Motor Court, when I retreat into my head, this is our sunset ritual: Dubourg grabs the boy, who at two is extraordinarily healthy and fine and light in Dubourg's strong arms, Dubourg holding him flat like he's surfing the air, flashlight in Boy's hand, bouncing him so that he never gets a good bead when the mole crosses open ground, jumping from rock to plant, the pregnant Ursula pulling the string from the swinging bench.

When I am not in an episode of paralysis, I tell Boy every night before bed about his biological mother Ruth who is a great star traveler, and we see a few stars coming out in that impossibly purple light as we stand on top of a hotel, him not understanding yet what it means to be traveling among the stars.

That's where Ruth is, or at least she's somewhere in the asteroid belt for the next two years, and I can't help but think that this isn't much different from Randolph traveling toward Chava Norma, but

Ruth is much slower and will never get to a destination. Her travel is not much different from death, except that we can send his mother messages via computer and wait a few days for her response. All the important women in his life come from the sky: Ur, who comes to see him; Ruth, sending him messages; Elizabeth, who I tell him fantastic stories about but whom he can never communicate with. I would do anything to have one more night to talk to her, to go back to that hotel room in the blue light and talk to her in her Gypsy Sky uniform. Even if it were a dream. Would she look around at us here and think it was all worth it? I don't care. I miss her so.

We were at the Grand Aerodrome's pool when the boy was born, the paralysis coming on me slowly at that time as if it were the actual grief of losing my mother. We were trying to unravel the mystery of why the sound from the planet had suddenly quit. It took three thousand years to get here and they couldn't have known we had sent Randolph at that exact moment. Ruth had scanned the body of Butch and found no data on the microchip, and I think we all, late at night, wonder if any of it was real. It's no more real than the past ever is.

We scattered Elizabeth's ashes from the top of the Grand Aerodrome. All five of us witnessed that and have that stored, shared memory. Elizabeth's ashes went with the wind toward the airport. So much of the past you have to take on faith.

I'm telling it like I remember it, though I have nothing to offer as proof other than four witnesses, one of whom isn't here on Earth, and Dubourg refuses to talk about it. Ursula believes aliens are still here. Charles Van Raye should be writing this book, not me.

Van Raye, who had nothing now, had nearly quit talking to any of us, even by that night of the boy's birth. He was in some state of shock, legless, without even his sound of a distant civilization to show the world.

Ruth, swimming normally in the pool that night of the birth, gave no indication anything was about to happen to her. She squatted in the shallow end and reached between her legs and lifted this thing out in a brown swirl of water, lifted it by both legs, umbilical cord running along its prune face, hands over its head as if indicating a touchdown. Ruth said, "Boy."

Ruth signed up for some crazy, privately funded mission that sent three astronauts straight into space, a so-called self-sufficient craft, or at least sufficient enough for the astronauts to survive their normal lifetimes if no disaster struck, all we can ever hope for. She simply couldn't stand not being in space. I reminded her that space was where she'd been terrified. "Maybe that's why I'm going," she said.

Ursula jerks the string and makes the mole jump in the air, and Dubourg takes the boy bouncing off in the wrong direction, the air thick with dust kicked up by his priestly black shoes. Ursula sees me looking at her. "You still think you have something to do with this?" She touches her stomach.

I blink once—yes.

What happened to Charles?

Van Raye is easy to locate. When I need to see him, I check the race schedule.

Elizabeth, never really being able to separate from him, left in her will that he be provided for in order to maintain his "current lifestyle," which is vague, and left to the trustee's discretion. That's me.

There are thirty-six races in a NASCAR season.

Last time I hunted him down in Bristol, Tennessee, Ursula flying me in a pressurized Beechcraft Baron. She flew us into a tiny airport packed with private jets, releasing the air seal around the door when we taxied to the terminal. She shut down the right engine so I could safely get out. I gestured for her to take the headphone away. She cracked one side to hear me.

"Come with me," I said.

She let the earphone go and shook her head, eyes hidden behind the dark glasses, which is exactly the answer she gives when I ask her to marry me. "Fundamentally different philosophies," she says, but I feel her caving. Those nights when we are sleeping together, finally, after all those years, I know she loves me and another baby is on its way.

In the airplane, when she threw her thumb to tell me to get out, the screen of her wristwatch (still worn backward) sparkled and her belly peaked from beneath her pilot's shirt. This baby is going to be so brown. She just doesn't understand. Like Elizabeth said, the Indian genes will dominate.

When I shut the door, and she locked it from inside and turned the plane, she hit me with a blast of prop wash. I caught a ride to the campground beside the racetrack to find Charles.

There is a huge coliseum built in the middle of the hills of east Tennessee where humans race cars. That night I went looking for Charles, the day's racing done, and the parties had started. There were miles of RVs in every direction, music intertwining with other music, laughter and shouts, the sound of beanbags slapping in a cornhole game. The dark air smelled of campfires and port-o-potties, and I searched for his row. A country music band jammed in a dilapidated house at the corner. I used the tracker on my phone to find his, the sewage truck passing me on the gravel road, kicking up dust. I took out my handkerchief, and put it to my nose until I saw a group of race fans beneath a string of cactus lights staring at me. They drank beers, watched me in my button-down and slacks, handkerchief covering my face.

I saw Van Raye sitting in a reclining chair, hands behind his head. "Sandeep!" he yelled and the patio recliner tilted, but he remained seated. "It's my son!" he shouted.

"Hello, Sandeep," one of the men said to me, Bill something, one of the race regulars with Charles.

Charles didn't get up, but I bent and took his hand and put my face against his face and kissed him.

"Want a beer?" Bill said, already going into the cooler.

I sat by a campfire built inside a metal ring and asked about the race today, and the one tomorrow night, drank beer and kept seeing flickering lights in the sky, not an airplane but yellow glowing orbs of floating lanterns rising from the massive campgrounds. Van Raye kept pulling out his phone to check race news, fingering it off. He'd always loved driving fast cars, but how did he end up here?

Van Raye reached and touched my shoulder and whispered, "Sandeep?"

"Yes."

"I got a pit pass. I was *this* close to Austin Harris. I've got pictures!" He turned his phone on and started showing me pictures.

"The family is fine," I said, ignoring the pictures.

"I'm glad. Ursula and the baby? Okay?" He looked at the pictures himself.

"Yes."

"Wonderful."

The campground was one big party, people wandering up and down the gravel road, beers in hand, golf carts dragging effigies of different drivers through the dirt. A guy staggered up and asked if he could use someone's bathroom, said that he was lost. When he was done, he came back out of the neighbor's RV and sat in one of Van Raye's folding chairs and simply declared, "I'm from Canada," and waited to see what reaction he got about this news. There was none. Harold from Maryland gave him a beer.

"Are you happy?" I asked Van Raye.

"Of course! This is great, isn't it?"

"Sure," I said. "Why are you so interested in this?"

"In what?"

"Racing. NASCAR."

"I've always been," he said.

"No, you haven't. Did you ever go to a race, I mean, before?"

"I *followed* it."

"No, you didn't. You drove fast cars, but I never saw you watching a race. You've got some kind of false memory. I never even saw you watch television."

"Watching sports is for imbeciles," he said. "*This is racing.* I've always loved racing. I just didn't have much time to do it before. Retirement is great."

The word "retirement" gave me a shot of pain for Elizabeth to have lived long enough for it.

Across the road, people held open a paper lantern and someone lit a tiny block of wood at its base, filling it with light and hot air. They raised it and let it go on the breeze, which carried it over the campers and the campground, rising ever higher. At one point there were dozens of them in the sky. "Redneck UFOs," a guy name Marty said.

"You know what this reminds me of," Van Raye said to me and pointing to the surrounding hills of this Tennessee valley. "All these campfires?" I waited. His hand dropped. "The night in Georgia, that night, all the campfires and the soldiers."

"I don't want to remember it," I said.

"Of course not. You certainly don't want to," he said. "I'm sorry. What was I thinking?"

When four silver empty cans of beer stood beside his chair, he rose using the pole of his awning. Charles pulled his pant leg up. Velcro ripped and he took his prosthetic leg out leaving the pant leg empty.

"Oh Jesus, he's taking his leg off," Marty said.

"Things are getting serious, the professor is legless," Bill said.

"Gentlemen," he announced, "I lost this leg in the pursuit of extra-terrestrial life." He pivoted and plopped back in the lounger, holding the leg across his body like a guitar.

"Have you found intelligent life yet?" one of the men asked and the others laughed, one saying, "Not around here!"

This is the first joke any fool would think of, but Van Raye didn't blink and said, "I have! I really have. Sandeep will tell you. We did it, didn't we?"

"Yes," I said, "you did."

"Don't start with the alien crap," Bill said. Then to me, "You know he's drunk when he takes his leg off and starts in about aliens."

"Hunting them used to be his job," I said.

"Well, he knows how to retire," Bill said, raising his beer.

"Hear, hear, to the professor," someone said, "intelligent life in Thunder Valley!" Everyone raised beers, and I did too, though it felt faked. When the toast was over, the Canadian announced that he'd wet his pants. Everyone laughed and Van Raye said, "That's my chair, asshole!" A four-wheeler came by hauling a trailer with a hot tub full of people in cowboy hats. Elizabeth would have asked, "What kind of country is this?"

"Listen, Charles, I'm going to write everything down. A book."

"Why?" he said. "I'm going to write one."

We both knew he wasn't going to do it. This was his old life.

He thought about this a second, and his chest relaxed, and he said, "Well, don't mention the dog, okay? Someone might misconstrue my handling of the dog."

"But how could I ever tell this story without the dog?"

He didn't answer. It made me realize that Van Raye's books, the articles, they were all bullshit, not in the sense that he ever lied about anything, but in the sense that they were chosen, edited, and elaborated to serve the image that he had of himself, and more importantly, he'd lived his life thinking first about the essay he would write, done things simply because it would make a better story. Even science, physics, mathematics were just frames to stretch the canvas of himself on and show the world who he thought he was, leaving out the parts he considered boring, uninteresting—father, husband, shitter, pisser, bankrupt man. Now he was simply old.

The next night I went to the race with him, and the roar of forty-four cars going around on a half-mile track was unbearably loud even though I had those foamy earplugs in. I looked over and Charles was filming the green-flag start with his phone, body tilted back so he could see everything in the tiny screen, his mouth formed into a holler though no one could hear him. Van Raye had obtained a rare pleasure in this life: he had let go.

I had gone to the demolition of the Grand Aerodrome because I wanted to see if I felt the memory of all the old lives lived there, those that had crossed through that hotel finally disappearing in the great cloud of dust. Of course I couldn't. The hotel is gone and there is no way ever to go back into the hotel room with the blue light and talk to Elizabeth.

When I fly through Atlanta, I take a cab to that totally industrialized side of the airport, passing the Gypsy Sky Cargo compound that will be there until the end of times. I stand on the bare dirt in the place that was the Grand Aerodrome and watch the sky and the Gypsy compound, and there is a small part of me that watches for Elizabeth's posture over there on the other side. I really can't fathom that I'll never see her again. I need her so badly every day. Sometimes I catch myself thinking, *The next time I see Elizabeth I'll tell her . . .* Memories overlap between people, and as each person dies, certain memories disappear. Perhaps that instinct to believe I will one day see her, this is where the concept of heaven comes from, an archetypal image of the place we will reunite and began new memories and talk about the old ones. I'm pretty sure there's no heaven; the world, the universe, simply doesn't work like that. I've certainly seen no evidence of it other than an alien that knew a few things that seemed incredible, an alien that doesn't exist to me now. Writing about it makes me close to the feeling one last time before I let it go forever. Writing about it is as real as it will ever get.

Ursula swings. Dubourg carries Boy on the hunt for the mole in the backyard. The child Ursula is carrying is not a hybrid of Ursula and some alien, but I say nothing to her. When the new baby arrives, it will look Indian. There'll be no denying it's my child, but do the truly converted ever face facts?

We'll raise it just like we do Boy. Ursula will find reasons why his or her skin is dark like mine, and I'll never say anything to convince her otherwise, and hopefully we will make more. The idea of her not believing in what she wants to believe scares me, just like it would if Dubourg wanted to know what was in his case, or if he stopped believing in God.

Ursula flies in and lives with the boy and me in hotels across America. Dubourg comes when he can.

There is never a time when I don't walk into a new hotel room, weary from the road, and plop facedown on a bed. Boy stares at me. My body makes the crater in the comforter, and that's when I think about Butch's body on the bed and remember the gravity we all make and this is what being is: an existence, a created crater. We all just simply go away, and our gravity disappears.

Boy travels with me just like I did with Elizabeth, me rolling our luggage with one hand, carrying the bag of water and the fish for him through the airports, finding kind TSA agents who will let a boy and a betta fish into the Airport Zone, the fish inside warping big, small, big, small.

When we are alone, I change my voice and say, "I'm Randolph, never Randy. Hello, Number 2, what is this place we are in?" but either he's too young to understand or he doesn't buy it. But the boy loves the Desert Motor Court, and, by default, must not hate my periods of paralysis because that's where we go together and slow down.

Here in the desert the fantastic and mysterious mole lives, and Boy gets to go there, and Dubourg is there and his Earth mother, Ursula, and he can search for the mole, the mole always just outside of Boy's beam of light.

The ritual of the mole is this: When I am paralyzed, I lie in the reclining chair beneath the darkening sky, Leggett staring at this weird nuclear family from the glass cube of the Desert Motor Court's lobby. Dubourg lifts Boy up in his arms and carries him horizontally, flashlight in Boy's hand. Boy tries to shine the light in the sage and the bushes looking for the mole.

Ursula asks Boy, "Who are you looking for?"

"The *mole*," Boy says, eyes wide, and the way he says "mole" makes it sound like the most incredible, unbelievable, wonderful, most mysterious creature in the universe—*the mole*.

"When does the mole come out?" Ursula asks.

"At night," Boy responds.

"Where does the mole live?"

"Underground," the boys says.

I can see why someone outside of our group would think everything I've told you is unreal—headlights, a dog's eyes, an alien—but to me the problem is it's too real, and it's all going by in such a hurry. How many time mines are out there waiting for me, those terrifying moments when your life leaps forward, and you'll just find yourself at the end? We are always only one answer from the end.

The flashlight beam bounces over the yard thanks to Dubourg's purposefully shaky carrying, but there is a black shape that leaps from one bush to the other. "There!" the boy shouts. Dubourg plays along and chases, shaking the boy so that the beam can't quite be still. The black shape scoots along the dirt, bouncing, and jerks into the next bush. "The mole!" the boy shouts, Dubourg carrying him after it. "The mole! The mole! The mole!" The game ends too quickly, Ursula reeling the last of the line in and hiding the black sock beneath her leg. "The mole," Boy shouts, Dubourg out of breath, and the boy knows the mole can't be found.

"Where has the mole gone?" Dubourg asks.

"Underground!" Boy shouts.

I want very badly to believe in the mole.